Would I Lie to You?

By Clare Dowling and available from Headline Review

Expecting Emily
Amazing Grace
My Fabulous Divorce
No Strings Attached
Going It Alone
Just the Three of Us
Too Close for Comfort
Would I Lie to You?

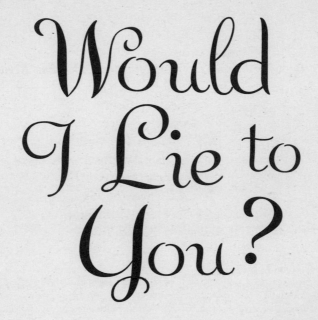

Would I Lie to You?

CLARE DOWLING

headline
review

First published in 2012 by HEADLINE REVIEW
An imprint of HEADLINE PUBLISHING GROUP

1

Cataloguing in Publication Data is available from the British Library

Hardback ISBN 978 0 7553 5979 0
Trade paperback ISBN 978 0 7553 5980 6

Typeset by Palimpsest Book Production Limited,
Falkirk, Stirlingshire

Printed and bound in Great Britain by Clays Ltd, St Ives plc

Headline's policy is to use papers that are natural, renewable and recyclable
products and made from wood grown in sustainable forests. The logging and
manufacturing processes are expected to conform to the environmental
regulations of the country of origin.

HEADLINE PUBLISHING GROUP
An Hachette UK company
338 Euston Road
London NW1 3BH

www.headline.co.uk
www.hachette.co.uk

For Stewart

ACKNOWLEDGEMENTS

Firstly, I'd like to thank my editor at Headline, Clare Foss, for all her hard work on this book, from her editorial notes to developing the gorgeous new cover. Thanks also to Emily Griffin for always being at the end of an email, Yeti Lambregts for the great design work on the new look, Jo Liddiard and Helena Towers for the crash course in social media, and all at Headline for making another book happen.

Thanks also to Breda Purdue, MD of Hachette Ireland, and the team in Dublin for marketing my book in Ireland – particularly Ruth Shern, who tirelessly drives me up and down the M50 every year to sign stock, and Margaret Daly for bagging me some great publicity.

As always, a big thank-you to my agent, Darley Anderson – the wisest man in town.

Thanks to fellow writers Sarah Webb, Martina Murphy, Martina Devlin and all the Irish girls for being great colleagues and friends.

Closer to home, I'd like to thank my husband, Stewart, for putting up with me, and my children, Sean and Ella, for letting me know when it's time to shut down the computer and have some tickle time.

Finally, thanks to all the readers who have gone out and bought my books and supported my writing over the years. I truly appreciate it. Check out my new website at www.claredowling.ie.

Part One

Chapter One

It was a good flight, except for the male flight attendant hovering nervously about my seat. He was concerned about my swollen eyes and nose. Eventually he plucked up the courage to tell me that the in-flight roll had contained traces of peanut – was it possible I was suffering some kind of allergic reaction?

'No,' I said apologetically. Clearly he was dying to get his hands on an EpiPen. 'I'm just crying.'

'Sorry.' He began to back off fast. They mustn't have covered that in the manual.

But then Barbara reached over and grabbed him. 'Hang on. We'll have two vodkas and tonics while you're there.' She turned to me. 'Do you want crisps with that?'

Crisps? I looked at her askance. The lump in my throat was so big that I could hardly breathe, never mind choke down a mini-tin of Pringles.

Barbara instructed the attendant, 'No crisps,' a little crest-fallen. She knew it would be bad form to tuck in on her own. 'Good lad.'

When he was gone she looked at my watery eyes in a kindly fashion. Then she opened her enormous bag, rummaged about through its diverse contents – a chicken sandwich, all her phones, *Teach Yourself Russian* – and extracted a wad of tissues, which she pressed into my hand. 'You'll have to stop that now, Hannah.'

'I know.' The thing was, I'd been absolutely fine up till then. Well, obviously I'd been devastated and humiliated and anything else you can think of, but in terms of crying and carrying on, I'd done hardly any. It was only when we'd reached the airport and run slap-bang into a wedding party from Kerry on their way to Majorca to get hitched, and who were trying to check in a wedding dress the size of a caravan, that I felt the full extent of my shock and upset explode to the surface.

It wasn't that I had a great hankering for a hideous wedding dress, or even a wedding (well, OK, maybe a bit). Besides, at our age, Ollie and I were a bit long in the tooth for the full church works. But I'd thought maybe a dignified ceremony in the registry office at some convenient point in the future, and a bottle of champagne in the Shelbourne Hotel afterwards. That's if I'd thought about marriage at all. Because, after ten long years together, and one beautiful child, I felt as if we already *were* married. I thought he did, too.

I'd been wrong. The last I'd seen of my beloved Ollie was his tail lights two nights ago as he'd driven off down the road and out of my life, going so fast that he'd taken the corner on two wheels.

I bawled, right there in the airport. Then, petrified that I would be spotted by one of his friends or extended relations, of which there were many, and they always seemed to be flying somewhere, and he would find out, I hid behind a pair of Barbara's hideous mirrored sunglasses as we checked in our bags and got through security. Except that I set off the alarm, twice. Barbara says it's all the fillings I have in my teeth and that I should have them removed before I die of mercury poisoning. She's the cheery sort. Several unsmiling guards took me aside and gave me a good frisking, which, I have to say, I quite enjoyed. At least it took my mind off things.

I was a bit worried they were going to go through my carry-on bag, too. When I'd packed it earlier I'd been in a bit of a state, and it wouldn't surprise me at all if I'd popped in a couple of kitchen knives. But no, they smartly turned their backs on me after the frisking and I felt a little deflated, although I was getting used to being dumped by now.

'Still, it'll be lovely to see Ellen, all the same,' Barbara announced, in a brisk attempt to head off more angst at the pass. She didn't mind tears, she just began to lose patience once a certain quota had been cried, usually about two millilitres worth. Then she said she began having uncontrollable urges to shout, 'Pull yourself together, for the love of Christ,' whilst delivering several sharp slaps to the poor unfortunate's face.

Her crushing practicality had come in very useful, though. The minute I'd broken the news of Ollie's departure, she'd been over like a light. She'd gently bullied me through the last forty-eight hours and all the business of getting ready to go away – 'The large suitcase, Hannah. That's right. And you'll need more than two pairs of knickers. And don't forget to pop round and leave a set of keys with that nice couple next door, what are they called, Josie and . . . oh, it begins with an M, it's on the tip of my tongue.'

'Peader.'

'That's it. Chop chop.'

Ordinarily, Barbara might have phoned up Ellen and said, 'Look, poor old Hannah's just had a terrible kick in the teeth . . . I know, I know, I can hardly believe it either. I mean, *Ollie* . . . This time we really *can* blame the parents . . . Anyway, it'd probably be a kindness if we called off this year's trip and let her stay at home with a couple of bottles of something strong.'

But there was another complication in all this. On Saturday, it was my birthday. I would be thirty-eight. That's right: two years from shagging forty. We were joining our best friend Ellen in France to 'celebrate'. I could have feigned illness or just plain refused to go, except for one further complication: Ellen was thirty-eight, too. On the following Tuesday. So we were 'celebrating' together, like we did every year, and it had all been great fun up until three years ago, when Ellen had suddenly shoved aside the champagne bottles and said hoarsely to me, 'Did we just turn thirty-*five*?' It had been a tremendous shock to both of us.

'Did Ellen tell you that they just had a new litter of pigs?' Barbara went on relentlessly. It was fine for her; she wouldn't be thirty-eight until next year.

'Really?' I tried my best to look interested. 'What breed?'

'I don't know. I think she might have said saddlebacks.' Then she gave a sigh. 'Oh, who gives a shite? Where's that cabin boy with our drinks?'

We weren't normally drinkers but whenever we went to France to visit Ellen, we hit the bottle hard, starting on the plane. You had to, to keep out the damp chill that settled in your bones the minute you heard the words 'north-east Brittany'. Five years ago, when Ellen and Mark had first moved over and started renovating the house, like something from one of those programmes *So You Fancy a Swanky Pile in the Sun!*, Mark had drawn up ambitious plans for a sunroom, a massive patio that wasn't just an extra room, it was an extra *house*, and all manner of little nooks and crannies that he assured us all would be 'guaranteed suntraps'. Being Irish, Ellen and Mark had long, bitter memories of being pelted with freezing downpours in July, and so they were looking forward more than most to basting themselves gently in the sunroom/patio/suntraps.

But there were problems with the sunroom. The details were vague;

paperwork mostly. The French loved paperwork, apparently (this was always said a bit tersely by Mark) and the planned extension seemed to require a lot of forms, which had to be approved by various different departments, at several different levels. At one point it looked like the suntrap forms might have to go before the actual French government.

Then there was some kind of falling-out with the builders; again, the details were sketchy, and Mark's face went a bit funny whenever it came up. He was now doing the job himself, which was probably just as well, as apparently he was brilliant at that sort of thing.

But the biggest surprise turned out to be the weather. Oh, if only they'd relocated a hundred kilometres further south . . . As it turned out, parts of Brittany had weather surprisingly like Ireland's: wet, cold, miserable in the winter, with the occasional week or two of sunshine in the summer. And the rain. Sweet Jesus, did it ever *stop*? Buckets of the stuff fell morning, noon and night. Every time you set foot outside the house you were soaked to the skin. Let's not forget the wind either. 'Exposure to the Atlantic airstream means that Brittany is a blustery region,' my French guidebook warned gloomily.

But go a few kilometres further south, to the bottom of Morbihan, for example, and you couldn't lash on the Factor 50 fast enough. A friend of theirs had left his dog in the car for two and a half minutes once and had come back to find it on its back, with its tongue hanging out, fried. Well, that was an exaggeration. Mark liked to play it up to make people laugh. Even if your holiday packing was routinely wellies and a raincoat, you always left after a stay with them with a smile on your face.

'How could they not have known the place was the very same as fucking Ireland?' Barbara demanded furiously every time. She took it all very personally, their failure to move to somewhere where she might actually get a tan. 'Did nobody do their research?'

Hmm. Yes. Ellen always looked a little embarrassed about that. Mark had found the place, apparently. But, as she pointed out, the two weekends that he'd flown over to do a recce had been unseasonably warm and sunny, and how was he to know that these were blips that would scarcely ever be repeated?

I gave a little shiver, and it wasn't just in anticipation of all the rain. 'Do you think Ollie will ever come home?' I asked Barbara in a small voice.

For a minute I thought she hadn't heard. Or maybe she was buried in that Russian book again – six months of study and all she seemed able to say in the language so far was 'Hello', and 'Do you know the way to the train station?'

But no. She was considering my question. Barbara wasn't the kind who gave an impulsive answer to anything.

'Very likely,' she eventually pronounced.

I'd have preferred something a little more definitive, such as, 'Absolutely! Give him five minutes and he'll be crawling back on his hands and knees just begging for a second chance.'

Barbara saw the naked hope on my face. 'Look,' she said, 'who knows what's going on in his head right now?'

She was right. Susie, his mother's dog, had only gone missing the previous weekend. I cursed his bloody parents all over again.

'The best thing you can do is let him get on with sorting stuff out at home,' Barbara counselled, clearly getting into the swing of this agony aunt thing. She even made a little steeple with her fingers and rested her chin on them. 'Don't put any pressure on him. And in the meantime, you make sure you enjoy your holiday.'

She'd been doing quite well up to that point. But the possibility of me kicking up my heels in France, whilst trying to face the fact that my relationship was hitting a brick wall, was practically zilch.

Barbara recognised the folly of this, too. 'Well, drink loads, anyway,' she hastily amended.

The toilet door swung open at the front of the plane, and we both quickly sat up. A little head came out. There must have been a body too, but I couldn't see it over the heads of the rest of the passengers. Cleo.

I immediately tried to prise my swollen, piggy-like eyes open as far as they would go, and gave my nose a quick wipe. There was no way Cleo was going to become embroiled in all this bad behaviour. So far, all she knew was that Daddy had temporarily gone home to look after Granny, who was under the weather. In other words, gone postal. Even more than usual.

'Right,' Barbara warned, in case I hadn't spotted Cleo. 'Put your best face forward.'

Chapter Two

Cleo was my daughter and the most beautiful girl in the whole world. I knew this because, when she was born eight years ago, I sneakily compared her to all the other babies in the post-natal ward, and she was a clear winner in the categories of skin tone, shape of the head, and how well she wore a nappy.

'She's the most beautiful, isn't she?' I said to one of the nurses. I wasn't being big-headed. I was just stating a fact.

'By a mile,' she assured me, and she must have seen *thousands* of babies.

Cleo was a little fretful, though. In the hospital, she didn't sleep much in her cot beside me, and the two of us would sit up crying together most of the night while the other mothers and babies brought the ward down with their snoring. Whenever I picked her up she would jump violently with fright, and no matter how much I coaxed and pleaded under my breath, she never seemed to have more than an ounce or two at feed-time. But then it was so hard to know how many ounces a breast contained. Since the birth, my own two had puffed out like a couple of inflatables, and were crisscrossed with fat, blue veins. I figured there must be at least two litres in each, if she would only drink.

'She's getting plenty. You just need to relax,' the nurse told me.

I had liked her up to that point.

'Really?' I made my voice politely sceptical. All the pregnancy books I'd read — twenty-two in total; I was nothing if not thorough — had included a patronising little section for new mothers on how to cope, the basic tenet of which was to 'relax'. Completely useless advice when faced with the myriad things that could happen with a new baby.

Ollie and I used to laugh our heads off at the idea. 'Worried about nappy rash?' Ollie would say to me sternly.

'Relax!' I would shout back.

'Have you ginormous, cracked nipples with funny, crusty bits on top?'

'Chill out!'

'Do you suspect your baby has colic?'

'Kick back and make a cup of tea!'

Boom boom. How we enjoyed those pregnancy books. They sustained us through six long months of pregnancy. (I was nearly eleven weeks gone before we'd noticed I was with child, so we kind of missed the first three months. It wasn't because we were on drugs, or anything. We'd given them up ages beforehand. I just had very irregular periods.) Ollie would make me Japanese food on a Saturday night – I'd an insatiable craving for vegetarian sushi, which was slightly inconvenient as they were buggers to make, but he never complained – and then we'd swap whatever new books we'd each bought during the week, and have a good old laugh.

Our favourite bit was the suggestion in one of them to make little sandwiches for the birth partner and pop them in the freezer. 'The sandwiches or the birth partner?' Ollie had wondered. Then, on the big day, they could take them to the hospital with them in case they got a bit peckish while watching you try to expel seven pounds of humanity through the 'birth canal'. Which we both agreed they should just call a fanny and be done with it. It was hilarious, all of it – right up until the moment I gave birth. Then I realised, with a terrible jolt, that I hadn't a flipping clue.

When Ollie arrived at the hospital ten hours after the birth of Cleo, bearing a massive bunch of flowers and a dreamy grin, I shot out of bed and pinned him up against the ward door.

'Did you bring the fucking books?'

'The books . . . ?'

'The pregnancy books. I texted you. The ones you were so busy laughing your arse off at.'

Ollie reared away, afraid. I couldn't blame him. The last time he'd seen me, I'd been out of my head on pethidine and cooing, 'Look at her, she's so beauuuutiful,' over and over again, while he'd told me, quite rightly, that I was the cleverest woman in the world. In the intervening hours, though, I had been replaced by some crazy-eyed, foul-mouthed harridan who'd razed a path through his lovely flowers, and had an indeterminate brown substance all the way down her fetching 'post-birth' pyjamas.

But didn't he realise? Everything had changed. I wasn't happy-go-lucky Hannah any more, if indeed, I'd ever been. I was now – and I know this happens to a lot of women, so I wasn't trying to be big-headed or overly dramatic, it was more the shock – I was a *mother*.

To illustrate the point, I grimly led the way back to my bed, where Cleo, the most beautiful girl in the world, was bawling her lungs out in the cot beside it.

'See?' I said. And I pointed in case he wasn't getting it. 'She hasn't stopped since she was born.' I was hoping there might have been some solution in one of those books. Infanticide or something.

The look on his face drove me mad; all calm and zen-like. 'Well, she's a baby,' he reasoned with me gently. 'I suppose that's what babies do.'

Since I'd met Ollie two years previously, on a tour bus in Majorca, both of us wearing fluorescent orange uniforms with 'I'm Your Holiday Rep!' emblazoned across the back – he had a fantastic arse in those shorts – I'd experienced many emotions, ranging from lust to love to a deep contentment. Hatred and an insane urge to scratch his eyes out had never featured amongst them.

I didn't go for him with my nails. Instead I burst into tears. He let me for a while, because I could get a bit excited if someone tried to comfort me before I was ready. Eventually I quietened down enough for him to put his arms around me and I snuggled in, feeling small and frail, even though my belly was, no exaggeration, still humungous (an awful thought: could there be another one in there?), and I probably outweighed him.

'You're just tired,' he said.

Tired? Seriously, was he for real? I was *exhausted*. It had been thirty-six hours since I'd had my first contraction and I hadn't slept since. I was delirious with the sheer lack of shut-eye, having been used to nine hours a night up until then, working up to twelve at the weekends, especially if we'd stayed up watching a box set of *The Sopranos*.

On top of it all, every time I looked at Cleo, I was gripped with a fear so strong that I actually reached up to put my hands on Ollie's shoulders to steady myself.

I looked into his brown, non-hysterical eyes and said hoarsely, 'What are we going to do?' I jerked my head towards the cot. 'With the baby.'

I was afraid of her, I decided. She didn't even look like me. *Anything* like me. That's when it occurred to me: there had been a mix-up in the labour ward. Of course! That was why this baby went mental every time

I took a foot in her direction, and tried her hardest to push away my gigantic breasts at feed-time (mind you, I would have, too). Because she wasn't my baby. The real Cleo was asleep in a cot somewhere, waiting patiently for the mistake to be discovered and to be returned to her rightful owner.

'We're going to take her home,' Ollie said, in that irritating, I-know-exactly-what-I'm-doing voice again.

'We can't,' I nearly shouted at him. 'She's not even ours, you fool. Can you not *see*?'

But Ollie wouldn't entertain the swapped-baby scenario, even when I tried to demonstrate how easily the identity bracelet could be slipped off the baby's wrist. Not that easily at all, as it turned out. But by then Ollie had picked Cleo up and was rocking her and cooing and growling some shite Bob Dylan song in her ear when – get this – She Stopped Crying.

The betrayal was so awful that I could only stand there, slack-jawed. For nine months I'd carried that witch around in my belly. I had two whacking great stitches holding together my previously beautiful birth canal, thanks to her. I was wrecked. But she stops crying for *him*? And Bob Bloody Dylan?

Then, thank God, she started up again, even louder than before. She cried like he was pinching her, hard. She cried like he was trying to murder her.

'What's wrong with her?' he asked, looking a tad rattled as mothers up and down the ward lifted their heads at the commotion.

'Oh, give her to me,' I fussed, ridiculously pleased. She mightn't like me, but she really couldn't stand him.

I put her in the crook of my arm gently, but not over-familiarly, as I sensed she was the kind of person who didn't want to get too pally, too quickly. She wanted to know what kind of stuff I was made of before she would entrust herself to my care. Which was fine by me; I was beyond pally at that point. I just wanted a cup of tea in peace, and maybe a quick read of my *True Stories* magazine. (One of the pregnancy books had advised me to bring in books and other reading material to 'pass the time'. More damn lies. There *was* no time any more.)

So we sat on the edge of my bed, the two of us. She was still crying, but a bit less breathlessly now. Good. I leant down to her, and whispered so that only she could hear: 'OK, pack it in. This isn't pleasant for either of us. But I'm trying my best and you're going to have to do your bit, too. Please. Also, I think there might be another one of you in there –'

I pointed to my bulging belly, ruling nothing out yet – 'so I'd get on my good side if I were you, or I might like your twin better.'

Clearly a firm hand and treating her like an equal was the right way to proceed, because she *did* pack it in. She gave one last shuddery little cry, before turning her face in towards me, like she was giving me the benefit of the doubt – reluctantly, mind – and then she conked out.

So did I.

Chapter Three

But all that's ancient history. Cleo didn't like me going on about her birth, even though I never got tired of it. In the same way, she'd started to discourage me from standing outside her classroom window at home time, jumping up and down and waving in wildly at her.

Anyway, there she was, clunking down the aeroplane aisle towards me in her new boots: cherry coloured, with daisies on the side, and these toy yokes in little chambers in the sole of each boot, which was completely ridiculous – I mean, a *toy*, in a *shoe* – but she begged for them, and I, as usual, gave in, after ten minutes of telling her firmly, 'I'm not going to change my mind, you know. You can plead all you like, young lady, but all you're going to do is make me more determined.'

She still looked nothing like me. She had Ollie's chocolate-brown eyes and sallow skin, lucky girl, but not his hair, thankfully, as he had a bit of a rasta look about him at the best of times. Mum, to give her her due, always said valiantly, about once every six months, more hopeful than anything else, 'You know, I think she's getting a bit more like you.'

'Which bit?'

Mum would um and ah and look at Cleo from all angles. 'It was there a minute ago.' Then, in a clear attempt to divert attention from her blatant lying, she would usually insist strongly, 'Well, she has your personality.'

Poor Cleo always looked as though she didn't know whether to be pleased or alarmed by this, especially if I was wearing my T-shirt with 'What If the Hokey Cokey Really *Is* What It's All About?' splashed across the front.

But of course Mum just didn't like Ollie. She never said it, of course – she was far too afraid of me for that. Instead she went on about his facial hair. 'Is he growing a beard or is he not?' she always wanted to know, in a state of some agitation. 'Because if he is, then why doesn't he just grow it? Why does he keep it all stubbly like that? Believe me, I know it's hard when you get to that in-between stage — I was trying to grow out that bloody bob for ages, do you remember? My heart was broken — but he just has to stick it out.'

Then, one Christmas — and I secretly admired her audacity — she brazenly bought him a Philips electric shaver, the same make my father used to use, bless him. I still remembered lying in bed when I was small, listening to the whirr from the bathroom. He was always very particular about his appearance, my dad. He wore a formal shirt every day, even after he was retired, and he always had a chin as smooth as a baby's bottom. He shaved right up until the end, and the undertakers told Mum, very impressed, that they'd hardly had to do any work on him at all, he was so well turned out.

I thought Ollie would go mad over the shaver. But he just said to Mum, 'How thoughtful. Just what I wanted,' and never mentioned it again.

I forgot all about it until Mum rang me up four months later in great distress. 'Do you know what Ollie sent me for my birthday?'

'What?' I didn't even know he'd got her a present. I'd nearly forgotten about her birthday myself, and had had to dash into Brown Thomas after a meeting in town and spend twice as much as I'd intended to. And now Ollie had been one step ahead and sent her something already?

'A . . . a . . .' Her voice dipped alarmingly, like she was on the verge of fainting.

'Mum?' I hoped to God it wasn't a puppy. My mother hated animals.

'A *vibrator*.'

'What?' Even I was shocked, although I was used to Ollie's sense of humour by now. But my poor mother . . . 'Are you sure? It's not a foot massager or something like that?'

'I think I know a vibrator when I see one.' She sounded more robust now; confident even. 'Anyway, it has instructions.'

'I see.' I didn't know what else to say. I mean, what *could* you say to the news that your boyfriend has bought your mother a Rotating Rabbit for her sixty-seventh birthday?

'What do you want me to do to him?' I asked at last. Because I was at a complete loss myself.

But my mother just said, 'Oh, nothing,' as though Ollie were completely beyond redemption.

Ditch him, was what she really wanted me to do, of course, instead of hanging around waiting for him to make an honest woman of me, even though nobody cared about that except her. And me, just a teeny, tiny bit, and only after two glasses of white wine.

Well, he was never going to marry me now, that was for sure. Even if we did get back together, I had a very strong feeling that Ollie had been put off marriage permanently.

Cleo, in her new boots, squeezed in efficiently past me to take her seat between Barbara and me. She plonked her sturdy little body down with a sigh and wiggled back determinedly until she was sure she was comfortable. There was a part of Cleo that was middle-aged already.

At the same time it seemed like only yesterday that she was happily singing along to Barney about the benefits of looking both ways before you toddled across the road. Now? I wasn't allowed to hold her hand in the shopping centre any more, for fear that someone from school might see.

But today was different; due to exceptional circumstances, the rules were relaxed, at least on my side. When Barbara was busy tucking into her chicken sandwich I sneakily reached a hand out towards Cleo. To my relief, hers snuggled into mine like a hand into a mitten.

'The toilets smelt,' she told me gravely.

'Did they?'

'I don't think they cleaned them very well.' She was concerned about these kinds of things; she would often sit up in bed as Ollie and I were headed that way ourselves and hiss, 'Did you remember to turn the electric fire off?'

I used to get very paranoid about this. I would fret to Ollie that she obviously felt the pair of us were flakes, and that it wasn't safe to go to sleep at night in case we set the place on fire, or failed to lock the front door against vicious burglars, or just plain forgot to turn the tap off after we'd brushed our teeth (once, it had happened. Once).

But as she got older we realised that she was simply very earnest, and that while she might well regard the two of us as flakes, she would simply see it as a bonus that she herself was most definitely not. Already she had a spare key to the front door buried in the garden for those times – again, it just happened the once – when I managed to lose mine.

She looked at me now and said, 'Are you upset?' Some part of her busy little brain had obviously registered that something more was afoot than Granny Muriel going bonkers, which had been happening regularly since last summer, so much so that nobody batted an eyelid any more.

What was new was this whole business of Ollie moving out 'to look after her'. If you wanted my opinion – and, actually, nobody seemed that interested in it – I'd have told Granny Muriel exactly where to go.

'Maybe a little,' I said, cagily.

'Me too,' Cleo declared, although I wasn't sure whether she was referring to Granny Muriel's mental state, or her daddy being gone.

Barbara's hand went to her massive handbag again; this time it emerged with drugs. 'It's just a relaxant,' she hissed over Cleo's head. 'It might help you sleep.'

Honestly? I was tempted. A few hours' oblivion was exactly what I needed. I'd barely slept for two nights running now, and my brain felt like a big ball of cotton wool. And now there were more than two whole weeks of other people to get through. They were friends, of course, but still. The *effort*.

'Where did you get them?' I stalled.

'I have contacts. Look, they're Daddy's, from that time he thought he heard voices. I'll look after Cleo for you,' she assured me. 'It'll be good practice for me.'

At that Cleo bolted upright in her seat and looked at me with pleading eyes; *nooooo*. Barbara was always trying to 'practise' on her. She liked to do things like check her hair for nits, and take her on shopping trips to Next, where she would buy her Dora the Explorer T-shirts and days-of-the-week knickers.

'Don't let her, Mum,' Cleo whispered to me urgently. 'Why does she always have to treat me like a baby?'

'You know why.'

But Cleo was no longer buying that. 'She's never going to get one herself,' she said, looking highly concerned for Barbara. 'She should just give up on that guy.'

'Cleo!' That was blasphemous, even from an eight-year-old. I looked over at Barbara quickly, hoping she hadn't heard. She'd go mental. And we were in a confined space, too. 'She will. Dimitri promised. He's a professional.'

'He's stringing her along,' Cleo whispered resolutely. She had no time for injustice. I wouldn't like to come up against her in a court of law.

But sometimes it did appear that Dimitri wouldn't come through for Barbara. Then, fearful that Barbara might actually read my thoughts

– because sometimes she could – began singing *la-la-la* loudly in my head. If she had a peek in now, she'd just think I'd gone a bit cracked with grief over Ollie.

Which I had. I was due another cry about now, but actually I was exhausted. I was also in semi-shock. I was so used to being part of a couple, part of *Ollie*, that being on my own, with just Cleo, was profoundly disturbing, and I kept having to repress a natural urge to look over my shoulder to see where he'd gone.

But he wasn't here, even though I looked. He was in Ireland, and I was here, and we were no longer together.

It took great willpower to turn down Barbara's drugs, but I did anyway, and she reluctantly put them back into her massive bag.

'I checked the forecast before we left,' she said anxiously, with a look out the window in case she could see a cold front coming to settle over north-east France. 'I don't think it's too bad. But better get an update just in case.' The hand disappeared into the bag once more as she searched around for her phone. She had three of them. One for work, one for personal use, and one for Dimitri.

After about ten minutes of rooting, and sighing, and peering in, she extracted the Dimitri phone, as I knew she would.

'Any news?' I asked, more out of habit than anything else. There never usually was. But over the years everybody asked it so often that it had become a form of greeting: 'How're-you-Barbara-any-news?' Every time Barbara rang anybody, she always began with the clarification, 'Just-me-no-news, listen, are you free for a pizza on Friday?'

She checked the phone now. The look of hope on her face would break your heart; as if there was the remotest possibility that she might actually have missed a call. That phone went everywhere with her, pressed to her skin, I suspected. She never turned it off. It had rung during a funeral last year – Miriam Feelihy's father's – just as the coffin was being carried out past her. 'Oh my God,' she'd blurted out loudly, fumbling for the phone. Half the congregation thought she was launching into some kind of prayer; they looked at each other in confusion and started up, 'Oh my God, oh my *God*,' as the coffin went by, as though they'd just realised there was a dead body inside it. In the end, the call had been a wrong number.

Barbara put the phone back into her bag. 'No.' But there was no despair. Only the stoicism of one who understood what it was to wait. 'Next week, maybe.'

17

'Yes,' I told her encouragingly. I was excellent at fostering delusion, usually in myself. 'Maybe even as soon as Monday.'

'Do you think?'

'Well, he has to get in contact with you *sometime*.'

Cleo gave a little warning look, as though to say, 'Don't go getting her hopes, up.'

But it was too late; my words had put Barbara in great form, and when the vodkas finally arrived, she insisted on tipping the flight attendant. 'That's for yourself,' she said, pressing two euro into his young, unformed hand. 'Oh, and a juice for Cleo here.'

I drank my vodka back quickly, as Barbara forced a game of snap on Cleo. But Barbara wasn't able to curb her competitive streak, even for an eight-year-old, and pretty soon all I could hear was, 'I won again!' while Cleo stoically said, 'Yes, well done.'

I would intervene in a minute, I decided, if Barbara got too carried away.

But the next thing I knew, Cleo was shaking my shoulder. 'Mum? Wake up. We've landed.'

Chapter Four

Ellen met us at the airport, swamped by an enormous dress that billowed out as she waved frantically at us.

'Jesus, she's getting worse,' Barbara said in alarm.

Since moving to France Ellen had dropped all her skinny jeans and Ugg boots and taken up with these gypsy-like frocks instead. They were made of some strange, coarse material, like those bags farmers keep corn in, and were dyed in 'country' colours of beige and cow-shit green. The material was low-cut over her modest breasts, before being suddenly and viciously yanked in immediately under them, which had the effect of squeezing them together and up in a most suggestive fashion. She looked like a slutty milkmaid. And, at only five foot one, a very short one.

I had no idea where she got the dresses. Off the Internet, I suspected, on some fetish site. Certainly, nobody in France wore them. Other passengers alighting from the flight looked at her like she was an extra from a period film. Some of the men clearly hoped one of her breasts would tumble out, and that they could gallantly dash forward and rescue it for her.

'What kept you?' she bellowed cheerily at us from across the barrier, as though we had a whit of control over when flights decided to take off and land. The next question on her lips would be, were we pissed?

But she held off; instead she watched me keenly for signs of mental disintegration.

'How much does she know?' I asked Barbara, bracing myself.

'Everything,' Barbara assured me.

I hadn't rung Ellen since Ollie had left, two days ago. Along with Barbara, she was my closest friend in the world. We'd had our babies together; I'd been bridesmaid at her and Mark's wedding; Ollie had been a pallbearer at her mother's funeral. If anybody could provide a bony shoulder to cry on, she could. But there was a nugget of something stopping me picking up the phone and letting rip down the line to France.

I think it might have been shame.

There goes Hannah, fecking things up again. If I'd nailed him down *before* we'd got shacked up together and had a child, like other, normal people – like Ellen – then maybe none of this would have happened.

Ellen was oblivious to my emotions. 'Come here to me, you poor pet,' she shouted, alerting the whole airport to my misery. I'd barely got to the end of the barriers before she was on top of me, hugging me hard to her chest. God, but she was strong. It was from her job as resident midwife on the farm. I'm not joking. She 'birthed' a calf last year by hauling it out of its bawling mother, who apparently couldn't be arsed to push. She'd always been wiry and thin, but five years of physical labour had made her even leaner. Barbara and I hated wearing sleeveless tops around her, because there she was, all sculpted and firm, whereas we wouldn't have been out of place in a bat colony.

'Happy birthday, eh?' I mumbled into her masses of hair, in a jokey voice. I wanted to get in there first: don't go feeling sorry for me, because I'm doing a grand job all by myself.

'Oh, it's just crap, isn't it?' she said, looking like she was going to cry herself.

'Don't you start.'

'I'm just so shagging up*set* for you.' She hugged me harder.

To add insult to injury, she looked nowhere near thirty-eight. There wasn't a mark on her face, despite all the hours spent in the bracing wind, cleaning out sheds. Her skin was horribly healthy-looking, the only lines being some jolly laughter ones around her mouth. Her hair was still as wild as ever – dark red corkscrew curls that were forever bursting out of clips and buns in a most provocative way, Barbara regularly complained.

How did she manage to look so well, everyone at home said. The fresh air, was the general consensus. And all that organic food (they reared their own lambs and promptly ate them). Lack of stress, too – what worries could she possibly have, living out in the middle of the countryside with her family, amongst nature, sculling back cheap, delicious wine and shooting the breeze with their authentic French neighbours?

Barbara and I knew it was none of those things. It was SEX. She and Mark went at it relentlessly. We had first-hand experience of this, because the guestroom where Barbara and I usually slept (Ollie was always banished to the sofa downstairs) backed onto their room, and we would reverberate in our beds every time their headboard crashed against the dividing wall.

'Not *again*,' Barbara would moan, lurching for the bottle of Jack Daniel's that she normally brought to bed to ward off the cold. 'Don't they have to be up at six to milk the goats or something?'

But even as we complained, and pulled our duvets up over our heads to drown out the noise, I think both of us were just the teeniest bit jealous. There we lay, in our austere little single beds, untouched and unloved, unless we went at it ourselves, and it'd take more than one bottle of Jack for that to happen.

Seeing her again now was marvellous; like comfort food or something, and I relaxed, as much as it was possible, into her twig-like arms.

'How're-you-Barbara-any-news?' she said over my shoulder.

'No,' Barbara sighed. 'But maybe Monday.'

'Yeah, yeah,' Ellen sneered. She wasn't as good at delusion as I was, and fairly pathetic at hiding it, too.

She eventually released me. My front teeth had left an indent on her right boob.

'How are you?' she demanded tenderly, holding me firmly by the shoulders, the better to get a good look at me. She had one of those hoarse, cracked voices that sounded like she hadn't been to bed in three days because she'd been busy drinking neat rum whilst balancing a pogo-stick on her belly-button (Vegas, sixteen years ago, she'd been young).

The concern in her voice, the loyalty, the *love* – I was starved for it – nearly had me crying again, and gushing forth with all kinds of intimate details right there in the airport, such as, 'I should have guessed, what with that gang he's started hanging around with recently. And we haven't had sex since Gemma O'Neill's forty-fifth in November . . .' while Ellen would croon, 'You poor, poor thing . . . Hang on a second, Gemma O'Neill is forty-*five*?'

While Barbara was great in a crisis, Ellen was the acknowledged expert in feelings. No stone would be left unturned until every drop of emotion and angst had been wrung out of a particular situation. Ellen and I could talk for hours about What He Had Actually Meant, and, Where in the Name of Christ Is My Life Going?, and occasionally, if we were very bored, Is There Really Anything After You Die?, while Barbara would sigh and despair, 'For feck's sake, lads, we're never going to know any of these things for sure,' before giving up and going out for chips and two battered sausages.

21

Barbara just didn't get it, we both agreed; this whole shite-talk thing. But we loved her all the same; adored her, the way you would a rather eccentric yet endearing child, the one who brings in fifteen worms in her pencil case and frightens all the other, nice, little girls.

'I'm OK,' I tried to reassure Ellen.

But her eyes continued to worry at my face. 'Was it the . . . dog?'

Christ. Even *she'd* heard about it, in France. Stupid, stupid Harry, even if he'd only been getting his own back.

'I think it might have been the final straw all right,' I confirmed tightly, aware all the time that Cleo was trundling towards us with the luggage trolley, having insisted on being left in charge.

Ellen took the hint. 'You're tired. Let's wait till later.'

'Yes,' Barbara chimed in. I could tell she was getting hungry. She was looking around for a kiosk or a coffee shop that might sell her something carbohydrate-y, although she had few objections to protein or fat either. She spotted a vending machine by the exit doors. 'Should we . . . ?'

But now Ellen was pouncing on Cleo in delight. You could barely see Cleo over the pile of suitcases, most of them containing Barbara's supply of Christmas jumpers, which she'd knitted herself.

'Cleo!' Cleo was grabbed by Ellen and treated to a face-full of the slutty breasts. 'Don't tell me you've grown again.' Ellen made her stand there while she walked around her appraisingly. 'You're at least an inch taller,' she declared.

'Two,' Cleo corrected shyly.

'Two! What are they putting in that milk in Ireland at all?'

Cleo squirmed with pleasure. Auntie Ellen was so much *easier* than Auntie Barbara, she always said, even though neither of them were her aunties at all. But both of them enjoyed the title; nay, insisted on it. Auntie Ellen knew how to talk to kids, probably on account of having a couple of them herself, and she never asked pointless questions that people with no children asked, such as, 'How are you enjoying school?' Answer: 'Not.'

'Sophie and Sam can't wait for you to arrive,' she told Cleo. Sophie was eight too, born a month before Cleo. Sam was only five, born two days after they'd relocated to France, having been jolted out early by the rigorous journey across the Irish Sea. They were gorgeous kids with Ellen's mad red hair and tanned skin, despite the weather, and a great love of baguettes. 'They're so excited. And they've got a new tree house in the garden; Mark built it for them. You can sleep in it and everything, if you want.'

I could see that Barbara was really pissed off now. Days-of-the-week knickers couldn't hold a candle to a tree house, although technically you could sleep in both.

Me? I was delighted. It was one of the nicest things about coming to France; how well Cleo and Sophie and Sam got on. We'd sit out on Mark's massive patio on the summer evenings, wrapped in blankets and weather-proof jackets, and listen to the chatter floating up from the garden. Sophie and Sam had these fabulous little accents, on account of having lived in France for the past five years, and which always seemed to become more pronounced when they were with Cleo, who was Dublin through and through. Her accent also seemed to go up a notch.

'Will wee play Mummies and Daddies?' Sophie. She was very girly.

'Only if I get to be de da.' Cleo.

'But you were ze daddee ze last time.' Sam. He had a very good memory.

'Got a problem wit dat, have ya?' Cleo, slightly exasperated. In fairness, she hated playing Mummies and Daddies, feeling she and Sophie were far too old to be sticking cushions up their T-shirts before producing triplets. Sam wasn't crazy about it either, preferring to be bashing at something breakable with a large stick, but Sophie somehow seemed to get her way.

'They're at home baking cookies for you, God help you,' Ellen warned Cleo. She linked her arm through mine. 'Come on. We need to get you home too.'

Home usually meant a big feed of comforting casserole, probably of their pet lamb, washed down by lots of indecently cheap but gorgeous wine, and a good old natter long into the night. Right now, I couldn't think of anything I needed more, although I always felt a bit guilty for depleting the livestock. 'Isn't it much better than picking up some cheap chicken from the supermarket wrapped in plastic that probably spent its life in a tiny cage looking at its feet?' Ellen always said.

'Yes, yes,' Barbara and I always bleated, although perhaps that was an unfortunate choice of word.

She led the way out of the airport, pushing the huge trolley one-handed as though it weighed no more than a feather, her skirts swaying and her red hair bullying its way out of the knot on the top of her head.

'Let's hope she didn't bring the tractor,' Barbara muttered sourly as we trailed behind her, feeling wildly overdressed in our city coats and boots.

She hadn't. She'd brought the huge, mud-encrusted Range Rover instead. Barbara gallantly insisted that I sit in the front, while she and Cleo climbed into the back, Barbara brushing aside a ratty old brown rug that actually turned out to be a dog.

'Sorry,' said Ellen, as Barbara clutched her chest in fright. 'He has worms. Don't you, you poor old fellow?' And she reached back and gave him an enormous tickle, which he responded to by jumping around like a mentaler and barking his head off. 'I thought I'd get to the vet before collecting you but I ran out of time.'

Barbara was nearly in the boot at this point. 'You're not thinking of going now, are you?'

'It'll wait till tomorrow. Oh, sit down, Barbara. It's not contagious or anything. At least, I don't think so.'

I looked over my shoulder to find Cleo grinning beside me. She reached forward and squeezed my shoulder as though to say, 'You're all right now. You're with the other lunatics.'

And, funnily enough, I did feel better.

Chapter Five

Barbara, Ellen and I went back twenty years; 'two whole decades,' Barbara often said, in case one of us didn't quite get it.

We'd been seventeen or eighteen, only babies really, and just about to start college. Our parents had put us all into the same digs in a house in Stillorgan. The place was run by Mrs Dullard – unsurprisingly, a large, dour woman with a vicious moustache and a dry cough. She was aided and abetted by her husband, a little whippet of a man who was always up ladders fixing things or popping out of nooks and crannies and giving Barbara a fright.

Mrs Dullard was a fan of tassels. They were everywhere: fringing the couch, dancing around lampshades, adorning tablecloths, rugs, bedspreads, blinds. She even had a pair of earrings that looked like couple of runaway tassels. For years afterwards, I would have little tassels floating in my line of vision, like black dots. 'Me too!' Ellen had declared recently, like it was a terrible secret she'd been holding in.

I was to share a twin room with Ellen. Barbara was next door, in a room of her own. Mrs Dullard had decided it was better that way, on account of the fact that, back then, Barbara was a sleepwalker, and it wouldn't be fair on another person to wake suddenly in the middle of the night to find her looming over them.

My first sight of Ellen was this pixie-like creature with orange hair, sprawled across one of the twin beds. She lit a cigarette – I was shocked – inhaled like Dot Cotton, and said to me, 'Nice Doc Martens.'

That was the trend back then; big lace-up boots teamed with floaty, romantic dresses and blouses, topped off with piles of plastic jewellery. When we looked back at photos of ourselves, we were like a joke version of Bananarama, although Barbara was never sure which one of them she most resembled. A member of the crew, we eventually decided.

'Thanks,' I said, thrilled that I'd got one thing right. I was very eager back then.

She took another few sucks of her cigarette, trying not to cough. 'I can't get the hang of these at all,' she said worriedly. 'Do you want a go?'

It was exactly the kind of thing my mother had nightmares about. Her main reason for putting me in digs in the first place, as opposed to a flat, was that she was worried that I might be easily led.

'Go on, then,' I said, confirming every one of Mum's suspicions. I would remain enslaved to the weed for the next ten years, only giving up after seeing a documentary showing the inside of a smoker's blackened lungs. The smoker, it hardly needed to be pointed out, was dead.

From the minute I saw her, I thought Ellen was the bee's knees: good-looking, popular, thin, brainy, had a great laugh, thin, excellent at holding her drink, and did I mention thin?

In contrast, I was a heifer of a country girl, with marbled thighs and a wad of puppy fat around my middle. The frilly tops were no help either. Next to Ellen, I felt backward, inexperienced, unsophisticated. We were the same age, but she was streets ahead of me in every department. After only a week in college, she already knew the best pubs to go to, whereas I had come to the attention of the college authorities for nothing more impressive than persistently turning up at the wrong lecture halls.

'It's not that I don't care,' I insisted to my personal tutor. He looked like my dad, and I was mortified at having been hauled into his office after only seven days in the place. 'I'm just a bit of a slow starter.'

That was true. I hadn't begun puberty till I was fourteen, for example. For years I was the smallest, weediest person in the whole class, alongside Patrick O'Keeffe, who looked like he was about seven with his little round, smooth face. I was so used to it, happy even, that when I'd woken up one morning to find that I was sprouting boobs and hair everywhere, I'd been mildly traumatised.

It could be said that change wasn't something I felt entirely comfortable with. When I made friends, I tended to keep them on a permanent basis, although I wasn't sure if Ellen was aware of this danger when she took pity on me following her around, and began coaxing me into flouting Mrs Dullard's rule of no staying out past midnight. She was very persuasive; I managed to overcome my natural fear of rule-breaking, and put my best foot forward through the door of O'Neills & Sons, Purveyors of Fine Food and Spirits.

Once I'd been slowly initiated into the culture of pubs, and drinking, I found that I actually loved it. It was my natural calling and something that I would enthusiastically keep up throughout my twenties, right up until the moment I discovered I was pregnant (which, funnily enough, had happened after a particularly boozy night in the pub, I worked out). I was so good at it that study and exams became merely minor annoyances that had to be seen to every now and again.

Ellen and I probably developed a reputation that first year as good-time girls; always up for a laugh, or a party, entertaining everybody with our stories about the Dullards, and how Ellen had opened the bathroom door suddenly one evening to find Mr Dullard on his knees on the other side of the door, 'fixing the lock,' he maintained. If anybody was moving flat and wanted to organise an impromptu housewarming, Ellen and I were generally somewhere near the top of the invite list – not entirely because of popularity, I suspected, but more because we were guaranteed to show up.

We didn't get on with Barbara at all in the beginning. She wore really hickey clothes, like corduroys and awful jumpers that we learned she knitted herself, and she had a desperate fringe, cut straight across like she was six. She'd never come out drinking, preferring instead to stay in her room and watch documentaries on whaling on her black-and-white television. Plus, the whole sleepwalking thing was a bit freaky. I bumped into her on my way to the loo in the middle of the night once, and she looked through me like I didn't exist.

But Ellen maintained it was a sham, just put on to seek attention.

'It's not,' Barbara defended herself stoutly.

'Why don't you walk with your arms outstretched then, like they do in *Scooby-doo*?' Ellen challenged. We had noted that Barbara's arms remained firmly at her side during these so-called sleepwalking episodes.

'I don't know. I have no control over it. But next time I'll try, OK?' Barbara said, exasperated.

Barbara wasn't a bit impressed with our rampant socialising, or Ellen's innate ability to attract good-looking men into our vicinity. All she seemed to do was study, eat, and go home on the bus at weekends to Ballyhaunis, where she was from. For her part, she treated us as though we were the worst pair of eejits she'd ever had the misfortune to end up living with. The fact that we were doing Arts degrees was proof enough to her that we were airheads with no ambition and no clue as to what we really wanted to do.

She probably had that much right – when it came to me, anyway.

The three of us were forced together every night in Mrs Dullard's chilly, sparse kitchen. As part of the deal, we got our dinner cooked for us each evening; nearly always something with mince in it, like a tiny slice of meatloaf or a starter portion of shepherd's pie, accompanied by a few sticks of carrots and two small, hard-boiled potatoes. The grand finale was some jelly or custard, served in little metal bowls like they gave to people in institutions.

'It wouldn't feed a fecking sparrow,' Barbara regularly and bitterly complained.

For once, we had to agree with her. Mrs Dullard's food provided hardly any lining for our sessions in the pub; over the course of that first term we all lost on average half a stone, which was great. The downside was that we had to waste good drinking money on proper lunches in the campus canteen so that we didn't start collapsing during lectures.

Barbara felt the food deprivation most keenly. She came from a family that felt that no meal was complete unless accompanied by a white sliced loaf spread thickly with butter, and followed by a large apple tart covered in custard. Then, to finish up, tea and biscuits. If anyone was still hungry after that, they could always have a slice of roast beef left over from the day before, between more slices of bread.

Under Mrs Dullard's regime, Barbara's corduroy trousers were beginning to hang off her large frame and she took to nibbling the top of her pencils. Then one night the hunger pangs brought on a sleepwalking episode. One minute, she said, she was switching off her reading lamp and turning over in bed; the next thing she knew, she was standing barefoot in the kitchen, the fridge door swinging open, and her mouth stuffed full of ham, cheese and a hunk of bread. Mr Dullard was standing beside her in a pair of stripy pyjamas and holding a hurley, looking shocked.

Apparently, by the time he'd arrived on the scene, Barbara had put away most of the weekly shop, including a box of Mr Kipling French Fancies that Mrs Dullard had got in especially for when her sister came round to visit. He'd discovered the pillaged box hanging limply from one of her outstretched hands.

There was terrible trouble. Mrs Dullard was so outraged at this 'breach of privacy' that she went and wrote a letter of complaint to Barbara's mother, making some very personal remarks about Barbara into the bargain. Barbara's mother was no pushover and fired a letter back, alleging that Mrs Dullard was 'meaner than a junkyard dog'.

The following night we got *two* slices of meatloaf along with the boiled potatoes and carrots, and a loaf of bread was left out, as well as a block of (cheap) cheese.

'I might try this sleepwalking lark myself,' Ellen said, delighted.

Barbara looked at her calmly. 'Who said I was sleepwalking that time?'

Our heads snapped up: Barbara, and *treachery*?

'I had my hands outstretched in the kitchen, remember?' She couldn't resist getting the dig in. 'I just did it to fool him. I have a load of stuff stashed under my bed from their presses.' She gave us a doubtful look. 'You can share it, if you stop that stupid laughing that you do all the time. I can hear you through the walls.'

'*Well*,' Ellen began, all in a huff. Then she must have remembered the French Fancies, because she gave a shrug of her elegant shoulders and said, 'Fine. But only if you stop that noise you make blowing your nose. We're not deaf either.'

Barbara staged three more daring 'sleepwalking' raids on the kitchen over the next month, but then Mrs Dullard put a lock on the fridge door at night and that was the end of that. By then, we'd talked Barbara into wearing jeans instead of baggy corduroys – 'You've got quite an OK bottom,' Ellen told her encouragingly – and Barbara had taken to coming into our bedroom on a nightly basis to trade insults with us.

'Hungover again? You're such a pair of losers.'

'Yeah? Bet you're still a virgin,' we'd sneer back, not to be outdone. (Although so was I. I wasn't at all sure about Ellen.)

'Of course I am,' Barbara always said proudly. 'Although I reckon I've probably broken my hymen from riding the horses at home.'

'*God*, Barbara. Like anybody's going to check.'

'I hope they don't go looking for *yours*,' she said to Ellen. 'I'd say it's already gone into early retirement, has it?'

We really began to respect her. The clincher came at the end of the last term, when we had to hand in a load of final assignments, none of which we had done. We'd simply run out of time, and were suddenly facing the possibility of failing the year. 'Our parents are going to kill us,' Ellen stated, looking scared. Barbara, of course, had handed hers in weeks early and came round to our room one night close to the end to enjoy our distress. But she surprised us by volunteering to sit at one of the massive, ancient Amstrads in the computer room at college – 'out of the goodness of my heart, not because I like you or anything' – and typed with surprising speed while we hurriedly plagiarised textbooks and past students' assignments that we'd managed to buy from a dodgy guy called Gonzo. We submitted the assignments in the nick of time, managing to accumulate enough marks to scrape through.

After eighteen months in Mrs Dullard's, and with Barbara a stone lighter, and with streaks in her hair (Ellen was working wonders on her), we eventually moved into a flat together, and then a house. After graduation, we decided to take some time out to travel. We started off in Sydney, where Ellen trumped our menial jobs in ice-cream parlours by landing a gig as a 'hostess', wink wink, although she maintained that she'd never been asked to do anything improper. Barbara finally lost her virginity to a very nice Aussie called Fred, who promptly asked her to marry him. 'You were that good?' Ellen said in plain disbelief. But then Barbara got offered a high-powered job back home and she broke poor Fred's heart, and ours, by abandoning our world trip midway through to go home to Ireland and earn sixty grand a year doing something in science. Many times we had to ring her up from Toronto or Mexico City and beg her to wire through emergency funds. She always came through for us, fair play to her, although her interest rates were on the steep side.

Then Ellen got a job back home too, when we were in Kos. I hadn't even known she'd been applying, and I was a bit hurt. 'We've been away two years,' she reasoned with me. That came as a bit of a shock to me; I thought we'd been gone about six weeks. But time flies when you're having fun; so much fun, in my case, that I was looking a bit jaundiced.

I could have just gone home too, of course. But I decided I'd stick around for the summer, as I'd just landed a job as a holiday rep. It would be another eight years before I finally came back to Dublin, with Ollie in tow – another fully paid-up drifter with a computer degree and a great love of weed and playing guitars on faraway beaches at sunset. By that time, of course, I was pregnant with Cleo, and when I landed in Dublin Airport, I remembered thinking excitedly that I'd had my wild youth, quite a few years more of it than most people, in fact, but I was home now and my real life was just about to begin.

Chapter Six

Ellen always maintained that it had been a joint decision to relocate to France.

'Ahem, right,' Barbara and I always said behind our hands.

'It bloody was. Why do you two always think it was just Mark's?'

Possibly because Ellen allegedly had never set foot outside urban boundaries until she'd been forced on a school trip to a bog in Louth, where she'd spent the whole time teetering on the edge of it, trying to put on a pair of lovely polka-dot wellingtons she'd sourced in town for the occasion. Even now, Barbara strongly suspected that Ellen's air of contented countrywoman was a complete façade, and that if we ever got her to Paris for a day, and to all those lovely, expensive designer shops, she'd unravel like a jumper from Primark: 'To hell with the countryside. Gimme me clotheeesssss.'

It was an attractive theory, but I wasn't so sure. Apart from the questionable dresses, she seemed to have thrown herself into the whole adventure heart and soul. The other side of it was, even if it was all going belly up and she was desperate to come home, she would never let anybody know. She was like that; completely pig-headed, and proud with it, even with us.

All the same, she could insist all she liked about the move to France being a joint decision, but there was no doubt that the dream had been Mark's. His best friend's father used to have a farm, before he'd got addicted to on-line poker and lost it all to a sixty-year-old lady from Arizona. Mark would recount fervently to us many happy childhood memories of visits to the farm, and of being chased around the yard by demented turkeys in the run-up to Christmas. He'd dug up potatoes too,

31

and eaten blackberries off the actual branches without even washing them first (his eyes always grew misty when he told us this). It was in his blood, he maintained, and even though life was good and right as an overpaid IT consultant, he kept feeling the pull of the land, to the extent that he began growing things in pots around the Dublin 4 penthouse. It started with basil and coriander, which was harmless enough, but soon he wanted more; the balcony became home to dozens of tomato plants and bags of compost. He began taking little pots of his early produce to dinner parties: mottled-looking mushrooms with strange, wart-like growths, and tomatoes of a queasy orange hue. 'Could he not have brought a box of After Eights?' the hosts would complain, as they made a show of trying to find room for the deformed vegetables in their pristine fridge.

'All organic,' Mark would tell the rest of the guests, his dark eyes burning with the light of a zealot. 'They've never been sprayed *in their lives*, can you believe that? Go on, taste one. No, I'm not being weird, I just want to illustrate something. Let me pop one in.' It was nearly always a female guest, and she nearly always consented to Mark popping one in. 'Roll it around your tongue. That's it. Slowly. Does that taste good? Yes, I thought it might.'

The female guest would be nearly orgasmic at this point, such was the passion and seductiveness in his voice. By the end of the night they'd be lining up, all with their mouths open.

In the early days of this, before she'd got drawn in, Ellen could reliably be found in the kitchen, flinging her eyes to heaven behind his back, and getting pissed: 'Him and his fucking vegetables. God give me patience. I can't even hang a clotheshorse out on the balcony any more. Hopefully it's just a phase.'

So no: France had not been her idea, but his. And she'd gone along with it because she loved him. Simple as that. And the sex was undoubtedly marvellous. I think I may have mentioned that before. But both Barbara and I agreed that whenever we thought about Ellen and Mark, we always imagined them having sex. Barbara used to be very disturbed by these thoughts: 'Do you think it means I want to have a threesome with them?' She'd been relieved to find I was having the same problem.

Barbara was still a little dismissive that Ellen had uprooted her whole life for a man, especially as we were all supposed to be feminists. At least we had been back in our twenties, when we'd gone to lectures on 'The History of Birth Control' (which had let me down badly) and passed around a dog-eared copy of *The Beauty Myth*. Barbara had gone for months without shaving under her arms after reading that. In fact, we still weren't sure whether she'd ever gone back.

'I've seen those programmes on the telly,' Barbara maintained stoutly, when Ellen first voiced her and Mark's plans. 'About people who jack it all in for some harebrained idea – usually the man's – to make a living growing blooming vines on a rocky hillside in a foreign country.'

'We aren't growing vines.' Ellen rolled her eyes. 'We won't get enough sun to grown vines.'

How right she'd been.

'So what exactly *are* you going to grow then?' Barbara persisted officiously, as though she would recognise a head of kale from a head of cabbage. And I wouldn't, either.

'We haven't decided yet. Mark has lots of ideas, but we need to talk to the local people first, get their advice.'

'Yeah, because you both speak loads of French,' Barbara scoffed.

Ellen began to throw around her red curls, always a danger sign. 'No, we don't. But we're learning. God, Barbara, don't knock it just because you haven't the nerve to do it yourself.'

Barbara wasn't in the least bit offended. 'I don't want to go live in France. And you didn't either, until Mark woke up one morning and decided to uproot his whole family and relocate to a place he'd seen on the Internet.'

I knew Barbara was only speaking out of concern for Ellen, and it was true they'd bought the house on an ex-pat-type website from someone who was offloading it cheap. But could she not see that maybe it wasn't selfishness driving Mark, but passion?

Barbara had no time for Mark's passion. I, on the other hand, had been in his company the time he'd described growing his first tomatoes from seed, and I'd been hooked. Couldn't remember a word of it afterwards, of course, but the way his eyes had flashed excitedly, and his strong, square hands had made round, tomato-like shapes, had stayed with me for quite some time.

When they'd finally confounded the sceptics and actually moved to France, I think we were all a bit envious of them, including Barbara. We might have laughed our heads off at the first pictures that floated home of them, both wearing stripy tops and Mark with a black beret – hysterical – but when we dried our eyes, we were all still in the same old jobs, still stuck in the city, still eating beautifully shaped, tasteless, and probably radioactive vegetables from the supermarket.

Somehow we all felt a bit flat.

But that was the effect Mark and Ellen had on people. They made you feel that your own life, no matter how brilliant it looked on paper, was ever so slightly boring. Not intentionally, of course. It wasn't their fault they were cooler, better-looking and generally more exciting than your average Jo and Josephine.

It was enough to make you just the teeniest bit green around the gills.

Chapter Seven

We left the airport and began the drive up towards the house, ignoring Barbara in the back, who began doing up buttons on her coat the further north we went, and blowing on her fingers. Ellen, as always, gave us a running commentary on our surroundings, which we privately called her tourist information broadcast.

'Agriculture is one of Brittany's main economic activities,' she lectured us. I'd hoped that she would kick off with something a bit more fun like, say, its rare bird sanctuaries, but it looked as though we were in for a heavy-duty session. She shot a look across at me before proceeding. 'That's BriTT-any, as opposed to Britney, the singer.'

I'd once dropped the T. I wasn't allowed to forget it. Along with her hitherto undiscovered passion for organic farming, Ellen had been infused with a mad patriotism towards everything French. You couldn't have a simple joke by crassly taking off the French accent without having the head bitten off you. 'That's racism, you know. How would you like it if the French went around saying, "Bejaysus", and "Mighty" and "What-The-Fook"?'

'How's Mark?' I asked, hoping to head Ellen off at the pass.

I liked talking about Mark. Most women did. I probably fancied him too, but I wasn't allowed to say it, or even think it, because he was married to my best friend. All I knew was that I got a bit goofy and tongue-tied in his presence, and I enjoyed watching him bend down to pick things up. Once I purposefully let a book fall to the ground just so he'd pick it up. But it was OK, because Barbara did it once too, even though she maintains to this day that it was an accident.

If you saw Mark you'd understand. He was tall, very tall – six foot

two, I would wager — and built like a rugby player. That is, for the uninitiated, stocky, but — and this important — *not fat*, with large, muscular
shoulders, and thighs that Barbara maintained were a little thickish for
her taste, but which I thoroughly enjoyed watching as they chafed friskily
against his jeans.

I also liked his hair, even though I suspected he spent quite a lot of time
on it. But why wouldn't he, when it was so springy and luxuriant, and
needed a little fix every now and again to stop it flopping into his eyes?

'Only poofs fix their hair that much,' Ollie had declared once in a
rare outburst of rancour.

Jealous, of course. His own hair was shocking. He was a firm proponent
of Wash & Go, and a visit to the barber maybe once a year. The result
was that he had enough for a ponytail, but that would be incredibly naff,
and so it just hung about his shoulders, giving him the look of a rock
star — well, in his dreams, anyway. I actually loved his hair, because in my
head I was still twenty and thought that longish, clean, rock-star hair was
the best thing ever.

But back to Mark (whom I didn't fancy, of course). More than his
good looks, he had charisma: what other Irishman on this planet could
persuade a woman with a job *as a film producer* to up sticks and move
from a penthouse apartment in Dublin 4 to a run-down farm in France
with just a crook of his little finger?

'Mark's great,' Ellen answered me now. 'He won't be back till tomorrow.
He's taken the Dutch on a trip to a couple of vineyards and they'll stay
overnight.'

'What Dutch?' I asked.

'Oh, just a couple of friends who are staying with us for the week,'
Ellen said, as though she'd already mentioned it, which I was pretty sure
she hadn't. 'They won't bother you. They're staying in the barn, which
we've converted into a living area.'

They had? That was all news to me. I'd thought the barn was a listed
building, it was so decrepit and old, and if not, it should have been. And
I didn't know anybody who called their friends 'the Dutch', even if they
were Dutch. Would you not say, Mary and Brian, or whatever the equivalent was in Dutch?

Ellen shot me another of her warm, sympathetic looks. 'He just can't
believe it.' She cast a careful look back at Cleo. 'You know, what happened.'

Could any of us? The shouting, the fighting, the threats to phone the
guards at 4 a.m. . . . .

And that was just his parents.

'Only last week they were shopping in Lidl together,' Ollie often said to me in disbelief. I didn't so much mind the drama as the way everybody was forced to take sides, to choose. We were talking about *adults* here. But when I tried to make Ollie see that, he couldn't. But, of course, by that stage he was turning all his fears and resentments onto me. And I hadn't done a blasted thing, except make casseroles and pies and taken them around to his mother, eejit that I was.

Maybe if I'd spoken up more, and not allowed our little family to become embroiled, none of this would have happened.

'Have you talked to him since he left?' Ellen asked, doing her best to be cryptic in front of Cleo.

Cleo, however, was no daw, having watched enough episodes of *Home and Away* to understand many an adult context. She was also worryingly clued into things I'd been sure she knew nothing about.

'He might change his mind,' she told Ellen rather sternly.

'Oh, er, yes.' Ellen gave me a look; she didn't approve of soaps, even though back when we all shared a house, we would lose entire evenings to them. Soaps were off Ellen's agenda now. She insisted that they just couldn't get them on their telly over here. But I reckoned that her viewing habits had gone the way of everything else: organic, home-grown and slightly sanctimonious.

And some day I would pluck up the courage to say this. Although, on reflection, probably not. More than likely I was just jealous, anyway. I mean, look at me – thirty-eight, still unmarried, and now a single mother. I'd frittered away my entire twenties when I should have been laying down the foundations for my future; or at least I should have had enough self-respect to pack in those badly paid jobs where I was required to stand on a tiny stage in my fluorescent orange uniform and help host wet T-shirt competitions.

And now my thirties seemed to have turned to dust as well. I'd been so full of plans when we'd finally come home, Ollie and I. We were going to do things. Achieve something. No more mucking around, pretending we were still twenty-two. We had a child now. We had to grow up.

I wondered what Ellen thought of me, arriving on her doorstep like some delinquent yet again, my suitcase in tow, only this time dragging a child behind me, too. My man had left me, and I hadn't so much as a lick of mascara on my face. If it wasn't for Barbara, I wouldn't even have any money, as I'd been too distracted to remember to go to the bank before leaving. And I suspected that I stank of vodka, even though we'd only had the one.

Really, all I was missing was the awful orange uniform.

A phone rang. In the back, Barbara jerked upright like she'd just received a thousand volts, and hauled her bag out from under the wormy dog. Could it be Dimitri? Then, beside me, Ellen nearly sent the Range Rover into a tree as she patted herself frantically all over, though it was hard to know where she'd secure a phone in that skimpy dress.

But it wasn't her phone, or Barbara's. It was mine.

They all watched as I dug around in my bag, then my coat, then my jeans pocket before finally extracting the thing. I didn't even have time to check the caller display before jamming the thing to my ear.

'Hello?'

Chapter Eight

There was the long, echoing silence that international phone calls everywhere seemed to specialise in, just to keep you guessing.

'Hello?' I said again, aware of three pairs of eyes on me expectantly.

Then a voice burst into my ear, 'Hannah? Is that you?'

Who else was it going to be: Shirley Temple?

'Oh. Hello, Harry.' My heart settled into a depressed sulk. The very last person on this earth I wanted to talk to right now was Ollie's father.

He sensed this; he wasn't slow. Besides, half the family had apparently told him in the past couple of days, 'You're the last fucking person on this earth that I want to talk to right now, do you hear me?'

The few who would still entertain him had professed their shock in no uncertain terms. 'We don't know what to say, Harry. We thought that kind of thing only happened in China. Frankly, we're not going to invite you over for dinner any more. We've all been feeling very queasy since we heard the news.'

'Is that Granddad?' Cleo piped up. She knew nothing about what had happened, and still thought he was great.

I put my hand over the phone. 'You can talk to him later, OK?' I knew I was being mean, but why should Harry have the benefit of a chat with his granddaughter after all the trouble he'd caused?

He continued to hang about awkwardly at the other end. 'How was the trip?' he asked. 'Did you get there OK?'

'No, pesky plane crashed, I've lost both my legs, but what can you do?'

Behind me Cleo gave a scandalised intake of breath. She didn't consider that kind of thing funny at all.

'Hannah,' Harry said reproachfully.

'Sorry,' I said with a sigh.

I couldn't understand this myself, but I was still mad about Harry, despite everything. Even though he could be the world's biggest idiot, he was a genuine idiot. There were no pretensions with him; he wouldn't know how. When I'd first met him in the living room of their family home – aargh, tassels, everywhere – he'd immediately tried to put me at my ease by informing me matter-of-factly, 'I got Muriel up the duff too, you know, before we got married,' not noticing that Muriel was slowly going purple in the face.

He dropped clangers like dandruff; he called me Fiona for about a year, even though we could never work out why. He insulted Muriel's cooking, dress sense and the size of her bottom unthinkingly, and heedless of the consequences, which was just as well, as she usually went mental. Cleo he regarded affectionately and distantly, as though she were mildly interesting but not enough to turn the telly off for. He lived in his own little world, like some small, plodding creature (he even had a thatch of thick, furry hair) that occasionally came out to socialise but who was really quite happy in his own little burrow.

That was until Muriel had come over all modern, of course, and dug him out.

I assured him, 'We're in France, OK? Ellen's just driving us back to the house now.'

'Oh,' he said, sounding relieved. 'Great.' He knew Ellen well, and had even been over with us once or twice over the years. He'd walked around the farm with Mark, blinking benignly as Mark had explained in detail about how he artificially inseminated the cows. 'It's a tough job, but somebody's got to do it!' Harry had unexpectedly ribbed a baffled Mark.

I wasn't in the mood for him today, however. He had *nil points* on my popularity rating at the moment.

'Harry, what do you want?'

He gave a long, heart-felt sigh. 'I just wanted to say sorry. About Friday. I feel like it's all my fault.'

'It *is* all your fault.'

'Now, Hannah—'

'Don't you "now, Hannah" me. I honestly thought better of you, Harry. You should be ashamed of yourself.'

I could see the girls looking at me; how could I be so mean to a poor, helpless pensioner like Harry? Not so helpless, though, that he couldn't turn the tables on Muriel in a way that had left us all fighting for breath. And many of us reaching for sick buckets.

To his credit, he took it on the chin. 'I can't believe I did it,' he said with a sigh. Neither could any of us. It was possibly the most out-of-character thing he'd ever done in his life. 'I just got so *mad*. She started it, saying all those things about me down at the Community Centre to everyone we knew. What was I supposed to do? Just suck it up?'

Harry watched even more television than we did, crime mostly, and often came out with inappropriately youthful phrases.

'Harry, I thought you phoned to talk about me? Not you.'

Again, more scandalised looks from Barbara and Ellen. They thought Harry was a dote, and didn't deserve all this bitch-slapping, no matter what he had done.

But it worked, because he went on urgently, 'I spoke to him today. Ollie. Asked him what the hell he thought he was doing. Walking out on a good girl like you? And then there's Cleo . . .'

I could feel myself getting a bit upset again, and I didn't want to, not there in the car with everybody looking at me. But Harry was so genuine, so upset himself, that I had to blink hard several times.

'I tried to talk sense into him, Hannah. Told him to put things right before they went too far. I said, "You'll be lucky if she takes you back at all, after the way you've behaved."'

Harry seemed to realise that he was very much in pot-calling territory now, and went silent. Honestly. Just when he and Muriel should have been kicking back and enjoying retirement cruises together, they decided to embark upon a nasty and bitter separation instead, and drag everybody else into it while they were at it.

'I'll ring Muriel, if you like.' Harry really must be anxious to make amends, if he was suggesting ringing the ex. 'Tell her to send him home. If he won't listen to me, maybe he'll listen to her.'

He had a point. So far, Ollie had fallen for Muriel's self-serving, low-down tricks. And if you think I'm being too hard on her, it's not because she and I never got along, even though we didn't. She never thought I was good enough for Ollie, which was gas, given that I was the one who'd finally bit the bullet and got a nine-to-five job, paid the mortgage, bought the car, and generally held the whole shebang together.

Anyhow. I had no head space for Muriel that day, even though she was probably propped up on a sofa at that very moment, fanning herself hysterically, while Ollie drip-fed her cups of sweet tea.

I suddenly had a flash of furious anger at him. The first one. It felt strange. We were never angry at each other. Life, we always agreed in our happy-clappy kind of way, was just too short. Why make war when you can make love? Or something like that.

'Harry, I have to go.'

'No, no, wait. We have to sort this thing out.' Now that his own life had bottomed out spectacularly, he seemed intent on fixing mine.

'We don't. This is between Ollie and me.' Now I was sounding unusually forceful. Normally I believed that life was too short for that too. It was always much easier just to bob along.

Well, feck that.

'Hannah,' he said suddenly, 'what am I going to do about Susie?'

Muriel had had her beloved dog, Susie, for fifteen years. She'd been missing a week now.

Or so it was alleged. I still couldn't believe Harry would use the dog to take his revenge on Muriel.

'I think you've done your worst on that front,' I told Harry coldly.

'You're not going to believe me, are you?' he said plaintively.

'I don't know what to believe, Harry, frankly.'

'I don't care what the others think, but *you* . . .' We had become very close in the past few months, and I knew what he meant. 'They're all very upset with me,' he said, sounding a bit small and lost. 'The family.'

'Yes,' I agreed. 'And can you blame them?'

'No,' he said at last.

It would do him no harm to realise, at the ripe old age of seventy-one, that actions had repercussions, and other people had feelings too.

'Goodbye, Harry.'

Chapter Nine

At the farm Sophie and Sam were being looked after by Rosalie, a stout woman who lived nearby and who helped out three days a week with the cooking and childcare, but who did not do cleaning. Let's get that one straight from the off.

We'd known her for years by that point, but she always opened the door to us like we were travelling saleswomen trying to peddle her something cheap and nasty.

'Hmm,' she said in greeting.

There were Sophie and Sam now, running out past her. At the sight of Cleo there was an eruption of hysterical 'AARRRGH's and 'OOOOH's and 'EEEEEKK's.

Rosalie proceeded to chat to Ellen in rapid-fire French. Ellen, fair play to her, responded with loads of French-sounding words back, while Barbara and I stood there uselessly, trying to remember the few phases that had been drummed into us at school.

'*Voulez-vous coucher avec moi ce soir?*' Barbara said suddenly, a light bulb clearly having gone in her head.

'No. But thanks for the offer.'

Sophie, meanwhile, had enveloped Cleo in a love-fest and was plastering her all over with sticky little lips. Sam couldn't reach and so didn't bother, and anyway, he looked vaguely disturbed by all this girlish stuff. He knew from bitter experience that he had two weeks of hell in front of him, mostly involving being dressed up in floaty clothes and forced to participate in wedding ceremonies against his will. No wonder he looked a bit depressed.

But Sophie had a firm hand on his plump little arm; he wasn't going anywhere.

She took Cleo in her other hand. 'You're in the top bunk,' she announced bossily.

Cleo hesitated. 'But I don't like heights.'

'You're in the top bunk,' Sophie reiterated, with steely resolve.

Sophie was the kind of child who had managed her own labour – six hours, not too much pushing and no drugs, thank you – and I could see that nothing much had changed.

Cleo was wondering whether to make a fuss, but then she pursed her lips up tight – dear God, it was my mother whom she looked like – and said, stoutly, 'O-K. But just for tonight.'

Peace restored, she allowed herself to be dragged off by the indomitable Sophie and the three of them ran out of the kitchen with a chorus of 'AAARGH!'s.

'Jesus Christ,' said Rosalie, slapping her hands over her ears. She was very contrary, according to Ellen. Oh, don't get her wrong, without Rosalie the whole operation would have fallen apart, but you had to be careful with her. No talking to her before 10 a.m., that kind of thing, as she was not a morning person, and she didn't like a crowd in her kitchen.

Which would be me and Barbara. We flattened ourselves back against the walls as Rosalie got her coat, took cookies out of the oven, washed up something in a flurry of suds, whipped out a fully prepared lunch from the fridge – she really *was* a marvel – and departed in high dudgeon.

'I'll see you when this lot are gone,' she said, in English, so that Barbara and I were left in no doubt as to her feelings.

'Yes, yes, I don't blame you, Rosalie,' Ellen said fervently. 'I'm terribly sorry.' Lick-arse. But, as she'd said to us often, if it was a toss-up between us and Rosalie, Rosalie would win hands down every time.

There were more goodbyes at the door, and more kisses, and then Ellen loaded Rosalie into an ancient car and waved her off and blew kisses, and by the time she'd finally left we were all flipping exhausted.

'Now. Tea!' Ellen announced happily.

Oh. We'd been half hoping for, 'Now. A bottle of wine!' but maybe it was too early. Ellen always complained that people assumed that life in France always involved getting scuttered at midday on table wine. Which we had done more than once, it has to be said.

Still, we hadn't eaten yet, and anyway, I was traumatised and avoidance of more alcohol was probably a good idea.

They had an enormous farmhouse table. You could play a game of five-a-side on it. Mark had built it from some beautiful old tree they'd had to cut down because it was developing some kind of fungus. I'm sure he told me the details but I confess I tended to drift in and out of these conversations about plants and trees and stuff, although I do remember enjoying watching his lips form around words that meant nothing to me: '. . . oak . . . three hundred years old . . . Ceratocystis fagacearum . . . sanded it down . . . varnished . . .'

There was a beer mat stuck under one of the legs of the table to steady it, but it was still a fine, fine job.

While Ellen made the tea, Barbara checked her phone under the table when she thought nobody was looking, and announced, 'You're getting too skinny.'

I perked up, thinking she was talking to me. Well, there had to be some upside to getting dumped, hadn't there? I'd barely eaten anything since Friday and I felt satisfyingly concave.

But her words were directed at Ellen. Barbara accused her of this every time we came over. If it were true, Ellen always countered, then she would be clinically dead by now.

'And you're getting plump,' Ellen said back.

'I know,' said Barbara smugly.

There was always a bit of this for the first day or two. It was a knee-jerk thing, the compulsion to trade insults. Then, by midweek, when they'd rubbed the corners off each other, they could relax and get tight again.

The only thing was, this time Barbara was right. Ellen *was* getting too skinny. Her cheeks were hollows and her wrists looked like a vigorous handshake might snap them.

'Are you working too hard?' I said. I was concerned. Also, it was great to talk about somebody other than myself for a moment.

'Well, of course I am,' Ellen said, exasperated. 'You try running a farm and see how much work it is. If it's not the weeds choking the vegetables, it's the damn sprinkler gone on the blink again in the greenhouse. And did I tell you that two of the piglets have to be hand-fed every four hours with babies' bottles because the others won't let them near the mother and we can't afford to lose them?'

'Really?' Barbara always looked satisfyingly disturbed by these tales. She could never understand why Ellen would want to spend her life with creatures who were so uncivilised. Already that worm-infested dog was romping around with the other dogs in the garden, as yet untreated, and I could see that she wasn't able to take her eyes off him. She'd also washed her hands twice already since we'd arrived. The second time she'd turned the tap off with her elbow, the way surgeons do when scrubbing up.

'Anyway, I don't mean to moan,' Ellen said, all cheery again.

'Moan away,' I encouraged her. 'That's partly why we're here.'

An integral element of the annual trip to France was the offloading of emotional baggage on the people who knew you better than anybody else in the world. There was only so much of your private life you could divulge to, say, your work mates, or your family – try talking to your mother about your sexual problems, for instance; *very* uncomfortable – but with Ellen and Barbara, I really felt I could tell them anything. I hoped they viewed me in the same light.

And so the pot of tea was made, the chairs were pulled in close to the vast table and it was a case of who would jump in first.

Generally, each of us had stored up a year's worth of gripes and worries; Barbara's concern over Dimitri, for example, had spanned two holidays now, so long was it all dragging on. The next villain (although Dimitri wasn't a villain, just misunderstood, mostly by Ellen) was her boss in work, who was, according to her, racist and intolerant and sexist, and who even hated it when women got pregnant and had to take maternity leave. He wouldn't hire a bloody woman under forty ever again, he'd been heard complaining, if only the discrimination laws would facilitate him; no sooner did they get their feet under one of his desks before they were up the spout and off on maternity leave. 'You're all right, though,' he'd said to Barbara in the pub once, as though it was a compliment. 'No chance of you going that way, eh?'

She'd put off telling him that she *would* be going that way herself, actually, please God, if everything went well. She'd put off breaking the news to him for ages, and now there she was, five years down the line, with motherhood about to strike any day or week now, and she *still* hadn't told the bigot. Darn fool girl, as Ellen and I insistently and repeatedly told her. It was only going to be worse, keeping it from him.

Ellen generally had a mixed bag of moans. Her mother's cancer had been the biggest worry for the past three years; then we'd tried to help her through her feelings of guilt at not being in Ireland when her mother had finally died. Well, it had been impossible, what with the kids and the farm. They'd just launched their farm tours, too, to make a bit of extra money, which had turned out to be a disaster, as Ellen had to keep making flying trips back to Ireland to her mother, and Mark had been left trying to do everything. The final farm tour had been conducted with poor

46

Sam being pushed around with the group in a wheelbarrow, with a blanket over him, as he'd had tonsillitis and couldn't be sent to playgroup and Mark couldn't get anybody to mind him (this was pre-Rosalie). Or hadn't tried hard enough, or something.

Ellen still missed her mother desperately. You could see it in her. Sometimes I got the impression that she didn't get the chance to speak about her much, only when we were over. Maybe our visits forced her to slow down or something, and she was able to talk.

I didn't usually bring an awful lot to the Table of Moans. Maybe some minor gripes about how boring work was – I was a recruitment consultant in, you've guessed it, the travel industry. I also had the usual complaints about being a working mum – too little time and too much housework – but all in all I was a happyish person, just chugging along.

But this year I'd brought the blooming kitchen sink with me. Ellen and Barbara would be catatonic by the time I'd finished detailing how my life had disintegrated so spectacularly. I wasn't much looking forward to it myself.

Ellen wasn't going to be drawn first in the moaning stakes. I could tell by the determinedly chirpy look about her. She was in hostess mode, which was always a bit frightening for the first day or two. 'Croissants? Fresh towels? Another cup of coffee?' you'd find barked at you several times an hour. Luckily she seemed to realise pretty quickly it was only us, and the courtesy would soon descend into, 'Get your own glass of wine, you lazy pig.'

They were both looking expectantly at me now, waiting for me to kick off with, 'Jesus, girls, I'm *so* miserable . . .'

My pride wouldn't let me. I'd hold out for a few more minutes, anyway. So I did the chirpy thing too, pointed to the window, and said, 'Ah, would you look!'

Outside, the kids were running across the lawn towards the tree house Mark had built. Sophie was clambering up to it as nimbly as one of the goats in the pen nearby, Cleo slightly slower in her new boots with the toy in the soles, which seemed a little impractical in this setting.

'HELP ME.' Sam stood at the bottom of the tree, roaring, trying to get one stout little leg onto the bottom rung of the wooden ladder, but having no luck. It wasn't entirely his fault. The ladder was too high off the ground for smaller children. Also, at least two of the rungs had already broken off halfway up.

'HELP ME OR I WILL TELL,' Sam tried now.

I saw then that he was wearing lipstick and what seemed to be blue eye-shadow. Up in the tree house, Sophie seemed in no hurry to come to his assistance.

'Nobody likes a snitch,' she called down triumphantly.

Eventually it was Cleo who climbed down again rather laboriously, huffing and puffing, her sturdy little haunches working hard. She caught him by the hand and tried to haul him up. That didn't work. In the end she got off altogether, grabbed him under the oxters, and, through sheer brute force, hoisted him up on to the first rung of the ladder.

We'd been going to try for another child, Ollie and I. We'd even got around to it too, which was unusual for us. But I'd had an early miscarriage, and lost heart for a good while. After that the years just seemed to fly by; suddenly Cleo was six, then seven. And I wasn't getting any younger either.

'Are we going to start trying again?' I asked Ollie one day last year.

'OK,' he said, readily enough, and went off to puncture little holes in his condoms.

But then of course Harry and Muriel split, and Ollie went off the deep end and began going out to pubs again like he was twenty-three, coming home too sozzled to take off his trousers, let alone have unprotected sex in an attempt to procreate.

I thought he was just letting off steam, with all the pub stuff, and taking up smoking again, even though we'd both given up years before. But of course it had been the beginning of the end. I'd just been too dumb to see it.

At that, I caved in. I took a mouthful of Ellen's strong tea to wet my mouth, and began, 'Jesus, girls, I'm so miserable . . .'

They were delighted. 'We knew you were,' Ellen said in great relief, reaching across the vast table to clasp my hands in her hard, brown, calloused ones. I made a mental note to bring her a tube of E45 cream the next time. For the first time, I could see little fine lines running across her forehead, and at the corner of her eyes. I'm sure she could see mine too. It was comforting, in a way. And also alarming.

'We're listening,' Barbara pronounced, like she was a host on one of those misery confessional programmes, where people admitted to fathering children with fourteen different men, only now they were a bit confused as to which one belonged to who.

It was unnerving, all this attention. Normally the two of them were so noisy and opinionated that often I'd be hard-pressed to get a word in edgeways. I seemed to have spent a lot of my life trying to interject with, 'But—' and, '*I* think—', with the occasional, 'Shouldn't we—' only to be completely drowned out.

But now their eyes were fixed on me with great tenderness and compassion, even Barbara's, and she'd already endured forty-eight hours of unrelenting misery from me.

'He's a dirty, rotten scumbag, isn't he?' Ellen said sympathetically, just to kick us off.

This kind of thing had worked perfectly well for us in the past. Whenever any of us split up with someone, the accepted code of practice was to run him into the ground. His personality would be torn apart, desecrated; his character disembowelled. There was no harm meant by it; it was just all part of the healing.

This time, though, it was wrong.

'He's not a dirty, rotten scumbag,' I pointed out quietly,

Ellen sighed and deflated. 'You're right, he's *so* not, that's why I just can't believe this.'

That opened the floodgates. 'I know, me neither.'

'It just makes everything that much harder, doesn't it?'

'God, I'm going to miss him!' That was from Barbara, and it was possibly a step too far.

A silence fell and Ellen turned to her, eyes narrowed, 'You can't be in contact with him any more. You know that, don't you?'

However much we might have liked each other's boyfriends, there were very clear boundaries; when it was over, it was over. For all of us.

Barbara looked highly offended. 'Of course I do. What do you take me for?'

'Not even about your fish.'

Now Barbara's eyes narrowed too. Ollie had looked after Barbara's tank of fish – so much easier than a dog – ever since her auntie, who used to do the honours, refused to believe that fish only needed a pinch or two of food a day, and had systematically wiped out her tank of tropical totty (they were all very good-looking) twice now.

'Not even about my fish,' Barbara ground out.

The tension lifted. Phew. Now that we were all on the same page again, Ellen gave a deep, troubled sigh, and took an enormous swig of her tea. 'The problem is,' she said to me, 'I don't know whether to tell you to forget about his sorry arse, or crawl over broken glass if that's what it takes to win him back.'

Chapter Ten

That was the problem with Ollie: he was great. Out of all the partners and boyfriends we'd ever had between us – and it came to quite a number – Ollie had emerged over the years as the clear frontrunner in the popularity stakes.

I don't really know what it was about him. I mean, he wasn't extra good-looking, although obviously I thought he was gorgeous, and I know his type of slightly scruffy, long-haired, cool look appealed to a lot of women. He wore a pair of jeans particularly well, and he was tall and sturdy, if not big, and he had a great laugh, the kind that makes you want to join in.

What else about him? He was laid-back, chatty, quite funny, although he didn't actually tell jokes, thank God. One of Barbara's exes was a frustrated comedian and would greet us all with, 'Did you hear the one about the road that got fed up of being crossed?' I can't remember the punch line now, that was how funny he was.

Ollie didn't make a huge first impression on people – he wasn't fond of dramatics – but he was always in good humour and never in too much of a hurry for a chat. Although, I suppose, you could look at that both ways, in that possibly he should have had a proper job and less time to chat. He had friends all over the world, from every kippy resort we'd ever worked in, and some nicer ones too, although we hadn't worked in as many of those. He was good at keeping in contact, and was always sending people bits of music and photos of Cleo, and offering our spare room for friends to sleep in. Frankly, this annoyed the hell out of me, as we were always having people – usually single, hungry-looking men – turning up on our doorstep, looking for a free bed for the night: 'Ollie!

Great to see you, man. Jesus, you still got that scrawny beard?' But we usually ended up sitting around the table till three in the morning drinking coffee and playing cards and having a laugh, and I was never cross for long, or at least not until it came to washing yet another set of used sheets and towels.

Ollie had so many friends that he'd been best man at seventeen weddings so far. We'd been all over the world to attend blooming weddings. Except our own, of course. Last year I'd told him no more weddings, unless they were in the country. We just couldn't afford them.

Ollie got on particularly well with women. He was able to talk to them without (a) getting embarrassed, (b) looking like he was trying to hit on them, (c) making their boyfriends/husbands jealous, and (d) making *me* jealous. He was unfazed by conversations about, say, childcare or hair dye. He just jumped right in there with his own hair dye experiences, of which he'd had a couple, both at stag nights (seventeen of those, too). But he never tried to take over the conversation, the way men can sometimes do, just to make sure the women knew how important and great they were. Ollie *was* great, but he didn't realise it, and if he had, he wouldn't have cared anyway.

His biggest claim to fame, though – and he'd probably like me to mention this – was that he scored a perfect one hundred points in a quiz called 'Have You Landed the Perfect Man?', or something like that, which we once did in a magazine.

'I don't want to pre-empt the results, but I think we both know you're in with a pretty good chance,' he told me smugly as he thumbed through the magazine to find the quiz. It was a rainy Sunday and we were clearly bored.

The questions weren't exactly *Mastermind* either. 'Does your man think with his head or his heart?' was the first off the starting blocks.

'Don't scoff. It's a serious question. And I could give a really rude answer but I won't.' Sanctimoniously, he ticked off (b), which was his heart, and drew a little love-heart beside it just for effect.

He romped through another dozen or so questions, including such conundrums as, 'If you were upset, would your man always, sometimes, or never know what was really behind it?'

'Always.' Another box ticked with a flourish.

'I think I'm supposed to be filling it in, not you,' I pointed out.

'Yes, but in question four, I ticked (c), which means that I am always completely in tune with your thoughts, so I know exactly what answers you would have given anyway. I'm just ticking the boxes to save you the effort, my little pumpkin pie.' (Another question had involved pet names.)

He came in at the top of the class, although I was suspicious at the level of proof required by the quiz, which was exactly none.

But sitting there on the couch with him, my legs thrown over his, and listening to the rain outside, I remembered thinking, I love him so much.

I did that a lot: made mental notes of how happy I was, or what a perfect moment I happened to be experiencing. I don't know why. Just trying to appreciate what I had, I suppose, as I was getting to an age where I knew that life wasn't always that kind.

Or maybe deep down somewhere I was thinking, well, this ain't gonna last so I might as well enjoy it while I can.

If I was, I seemed to be the only one thinking that.

'You're so *lucky*,' I'd been told many, many times. 'He's just so *lovely*. I could run away with him.' And indeed one or two of them had tried over the years.

But not Ellen or Barbara, at least not to my knowledge. They just doted on him completely. Whenever I was on the phone to him in their presence, it was all, 'Tell him we said hello!' and blowing kisses and generally being sickening.

I don't know which of them loved him more. Ellen relied on him heavily as a yardstick for acceptable male behaviour; if Ollie did it, then it was OK for other men to do it too. But if Ollie disapproved, then it was *not* all right. After she'd been with Mark for only two weeks, I got this phone call one night – Ollie and I were working in one of the ski resorts, which is mostly what we did in the wintertime – to announce that she was coming over.

'*Now?*' We normally didn't see her off-season, as back then she was a beach babe, who liked to strut her stuff in a variety of tiny bikinis.

'I'm bringing someone for Ollie.'

'I think he might already be spoken for.'

'No, I mean a man.'

'You can ask, but I just don't think he's going to be that interested—'

'*My* man, Hannah. I've met someone.' When she couldn't take a joke I knew it must be serious. 'I want Ollie to look him over.' she said. 'To see if he's, you know, all right.'

I laughed. 'And how the hell would Ollie know?'

'Because he's a really good guy, Hannah.' Ellen sounded a bit cross.

'Honestly. I'd have thought after all the eejits you've wasted your time on, you'd recognise a good one when you saw him.'

That was the first time I'd wondered whether this was serious for me, too. Up to then we'd just been having a good time, Ollie and me, going wherever the mood took us, like a pair of delinquents. We were mad about each other, but at the back of my mind was the thought that he viewed me as somewhat temporary.

I'd viewed him the same, but after Ellen's words, suddenly I wanted things to change.

'Are we a holiday romance?' I blurted to him that night.

He said nothing for a minute. Then, 'As in . . . finite?'

'Yes.' I hadn't realised my mouth was so dry. And all over a guy who wore Arsenal socks and told me that thunder was just God breaking wind (I was afraid of it).

He scratched his chin and mused, 'I don't suppose anything is for ever.'

He was winding me up. I could tell by the look in his eye. But all the same I felt a quivery nervousness in my stomach. 'If you're not careful, I'll go and sleep with that fat bloke in 4A who can't even manage the beginner's slope.'

He laughed. 'I won't let you. For your own sense of pride, not because I'd be jealous or anything.'

Then, as if he knew the joking had gone far enough, he cupped my face in his hands and stroked my cheeks with his thumbs. 'Even though I would be. Madly. I'd be so jealous that I'd probably go and strike him down with a sword, or a ski pole, or something.'

I went warm all over, in the way that only he could make me feel. I was so happy that I gushed, foolishly, 'I'm not asking for any big, you know, commitment.' Looking back, I should have nailed him down then and there, as big commitments were not particularly his bag, as I was to find out in the decade that followed. 'I just want to know if we're . . .'

'Going sh-teady?' he said in a thick country voice.

'Yes.'

'We are.' Then he looked a bit sad. 'Sorry that you felt you had to ask. I thought you knew by now how much I love you.'

I was getting so warm by that stage that I felt I might have to take a couple of paracetamol in case I over heated.

'Let's have sex,' I said.

'Of course,' he said, accommodatingly.

As we stripped our clothes off and threw them to the four winds, I said, 'Oh, and Ellen is bringing a man over for you to give approval to.'

Ollie was as puzzled as me. 'Why would she want my approval? I'm not her father. At least, I don't think I am.'

'Beats me. Just take a look at him and say he's all right.'

He pulled me close. 'Let's not talk about Ellen any more.'

Ellen and Mark duly arrived, and Ollie and I put them up in our little chalet, and listened as they had sex all night long.

'This puts us in the shade, you know that, don't you?' Ollie whispered to me, as the walls around us shook. 'He's very beefcakey, isn't he? Mark.'

I looked at him. 'Are you jealous?'

'Of *Mark*?'

I don't know what he was scoffing about. A lot of men would be. When Mark had walked into the chalet, I was sure he was a male model – they were attracted to ski resorts in the winter – who'd somehow lost his way coming off the piste.

'Well, I think he's gorgeous,' I said, just to wind him up.

'In that case I'll tell Ellen he's perfect, just so you have something to look at,' he assured me. 'Now get your pyjama top off. We'd better give them a run for their money.'

But Ellen wasn't happy until Ollie took Mark out to some après-ski joint and got him bladdered and, as she put it, 'sussed him out'. Ollie hadn't a clue what that meant, and so in the end, after about nine bottles of wildly expensive beer and some stilted conversation about football – Mark wasn't that into it – Ollie got him home and took out the quiz from the magazine, and made him go through it: 'Now, Mark, if I was feeling low, what would you do to cheer me up? Would you, (a) run me a bubble bath and light my favourite scented candle, (b) ask me if I wanted to talk about it, or (c) whisk me off to bed and suggest experimental sex? Bear in mind that I'm a woman, here.'

Mark, he'd said, had looked at him as though he was off his trolley. Made him feel about nine.

'He's just more sophisticated than you,' I assured him.

'He thinks he is, anyway,' Ollie said, looking a bit put out that Mark didn't get his cutting-edge humour.

I wasn't a bit sympathetic. It wouldn't do him any harm to be in the company of a man who was an actual grown-up. Mark had a great job and a car and an apartment, and he helped out at an animal shelter at the weekend. He didn't tell us any of this. Ellen boasted about it when she got drunk one night. Mark just shot me a mortified look, and I decided I liked him even more.

'Why do you always have to bring up the animal shelter thing?' he complained. 'I volunteered twice. *Twice.*'

'Yes, but you were great both times,' Ellen gushed.

Ollie was behind them in the kitchen. Behind Mark's back, he pretended to be sick. I looked away. Honestly. He really *was* like a nine-year-old.

When their visit came to an end, I asked what he was going to tell Ellen about Mark.

'The truth,' Ollie said gloomily. 'That he's perfect.'

I laughed at the look on his face.

'Although he's a bit heavy on the hair product, do you not think?'

I hadn't noticed.

'He's always *at* it. Adjusting it. Fixing it.' He shuddered. Men who bothered with their hair disturbed him.

Now that I thought about it, his hair did look very well cared for. But that was a good thing, surely. Nothing worse than an unkempt man.

Anyway, Ellen went home very happy, and I took no notice when Ollie complained afterwards that, along with an overuse of hair product, Mark was 'a bit intense or something'. But then again, Ollie himself was so on the other end of the spectrum that intense could mean simply wanting to plan tomorrow's dinner.

Barbara had never asked Ollie to test-drive any of her many men. Instead she rang him up to talk about boilers and her fish tank. They were both a bit geeky about technology and the Internet, and would start speaking at the drop of a hat in a strange language that included words like 'encryption keys' and 'double firewalls'. Often I would go to bed and leave them sitting over Ollie's computer at the kitchen table, oohing and aahing over something they'd discovered online, and I just knew it wasn't porn.

Barbara treated him like a trusted brother. She had three real brothers, but they were layabouts and spongers, according to her, and she would feel Ollie's loss keenly.

I felt like I was letting both Barbara and Ellen down. It wasn't my fault, of course; Ollie was the one who'd walked. But he was almost like one of the girls; not a fully paid-up member, of course, and he would never be part of our history together, nor privy to our deepest conversations (that would be treachery), but he was always on the periphery, available for a chat and to fix the odd thing for Barbara, or for Ellen to ring up and give out to about Mark. She still confided in him occasionally, just to get the male view, I think, although she never told me about these conversations, and neither did Ollie, and I have to admit to sometimes feeling a little excluded.

The last significant point about Ollie was his happy childhood. I won't go through the whole thing, as it was probably like a lot of other people's happy childhoods – climbing up trees, fighting with siblings, getting plasters and kisses on hurt knees, family holidays in caravans in Tramore, that kind of thing. They'd had a horse too, called Nellie, a big, gentle slob of a thing, and Ollie had a photo of himself up on her back. He must have been about six at the time, and all his front teeth were missing. Harry had been standing at one side of the horse, and Muriel at the other. His sister, Maeve, had been taking the photo, which was why the top of Harry's head was lopped off, but you couldn't mistake the big smiles on all their faces. Muriel's hand was on Ollie's back protectively, and Harry's chest was puffed out with pride at his family.

Ollie couldn't even look at that photograph now. He'd tried to tear it up only I'd stopped him. He said it was fake, all that happiness. That Muriel had said – stupid, idiotic woman – that she and Harry hadn't been suited from the start. Harry, who was just as bad, had retaliated by saying he'd only married her at all because she was pregnant.

Ollie said that there was no way that Cleo would grow up thinking that her entire childhood had been a lie too.

'But it isn't. It hasn't been,' I tried to reason with him.

But by that stage I already knew it was too late.

Chapter Eleven

I woke up very early in a strange bed. I wasn't sure where I was for a minute. But something had woken me.

Then: *Cock-a-doodle-doo.*

At least, it would have sounded like that had I been in an Enid Blyton book. Ellen and Mark's rooster, on the other hand, hollered like he put away forty smokes a day, and wasn't particular about his vowels either. Every time he let rip in outrage, it was like someone had just stuck something up his rear end. Maybe next time they'd finish the job off.

I looked over to the bed opposite me. It wasn't an edifying sight. Barbara was flat on her back, snorting and snoring and bubbling like some old geezer on the way out. On the locker beside her was her knitting, along with a pattern for a little white cardigan. There wasn't a huge amount of resemblance between the two.

I hadn't even heard her come to bed; I'd left her and Ellen downstairs at about nine o'clock, tucking into more tea. I'd been too exhausted to keep my eyes open a second longer.

Apart from Barbara and the rooster, the rest of the house was quiet. I had no idea what time it was. And did the clock go forward or backward an hour when you went to France? After such a long sleep you'd think I'd have been sharper, but no. I felt dull, leaden, disconnected.

I searched around for my phone to find out the time, but I must have left it downstairs in my bag. I could always reach across and check the Dimitri phone, which was, rather symbolically, on the locker next to the knitting, but I suspected that once I got within a foot of it, Barbara would jackknife up in the bed to disable me with a karate chop. *Nobody* touched that phone.

I once suggested, foolishly, as it turned out, that she ring Dimitri. Did it all have to be so one-way? How come she was continually hanging around for some communication from him, while it seemed somehow forbidden for her to pick up the phone and give him a tinkle?

'I can't do that.' Barbara rolled her eyes. She'd tried explaining it to Ellen and me many times but we were just slow, slow, slow. 'That would be hassling him. And I don't want to hassle him, OK?'

'Why not?'

I couldn't understand it at all. He didn't seem to phone much, rarely emailed, and any news was not imparted as often as it should be, in my opinion. Yet she was supposed to be happy to hang on in limbo, ignorant, while he . . . well, I didn't know what he did.

'He's waiting too,' Barbara clarified.

Ellen couldn't understand it either. 'What kind of a process is this, where everybody hangs around waiting all the time? It's been *five years*, Barbara, since you started all this. I mean, does *anybody* get there in the end?'

But apparently people did, lots of them, although they all seemed to be waiting for ever as well. Barbara would occasionally come off the Internet, ecstatic at some email she'd got. 'Michael and Angela got the phone call! They're travelling out on Tuesday!'

'Well, hurrah for Michael and Angela.' Ellen's voice would be dripping with sarcasm. 'What about *you*? You were there before them, if I remember correctly. How come it's taking so long for you?'

Barbara wouldn't blink. 'I'm divorced. That's why. So you can stop blaming Dimitri, OK? Because it's not his fault.'

I thought she might be dreaming of Dimitri now, the way she rolled over and ground her teeth rather viciously.

Then she settled down again to wait.

I put on one of Barbara's enormous hairy jumpers over my nightie, the wool of which immediately began to savage the back of my neck, and crept downstairs. I thought I might have a quiet cup of tea by myself, and ponder the vagaries of my life – something I'd always wanted to do, but never had the proper setting before. Surely in the peace and quiet of the French countryside, some startling insights might occur to me, and I'd go home a new woman.

Cleo and Sophie were fast asleep in the bunk beds in Sophie's room when I stuck my head in, their little faces flushed, although it took me a while to locate them amongst the hundreds of cuddly toys, princess duvet covers, and the haze of nail varnish fumes that hung in the air. Sam was on a mattress on the floor, looking troubled, even in sleep. It was unclear whether he'd chosen to bed down in the girls' room, or been persuaded against his will. He had a Thomas the Tank Engine train clutched firmly in his little hand, as though trying to hang on to his masculinity in the sea of pink.

I closed the door quietly on them in the hope that they would fog it for hours yet.

The kitchen was dark and a little chilly. I put the light on, let out an enormous yawn and had a leisurely scratch of an armpit. I nearly lost my life when someone said, 'Good morning.'

It was Mark. He was kneeling by the Aga, feeding it logs.

'Mark. Jesus.' I was clutching my chest.

'Sorry,' he said, with a lazy grin. 'Didn't mean to give you a fright.'

I was suddenly mortified by my hairy jumper and white, equally hairy legs. If I'd had an inkling that there was anyone in the house bar women and innocent children . . . 'When did you get back?' I managed.

'Late last night. We were going to stay over in a hotel but, well, the Dutch . . .' He threw his eyes to heaven and made a violent slashing movement across his neck. It was a very odd way to talk about his friends. But then he was smiling warmly and holding his arms out. 'It's great to see you, Hannah.'

We did the hug, hug, kiss, kiss thing, me aware that I hadn't brushed my teeth and that my breath probably smelled like a dog's. 'You too!' I said, keeping my lips as close together as possible so that he wouldn't faint.

When it was over I reared away and kind of stooped over so that Barbara's jumper came down as far as possible over my bare thighs.

'Are you all right?' he said. I thought he might be laughing at me. But then again, I often got the impression that I amused him, and not in a good way.

'Oh, just that bloody rooster,' I complained happily, hoping to divert attention from myself.

He duly looked towards the window, leaving me free to scuttle to the kitchen table, where I was able to take cover under the cloth, and relax a little.

'I know. I'd love to go out there and strangle the fucker with my bare hands,' he was saying with relish. 'But Ellen won't let me. She's mad about him, for some reason. Plus, the guests love him. They think it adds to the "authenticity" of the experience.' He laughed at that, and so did I, overly anxious to please. I was a bit that way around him: laughy and a little crawly. I suppose you could look at it as embarrassing. But he was just so good-looking, I defy any woman not to act like a bit of an eejit around him.

'Oh, we do, we do,' I said, even though I could do without the rooster.

He looked a bit surprised. 'I didn't mean you and Barbara. I'm talking about the paying guests.'

I was confused. For some reason I looked over my shoulder. What paying guests?

Mark was bending down again, and peering into the Aga like he was trying to see his future. 'I don't know why it won't light this morning.'

My eyes were irresistibly drawn to his backside. I knew it was wrong, I knew it was unseemly, but come on, I had no witnesses, and it wasn't like I was going to touch it or anything. Plus, I was single now. If, as a single woman, I couldn't ogle a bottom guilt-free then I didn't know what the world was coming to.

He reached for another log and the jeans slipped lower. GO ON! I wanted to roar, and for a horrible minute I thought I'd bellowed it out loud, like some drunken tart on a hen weekend. Honestly. What was wrong with me?

It was the lack of sex. Definitely. Ollie hadn't touched me in months; I hadn't let him. Even my mother, with her newly acquired birthday present, was getting more action than I was.

Enough of this bawdy behaviour. I dragged my eyes from Mark and fixed them demurely on the tablecloth while he continued to wrestle with the Aga.

'Come on, you bastard, light,' he said. He gave me a bit of an embarrassed look.

The Aga had been Ellen's idea, of course. She said you couldn't have a proper country kitchen without a whacking great cooker in the centre of it all. Never mind that the thing seemed to have a mind of its own and refused to fire up for anybody except her.

Mark eventually gave up. He pushed back his hair – still quite a lot of hair product, but it suited him – picked up the electric kettle and said, wryly, 'I'll guess we'll have to boil water the old-fashioned way instead. Tea?'

'I'd love a cup,' I said gratefully.

An odd thing was happening. He wasn't mortified around a newly broken-hearted woman. A lot of men would be, in the circumstances. Take Peader-next-door, for example. When he'd opened the door to me two evenings ago, he'd looked . . . shifty. It was the only word for it. He'd tried to hide it, of course, behind a big smile and a hearty, 'Of *course* we'll guard the place from the legions of burglars while you're away in France.' But I saw. I knew. Before Peader got a word out, the conversation was already going on behind his eyes, along the lines of, 'Fuck, she's been dumped. What do I say? Is, "I'm sorry for your troubles" appropriate?'

Being dumped posed a set of conundrums for people. Should they bring it up at all? Or was it better to pretend that nothing had happened? People were thrown into dreadful confusion. They were barely able to look you in the eye in case they inadvertently passed judgement – because, clearly, there was something wrong with you, a deficiency, as otherwise you wouldn't have been dumped, would you?

'Sugar?' Mark enquired. 'No, hang on. I remember. Half a spoon. Am I right? And plenty of milk?'

'Yes,' I said, ridiculously pleased.

He put a lovely, steaming mug of tea down in front of me before sitting down at the table with a mug himself.

I got all squirmy again, and a bit eejity, like the coolest guy in the class had just sat down at the lunch table with me. Underneath the table my legs began to hop up and down nervously.

'Listen,' he said, fixing me with his lovely dark eyes (which matched his lovely dark hair), 'I was really sorry to hear about you and Ollie.'

My first instinct was to brush it off as fast as I could, maybe with a flick of my hand and a jolly, 'Oh, well, these things happen, what can you do, eh?'

But as Mark had had the decency to be honest, then I felt an onus to be the same. 'It was a bit of a shock, all right,' I admitted. 'Well, for me, anyway. I suppose Ollie must have seen it coming.'

For months now, actually.

Mark said nothing for ages, just kind of sat there, swinging one foot back and forth. (Huge feet. Just for the record.) In the end he gave a sigh, shook his head and told my sleep-swollen face, 'Well, I think he made a big mistake.'

I knew he was just being nice; that I was one of Ellen's oldest friends and that he probably felt obliged to jolly me along. But it was still nice to hear it.

'And if you don't mind me saying so, I think you're better off without him.'

Better off? Without *Ollie*? Was he insane? Ollie was my life and soul, my bread and butter, my . . . oh, whatever. He was *half* of me. Could he not see that I was a woman who only barely existed? Well, in spirit anyway. There was plenty of me left physically, as a quick peek under the table at my white, lardy legs would testify.

But Mark ignored the shock on my face and said, quite decisively, 'He was always a bit immature.'

Colouring all this was the slight antipathy Mark and Ollie had always shared. It wasn't just that stupid magazine quiz that Ollie had made Mark do all those years ago, although I know that Ollie had lost a lot of Mark's respect over that – if he'd had any of it in the first place. Shorts-wearing, scruffy-haired, wise-cracking, guitar-playing louts weren't entirely Mark's bag, I knew. Certainly, in Dublin, Mark hung around with other rugby-playing-lookalikes, all of them good-looking and jocular, and almost entirely employed in either IT or finance. Ollie just wouldn't fit in with that scenario, even if you'd cut his hair and stuffed him into a suit.

Mark was a fan of the kind of 'friendly' punching that men did of each other's shoulders and stomachs, and he would launch himself at Ollie with a cry of, 'Hey', and Ollie would find himself pummelled and, occasionally, in a headlock, with the top of his head being ritually pounded by Mark's huge fist.

'That was fun,' Ollie would say afterwards, with huge sarcasm, but Mark would just laugh and order him a filthy pint of Guinness, even though Ollie preferred bottled beers. 'Only wusses drink bottled beers,' Mark would rib him. 'Get that down you and I'll introduce you to Rod and Chopper.' His friends were always called something penis-like. 'They've got their own computer company if you ever felt like a getting a proper job.'

'He's a pain in the arse,' Ollie would complain to me bitterly afterwards. 'All that macho shit. Honestly. That guy has issues. Look at that fucking bruise on my shoulder from where he punched me.'

He was just very male, Mark. And Ollie wasn't. He shouldn't let it upset him.

The big falling-out, though, had happened when I wasn't even there.

Just after Mark and Ellen had first moved over to Brittany, Ellen had popped out Sam almost immediately, throwing things completely out of kilter. They'd hoped to have at least a month to get the farmhouse habitable. Now, not only was Ellen laid up in hospital with a newborn (she had a postpartum infection and would be kept in for two weeks), but the house turned out to be in a worse state than they'd thought – as in, no roof.

'Would you not rent somewhere for a few months, give you all some breathing space?' I'd urged Mark.

But he was having none of it. 'No, no, just so long as I can get the roof fixed for when she gets out of hospital. She says she doesn't want to go into a rented house, she wants to come home, and I'm going to make it happen.'

I was impressed by his zeal and energy. He worked day and night for a week, but progress was slow, and he was hampered by bad weather.

It was Ellen who eventually rang Ollie from the hospital, asking him would he go over and lend a hand. 'You're good at that sort of thing,' she'd pleaded.

'Me?' said Ollie afterwards. 'Does she know *anything* about me?'

But he was too good-hearted to refuse Ellen, especially as she was laid up in hospital, and so he packed a sleeping bag, borrowed a massive toolbox from Peader-next-door, and went over on the next ferry.

'Man, it's bad,' he ranted, when he rang me. 'They never told me it was going to be like this. No roof. No heating. Wet. And *Mark* . . .'

'What about him?'

'Nothing,' said Ollie, in a big fat liar voice. 'Look, I have to go. He's up a ladder and to be honest, I'm not too sure he's not going to fall off.'

Mark? Fall off a ladder? Ollie was exaggerating, I was sure. While he was great when it came to computers and guitars, hard, physical labour and he were strangers that were in no hurry to get acquainted.

He spent four days in the house with Mark, sleeping on the damp floor, according to him, and having lukewarm pizza for dinner every night. There was no television, or radio, or anything at all to entertain them, except for an old mandolin left behind by a previous occupant, and so Ollie would pluck away after dinner and fill the silence with songs until one night Mark asked him – tersely, I believe – to stop, and that was the end of that.

'Fucking hell. Now we're just sitting there, reading the pizza box,' Ollie told me in his nightly phone call, which was becoming more and more tense.

I wasn't sure what had happened in the end. Again, something to do with a ladder, only this time Ollie was up it, and Mark was shouting up instructions, detailed instructions, apparently, at roughly thirty-second intervals. Eventually, Ollie, who had been getting on fine on his own up to that point, he maintained, lost his rag and there had been some threatening gestures made with lump hammers and that kind of thing. Phrases like 'couldn't organise a piss-up in a brewery' had been thrown around, it was unclear by whom, but I had a bad feeling that Ollie hadn't been up to scratch.

At that point the two boys had sensibly decided that the best thing to do would be to get in Marcel, Rosalie's husband, and several of his friends, all of whom were very *au fait* with ladders and suchlike. Ollie split three days ahead of schedule and took himself, his sleeping bag and Peader's toolbox back on the next available ferry.

'What happened?' I demanded.

'I don't want to talk about it,' said Ollie. Then he burst out, 'Nobody can work with that man. Nobody.'

I tried to be diplomatic. 'It's because he's a perfectionist.'

'A perfectionist!' Ollie said, slightly hysterically. 'What the fuck is he doing, taking on a pile of rubble like that so?' Then he reined himself in again. He knew it wasn't the done thing to criticise the husband of your best friend. He contented himself with one final shot. 'All mouth, and no action.'

I didn't believe that. Mark had powered the entire move; I'd seen the spreadsheets he'd drawn up for the farm; he had it planned right down to what crop would go in which field. How could Ollie suggest that he was somehow workshy when it came down to it?

I suspected the fault lay with Ollie. He'd been too laid-back. Too jokey and wanting to stop for cups of coffee. That wouldn't suit Mark at all, especially when the pressure was on to get things finished for Ellen's discharge from hospital. Ollie simply hadn't taken things seriously enough.

Story of his blooming life.

Anyway, nobody mentioned Ollie's DIY foray to France again. We were all adults, after all, and everybody recognised the benefits of brushing something like that under the carpet. When we went to France six months later, the roof was on – a beautiful job, I might add – the floor was fixed, and there was a brand-new kitchen installed. I thought I saw Mark give Ollie an 'I told you so' look, while Ollie bristled but, thankfully, held his tongue.

Things had remained cool between them to this day.

And now here was Mark watching me across the kitchen table, swinging those enormous feet, and feeding me tea and sympathy.

It was lovely.

So lovely that for a minute I was worried that I was going to well up again. Jesus, not more tears. There was no way Mark would be able for *that*, too.

But Mark was clearly made of stronger stuff than I'd given him credit for – I'd thought him a bit lightweight on the emotional intelligence front, to be honest – because he said, slightly awkwardly, mind, 'It'll do you good to get away. The girls will look after you. In fact, there's probably nothing they'd like better.' He cracked a grin at me. 'The Table of Moans is going to be busy.'

'You know about the Table of Moans?'

'I do. And I think it's a great idea. Us men just bottle everything up.'

'And what have you to be bottling up?'

He was grinning openly now. I was grinning back. Probably too much.

'You don't want to know,' he said gravely.

I laughed like a drain. Dear God. But I was just letting off steam, I consoled myself. My heart had just been through the wringer. If there was one thing I needed right now, it was a seriously easy-on-the-eye man and a good laugh.

But it was over now. I watched with disappointment as Mark put both enormous feet on the floor and stood up. 'Right,' he said, knocking back the last of his tea, 'I'd better go dig a ditch.'

'Why would you want to dig a ditch?' I was probably spinning the conversation out a little now.

'I have no idea.' He pointed to the ceiling. 'I just do what the boss tells me.'

We could hear her now, moving around upstairs. Ellen. In a minute she'd be down and darting around the kitchen like some manic landlady, making mounds of breakfast for everybody whether they wanted it or not.

'It'll be good for Ellen to have you and Barbara here too,' Mark said unexpectedly.

He watched me closely, as though wondering whether he could trust me. Gratifyingly, he leaned in. 'I don't know if you've noticed, but she's not herself at the moment. She'd kill me for saying it, but I think she gets lonely now and again, stuck out here with nobody for company, only me.'

Lucky fecking bitch. The thought struck before I could stop myself. Then, feeling like the jealous cast-off that I was, I moved quickly to make amends to my lovely friend Ellen, who didn't deserve my envy. And who did seem a little out of sorts this visit. Stressed, or something. 'Don't worry. Barbara and I will cheer her up.'

Mark gave me a beautiful smile. 'Thanks, Hannah. It's good to have you here.'

Chapter Twelve

Ollie and I began to break up six months ago.

Not that we knew it at the time. We were just minding our own business, clueless as to the catastrophe that was about to befall us.

It was a Friday evening, if I remember correctly. I'd had a frantic week at work and was wrecked. It was Ollie's slow season, and I wasn't being funny. Most of the holiday bookings made through his camping website came in during the spring. In October everybody was still paying for the summer holidays they'd just been on, and the only enquiries he got were from over-eager people anxious to get the following year's holiday nailed down.

'Dear Oliver,' a lot of these emails would begin, usually from older people. 'We enjoyed our camping experience in Spain so much (thank you for that tip on the nudist beach, we had no idea we would enjoy it as much as we did) that we already want to go back.'

Ollie had a huge bank of repeat customers, mostly because he got personally involved in their holidays. He couldn't help himself. He never sold a pitch in any campsite that he himself hadn't stayed in, and liked, and so he had loads of tips about such things as local attractions and nightlife, the best beaches to party on, the authentic bars where you were most likely to meet hot native girls, as opposed to Bernadette from Baldoyle.

'Dear Jack/Fionnula/Alojzy, I'm pleased to inform you that your booking has been successful,' his client emails always began. 'And you didn't hear this from me, but the tapas isn't the best in the restaurant on-site. You're much better off going to this little place about half a mile down the road. When you come out of the campsite, hang a left, and keep going until you pass two barking Alsatians . . .'

66

His site was officially aimed at the eighteen-to-thirty-five age group, but quite often unsuspecting families or pensioners stumbled across it and innocently booked. They would find themselves in the middle of a gay beach in Mykonos, or maybe wandering through fields of poppies in central France. Everybody seemed to like where they ended up though, and were always posting reviews about 'that great Irish guy Ollie'.

He'd got another one that particular Friday, which he insisted on reading out to me as he cooked.

'They said I was fantastically wonderful and very good-looking. People are *so* kind.'

'How can you be good-looking when they've never laid eyes on you?'

He waggled a finger. 'Jealousy will get you nowhere.'

Maybe I *was* jealous. He got to do the fun stuff all day, making people's holiday dreams come true, while I got to make up the yawning gap in our finances with a distinctly un-fun job in travel recruitment. Which meant finding fresh eejits to do the same holiday rep jobs that Ollie and I had done years before for peanuts.

'You'll have a blast,' I told the lucky few who finally landed the gig. 'I did.' Although I never told them for just how many years. 'My advice is to try not to drink too much, OK? And sleeping with the guests is a fireable offence. I don't care what you do to each other.'

If they were smart, and a lot of them were, they'd try and soak up some of the local culture on their days off instead of just getting pickled. And if they were really lucky, like me, they might even find true love.

'You like your job really,' Ollie was always saying to me. 'You just enjoy a good moan.'

OK I *did* like my job. I enjoyed picking the best of the crop and training them in, which usually involved a lot of role play.

I'd always be the guest, and would choose a scenario with which to challenge my trainees. 'Did you hear what I said, or are you just stupid?' I'd shout excitedly. (I was quite good at it by now.) 'The shower in my apartment is broken. I stink. What are you going to say to *that*?'

'You're right, you *do* stink. Now fuck off.'

'No, *no*, Stephen. You can't talk to me like that.'

'But you're obnoxious. I'm not taking crap like that from anyone.'

'You've got to calm the situation down. Ask me not to speak to you that way, or you'll have to report me to your superior. Never raise your voice, even if they do. OK?'

A big, doubtful, sigh. 'O-K.'

At the end of the training session, I would give them all a little badge and a good luck hug, and a lot of them sent me postcards from Majorca or Tenerife, or wherever they ended up.

Ollie handed me one that had arrived that morning. It was of a topless woman, from that lad Stephen.

'Dear God.'

'It's a compliment. He clearly thinks you're hot.'

'Are you sure it's not to taunt me?' I eyed the enormous, pert breasts of the blonde model on the postcard.

Ollie looked at mine appreciatively. 'Baby, you've still got what it takes.'

Years ago he might have made a grab at them and we'd probably have had exciting sex on the sofa, particularly as Cleo was gone on a sleepover. But we were too comfy with each other now to be bothered flinging our clothes off – and it was a damp night, too – and so we happily settled for a glass of white while Ollie's dinner cooked: piri piri chicken which, he assured me, would blow my head off.

'I got some holiday brochures,' he said.

'Oh, no. Please don't make me.'

'I know it's hard, baby. I know the very idea of a summer holiday makes us both sick. But we don't have to go to any of those places that we sell. Let's do it for Cleo, if nothing else.'

'All right,' I conceded. 'But just for one week. I don't think I could handle two.'

Besides, we'd just been to France for three days during the October school half-term, to see Ellen. But that wasn't considered a holiday as such, just a catch-up. Having spent so much of my life involved in travel, I honestly think I would be happy never to leave Ireland again.

We'd just settled down with the brochures – picture after picture of fabulous beaches; it'd turn your stomach – when Harry arrived.

Ollie let him in. I listened from the living room, expecting the usual exchange at the front door, which always went something like this:

'Hi, Dad.'

'Your front lawn needs mowing before the winter sets in.'

'I know.'

'I can bring the lawn mower over tomorrow, if you want.'

'It's fine. I'll do it myself.'

'You won't, though. That's why you've got moss. Moss is a bugger to get rid of, you know.'

'I know, Dad. You've told me before.'

'Did you try washing-up liquid, like I told you last time?'

But tonight there was no talk of moss. Instead, the door burst open and Harry kind of lurched into the living room, very sweaty and red-looking. His mouth was hanging open, like he'd received a blow to the jaw, and he looked at us in bemusement and said, 'She's after fecking me out.'

I didn't get it for a minute. 'Who?'

'Muriel. She told me not to come back.'

It was a terrible sight to behold. A lovely, inoffensive man like Harry, standing there like a lost puppy and holding . . . I looked more closely . . . a violently flowered Laura Ashley carrier bag.

His eyes drifted down to it too. He seemed as thrown by it as we were. 'She gave me this. It's got my toothbrush in it, she said, and under-pants and socks. She said she didn't bother putting any clothes in it as I've worn the same thing for forty-two years now, and I might as well get buried in them.'

Ollie and I looked at each other. Shocked. He must be drunk. Or had banged his head, or something. Maybe he'd been driving the car and had accidentally driven into a tree and had wandered from the scene, totally confused, dreaming up this story of Muriel having thrown him out without even a change of clothes.

But then we couldn't help it; we looked at the poor man's clothes. His grey flannels were baggy and shiny around the backside from constant wear, and his jumper . . . well, the best you could say for it was that it was indistinguishable from all the other jumpers he owned. Grey-ish, patterned, the hint of a gravy stain down the front.

We made him sit down. I got him a brandy, and tried to take the Laura Ashley bag from him, but he had it in a death grip.

'Now, Dad, what's all this?' Ollie said, like you would to a toddler who'd eaten a whole packet of Skittles by himself. 'Have you and Mum had some kind of a fight?'

They didn't normally fight, Harry and Muriel. Well, nothing vicious, anyway. Just the usual sniping and flinging of eyes to heaven that Muriel enjoyed – in fairness, she had to let off steam somehow, because Harry *would* drive you mad – and the odd crack from Harry when Muriel took forty-seven minutes to 'put her face on', and him with the car engine running.

Harry was staring rigidly ahead, the Laura Ashley bag on his knees. He looked like Miss Marple. 'It's over. Me and your mother. We're separating.'

Over? I looked at Ollie, but he was gawking at Harry as though he should call a doctor.

'She says she can't stand to waste another day of her life looking at me. That *Cosmopolitan* magazine says that seventy is the new forty, and she says that she wants to be an independent woman who can go and play golf if she wants to in the mornings, instead of having to cook a big fecking roast at lunchtime for me because of my ulcer.'

Harry had had stomach ulcers for years. He couldn't eat large meals close to bedtime, so for as long as anybody could remember, they'd had their dinner in the middle of the day and something 'light', like a boiled egg, at teatime.

Ollie still looked as though this might be a very bad joke on the part of his father, although Harry had never been much of a one for jokes. 'But she doesn't even play golf,' he pointed out to his father.

'She says she's going to take it up. And poker too, and go on cruises and read books about sex.'

We all digested this. It could be the pension. A lot of people went mad when they first got it; started getting notions above themselves, wanting to do crazy things, all because they had a bit of money from the Post Office every week that they didn't have to scrimp and save up by buying dry, own-brand ginger biscuits instead of nice expensive ones.

But she'd been getting the pension for five years now. If it was going to go to her head, surely it would have done it before now.

'Is there . . . someone else?' I asked.

Ollie gave me a terrible look. I suppose the image of his mother astride a younger model wasn't a pleasant one. An older model was even more unpleasant.

'No.' Harry gave a deep sigh. It was almost like he wished there was. 'It's me. She says she thought things might change when I retired, that I might have more get up and go. But she says that the way we're going, we might as well be dead already.'

Strong words, even if I suspected they'd also come from *Cosmopolitan*. And the feminist part of me had to sneakily admire Muriel for striking out for what she wanted.

It was one of the few times in the entire mess that I would admire either of them. Because everything went downhill from there.

We'd just fixed up Harry on the couch with a cup of tea and a big plate of Ollie's piri piri chicken – we only thought of his ulcers afterwards – when Muriel got on the phone.

'Is he there?'

I had the misfortune to pick the phone up. I looked over at Ollie. He was still being very calm and mature at that point and, I suspected, very sure that the whole thing would resolve itself in a day or two. They'd been together for forty-two years, after all. They had three kids – Ollie's sister Maeve was in Australia and Orla lived in Canada, which, I would later realise, had huge implications for the way this whole thing would pan out. As in, they weren't around physically to deal with all the crap, and contented themselves with long-distance meddling on the telephone instead.

'Yes, he is here. And he's quite upset. I don't know what's happened between you two—'

'*He's* upset?' Muriel burst into tears then. It sounded genuine. 'What about me?'

'But you fecked him out, he said.'

Behind Ollie, Harry stoically munched his way through the chicken. He looked like he was waiting for someone to take charge of him.

'Well, someone had to do *something*. And it wasn't going to be him, was it? He'd put up with anything, so long as it didn't interfere with his television schedule. Do you know what he's following on the telly these days? *CSI: Miami*. Obsessed with it. All that blood and gore, and corpses laid out in medical examiners' offices. It makes me go weak, but he doesn't care. And I can't sleep after those programmes, what with the worry that someone is going to break in and carve their initials into the skin on our backs. So I lie awake all night listening to him snoring. I'm telling you, I can't stand it any more.'

Harry prudently avoided my eyes. Could he possibly be a murder-obsessed crime-scene freak? No. Surely Muriel was just being a little over the top.

I could hear Susie start up yapping in the background. The only good thing I could see coming out of the bust-up was that Harry would get some respite from Susie, if only for a short time. None of us was keen on Susie, but Harry had a special dislike for her, and he was not a man who was given to strong emotions. She sensed this, of course, and spent her time cosying up to Muriel sickeningly, always sitting on her lap and turning over to have her belly tickled.

They'd got Susie from the dog pound, to keep Muriel company. She was a little fart of a thing, white and skinny, and always yipping around people's feet disconcertingly. She'd tripped Harry up on numerous occasions – too often to be accidental, he maintained.

71

Her bark drove him cracked: high-pitched and incessant and always when he got on the phone. There he'd be, trying to sort out the gas bill while she yipped and yapped and tried to bite his shoelaces. He'd kicked out at her once, and that's when the real trouble started; he maintained that she had a vendetta against him ever since. 'A vendetta!' Muriel was incredulous. 'For God's sake, Harry, she's a dog. If you were a bit nicer to her she'd like you more.'

Muriel fussed over her sickeningly. She bought blankets for her, and the most expensive brand of dog food – 'I could buy a steak for that!' Harry loved to complain – and she lined a basket with cashmere and put it in the corner of the kitchen for her. And the way she *spoke* to her . . . 'Who's a pretty girl, then? You are! You are!'

Harry maintained it went to Susie's head. She began to get notions about herself. Thinking she was more important than anybody else. He would go so far as to allege that she thought of herself not as a dog, but as a *person*. As the years went by, he believed that she began to turn into Zsa Zsa Gabor; wouldn't eat own-brand food any more, that kind of thing, and went all sniffy if Muriel went out for more than an hour.

But, worse, she began to treat Harry with contempt; turning up her pointy little nose at him in disgust, just like Muriel. She pooped in his shoes – an accident, Muriel maintained – and chewed up his copy of the *Sun*. Oh, they were well suited that pair, Harry had said to Ollie once in an uncharacteristic burst of venom.

Ollie took the phone from me now. He was still in his this-is-all-a-temporary-glitch mode. He raised his voice to be heard over Susie. 'I'm going to drive Dad home as soon as he's finished his piri piri chicken. And you two are going to sit down and talk.'

That's when Muriel torpedoed Ollie's entire bank of happy childhood memories, including that of him sitting up on Nellie's fat back, his parents beaming oh-so-contentedly either side of him. I knew she wasn't really aware of the damage she was causing, that she was totally wrapped up in herself and didn't intend to cause any pain to her children. But the look on Ollie's face was terrible when she said, 'There's nothing to talk about. There never has been. We only stayed together for the sake of you kids, that was all.'

Chapter Thirteen

Ellen's Dutch guests had swallowed.

'Ideally, you wouldn't swallow,' Ellen explained to them kindly. 'You would swirl and spit.'

'Swirl and spit.' Femmie clutched her head with both hands and rocked back and forth. 'That was where we went wrong.'

Ellen clucked over her in a matronly fashion. 'Do you want to go back to bed?'

Femmie's husband, Denis, was also in some considerable pain. 'No, no,' he insisted. Mark had taken them on a tour of three different Muscadet wineries down by the Loire – their first ever wine tasting – and when they'd seen other people taking mouthfuls of wine, washing it around in their cheeks as though they were putting it through a spin cycle, and then, *then*, they told us in appalled voices, gobbing it out into a metal bin thing, well, they'd been shocked. What disgusting manners. And the hosts in the vineyards didn't bat an eyelid! Just refilled these horrible people's glasses and stood well back as they'd all swirled and hawked and spat out another mouthful of perfectly good wine as though it were poison.

Femmie and Denis didn't cotton on that you were supposed to do that. They'd politely swallowed every single drop, and nodded enthusiastically when everybody else marvelled over the 'yeasty aromas' and 'minerality' of the Muscadet, even though Denis told us that he was damned if he could smell yeast anywhere except from that chap's armpits whom he'd been standing next to. By the time they'd arrived at the third vineyard, having had only a light lunch along the way, they were completely rat-arsed.

Femmie liked to sing when she was drunk. 'Dancing Queen', in particular, complete with movements, according to Mark. She also knew all the words to 'Too Shy' by Kajagoogoo, and had been accompanied by Denis, who played two spoons he'd liberated from a pizza restaurant that Mark took them to, in the vain hope that a Quattro Formaggi might sober them up.

It hadn't. Mark decided that it was time to scrap plans to stay over, and just shoot for home. He'd belted the pair of them into the back of the car – 'No more singing, OK? I mean it' – and driven several hundred kilometres in the dark while they'd slept it off.

Not that they seemed the better for it. They were grey and pickled-looking across the breakfast table from me and Barbara, who'd finally got up.

'Bit old to be friends of yours, aren't they?' Barbara had said bluntly to Ellen a minute ago, *sotto voce*. Which, for Barbara, was more like a bellow. 'They must be sixty.'

I wasn't sure whether Femmie and Denis had heard this; either way I tried to make an effort with them, even though I didn't feel like it. I'd thought it would just be the old gang in France that week, people I was comfortable being miserable around. But that was just me being selfish.

'So how did you guys and Mark and Ellen meet?' I asked them politely. Mark and Ellen had never mentioned them before now.

'Through the tourist board of Holland,' Femmie said. 'And you? Did you find them over the Internet? Most people do.'

I could see Barbara looking at me. Cracked, her face said back. And probably lushes to boot. Don't encourage them, for Chrissake.

Ellen, who was rustling up a non-traditional French breakfast of rashers and sausages and black pudding that Barbara had smuggled over in her suitcase, got very busy at the cooker.

And I remembered what Mark had said earlier about paying guests.

'No,' I said. 'We're old friends from college.'

'Well, it's very good of you to give them the business,' Femmie said warmly.

Ellen still resolutely avoided my eye.

Denis, meanwhile, seemed to be recovering somewhat from his hangover, and was giving Barbara and me a thorough once-over from behind a pair of John Lennon wire-rimmed glasses.

'Your Irish ladies are lovely,' he complimented Ellen.

'Thank you,' she said. 'I try my best to provide a nice selection.'

I laughed obligingly but Barbara was rounding on Denis with some hostility. 'Would you like to see our teeth?' she asked him.

Denis looked delighted. 'Feisty,' he told his wife.

Femmie nodded her head vigorously. 'Much better than those bloody Irishmen.'

OK, now I was really confused; there were other Irish people staying as well? And where were they?

Barbara and I looked at Ellen for clarification, but she was busy flinging more rashers onto the pan. 'Eat up,' she trilled, even though we hadn't actually been given any food yet.

'They're in Paris on an overnighter,' Femmie informed us chattily. She was very thin and tanned to a deep walnut, with a head of ash-blond hair and a slash of frosted lipstick which, thanks to a surplus of Muscadet the previous night, had overshot her lips slightly at the last application. 'They'll be back tomorrow, though,' she warned us.

'We have excellent English, don't we?' Denis suddenly challenged me.

I nodded enthusiastically. 'Absolutely. Top notch. Better than mine.'

'In Holland we learn English from when we are so high.' He reached down to hold his hand eighteen inches off the floor. The effort unsettled him and he nearly fell off his chair. 'We make the effort, you see. Not like you English-speaking countries. You think, oh, we are top dogs already because it's our first language, so we don't have to bother our backsides learning anybody else's language.'

'Shut up,' Femmie told him. 'I apologise, girls. He is a crashing bore.' And she laughed. So did Denis, merrily.

Ellen interrupted to plonk a fry-up in front of him and Femmie. Both of them reared away, turned greenish and began stumbling to their feet. I suspect it was the effect Ellen wanted.

'Mark is going to take you to the coach in a minute,' she told them.

Femmie and Denis froze. 'I don't want to,' said Denis.

'But you're booked in.'

'Again?' said Femmie, viciously. 'So many tours. We've been on one every day this week.'

'I know,' Ellen said sympathetically. 'But Le Mont St-Michel is wonderful. Historic.'

Femmie looked at Denis, torn. 'We had better do it. The bloody neighbours will want to see the photographs when we get back.' With sighs and groans they made to leave the kitchen.

'Goodbye, lovely ladies,' Denis said.

75

'Goodbye! Have a nice day!' we sang back, quite fond of them now.

A moment later we saw them crossing the yard towards the converted barns, propping each other up.

Ellen finally sat down. She'd been on the go for two hours by that point, feeding the kids – they were gone out with Mark to bottle-feed the new piglets – and putting on washes and then making breakfast for us all.

'Sorry about that,' she said. 'Usually Femmie and Denis are up very early, and would normally be gone off somewhere by now. I booked them into everything I could, just to get them out from under my feet.'

'They're not friends at all, are they?' I said. 'They're paying guests.'

Barbara did a swift intake of breath, like they'd just been unmasked as drug dealers. She was wearing the same hairy jumper as I'd had on earlier, only teamed with a pair of jeans that had a stiff crease ironed down the middle of each leg. Since Ellen had moved to France, Barbara's fashion sense had deteriorated radically.

'OK,' Ellen admitted slowly, 'they're tourists.'

Even worse than drugs dealers.

She continued to look wretched and guilty. 'I didn't want to tell you because, well, you'd think we were pathetic.'

'Why would we think that?' Barbara enquired. Now that the drama was over, she helped herself to several rashers and sausages, and half a baguette.

'Because it wasn't part of the plan, was it, to take in tourists? We were so full of ourselves five years ago, boasting about how we were coming over here to live off the fat of the land, do you not remember?'

'No.'

'Yes,' Barbara chimed in. 'You were pretty unbearable.'

Ellen shot her a look before turning back to me. 'Telling everybody how we were going to make a small fortune growing and selling vegetables to the French. Like the French had never heard of vegetables before. Like we were going to invent them or something. Christ, I'm mortified.' She did look fairly morto, all right. It was a rare sight, and one I'd have enjoyed if I didn't realise how upset she was. 'Two Dubs, two eejits, getting off that ferry with a couple of suitcases and a book on how to rotate your crops.'

'And *The Essential Guide to Animal Husbandry*,' Barbara chipped in. We'd bought it for Mark as a joke. He'd said, 'Great! I've been looking for this.'

'OK, Barbara, you've had your fun,' Ellen snapped.

We both looked up at Ellen in unison, me and bold Barbara. Something was wrong here.

'So you were a bit green around the ears,' I said to her. 'It's nothing to be ashamed of.'

Ellen examined the calluses on her hand. She had two very impressive ones. 'They were laughing at us, Hannah. All of them. Only we were too thick to see it.'

I'd never heard any of this before. She'd spoken of challenges, sure. And Mark had always amused us with some story of one hiccup or another. But the way Ellen was talking, it had been a disaster from day one.

'I'm sure they weren't laughing at you,' I said, trying to gee her up.

'They were. Rosalie confessed recently that they used to walk past at the bottom of the road to have a look in to see what we were digging up that particular day. Mostly it was water pipes. Mark cut off the whole village for three days once – I never told you that, did I?'

Barbara gave an involuntary snicker before quickly restraining herself. 'Come on,' she said. 'That was years ago. You can't beat yourself up over something like that now.'

'Another time we got this massive electricity bill and discovered that the wiring was earthing all over the place,' Ellen went on gloomily. 'We probably electrocuted every slug within a five-mile radius.'

Barbara couldn't help herself now; she was laughing openly behind her hand. I was trying my hardest not to.

Even Ellen allowed herself a small smile. 'It was a disaster. Everything. Nothing would grow, no matter what we did. Or else it would look so strange that we couldn't sell it. We'd be stuck eating cauliflowers for months, or pickling millions of miniature beetroot, which refused to grow beyond the size of a golf ball.'

Barbara began to pour tea, now that it appeared that the Table of Moans had kicked off, and at an impressively early hour too. 'Fire ahead, girl,' she encouraged.

Ellen looked towards the door. I knew she was making sure Mark wasn't around. Once the coast was clear, she was free to give him a good slagging behind his back. 'We had Health and Safety out twice, after the goats kept chewing through the fencing Mark put up, and escaping out onto the main road. And then he bought a tractor off some guy who gave him a "good price" and, well, you can guess the rest. I think he spent the best part of a year with his head under that tractor's hood. And it still wouldn't start.'

Barbara was creased with mirth now. I hadn't seen her having such a good laugh in years. 'More,' she said.

'We don't have cock-ups just to entertain you, Barbara. And you're not to tell anybody else, OK? Mark would kill me if any of this reached Dublin.'

Yes. It wouldn't look too good for the sharply dressed lads back in banking and IT in Dublin, if indeed there were any of them left after the recession, to find out about his pipe-cutting exploits.

I thought again about the roof, and the time Ollie and come over. Maybe it hadn't been as one-sided as I'd thought.

Ellen gave a deep sigh that rattled her skinny bones. 'So here we are, five years down the road. We're not making the neighbours laugh any more but we're not making any money either. Or, not enough. And so we're taking in tourists to make ends meet.'

She made it sound like she was hawking her body on the village green every Saturday night.

But I knew her pride had taken a battering. It wasn't easy to admit that the dream hadn't quite worked out. She probably wouldn't have told us at all if the Dutch hadn't been staying.

'Are there really a couple of Irishmen as well?' Barbara asked.

'Yes. But don't get your hopes up. They're gay.' Ellen had a bit of colour back in her cheeks now, I was glad to see. It was true; a good moan worked wonders. 'It was my idea to take in paying guests. A lot of people like to stay on a real, live farm, if you know what I mean. They choose us because we're Irish and they think we're going to be great craic. But, failing that, they get to see the animals up close, and Mark takes them on tours of the local tourist joints, and talks up the whole living-in-the-country thing to them.' She added flatly, 'He's good at that.'

I looked at her quickly, but she just picked up a piece of baguette and said, 'I didn't tell you about the Dutch and the Irishmen, because I was afraid you'd think there wouldn't be room for you, and you wouldn't have come.' She flicked back her curls a little defensively. 'And maybe I didn't want you feeling sorry for me.'

I did a bit of incredulous spluttering, as expected. 'Feeling sorry for you! Why would we do that?'

'He thinks it's a climb-down. Mark. We were going to have this great farm, and we end up running a glorified B and B.'

I suppose in a way I could see his point. In all the talk about moving to France, he'd never once expressed a wish to ferry groups around wine tastings.

Ellen clearly felt she'd been disloyal enough because she got up and began to fill the sink with soapy water. 'It's just during the summer months, until we can find ways of making the farm more profitable. And I quite like the company when Mark is out on the farm all day. Sometimes I take them over to Marcel and Rosalie's.'

They lived three fields over, along with a whole rake of wild-looking goats from which they produced some of the most eye-watering cheese I'd ever tasted in my life. When the wind was a certain way, you could smell the stuff from Ellen's back door.

Marcel was great with foreign people. He usually pretended he hadn't a word of English, and he had a horrible old black beret, which he put on especially for them, and he'd usually have a quick chew of a garlic bulb beforehand.

'Funny old geezer, isn't he?' Barbara had loudly said in his presence, the first time we'd met him, clueless that he was having us on. 'I suppose we'd better not mention the war, eh?'

'Was that the war the Irish didn't bother getting involved in at all?' Marcel enquired in a perfect, mid-Atlantic accent, nearly giving Barbara a heart attack.

I knew that Marcel and Rosalie had taken Ellen and Mark under their wing quite soon after their arrival (possibly after the village's water supply had been cut off). Rosalie was great with the kids every now and again, and Ellen, I knew, drove the old couple to hospital appointments and the dentist and that kind of thing.

I also knew that Rosalie had been a great comfort to Ellen since her mother had died. It always made me feel better, knowing that she had someone over here; that she wasn't on her own.

Which of course she wasn't. She had Mark, hadn't she?

Chapter Fourteen

'I hate her. I hate her,' Sam sobbed pitifully.

Cleo and Sophie exchanged looks; which one of them did he mean?

'Sophie,' Sam clarified, swinging a bloodied finger and pointing it squarely at his sister. They had been re-enacting the game of the little boy who had stuck his finger in the hole in the dam; Sam had obviously landed the plum role. The problem was the hole, which Sophie had persuaded him was in the thin wall of the wooden stall housing the bottle-fed piglets. The piglets, seeing Sam's pink, plump finger, thought it was feeding time all over again and had set upon it with delight. Sam had withdrawn rather too rapidly, but the wound, we were all glad to learn, was merely surface deep.

'Your finger is too fat,' Sophie told him silkily.

This threw him into fresh distress. 'My finger is not fat!' He held it up, seized with doubt. 'Is it?'

'It's a lovely finger,' Mark assured him, carefully applying a plaster, which was a Barbie one, to add insult to injury.

'I thought you were keeping an eye on them?' Ellen snapped to Mark.

'I was,' he said mildly.

She found a biscuit for Sam, which helped. Sophie got no biscuit; nor did Cleo.

'What were you girls thinking?' Ellen said to them.

Sophie announced. 'It was Cleo's idea.'

Cleo looked shocked. 'It was not!'

Sophie looked at her reproachfully. 'You said, I wonder what it must be like, to try and stop a dam with your finger.'

'Well, yes . . .'

80

Sophie shrugged and said to Ellen, 'See?'

Cleo looked at me; that is *so* not what happened, her eyes screamed at me. I gave her a look back: I know, but just button your lip, OK?

'There,' said Mark to Sam. 'All better.'

'No thanks to you,' said Ellen. She wasn't going to let this go.

Now he began to get a bit tetchy. 'I was trying to load Femmie and Denis into the car at the same time. I was busy.'

Her look said, oh, and I wasn't?

Barbara and I exchanged a glance. Barbara couldn't stand domestics and was inching towards the door. I knew she was dying to go back upstairs and fiddle with her Dimitri phone, something always best done in privacy. Sometimes she would have imaginary phone conversations with him. 'Dimitri! Listen, I'm really sorry to bother you. Normally I don't pester you, you know that. I let you get on with things. But I was just wondering, on the off-chance that you might have forgotten to phone me or something, not that you *would* . . .' Sometimes she got herself in a bit of a knot at that point. 'Look, Dimitri, the thing is, could you tell me . . . is there any news?'

I could do with getting on the phone myself. I'd already dodged calls from two of my friends. Word was leaking out about Ollie moving out. I would have to let people know sooner or later, but didn't have the heart after the conversation I'd had with my mother earlier, in which I'd broken the news.

She'd given a big sigh, a couple of comforting clucks, and then she'd announced, 'God loves a trier.'

'What do you mean, "a trier"?' I enquired, stung.

There had been previous attempts, of course, before Ollie. But not too many, relatively speaking. It wasn't like I'd broken into, say, double figures. So it wasn't quite a case of, 'Oh, just give up, love, because at this stage we're all a bit embarrassed.'

But my mother hadn't meant that at all. 'You've given him every chance. And if he doesn't want to make good on all those years you've given him, well, then maybe you're better off without him.'

Marriage. She was going to bang on about that again. I thought I would scream.

But then she veered off topic and said, 'I heard the most extraordinary story today about Harry, and Muriel's dog—'

'I know, Mum.' Great. Even my own mother had got wind of it.

'Is it true?' She sounded horrified.

'I have no idea. Listen, I have to go. I'll ring you next week, OK?'

If at all.

Back in the present, Ellen was saying, 'They're waiting in the car. Femmie and Denis.'

'I didn't know they were waiting in the car, did I?' said Mark. He managed a smile for the kids.

'If you don't take them soon, they'll miss the tour.'

'I hear you. Loud and clear.'

Chapter Fifteen

Ellen and Mark's piglets were very cute. The sow wasn't so cute; she turned her broad pink body around to give me the evil eye as I sidled up to admire her offspring.

'It's all right,' I assured her. 'I've only stepped out for some fresh air.'

The sow wasn't convinced. Her little eyes squinted at me suspiciously and she lifted one large, hairy trotter as if to say, 'See this? Lay a finger on them and I'll bleedin' brain you.'

But then she seemed to dismiss me as a threat, and lumbered off into her little shed at the side of the pen. There, she lay down on the straw tiredly and exposed her vast, pale belly. It was like someone had shouted, 'Feeding time!' because suddenly there was a stampede: the piglets raced in and jumped on her excitedly, grabbed her nipples in their teeth and pulled them hither and thither. Some of them seemed to delight in stretching the nipple assigned to them out as far as it would go, like it was Plasticine, before releasing it so that it pinged painfully back into place. My own two shuddered in sympathy, and retreated as far back into my bra as they could. Little savages (the piglets).

I left the bacon to it, and set off for the goats. I was joined at that point by the wormy dog (no fresh efforts to de-worm him had been mounted). 'Hello, boy,' I said to him. I even reached down to pat him, but almost immediately regretted it. However challenging my life was now, it would get a whole lot more so if I contracted worms.

The goats were very pleasant. They had little old-man beards and starey eyes, and weren't that keen on being petted, so I didn't press the issue. I was beyond forcing my affections on creatures that plainly didn't want it. That included Ollie.

Damn. I'd hoped to concentrate on some quality time for myself, and not think about him at all, but *now* . . . I steeled myself and banished him from my head. I was strong again.

Wormy and I visited the milking parlour next. It was empty, as the cows had apparently been milked at four thirty that morning, or something obscene like that, and were now grazing peacefully in yonder field (it was eerie how fast I was becoming countrified). But they'd left behind a lovely pail of milk, all creamy and white-looking, like something you'd see from an ad. I was half tempted to have a sip of it as, what with it being organic and freshly squeezed, it was bound to be the best milk I'd ever tasted.

But old Wormy jumped in there before me and began to lap it up. I made a mental note to ask Ellen whether the milk in her fridge was from the shop or from the same bucket there that Wormy had his big, hairy, parasite-ridden head in now.

When he'd had his fill, and even managed a polite burp, we wandered companionably out into the yard again. The sun was breaking through, the breeze was fresh, and there wasn't a sound in the world apart from the birds twittering and the dog by my side softly panting.

The fucker hadn't even phoned to enquire after his daughter. Not one lousy phone call.

There I went again. Giving him head space. Getting sucked right back in again.

But, seriously, he should have phoned. Even Harry had phoned to make sure the plane hadn't disintegrated upon approach. But Ollie couldn't be bothered to find out whether I was OK after what he'd done to me.

He hadn't phoned me even once since he'd walked out to go to his mother's. Not once. All right, so he'd picked Cleo up on Saturday morning and dropped her at her dance class and then home again – he hadn't entirely abandoned her – but for me, there had been nothing.

We'd talked about it before – you know, the etiquette of breaking up – never suspecting that it might happen to us. But we'd had plenty of friends whose relationships had gone bust, so we knew what happened to other people. It was Ollie who'd remarked on the strange phenomena of the phone calls; two people break up, but end up in constant phone contact. These phone calls were always driven by the guilty party, the one who'd finished it, who would go ringing up the other poor wretch every day religiously, 'just to see how you're doing. Oh, contemplating slitting your wrists? God, Alice/Peter/Susan, I'm really sorry. It's all my fault. Tell you what, I'll ring you tomorrow to see how you're feeling, OK?'

Just fuck off. Isn't that really what you want to tell them to do, Ollie maintained. Bit bloody late to be worrying about the welfare of a person you've just gleefully ripped the heart out of. But instead of letting them get on with grieving, or flirting with cliff-tops, or whatever it is that's going to make them feel better, now they have to hang about for the daily phone call, 'Just to see how you're doing,' and to listen to just how much their bastarding ex *cares.*

'I'd never do that to you,' he told me.

I wasn't that happy with the conversation, which had started off theoretical, being brought back to us. 'So, what, I'd never hear from you again?'

'No, I just mean I wouldn't mess with your head that way. It's not fair.'

It seemed that he was putting into practice what he'd been preaching. He'd finished with me – without actually saying so – and now it seemed I could look forward to absolutely no phone contact from him ever again.

'Don't do it.'

I jumped to find Ellen beside me. She was carrying a bucket of feed for the chickens. I looked into it; they were getting better grub than we were.

'Do what?' I enquired.

She pointedly looked at the phone that I'd been trying to slip back into my pocket.

'I wasn't going to ring him.'

'Yes, you were.' I'd never been able to fool Ellen; Barbara yes, often and elaborately, but never Ellen.

We walked on to the chicken run. French chickens were a stylish bunch; they stalked about haughtily, showing off their silvery grey or deep russet feathers, and feigning boredom. None of them had nasty bald patches around their rear ends, like most Irish chickens that I'd come across.

'Chook-chook-chook,' said Ellen to them.

I thought she was having a laugh at first. 'Chook-chook-chook!' I joined in, elbowing her playfully in the ribs.

She looked at me like I was deranged. 'I'm calling them,' she said.

'That's how you do it. They're hardly going to understand, "Breakfast time, guys", are they?'

'Oh.' I felt like a right plonker. But honestly. *Chook?* Wait till I told them back home.

I delayed until she was into the whole experience, clucking like a mad thing under her breath, and scattering feed in soothing motions.

'You and Mark . . .'

'Oh, I know,' she said, with a casual laugh. 'Sorry about all that in the kitchen. I could take a saucepan to his head sometimes. As you can probably tell. Honestly. Aren't men just flipping hopeless?'

'Yes,' I said grimly.

I could feel her watching me. 'Maybe Ollie just needs some time, Hannah.'

Before I could explode, she pressed on gravely, looking like some kind of female guru in her sackcloth and bucket of chicken feed, 'Look at his situation. Caught in the middle of his mad, warring parents. Can you imagine what that must be like?'

'I couldn't give a—'

'Yes, you could. You're just saying that. If the situations were reversed, he'd feel sympathy for you.' I hated it when she went all wise and organic on me; usually she was right.

'How do you know what he'd feel?' Just because she'd taken up a life in a rural wilderness didn't mean she had access to all areas of Ollie's mindset. I'd been his partner for ten years, and *I* didn't have a clue.

'I'm trying not to take sides here, Hannah. Especially if there's a chance of you two getting back together. If that happens, you'll always resent the fact that I said he was a womanising loser with bad breath.' She reassured me, 'I'm just using that as an example, OK? But do you not see? Fine if it's definitely all over, but until then it's better that I straddle the fence.'

I didn't want her straddling fences. I wanted her on my side.

She saw this and she said, 'I'm just looking out for you here, OK? Let no man tear us apart.'

That used to be our motto, just before we'd wade into some packed nightclub back when we used to go to such places. We'd always arrange to meet at a certain time at the end of the night, regardless of whether any of us pulled or not. 'I don't care how gorgeous he is,' Ellen always warned us sternly.

It was comforting to know that the old ways still held. But I was still a bit sulky. 'So what I am supposed to do now, seeing as you know it all? Just hang about while he gets his head together and decides whether he wants me or not?'

'Of course not,' Ellen soothed. She gave a dangerous cackle, just like her old, non-organic self. 'You're going to get laid.'

Chapter Sixteen

We never got to the bottom of precisely what set Muriel off that day she kicked out her husband of forty-two years, with nothing to his name but an embarrassing bag.

'Was it something you said?' Ollie kept badgering Harry. 'No? Well, did you forget a special date or something? You know what she can be like about birthdays and that kind of thing. All right, look, I don't particularly want to go here, but was it . . . bedroom related? No, don't shake your head before you've even *thought* about it, Dad. Were you pestering her? Were you getting Viagra from the GP and trying to get up on her the whole time?'

At that point I would have to intervene. 'For God's sake, leave him alone, Ollie. He's seventy-one.'

But Ollie wouldn't be placated. 'There must be some reason. She can't have thrown him out for nothing.'

To my mind, the reasons for the break-up had already been laid out by both parties and were crystal clear, but Ollie was refusing to listen. He persisted in treating the whole thing as a temporary aberration that could be fixed if Harry could just learn to put his socks in the wash after use, and Muriel could just ease up on the nagging a little.

It was like he'd blanked the phone call from Muriel from his mind entirely, or put it down to female hysterics. 'Don't mind her,' he said to me. 'She always gets that way when she's a bit excited.'

She didn't, though. She'd never said those kinds of things before – about having had enough, about being desperate for change – or at least not to us. She may well have said them to Harry numerous times, if his hangdog expression was anything to go by.

But he wasn't quite as downtrodden as we'd expected.

'Come on, Dad. Get your coat on. We'll go round this morning,' Ollie informed him. I'd tried to talk him out of it but he was going to get his parents back together whether they liked it or not. 'She might be in a better mood.'

Harry had been in our spare room for three days at that point. The first night I'd heard him get up around 2 a.m., and shuffle down the stairs rather pitifully. Then, the kettle being switched on. Making himself a cup of tea, the poor old devil. No doubt wondering what in the blazes had happened to his life.

I was about to get up and keep him company, but then I heard a gunshot from downstairs, and I nearly passed out with the fright.

'What the hell?' said Ollie, catapulting up in the bed beside me, wild-eyed.

'We should have searched the bag,' I said, as we fell over each other in our haste to rush downstairs and discover a blood-spattered Harry. 'The fecking flowery bag.'

Then there was another gunshot. We froze. Finally, as if the job wasn't quite done, a third.

OK, now it was just weird. Had he missed the first two times?

Clutching each other, we entered the living room fearfully, unsure of what terrible scene we'd find there. But Harry was comfortably propped up on the sofa, a hot toddy in one hand and the remote control in the other. A quick glance at the box revealed that he was watching a back episode of *CSI: Miami*. It was a particularly lively one, involving what seemed to be gang warfare.

'Sorry for waking you,' he said. 'Do you want to join me? It's really very good.'

He watched another episode the following night at around 3 a.m. It was quite nice to be able to get up during the night if he felt like it, he informed us at breakfast. Muriel went ballistic if her sleep was disturbed. Often he'd be lying in the bed beside her rigidly for hours, trying to hold in a wee.

And now he was refusing to go and patch things up with her. 'She fecked me out. If she wants to sort things out she can come over here,' he said, revealing a hitherto unknown stubborn streak.

'Dad, this is no time for stupid game-playing.' Ollie's this-is-all-a-temporary-glitch mode was starting to fray a bit at the edges now. 'She's your wife and you belong over there.'

But something was happening to Harry. He may have thought it was a taste of freedom. My own opinion was that he was just in shock.

'I'm not going where I'm not wanted. No, I'm all right here for a couple more days. Besides, it's nice to spend some time with my grand-daughter . . .' He searched about for her name.

'Cleo,' Cleo helpfully supplied.

'Yes, of course. Cleo.'

In fairness, he had about seven or eight grandchildren at that point. Ollie's sisters, Maeve and Orla, were prolific breeders. Orla was on a plane home at that very moment, *sans* children, to console Muriel.

'Well, you've taken Dad in, Ollie. How do you think that makes her feel?'

'But she threw him out—'

'I know that. But the fact that you're putting him up makes it look like you're taking sides.'

'I'm not taking sides. What do you want me to do, send him to a hotel?' Poor Ollie was no match for either of his sisters.

'You just have to be careful, Ollie, that's all. You can't go around making things worse.'

And then the other one, Maeve, got on the phone every night to wreck his head more.

'I remember them fighting,' she said sadly.

'Fighting?' All Ollie could remember was that damn horse. And the summer evenings playing in the garden, with his parents sitting in deck chairs, his mother with her skirt pulled up to sun her knees. Nobody had been hitting anybody else over the head with a rolling pin, as far as he could recall.

'Oh, you were too young to remember,' Maeve told him, which made me really mad. Not only was Ollie doubting his own memories, but now he was being told he'd missed all the action anyway. 'I could tell even as a child that things weren't right,' went on the ray of sunshine.

'I saw nothing,' Ollie said to me afterwards, bewildered. 'I thought we were all having a great time. Was I in a different family altogether?'

'Look, I'm sure they had their bad patches, like everybody else,' I consoled him. 'But they obviously loved you all enough not to let it show.'

'Maeve saw.'

'Don't mind Maeve.' She was the gloomiest person I ever knew. When something bad happened, she was the first to shoot up her hand and bleat, 'I always suspected something wasn't right there.' I don't know why she didn't just take up fortune-telling, if she knew that much.

Ollie had been able to dismiss Muriel's nonsense of a long history of unhappiness, but now he had corroboration from that stupid Maeve. 'Imagine what it must have been like, them having to stay put just for us,' he said, looking stricken.

'OK, now you're making huge leaps.'

'But Mum said it. That they only stayed together for the sake of the kids. Us.'

I tried to water it down. 'If that was the case, they'd have split the minute you reached eighteen. But they didn't. They kept on going another twenty years.'

But Ollie was shaking his head vehemently. 'I wasn't even in college at eighteen. How could they have split up? And then there was all that business of Orla getting married, and then Maeve a year later; they could hardly break up in the middle of all that, could they? Then you and I had Cleo, and the girls started having *their* kids, and if Mum and Dad weren't flying between Canada and Australia they were over here baby-sitting. Do you not see? They stayed together because they never got a minute to break up until now.'

'Ollie, now stop it, or I'll give you a good slap. They were adults, free to make their own choices—'

'Ollie?' It was Harry, calling from the kitchen. 'How do you work this toaster?'

Harry was hopeless in the domestic arena. Muriel had done everything for him, short of squeezing toothpaste onto his toothbrush at night. He didn't know how to make simple meals, or sort out a dental appointment for himself. Supermarkets baffled him, and he'd never used a PIN in his life. Every half-hour, it would be, 'Hannah, I wonder could you help me with this?' and, 'Woah! Damn thing exploded.' (An egg he'd been trying to boil. He really was that bad.)

As the days turned into weeks, there was no sign of him trying to sort out alternative accommodation for himself. In fact, in a daring operation, he went over to his own house when Muriel was out getting her hair done (he knew her schedule to a T) and came back with two massive suitcases of belongings, and a large spear that someone had brought back from Africa for them years ago.

'She's not getting this,' he'd said, waving it over his head excitedly, and looking like an ageing warlord in a patterned jumper.

Cleo, wiser than us all, was the first to point out the obvious. 'I think he's going to live with us from now on.'

She was missing her soaps, the little pet, what with the TV continually tuned to grisly crime programmes. And Harry never thought to give the bath a wipe down after himself, which she found a little disturbing. So did I.

We could put up with the inconvenience, though, if it was only for a couple of weeks. But what if Cleo was right and he was there on a permanent basis?

I swung round to Ollie. But he avoided my eyes like crazy. I knew it wasn't fair to ask him to feck out a man who'd been fecked out once that month already, but we had at least to talk about it. We couldn't just let Harry enter our home and our lives by osmosis, breaking all our kitchen appliances and making the living room his own. Plus, he was in the bedroom next door to ours, and you can imagine how *that* curtailed activities. When I'd put my hand on Ollie's chest the other night, he'd jumped away as though I'd scalded him. 'My *father*,' he said.

Meanwhile, four miles across town was Muriel.

'How is he?' she would question Ollie anxiously several times a day. Then, almost immediately, she would pull herself up. 'You see? There I go again! Worrying about whether he's taking his calcium supplements like the doctor told him to. Or if his bunion is playing up. I've spent over four decades worrying about that man's bunion, whereas my leg could be falling off and he wouldn't notice.'

'I'm pretty sure he would,' I'd try to reason, even though I wasn't that convinced myself. I went over to visit her with Ollie every second night, in case there were any further accusations of taking sides. Between all the toing and froing, we were exhausted.

But Muriel — or Thoroughly Modern Muriel, as I was beginning to christen her in my head — continued to analyse her entire existence with Harry like she'd only just seen the light.

'I don't have that many years left, you know,' she would tell us, even though, three weeks into Harry's siege of our house, she looked younger than me. 'I have to make the best of them, don't I? And your father, well, he's not a bad man, Oliver, but he's not exactly the type who wants to push the boundaries, is he? I'd always try to get him to do things, you know, even when you were children, but he was always so afraid of anything new.'

'Mum, I'm not really that comfortable talking about Dad behind his back—'

'I bet he's dropping his dirty underpants on your bathroom floor, is he?'

She saw Ollie's guilty face before he could hide it, although I don't know what he felt guilty about. *He* didn't drop his kacks on the floor. 'See?' she went on, clearly anxious to get some stuff off her chest. 'He's never going to change. So I don't know how anybody can blame me for doing what I did.'

'Nobody's blaming you.'

'You are. You all are, you and Maeve and Orla. Orla told me that if we sold the family home, she'd be devastated.'

The thought hadn't entered Ollie's head until now; I saw him reel under this new blow. It wasn't that he spent a lot of time there any more, but the family home was a base, wasn't it? Always there if it was needed, whether you were seventeen or thirty-seven. For years now, we'd all met up in Muriel and Harry's for birthdays, christenings, Christmases and Sunday lunches.

But now the house might end up sold to strangers, and the proceeds split to buy two one-bedroom apartments with a communal lawn to house your elderly, divorced parents. Not much fun going *there* for the weekend.

'We might have to, I told her,' Muriel prattled on. 'It's not like we're rich. Always hopeless with money, your father. I tried to tell him, we need to have investments, pensions, but if it was up to him, all our money would be in a biscuit tin under the bed.'

Shut up, I wanted to tell her. Keep your opinions on your husband to yourself because it is TOTALLY INAPPROPRIATE to go tearing a strip off him to your children, because he's still their father, even if he *does* drop his dirty underwear all over the house.

But Muriel was oblivious. Over the coming weeks and months, she loudly bemoaned Harry's lack of hygiene, his relentless snoring or else the fact that he never slept (she was unhindered by inconsistencies in her complaints). She gave out about his fondness for plain meals, his dislike of travel, his meanness, his conversational skills, his friends (all as bad as he, apparently), his mother, even though she'd been dead twenty-seven years, and his 'awful, awful haircut'.

In the beginning I'd thought that maybe she was doing it on purpose, slandering Harry to get the kids on her side, but I realised later that it was merely stupidity. If Ollie had still been seven, or ten or even nineteen, she'd have gone out of her way to protect him from the nastiness. But now that he was all grown up, she seemed to think he was fair game for her adult concerns. Not an evening went by when she didn't get on the blower, or ask him over, just so she could offload forty years of resentments onto his increasingly hunched shoulders.

Harry, on the other hand, busied himself in our house with several box sets of *CSI: Miami*, and by breaking our washing machine. 'The knob just came off,' he told us, bemused.

'I suppose you have to laugh,' I said to Ollie.

But Ollie didn't laugh. Ollie went out and bought himself a pair of tight leather pants.

Chapter Seventeen

Ellen had it all planned; I would have a fling, and hopefully hot sex, with one of the Irish guys staying in the converted barn.

'But they're gay.' Talk about stacking the odds against me from the start.

'Not at all,' she assured me. 'I just said that to wind Barbara up. No, I had my eye on them for you all along.'

'*Both* of them?'

'If you have the energy.'

She must be joking. She had to be. Me, a heartbroken woman, a mother, having casual sex with a randomer? Maybe even two of them, although hopefully not at the same time?

Ellen saw that I was somewhat reluctant. 'It'll do you the world of good,' she assured me.

'What, when I contract gonorrhoea?'

'Naturally, you'll use protection. And the two lads seem very clean. Look, I just think that your self-esteem is rock bottom and could do with a boost. How better than with a nice, no-strings-attached, holiday romance with an interesting, good-looking man?'

I wondered whether isolation had affected her brain; or maybe she fancied one of the Irish guys herself but couldn't make a play for him, obviously, and so was trying to live vicariously through me.

'And do I just walk up to them and start taking my clothes off?'

'I wouldn't,' she advised. 'Leave it to me. I'll create an opportunity.'

So she threw a big party that night so that we could 'get to know one another'. Not a birthday party, because that was going to be on Saturday night. No, she billed it as a mid-week welcome party for Barbara and

Cleo and me, even though we'd come over every year for the last five years, and had never warranted a party before.

'She probably feels sorry for you,' Barbara observed. She didn't know about the plan to bed the Irishmen.

'Barbara, sometimes you're supposed only to think things, not say them out loud.'

The preparations were ferocious. Things slow-cooked all day in enormous pots in the cooker: great hunks of meat, bean casseroles, and nearly one of the children before they were hurriedly banished from the kitchen.

'Go and pick me some broad beans,' Ellen instructed them.

Cleo looked at me: what the hell were broad beans? And what TV show might we have seen them on?

Sophie was right in there, little Miss Bossy. 'I'll show you,' she said.

But while she might rule the roost normally, she was no match for Barbara, who pulled down her hairy jumper and instructed magnificently, 'Come with me, children,' like some mad nanny out of a 1950s musical. 'We'll pick them together. Get those baskets, Sam.'

Sam ignored her. He had taken a quiet moment to himself, while the girls were otherwise occupied, to systematically squash a line of red ants that were infiltrating the kitchen via a windowsill. His thumb was covered in blood and carcasses and he was clearly having a whale of a time.

'Sam. Как называется ваша компания!'

He looked up warily; more females harassing him – and in a language he didn't understand, either – and making him do really boring stuff like pick vegetables. And he didn't even eat vegetables, only chicken nuggets and hunks of baguette. You could see his entire, chubby little body stiffen in revolt. But then Ellen gave him a ferocious look: *Move it, mister.*

I knew that he'd got the speech too, like the one I'd given Cleo; Auntie Barbara was waiting a long, long time for Dimitri, and she really liked looking after all her 'nieces' and 'nephews' and it would be great practice for when Dimitri finally phoned, right?

Sam, being a good child at heart, despite outward appearances, got to his feet with a heavy sigh. '*Bien sûr,*' he told Barbara.

It was astonishing how they were able to understand each other, even though Barbara hadn't a word of French, nor Sam a word of Russian. He trooped out with the baskets, the two girls following after.

'You're doing great,' Ellen told Barbara. 'And well done on learning so much Russian!'

Barbara beamed and went on happily after her charges.

It was only afterwards that Barbara confessed to me that what she'd mistakenly said to Sam was, 'What is the name of your company?'

'I'm worried about her,' Ellen said with a sigh, giving an enormous pink ham an unsettling caress. I wondered whether it had once lived down in the pen with all its mates, and whether it might explain all the hysterical squealing I'd heard from that direction early yesterday morning – pig-talk for, 'Don't kill him. Please. We'll do anything.'

'All this waiting,' she went on. 'And what has she got at the end of it? Nothing.'

Chapter Eighteen

When Barbara had first put her name down for international adoption five years ago, we'd all said jolly things to cheer her up like, 'You never know – Santa might be coming to your house next Christmas!'

'Don't be stupid,' Barbara would say, annoyed. 'I won't even have started the assessment by then.'

We thought she was being pessimistic. They'd pull all the stops out when it came to poor, orphaned children, right? But no, a year crawled by, then nearly another one before she was finally called to a preparation course, and after that, her assessment by social workers. Barbara was very nervous about it; she'd read newspaper articles where prospective adopters were asked probing questions about all aspects of their lives, including their sex lives.

'Are you serious?' We were all appalled. 'Filthy minds, those social workers. Honestly. Wouldn't you think they'd get their kicks elsewhere?'

Barbara had been turned inside out; every facet of her life questioned. Was she sure she could cope? What about her job? Where would she turn if something went wrong? Did she have enough put away for a rainy day, because who knew when it might be lashing?

She had a clean slate on that one. She'd been saving since she was seven and had the equivalent of the national debt stashed away in various bank accounts. She could retire tomorrow if the mood took her.

She told us she made the mistake of saying that – she'd confessed to being a bit boastful – which unleashed a whole new round of questions: was she seriously contemplating giving up work, which she already said she'd cut down to part time? How would she cope at home all day long with a child, given that she'd said in session two, question nineteen, subpart (c) that work was one of the main satisfactions in her life?

'I'm fucked,' she shouted at me down the phone that night. I'd never heard her so distraught. 'I should never have opened my big mouth. He thinks I'm a lightweight, looking for an accessory in the form of a child whom I can dress up and parade around on my arm for the benefit of my family and friends, whilst refusing to change my previously comfortable life in any fundamental way.'

'He said that?' I was shocked.

'He's not allowed to, but I can see it in his eyes.'

Her social worker seemed a very pleasant and reasonable man, from what she'd told me, and I couldn't imagine him thinking bad things about anybody, but you couldn't say anything like that to Barbara. If you even brought up his name she broke out in a sweat and began looking over her shoulder in a hunted fashion. Once, when we were out for the night, she wouldn't even have a glass of wine in case she was 'spotted' and 'reported'.

Then her social worker wanted to interview her referees. She'd put me down as one, and was clearly starting to regret it.

'Don't tell them anything incriminating,' she ordered me. 'Nothing about drinking, or not cleaning my house once a week, and definitely don't mention sex.'

'Will it not be the first thing out of his mouth, though?' I worried, remembering the terrible newspaper articles. Also, there was a vicious rumour going around that they ran their finger along the skirting board in the living room, even of the referees. I'd already spent two days dusting.

Barbara went on feverishly, 'Say that I'm chaste and modest and have no interest whatsoever in casual sexual encounters with men. No, no, hang on. He'll probably think I'm a raving lezzer. Shit.' Her hands flew to her hair (she was convinced she was losing it, through stress). Then she totted up on her fingers. 'Tell him I've had three boyfriends since my divorce. That's a reasonable number, isn't it? Although not at the same time. Say that all three broke up by mutual consent. Say that I just don't want to get married again. But – and this is important – that I'm not against marriage as an institution, OK?'

By that stage I was hopelessly confused myself. In the end I sat at the interview at my kitchen table too petrified to open my mouth in case I dumped Barbara in it. Her very nice social worker probably thought I was a bit dim.

'You can relax,' he said to me about five times. For the record, he hadn't even glanced in the direction of my skirting board, and I have to say I was a bit disappointed. 'So,' he said, consulting his notes, 'would you say Barbara has a sense of humour?'

'Absolutely not,' I was able to assure him confidently. Phew. First one over with.

'Um-hmm.' He scribbled. 'Has she got many friends?'

A tricky one. 'Yes,' I told him carefully. 'But we all pay our taxes, and really like children, and nobody drinks more than one glass of wine when we have a dinner party. Two, max.' I crossed my fingers under the table.

In the end he puts the notebook away altogether, obviously thinking that it was unsettling me. He was wrong. Now there was nothing at all to focus on except him, and his clear brown eyes seemed to bore straight into my soul. I could tell that years of rigorous training had honed in him the ability to spot a bare-faced liar when he saw one.

'Why don't we just have a chat?' he said casually.

Hell, no. Chatting was the very last thing I wanted. A list of questions, yes. But no casual stuff. Barbara had warned me explicitly against casual chat, because she maintained that was when I was at my loosest and most dangerous.

In the end the pressure got to me and I blurted, 'You don't understand, Mr Social Worker.' I'd forgotten his name in my fright. 'This is so important for Barbara. Did she tell you how it all started? It's not because she can't have kids herself, although I don't know if she and Derek ever tried, but I know she's not into casual sex —' it seemed like a good time to slip that one in — 'but she could probably get pregnant if she wanted to, so it's not like you guys are her last hope or anything like that.'

He remained politely interested. I ploughed on. 'She read a newspaper article once about how this orphanage had no central heating, right? And she couldn't bear the thought of all those children freezing in wintertime? And she held a series of coffee mornings to raise money?' I didn't know why I had suddenly started speaking in questions. 'The coffee was terrible, and her buns not much better, and people generally paid over the odds just to be let leave, but the thing is that she made five thousand euro. That's a lot of coffee mornings,' I impressed upon him. 'Then she added five thousand of her own money and she rang up the orphanage and told them to get somebody in to put a heating system in and she would pay. And she did.'

I lunged forward to wet my mouth with a slug of tea. Some of it splashed on the table. I saw him looking at it – another black mark – and I sprinted for the finish line, getting faster and faster. 'That's what got her started on all this; seeing those kids in a place like that. She said she couldn't sit by and do nothing, and that it wasn't enough to just put in a heating system. She knows she can't change the world, but she's got a nice house, and a good life, and she's a really decent person, despite outward appearances. And I truly believe she's going to be such a good mother to some child out there, otherwise I wouldn't be sitting here. So, you see, I *can't* say anything to you today that would mess it up for her, because she will kill me with her bare hands. And I really mean that.'

He hadn't written down anything else I'd said, not the coffee or the five grand, or the heating system for the poor freezing kids, but now he reached quickly for his pad and began jotting down furiously, probably something about Barbara's unpredictable violent tendencies.

'Would you like to open a couple of presses and have a look at how clean they are?' I asked desperately, hoping to distract him.

'That won't be necessary,' he told me, and left five minutes later.

I couldn't ring Barbara afterwards, not the whole day long. I waited until I knew she'd be fast asleep in bed and then I texted her: 'I'm so sorry.'

But, happy days, because she phoned me the very next afternoon to say that Dale, her gorgeous, lovely, handsome social worker – her words – had seemed extremely happy with the interview with me, not that he gave anything away because that lot never did – her words again – but he was talking like she'd just got another fat tick in her file.

She came round that night to us, with a bottle of wine in gratitude. We had to pull all the curtains and dim the lights before she'd accept a glass. It was about three months since she'd last had anything to drink and it went straight to her head.

'Only about another two and a half years of this shite to go,' she blubbered happily. 'Approximately. Depending on declarations, Garda Clearance, notaries, waiting times and other assorted odds and ends.' Then she put her glass down and fell asleep.

We used to say it was a shame that she had never popped out six of her own. But it wasn't like she didn't give things a go. After her success in Australia, she got a taste for men, and went through them with gusto. She tended to go for the unconventional: beardy, odd types with dogs that looked like they should be banned, or the IT geek in her office with the pudding-basin haircut who, according to Barbara, was a mad man in bed. Tall, short, fat, hairy, Buddhists, tax collectors – Barbara loved them all.

None of them seemed to last, though. Then she met Derek – vegan, goatee, poet – and got married, but after a year and a half it was suddenly all off. We don't know what he did, but we think it might have involved him writing poetry at home all day in his garret while Barbara worked her socks off in the lab, only to come home to a dirty, cold house, with not a sign of her dinner on, and Derek standing there in his socks waving his latest poem – 'It's finished!' – that nobody was ever going to read except her. *Your things are like buttermilk*, that kind of thing.

There was nobody serious after that. 'I'd rather have a cup of tea,' Barbara sighed derisively. 'Or I might try women.'

We thought that was an idle threat, but she duly had a couple of skirmishes with a short, dark girl she met at a muddy music festival in a field somewhere, and they experimented in a tent. But it just wasn't the same when Barbara got back to sobriety, and clean sheets, in Dublin, and she gave lesbianism up as a bad job.

That summer after her divorce was the first year since Australia that she'd had no one to go on holiday with.

'I'll have to tag along with you,' she said to me, not being one to sit at home.

Ollie had looked slightly alarmed at that (he didn't really know Barbara well at that point). Cleo, going on three, had been delighted, though. Barbara always brought her intersting things to play with, like plastic test tubes and broken Bunsen burners.

But Barbara came down with tonsillitis a day before we were due to fly. She spent her holidays in bed, sucking lozenges and catching up on a year's worth of Sunday newspaper supplements. It was there that she'd read about the orphanage with no heating system. There was a photo of some of the kids, with their hair badly cut and in coats too light for winter, and the sight of them cut her to the bone.

From that point onward it was like her life suddenly took on a sharper focus; she still went to work and to music festivals, and offended people regularly by not thinking before she spoke, but every month she sent money to that orphanage and her summer holidays now involved a trip out to it. Her suitcase would be packed full of toothbrushes, Calpol, thermal vests, pencils and paper – anything that was light and compact.

She would spend two weeks playing with the kids and telling them all about Ireland, and our gorgeous scenery, and our terrible politicians, and how we were all fed up with the whole world thinking that all we did was drink too much and eat potatoes, and how delighted she was at the opportunity to assure them that it wasn't true. The kids would laugh and climb up on her lap to hear more, even though they wouldn't understand a single word she'd said.

She put her name down to adopt after one of the kids in the orphanage was hospitalised for something that a round of antibiotics would have cured at home. 'It's disgraceful. It's disgusting. How can we all sit around and do nothing?'

We realised then that Barbara hadn't been cut out for the whole marriage scenario at all. Suddenly it seemed completely right that she would adopt a child and become a single mother. It was like she'd never been destined to do anything else.

Except that it was all taking so blooming *long*. Barbara was coping better with it than we were. There were hundreds of people all over Dublin, France, Australia and Dubai (one of her brothers was there) who couldn't wait for this baby, whoever he or she was, to come home. Barbara had applied to Russia. She'd managed to sneak in her application just before the rules changed – the rules were forever changing, it seemed – and now she was just waiting on her facilitator, Dimitri, to match her with a baby. We'd all urged her to slip a couple of thousand rubles into the envelope, preferably in used notes, in an effort to speed things along, as was the Russian custom, we all believed (Ellen had visited once and had declared this to be the case), but Barbara had been completely horrified.

'As in *bribe* them?'

'No, no, we mean just to help things along . . .'

Her face had been terrible. 'That would be called child trafficking.'

'Oh. Right. Sorry, we didn't know.'

'Do you have any *idea* how hard we have to fight this whole misconception that international adoption is nothing but sleaze and corruption?'

'God, we didn't, sorry—'

'Enough!' Another flinty look. 'I was going to ask one of you to be my child's godparent but I'm happy to inform you that I've now changed my mind.'

Jesus. It was like walking on eggshells, this whole thing.

Ring, damn you. Now, in Ellen's kitchen, I tried to channel Dimitri, who most definitely hadn't been bribed.

But maybe rudeness was bringing bad karma on the whole thing. I amended it to, *Ring, please. Anytime that suits you, that is.*

Outside in the garden, Barbara went on picking broad beans.

Chapter Nineteen

I needn't have worried about letting the Irish guys down gently, as it turned out they had no interest in me anyway.

It had started off optimistically enough. 'Can I get you something to drink?' the one called Damien asked. He was big, blond, enthusiastic. Lovely teeth. A little over-excited at being at an authentic French shindig perhaps, where kids were running around the place 'at, like, ten o'clock at night!' and everyone – Rosalie, Marcel, the Dutch, Barbara, Mark – was talking animatedly over each other like you see in the movies. I suspected he was mixing us up with Italians, but who was I to cast aspersions on the *Godfather*?

'Jesus,' he said, 'I never thought I'd end up in the middle of France.' Well, on the very north-eastern edge of it, but I let it go. 'I was supposed to go to Portugal, as usual – I love the sun, like – but I suppose a change is as good as a rest, eh?'

His energy was infectious, I decided. So I smiled back and accepted the offer of a glass of white wine.

He gallantly rushed to do my bidding, giving me a chance to look over his body. It was nice: firm, toned, muscular, etc. He'd already told me that he was a member of a gym back home – he went four times a week, he told me. The rowing machine was his favourite. He could do thirty minutes on it, no problem. Did I belong to a gym? He'd looked a little disappointed when my answer was in the negative.

He must visit the dentist fairly regularly, too; I enjoyed another mega-watt smile from him as he returned with my wine. He'd also brought a little dish of Mark's home-grown cornichons (gherkins, for the uninitiated), which were very tasty, even if they all listed slightly to the left.

'They're a bit weird-looking, like, aren't they?' Damien keenly observed.

'Yes, but they've lovely,' I said, biting into one. It was crunchy and delicious.

I searched out Mark with my eyes. Denis had him up against the sink and was talking at him nineteen to the dozen, while beside them, Femmie was rolling wine around in her mouth and viciously spitting it out into the sink.

Mark, sensing my gaze, turned to look at me. 'Delicious,' I mouthed, holding up a cornichon. The smile he gave me back made me feel a bit warm and I quickly turned back to Damien. 'Try one.'

Damien wouldn't be tempted, though. 'They look like they might give you indigestion, like.'

He didn't do wine, either – 'it upsets my stomach, especially white wine' – and stuck instead to cans of lager.

'So,' I said, ignoring Ellen as she gave me a lewd wink from across the kitchen island, 'how long are you here for?'

'Too bloody long,' he said, and I laughed. 'No, seriously, like,' he said, 'what do you *do* here all day?'

'Me? Well, there're all the animals, I guess.'

'The cows and hens and sheep, like?' He was fond of the word 'like'. 'Sure we have them back at home.'

'Oh. OK. I guess the scenery is pretty spectacular – quite different from Ireland. And there's the fresh air and the way of life . . .' How did you describe the joys of being in France in one fetching sound bite?

Clearly better than I was doing, because Damien was looking around again, a little restless. 'We've been here a week already and if it wasn't for the coach tours, I think I'd have gone mad.'

He may well be one of those intense, pent-up individuals that always had to be caught up in a whirlwind of activity. Exciting. Passionate. Maybe involved in the film or music industry or something?

'I usually go to Portugal with the lads from work. I'm in insurance.' He perked up. 'I could give you a very good quote on your house contents, if ever you needed one.'

'Oh, er, right . . .'

But he'd already moved on. 'But this year I got stuck tagging along with old misery guts over there.' He jerked a thumb disparagingly in a direction somewhere behind him.

Old misery guts turned out to be the second Irish bloke. He was hanging around the buffet like he'd rather be gouging his eyes out. He was the opposite to Damien – shorter, darker, older. Teeth fairly ordinary, but not *bad* or anything. His hair was passable, wiry and thick. Decent condition.

But it was his face that caught my attention. It was miserable. I mean, *really* miserable. Tetchy, brooding, sullen, narky.

Christ, I thought. Who took *his* lolly?

He picked up a slice of Ellen's delicious baked ham on a fork; then, as if it had somehow let him down, he carefully replaced it.

Miserable.

Then, clearly aware of my scrutiny, he looked up suddenly and fixed me with his tetchy brown eyes and gave me a look that said, unmistakably, *Fuck off and mind your own business.*

Fine. No problem. He'd give you indigestion, as Damien would say.

Damien was also watching him in despair. 'Can you imagine shacking up with *that* for a couple of weeks?' He grinned at me then, and I forgot he worked in insurance and had an unadventurous palate. 'And he snores. I'll tell you, I could do with a nicer sleeping partner.'

A little thrill ran through me. I didn't really fancy him, but he was definitely hitting on me and it was balm to my Ollie-inflicted wounds.

For a moment I was tempted. Would I? Should I? Did I have any condoms with me? Never mind, Barbara would probably have a couple of dusty ones lurking at the bottom of her voluminous handbag.

Ellen, doing her efficient hostess thing, was whirling around the guests with platters of things at unsettling speed: 'Olive? Miniature crêpe? Pâté on toast, made from our own ducks? It's OK, Sophie pet, don't cry, they didn't feel a thing, I promise.'

A moment later she was behind us. 'Go on, Damien, have two, you're a growing boy.' As he beamed with childlike pleasure, she said in my ear, 'Whoarr. Enjoy yourself.'

She danced smoothly on in her muck-coloured dress, Damien looking after her with his head cocked to one side. I hoped to Christ he hadn't heard.

'So,' he said, 'Ellen tells me you're recovering from a break-up.'

'Yes,' I said, surprised by the sudden lump in my throat. I was hardly recovering. More like still reeling. But I knew he wanted some light banter, not some grief-stricken woman on his shoulder, bawling, 'My life is OVER.'

'We'd been together ten years so I suppose it's been a bit of a shock,' I confided.

'I'm sure,' he murmured, looking at his miniature crêpe doubtfully. It was only pancake, for heaven's sake. Surely it couldn't do much damage to his digestive tract.

I ploughed on, 'That's our daughter over there, Cleo.'

She was playing one of those clapping games with Sophie that seemed to be incredibly popular with eight-year-old girls the world over, and that looked quite painful. They were slapping each other's hands in a complicated and vicious ritual, accompanied by nonsensical rhymes like, 'My heart goes BOOM BOOM A-mer-ica, BOOM BOOM Aus-tra-lee-a, yadda-yadda-yadda-yadda' (very fast hand-clapping now; someone was going to get hurt in a minute), 'PEPSI COLA!!!'

Then, with a final, ominous chant of, 'Fist, fist, fist, fist,' they crossed their balled fists over their chests and launched themselves at each other like a couple of sumo wrestlers, Sophie all energy and wiry strength and, to my eye, quite a lot of aggression. But Cleo, shorter and plumper, was like a little brick wall, and Sophie just bounced off her and fell into a rather pathetic heap on the floor.

'You did that on purpose,' she said to Cleo accusingly.

Cleo tried to help her up. 'I didn't do anything. I didn't even move.'

Sophie wouldn't take her hand. 'Muuuum!'

Ellen barely looked their way. 'Girls, keep it down.'

'She's lovely,' Damien said, sounding very impressed.

'Yes.' I felt that now would be a good time to clarify my position. Just in case he was getting any notions about my availability later on for a casual sexual encounter. 'The thing is, she doesn't know yet that things are definitely over between me and her dad, so if she was to, you know . . .' how to put this delicately? '. . . see me with someone else in France, it might confuse her and I wouldn't want that to happen.'

I really hoped he wouldn't be offended. He might even want to stay and harmlessly flirt a little while longer. It was doing my heart good.

'She's a fantastic cook, isn't she?' Damien said.

It took me a moment. 'Cleo?' The child could barely make a slice of toast, and only then if on the verge of starvation.

'Ellen.'

Ah. Now I got it. He fancied the pants off Ellen, but given that she was comprehensively unavailable, he was killing time in the corner with the plumper and less attractive best friend.

I was furious. Not about being plumper and less attractive than Ellen; I'd always known that so it wasn't like it was a shock. I was angry because

I'd been talking about my lovely daughter and he hadn't listened to a word I'd said.

'Yes, she is,' I told Damien with a brilliant smile. 'And she's witty and clever and kind and, I can tell you from first-hand experience, completely subversive in bed.'

Ah. Now he was interested in me. His eyes — little piggy eyes, actually, in a piggy face — flicked from me to Ellen, wondering if he could get some kind of sandwich thing going later on. At that point my glass of ice-cold white wine somehow slipped — oops — from my hands and the contents landed squarely on his crotch. 'Would you look at that!' I cried. 'I'm *so* sorry.'

He was pissed off, you could see that, and his willy was clearly drenched and probably shrivelled to the size of one of Mark's lop-sided cornichons. 'That's OK,' he muttered, plucking at himself in distaste.

'You might have to go and change,' I suggested.

'No kidding,' he said sarcastically.

I watched with grim satisfaction as he limped across the yard to the converted barn. His friend, old misery guts, gave me a wary look and took a step away when I swept past him to replenish my glass of white wine. When I'd finished knocking it back and feeling good about myself, I realised that on my phone was a missed call from Ollie.

'He didn't leave a message.'

'So ring him back.'

'I *can't*.'

'Why not?'

'Because I don't know what it was about.'

'How are you going to find out, unless you ring him back?'

I hated all this reasonable talk. It had no place in a discussion of man-based motives and patterns of behaviour. 'Anyway, if it was really important then he wouldn't have hung up, would he?'

'Maybe it *was* important but he just lost his nerve.'

I was getting really irritated now. 'And maybe he's just a gobshite — have you thought of that?'

I'd never spoken to Mark like that before. You know, like he was one of the girls. He certainly didn't look anything like one of us, sitting there bursting out of his jeans and with a bottle of beer in his big, manly hands.

'Sorry,' I said.

I hadn't even meant to tell him about the phone call. I'd escaped the noise of the kitchen in order to check my messages, sure that the message lady hadn't meant it when she'd told me twice, firmly, 'You have no new messages.' I'd flung myself down on the bench near the kitchen window, normally hogged by dogs and cats of questionable cleanliness, only to discover that I'd practically sat on Mark.

'Does Denis know I'm out here?' he'd asked anxiously.

'I don't think so.'

He'd relaxed. 'Great. He's trying to get me to show him how to milk a cow in the morning. It's only for the photos.'

We both laughed cruelly at Denis's expense. It was nice and balmy outside, although Barbara would probably call it freezing. Mark, probably loosened by a couple of drinks, like me, said, 'Look, don't worry too much about Ollie. Men do that. They have a few beers, realise what a plonker they've been, go ringing up their women to try to make it right, but then chicken out at the last minute.'

'I'm not his woman.'

'You don't know for sure that it's over, from what Ellen says.'

I was a bit put out at Ellen watering down my drama behind my back. 'It *is* over,' I stated. Rashly, wanting to impress him or something, I insisted, 'If not from his side, then definitely from mine.'

Mark didn't try to contradict me. 'You sound pretty certain.'

I was buoyed up on alcohol and his attention. I'd already dispatched one man tonight, so why not more? I stuck my nose in the air. 'Frankly, I think you're right. I don't think he *is* good enough for me.'

Mark looked at the window. 'For God's sake, don't let Ellen hear I was running him down. She'd kill me.'

'You only said the truth.'

'I know, but she says we have to stay out of it. And, as you know, her word is law around here.'

'She's sitting on the fence.' I felt I needed to explain her stance. 'You know, in case we get back together.'

I could feel him watching me in the dark. 'Don't you think you've given him enough chances?'

I rolled my eyes. 'You've been talking to my damn mother, haven't you?'

He laughed. Just a titter, but I enjoyed it. I liked making him laugh. For some reason, this visit, I wasn't just one of Ellen's goofy, left-of-centre friends that it was best to just park at the Table of Moans with a case of wine until it was time to drive me back to the airport.

This visit, I was interesting. Funny. He was looking at me like I actually had something to offer. And this was after I'd been dumped, too. Lots of other men would think, Christ, an emotional head-wreck, get me out of here.

But Mark looked like he was enjoying himself. Genuinely. He was half twisted on the seat, the better to give me his attention.

Naturally, I upped my game. 'That Damien guy fancies your wife.'

I had no idea why I'd lobbed that into the conversation. For some kind of reaction, maybe. I held my breath, suddenly sorry. Giving Mark that kind of information could be like handing him a loaded gun; would he hurl down his beer in a fit of rage and storm over to the converted barns and rip Damien's marinated testicles off?

Instead he threw back his head and laughed like I'd told him a hilarious joke. 'I know.'

I suppose a lot of men fancied Ellen. If he was to get excited every time and go tearing people's testicles off, he'd be worn out. And probably in gaol.

'Tool,' he said, casually dismissing Damien as any kind of threat against him or his wife, and I immediately felt better.

'He is, isn't he?' I said eagerly.

'I liked what you did with that wine,' Mark told me, a laugh in his eye.

'Well, you know, a girl's got to do what a girl's got to do.'

'They'll be gone by the end of the week,' he assured me. 'And if not, I'll kick them out, OK? Either way they won't bother you again.'

I felt warmed by his protection. He was looking out for me, when my own man had run for the hills. And even if he hadn't, Ollie wouldn't have dreamt of protecting me. I was a big girl and could look after myself, as far as he was concerned. In fact, once he'd cowered behind me when we got into a nasty spat with a man over a car parking space in the Dundrum Shopping Centre the day before Christmas Eve. 'Well, your T-Shirt said, *If You Look At These Again, They'll Take Your Eye Out,*' he'd said. 'I'm only wearing a polo shirt.'

It must have been about one o'clock in the morning by then. Sitting out there in the yard, I saw the sky was clear and full of stars – thousands of them – and for a moment I came over all poetic. 'Wow. And you get to see this every night.'

Mark looked up at them too, and stretched his legs out. God, he was sexy. Then he turned to look at me in the dark. 'Yep,' he said. 'Part of the reason we moved here. During the summer we sometimes sleep outside. The kids love it.'

OK, I wouldn't be so keen on that – God knows what animal you'd wake up next to the following morning – but I said enthusiastically, 'Sounds great.'

A movement through the kitchen window caught my eye. There was old misery guts, by the sink. Getting a drink of water, the life and soul of the party. He looked up and my eyes clashed with his: for a split second, it was like looking into a mirror. Looking back at me was my own pain, shock and betrayal.

Then he dropped his eyes, busied himself at the sink, leaving me wondering whether I'd imagined the connection, or whether maybe it was just the dim light.

Beside me, Mark stirred. 'Listen, chin up, OK? Maybe Ollie will ring again tomorrow.'

I couldn't believe how nice he was being to me. I'd always thought him a little, well, aloof and self-centred. But perhaps I just hadn't given him a chance.

'Maybe,' I said. I finished my wine. Suddenly I was a little embarrassed at having got so pally with him. 'Anyway! Sorry about all that, Mark. I didn't mean to offload on you like that.'

'Don't be daft. It's what friends are for.'

I shot him a grateful smile. Possibly some ice had been broken tonight in a way we hadn't managed in the previous decade. 'Yeah.'

I didn't see his hand move in the dark. I was looking at the stars again. But suddenly there was a warm, firm pressure on my thigh, and I froze.

The back door to the kitchen opened now and I could see Ellen framed by the light. She had a slice of nut tart in her hand, my very favourite dessert, and which she always made especially for me.

'Hannah?' she called into the darkness. 'Are you there?'

The hand was gone.

'Coming,' I said back, and I got up quickly and went to join her.

Chapter Twenty

'You're very quiet,' said Barbara accusingly.

'No, I'm not.'

'You are. You haven't said a word all morning. It's like going on holidays with a monk.'

'Well, I'm sorry I'm not the life and soul. I've just had my heart broken, remember?'

'Yeah, yeah,' said Barbara, as though I'd been banging on about it for years now. 'Come here,' she said. 'Did you see your man at the party last night?'

'Which one?'

'The miserable one, not the one with the teeth. Ellen was wrong. He's not gay at all.'

'Why, did you try asking him what his favourite Abba song was?'

'And he's not married either. Or at least he's not wearing a ring.'

I couldn't have cared less if he was a recovering sex addict with a stash of size ten ladies' shoes under his bed. 'Now's your chance,' I said to her.

I let her chew on that one as I wondered yet again why my own life couldn't be a little simpler. What had I ever done to anybody, man, woman or child – well, within reason, anyway – to deserve such shocking bad luck, and in such as short space of time too? Had all my stars, the really bad ones, aligned in my personal galaxy, ready to throw the biggest shit-hitting-the-fan party since the beginning of time?

'Stop feeling sorry for yourself,' Barbara, the mind-reader, flung over her shoulder.

Honestly. You couldn't have a private pity-party without being pounced upon.

'I know you don't want to hear this,' she continued her lecture, 'but at some point you're going to have to pick yourself up and move on.'

She thought it was only Ollie who was upsetting me, of course.

'It's only been five days, Barbara.'

But Barbara was giving no quarter. 'And you can start by pedalling.'

'I *am* pedalling.'

'Even the kids are going faster than us.'

Barbara and I were on a tandem. Barbara had bagged the front seat, declaring that she didn't want to spend the day looking at my behind. If she'd thought about it, hers was a far more shocking sight, especially in the tight khaki shorts that she was sporting. The shorts had about fifteen pockets and zips and pouches and places to store things, all of which Barbara seemed to have utilised, along with a bulging rucksack on her back. On top, she wore a tight vest over an industrial bra, and a panama hat jammed firmly on her head. She looked like something from an Indiana Jones movie – the slightly unhinged but enthusiastic traveller, perhaps, who will come to an untimely end in a rock-crushing machine in the second half of the film, with nothing left of her but her enormous shorts.

'Anybody for Factor Twenty? A sandwich? Some Vaseline in case your thighs are chafing?' she'd called at the last rest stop. There was nothing she didn't have in that rucksack, including a puncture repair kit.

'I'll have the Vaseline,' Denis had announced. 'But only if you put it on for me.'

Barbara had recoiled. 'Not even if you shaved them.'

'That could be arranged,' Denis told her, while Femmie laughed at the good of it. Strange people, but lovely.

I'd accepted two of Barbara's paracetamol tablets, taken from one of the pouches in her shorts, and nicely warmed from her bum. I was hungover, as were half the cycling party, but I suspected they'd all slept a little better than I had.

Anyway, so there we were, me clutching a handlebar at either side of Barbara's generous rear, as we travelled in formation down a long, narrow country road, with Barbara shouting over her shoulder at me periodically to, 'Slow down,' or, 'Sharp bend coming up in two hundred and fifty metres,' and sometimes, 'Oh, cheer up, for the love of God.'

Up ahead of Barbara were the girls – Sophie first, of course, the sun glinting off her little red head. Cleo cycled behind her, on one of Sophie's cast-off bikes, a pink Barbie thing with ribbons on the handlebars and other embarrassing paraphernalia. It was too small for her, and her knees kept coming up around her chin.

'You're too fat for it,' Sophie had announced earlier. Fat was one of her favourite words this visit, I was beginning to discover.

I'd waited for Ellen to swing around in horror and say, 'Sophie! Cleo is *not* fat.'

But Ellen had been too busy making hundreds of sandwiches for the bike outing and hadn't heard. It was up to me to say, 'I think what you meant to say was that Cleo is a little too old for a bike that size.'

Sophie had looked back at me coolly. 'Yes,' she'd agreed. 'Sometimes my English isn't so good.'

My eye. Her English was better than mine. 'Don't mind her, pet,' I'd said to Cleo.

'I'm not,' Cleo had said quickly, but I thought I caught a flicker of dislike as she looked at Sophie.

Following behind Cleo on our little trip was Sam, on a determinedly blue bike with things like 'Racer boy' written on it, and a picture of a skull on the mud flap. It seemed to inspire all kinds of recklessness in him that had been forcibly repressed for days now by the influx of oestrogen to his house, because he kept making daring breaks for the middle of the road and trying to go up on one wheel. Then, when we all started shouting at him, 'Get off the road, you pup, before you get run over by a tractor!' he would rejoin the line meekly.

A couple of feet behind me was Damien. I'd have known he was there even if I hadn't looked around, because of the heat of his dislike on my back. Tough. I didn't like him either, any more.

Old misery guts – he must surely have a name but nobody seemed too bothered to find it out – was the other rider on the tandem that they'd also landed. He was staring down grimly at the road like he was trapped in his own personal hell.

He also had an uncanny ability to know when I was looking at him – I hope to God he didn't think I fancied him or something – because he suddenly raised his head and nailed me with his eyes.

Again, I felt that jolt of connection.

What was going on? I hadn't even spoken to the guy.

Maybe we'd met in a previous life or something. As rats, or concubines or something.

I wrenched my eyes away, and back to Barbara's butt.

Leading us all, and on an enormous, shiny mountain bike with a big ringy bell, was Mark. 'Keep it up, people!' he shouted encouragingly back at us, with a trill of the bell. 'Only eleven and a half kilometres to go!'

It had been his idea to spring a bike ride on us all. Well, the plan had been to take the paying guests, hangovers and all, but the kids had wanted to go too, and Denis and Femmie hadn't wanted to get stuck on their own with Damien and his cheerless friend and, frankly, who could blame them? Suddenly we were all going, except for Ellen, who was staying home to whip up a five-course lunch for when we got back.

Mark turned his dark head to us, no doubt wondering what was keeping all the slow coaches.

I ducked down quickly. I couldn't look at him, in his shorts and his T-shirt and his sunglasses that hid his eyes. I hadn't looked at him all morning. I'd hidden in the loo while they'd all mounted their bikes in the yard, only nipping out at the last minute to hop on behind Barbara.

'All set, Hannah?' Mark had called.

'Yes, yes, yes!' I'd mumbled back cheerily, whilst thinking, what the fuck happened last night?

Well, I *knew* what had happened. I think. But why was he acting so normal? Had I imagined it all?

'Barbara,' I blurted. I might as well come out with it. 'How drunk was I last night?'

'Stop complaining and just pedal.'

'I'm not trying to get out of anything, I'm just wondering.'

'We were all a bit piddly-eyed,' Barbara assured me. 'Nobody blames you for what happened.'

My stomach heaved. 'What do you mean?'

'Pouring a drink down your man's pants.'

She threw a look around at Damien, nearly sending us crashing into a ditch. Once we had righted ourselves, the tension that had held me in its grip since the previous night began to loosen very slightly.

I had been under the influence. We had all been. And as for the . . . hand thing, it was entirely possible I had misread the situation.

I replayed the evening in my mind: party, nice food, everybody gathered happily in the kitchen, Damien, drink, wet pants. All fine so far. Then Ollie ringing. Still fine. Then me knocking more wine back and lurching outside full of annoyance and poor-me feelings, and I began to feel a bit queasy again.

I had thought we'd been having a great laugh on the bench, Mark and me. Bonding. And yes, I'd thought he was sexy, because he *was*, especially under the lovely moon and stars. I remembered feeling warm and fuzzy. Had I been horny? Jesus! Had I sent some kind of signal?

I had been laughing too much. Trying to be too witty. Leaning in.

'What's wrong?' Barbara enquired, looking alarmed. 'Your breathing has gone funny. Do you want to stop?'

'No,' I said between gritted teeth 'Keep going.'

There was a terrible question I had to answer: Had I Led Him On? All that boo-hooing over Ollie, and then, seconds later, insisting it was over. I'd enjoyed Mark's company – there was no getting away from that – but had I also been sending out mad signals that I was well up for it, if he was?

OK, I didn't like that scenario. And I wasn't sure it was true, either. Even though he was a delight to look at, he was also, well, Ellen's husband. End of story. I might fancy, but I would never *do*.

And what had actually happened, anyway? A light touch on my leg. Nothing more. Nobody had made a grab for my boob, or tried to jam a tongue down my throat. What if it had just been a reassuring, friendly touch between two people who'd known each other for over a decade? One of whom had recently suffered a traumatic break-up and was in need of comfort?

Yes. Thank God. Of course that's what it had been! Of course. We were talking about *Mark* here. Family man, crazy about his wife, happy in his life of tourists and muck. Why on earth would he want to fondle the flabby thigh of his wife's left-of-centre friend, in *full view* of the kitchen window?

I was very embarrassed now at my conjecture. The poor man had probably only tried to be nice to me. I could nearly hear Ellen now: 'For God's sake, be nice to Hannah, will you? She's in bits, after everything.'

And it wasn't as though it was the first time Mark had been asked to 'be nice to Hannah'. When we'd finally arrived home from our travels abroad nine years ago, Ollie and me, we'd been so broke that we couldn't even afford the deposit on an apartment. Ellen and Mark had lent it to us. I'd been absolutely mortified but, being pregnant, hadn't exactly been in a position to turn it down. Ollie had no job, and there were no signs of him getting one in a hurry. And so I'd been forced to accept a cheque from Mark one night at his lovely apartment in Dublin 4, my belly straining against my slightly grubby neon holiday rep T-shirt, the only thing that would still fit me. He'd been very nice about the loan, completely unpatronising, but I just knew he must have been thinking, Christ, what an irresponsible pair.

I'd paid the money back the very next month, and given them a case of nice wine as a thank-you, but it always hung there, between us, an embarrassment. Or maybe they'd forgotten all about it, and the embarrassment was just mine.

And now there was Mark being nice to me again, only I'd been about to screech, 'Are you making a PASS AT ME?'

Thank God I hadn't. In fact, what was I saying? The thought hadn't even entered my head – maybe because I felt as implicated in it as he, being full of wine and cosy confidences. No, I'd skedaddled into the kitchen after Ellen as fast as I could and shovelled down the nut tart, smiled and carried on as normal. When Mark had come in five minutes later, I'd pretended nothing had happened and so had he.

Because nothing had. No, I was quite sure of that now. Quite sure. We were all friends here, especially Ellen and I. I simply had to take care to ensure I didn't stray into any uncomfortable territory again, that was all.

'What's happened to you?' said Barbara, throwing a suspicious look over her shoulder at me. 'You're getting faster.'

I considered for a moment telling her. I could make it funny, and that would make me feel even better. And not like I was hiding something. I could say something smutty like, 'I'm going over to cry on Mark's shoulder again, in the hope that he might give my thigh another little squeeze.'

But I knew immediately that it wouldn't sound funny at all. Barbara's eyebrows would jump up and I'd open a can of worms.

So I just said, 'And you're getting narkier.'

'That's because I'm tired. And hungry.' She craned her neck to look at the top of the line. 'When are we stopping for food?'

Her plaintive voice must have reached Mark, because he turned round and called, 'Is that your stomach I can hear rumbling, Barbara?'

He led us on until we came to a picnic area with benches and tables in a nice pine clearing. We all stood around like groupies while he took charge: emptying picnic baskets; scooping off some bird poo from one of the tables; giving the kids the jobs of putting out plastic cutlery and napkins.

'Isn't he great?' Femmie murmured to Denis.

'Top drawer,' Denis said back.

Now it was our turn for his attention, and everyone squirmed with pleasure as he joked, 'There's a lake over there, if anyone fancies a skinny dip.'

I blushed. For no reason whatsoever. He wasn't even looking at me.

'I quite fancy a dip,' Denis announced, dutifully unzipping his shorts. Femmie had to stop him. 'No, no, he's just pulling your leg.'

But Denis had the idea in his head now. 'I'm going and nobody can stop me.'

He refrained from taking anything else off before setting off for the lake. Femmie grabbed her camera and went after him. 'I might post these ones on the Internet,' she said gleefully.

Damien looked after them in great disapproval. 'They're mad,' he announced, looking at Mark rather accusingly for having let such undersirables holiday on the farm.

Then he and old misery guts took off to a picnic table by themselves, with a box of sandwiches. Damien got out his mobile phone and spent the time texting away, while the other one . . . well, when he wasn't looking at the sandwiches like they'd offended him, he sat there brooding like somebody had ripped his heart out and flambéed it.

'Toilet emergency,' Sophie screeched, running up. 'Sam's wet himself!'

Sam came trundling up now too, his face contorted in rage and misery. 'I did *not* wet myself. I sat in a puddle.'

'If you'd sat in a puddle, then the *back* of your pants would be wet,' Sophie reasoned loudly. 'But it's the front that's wet. Look!' And she pointed out his shame to us all.

He tried to cover the offending wet bit with his bike helmet. 'Shut shut shut UP.'

'All right, let's go over there in the bushes and sort you out,' Mark said.

'I'll help,' Sophie decided. 'Cleo! We're going to the bushes.'

Cleo looked up warily. She'd kept her distance from the wetting shame, I noted. 'I don't need to go.'

'I know, but we need to help Sam. He wet himself.'

'I did not wet myself, you pisshead,' Sam wailed.

'Sam!' We all looked at him in terrible disapproval.

He hung his little tear-sodden face. 'That's what Mammy says.' It sounded like Ellen all right.

At that point Barbara weighed in magnificently with her Nanny McPhee impression. 'Why don't I take you all into the bushes?' She was delighted at the opportunity to get in a little extra tuition. Going to the toilet in tricky places was, she knew, a basic parenting skill, and she would have to get used to stopping abruptly on motorways and in the middle of supermarkets. 'It just so happens that I have a spare pair of underpants in my rucksack,' she told Sam. And she wasn't just being nice.

'If we're not back in five minutes, call search and rescue,' she instructed cheerily as she waded off into the undergrowth with Sam, Sophie and Cleo in tow, Sam still whinging and Sophie explaining in detail to Cleo what exactly had happened.

Then it was just Mark and me, him unpacking sandwiches and taking out flasks.

I was mortified. All my reasoning of earlier had deserted me and I just sat there, like I was waiting for some axe to fall.

But Mark just kept unpacking easily, confidently. There were no tortured looks, no outbursts of, 'Jesus, I'm so sorry about last night. I was completely scuttered. PLEASE don't get the wrong idea.'

Instead he smiled at me in a very non-threatening way and said, 'He's just broken up with someone.'

I was forced to raise my eyes from the table to his. Somehow they got stuck on his crotch on the way up – Jesus, Mary and Joseph – before I managed to lift them all the way to meet his eyes.

'Who?' I said, in a voice that sounded fairly normal.

'Nick.'

Old misery guts, I deduced.

'So I guess you two have something in common.'

What did that mean? My head spun as I tried to decipher the subtext. Was there even one? Was I just hungover and slightly mad?

And there was Mark, chattering on like he hadn't a care in the world. 'Did you enjoy the cycle?'

'Yes. Lovely. Bit sore, but fine.' Immediately I was sorry I'd said anything about being sore.

But he didn't dive under the table to examine my legs at length, kneading them up and down in a sexually charged fashion. He just smiled and said, 'If you think you're sore now, wait till the morning. None of you will be able to get out of bed.'

And suddenly the focus was off me, us, and onto the group again. Oblivious to their looks of boredom and misery, he called across to Damien and Nick, 'Lads! Come and join us.'

There, I told myself. See? Nothing had happened. Nothing at all.

Chapter Twenty-one

Ollie phoned again that night. I picked up straight away.

'Ollie,' I said. I wasn't going to say, 'Hello?' like I hadn't a blinking clue who it was. Especially as his pet name, 'Ollie the Ride', had flashed up on my caller display. Must change that.

'Is this a good time?' he asked cautiously, like we had to make appointments with each other now.

'It's fine,' I told him, amazed at how normal I sounded.

There was a little pause. 'What's that noise?'

'Oh.' The snuffling and snorting and squealing, he meant. 'Just the pigs.' Maybe I should have let him think it was me.

I was out at the pigsty. For some reason I found them soothing. In the few days that we'd been there, the piglets seemed to have doubled in size. The two sick ones, Bonnie and Clyde, were getting stronger too, and there were hopes that one day soon they might be rehabilitated into the group.

I gripped the mucky fence hard and pressed the phone to my ear. Despite my veneer of coolness, my heart was hurting and my stomach heavy.

'I was just wondering how Cleo was getting on,' Ollie said. 'How you're both getting on.'

In other words, this wasn't a 'Please, take me back' phone call. That was OK. I'd already known that.

'Fine, thanks. Cleo's having a great time, as usual. I'm getting the feeling that there's a little tension between her and Sophie and that she might possibly end up belting her one, but so far she's fine. They're inside doing magic tricks on Sam, trying to make him disappear.'

He gave a small, forced chuckle on the other end. I could tell that he was taken aback at my normality. Not that I would have wept pitifully down the phone or anything; he knew I'd never let myself down like that. But shouldn't I at least sound a bit sullen and uncommunicative? And maybe swiftly hang up?

But we were too old for that. Too long together to play games. And so I said, with some genuine concern, 'How are things your end? You know. With Muriel.'

Ollie gave a sigh and just said, 'Cracked as ever. But OK. In the circumstances.' It was the first time he'd sounded like himself.

'Yes, well, tell her I said hello.' Ordinarily I'd have been dying to tell him that my mother had heard what Harry had done, too. We'd have had a right laugh, as well as being horrified, of course. But all that easiness was gone now, along with everything else. Anyway, however much I disliked Muriel, she was still an elderly woman and Harry had had no right to do what he did with her dog. Even if he said it was a joke. She could have had a heart attack or anything. People did.

Then Ollie dropped his little bombshell. 'I got the rest of my stuff from the house,' he told me quietly.

Any last hopes I might have harboured of a reconciliation were brutally dashed. 'Right.'

'I thought it might be best, while you were away. Dad was there, though, of course. By the way, I think you might want to buy a new frying pan at some stage.'

He was contorted with agony on the other end of the phone; I could tell from his voice. No wonder he hadn't left a message last night. It had probably taken him three brandies just to dial the number.

'OK,' I agreed, although why I should be picking up after his bloody father, I had no idea. Except that I loved him. Both of them. In very different ways, of course.

Still, maybe it was for the best, him packing up, I tried to tell myself. However bad it would be going back to an empty house, plus Harry, it'd be ten times worse having to be there and watch while Ollie emptied out his sock drawer.

'You can have it,' he said, fast now. 'I don't want it or anything.'

'What are you talking about?' Jesus, had we moved on to the car? This was all going too quick for me.

Then I remembered we had two cars. At one time we had none. How we had come up in the world.

'The house.'

'The house . . . ?'

'In case you were worried. You know, that we'd have to sell it and split the money and all that stuff. It's yours.'

I hadn't been worried. I hadn't even thought about it. The idea of coping with practicalities on top of all the hurt . . . But of course we'd have to face facts: we had a child, didn't we? We needed to make proper arrangements. Access, money, who got what.

I began to feel hot. How did people do this? Unravel their lives after spending a decade, or more, together? Did they make bizarre lists? 'Here, you have the Duran Duran collection, I don't want it. No, really, I don't.'

But Ollie was already looking ahead. I tried to keep up, to look like I was as forward-thinking as he was.

'I can't take the house, Ollie.'

'Of course you can.'

'It's a *house*.' Quite a nice one, actually, that had cost us a lot of money.

'You'll need it for Cleo. I insist. You pay most of the mortgage, anyway.'

'That doesn't matter. It's yours too. You can't just give it away—'

He cut me off. 'Just take it, Hannah, would you, please?'

It was guilt, of course. We both knew that. He knew what he'd done and he was trying to pay for it in the only way he could.

'OK,' I said.

I could feel his relief. 'All right. Look, we don't have to decide anything else. Not until you come back. We'll sit down and go through everything.'

I didn't want to; to sit across from him at the kitchen table we'd bought in IKEA and pull apart the threads of our life together. To divide up all the knick-knacks and souvenirs we'd brought back from all the places we'd worked: the sombrero hats; the framed sketch of me in Minorca by a street artist who Ollie had paid a fortune to, but which made my nose look huge; the tavli set from Crete; the matching bathrobes we'd swiped from a really posh hotel we'd once stayed in when we got fed up of tents and hostels . . . They were *ours*. It wouldn't be the same if they were divided up, one-for-me and one-for-you.

But I said, 'OK,' because I was afraid I would start crying and I'd been doing so well up to that point.

There was a funny little silence now. With me and Ollie, there was *never* any silence, except maybe when we were hoofing back a big plate of something delicious he'd cooked for dinner. (God, I'd miss his cooking.

I was a shite cook. Would it be omelettes for the rest of my life, courtesy of Harry?) We were always nattering and swapping stories about what had happened that day, or else Ollie would have his guitar out and be singing daft limericks he made up on the spot just to annoy me. He'd stick a match in the corner of his mouth and pretend he was some farm boy from the Midwest, and make fun of me.

> There was a holiday rep called Hannah,
> Who had a peculiar manner
> She's always quite late
> Even on our first date
> She's a hippy who wears a bandanna.

Cleo would often turn off the television to join in the cruelty, banging a spoon on the table, and laughing along.

I could never think of anything to sing back, of course, and would have to retaliate with, 'What first date? You didn't even ask me out. Just brought a couple of beers to my tent and made yourself at home.'

'And it worked, didn't it?'

I missed him so much. More than anything in this world, I wanted for him never to have turned to me in the kitchen last Friday night, and said, 'I don't think we're working out, Hannah.'

''Bye, then,' I said, desperate to end that growing silence. This was not the moment to try to turn back the clock on last Friday.

Chapter Twenty-two

It started with the leather pants. Then the drinking.

It wasn't a case of an extra beer at night in front of the telly, or a sudden and strange flirtation with cocktails in the kitchen. It was full-on, hard-core, night-on-the-tiles stuff, where Ollie would disappear off into town and not come home until four o'clock in the morning, reeking of alcohol and doner kebabs.

I didn't mind at first. He was clearly taking his parents' break-up very badly and could probably do with letting off some steam.

He didn't ask me to come along, though. I'd always been quite good at drinking, even if I was a little out of practice now, plus I knew the inside track on all the Muriel/Harry stuff, so I would have thought I'd have been perfect company.

But I was left at home with Harry and Cleo while he danced the night away at Buffalo Bill's (I'd found a book of matches from there in his leather trousers pockets when I was putting them in the wash. Oops).

Buffalo Bill's was the sort of place you went when you were too old to get in anywhere better. The people that went there generally already had one marriage behind them and were drunk enough to think that a second one might be a good idea.

Ollie, in a place like that, was so *wrong*. His natural habitat was O'Reilly's pub down in the village, so old and battered that it was cool, and where sometimes a group of like-minded men with stubble and guitars would spontaneously break into a session in the corner over pints. And now he was hanging around clubs that were too boring even to be seedy?

Patience, I told myself. Yes. Patience, and forbearance, and swallowing the urge to give him a knee in the goolies and shout, 'You're fucking *forty*. So your parents have split up – get over it.'

So I sat in at home with Cleo and Harry. Just for something to do, we'd take to the kitchen and try to expand Harry's repertoire to dishes like spaghetti bolognese and macaroni cheese. Anything but eggs.

'No! No!' Cleo was nearly always shouting in alarm. Harry had set fire to his elbow by accident in one of our earliest sessions – long story – and Cleo was perpetually on high alert. Now if he even picked up a sharp knife, she was on her feet in seconds, ready to call the paramedics. Usually she had to go straight to bed after we cleaned up, she was so exhausted.

Then, one Friday night, the magic words. 'I think it's quite edible,' said Harry, in wonder.

Three of us gathered around his pot on the stove, and we gingerly dipped in spoons, and tasted his wares, and Cleo and I grew round-eyed.

'You did it, Granddad. You did it,' Cleo said, as though he'd just learned to walk again.

'I did.'

He was quite emotional. Well, it had been a tough week. A tough month. Muriel had been on the rampage with her tongue again, only now she was going outside the family with tales of her and Harry's marriage woes. Well, the fecking out business had to be explained to people, didn't it (although I didn't see why), and Muriel wasted no time in putting her case forward. Incendiary phrases like, 'I put up with him as long as I could,' began floating back to us, along with newly discovered crimes like the smell of his feet and the fact that he'd once taken Muriel to the Sellafield power plant for their wedding anniversary.

'We were passing *by* Sellafield,' Harry insisted miserably. 'We were on a tour of Wales at the time, we didn't go over specially to visit Sellafield. I thought it would be interesting to stop and have a look.'

Ollie found it very upsetting, his father's personal life laid bare like that for virtual strangers to pick over, and when Harry made no move to defend himself, he felt obliged to ring up Muriel to try to get her to stop.

'They're saying I'm senile,' Muriel told him furiously. 'For fecking out my husband at my age. They're saying I must have lost my marbles. And do you know what he told them? That I'd been losing them for years!' That would be a very Harry thing to do, in a jokey kind of way. Muriel wasn't seeing the funny side. 'Well, I haven't. I'm not going to lie and say it was mutual when it wasn't.'

'At least tone down the slander,' Ollie begged her.

'I'll tell it like it is.'

'Mum . . .' Ollie had a terrible hangover too, from being out the previous night.

'And you can tell him from me that the whole street knows now that he used to put our rubbish into other people's bins in the middle of the night so that he could wriggle out of refuse charges. They're pure disgusted. Oh, and will you please try and get him to come and pick up the rest of his things? I'm fed up asking him. I want to redecorate the house but how can I when his collection of ten-thousand-piece jigsaw puzzles is clogging up the attic?'

She'd been talking about redecorating for weeks now. She was going to transform the house into a place where she could hold cocktail parties and film nights for all her new friends.

Well, Emer anyway, a woman she'd met on her one foray to the golf club, and whom she'd had to seek help from in opening her locker. It had all been so intimidating that she hadn't been back.

In the storm of all this criticism, Harry did what he always did: broke things in my kitchen, and took refuge in front of the television. He'd run out of *CSI* box sets and had moved on to other crime series; darker ones, with dodgy lighting, and where everybody seemed to be muttering hoarsely to each other, 'It's payback time.'

'I'm afraid he'll explode one day and go over and kill her,' I whispered to Ollie one night.

Except that Ollie wasn't there. The bed was empty. He'd gone out for the first time in his new leather pants.

'Leather *pants!*' Cleo and I had stood around pointing and squealing with laughter. 'Look! We can see the outline of your undies! Oh, Ollie, that's the best joke ever.'

The trousers weren't a joke, though. 'The rap stars are all wearing them,' Ollie told us haughtily, like we were a pair of village idiots. 'These cost me a fortune.'

So now, in his head, he wasn't a middle-aged man any more with a mortgage and a kid and a woman he should probably marry, but young and hip and happening.

Another night he sashayed out past me wearing jeans so tight that his crotched screamed, 'Look at me! Amn't I huge, girls!' His shirts now seemed to be chosen specifically for their sheerness, so that once his crotch was finished with you, his nipples would assault you next. His aftershave was so plentiful and musky that poor Josie next door had to have two puffs of her emergency inhaler when she met him on the road outside.

'He'll come round,' Harry tried to tell me one night, as we sat in yet again, eating a shephered's pie that Harry had made all on his own. It was quite nice too, except for the fact that he'd forgotten to peel the potatoes before he'd boiled and mashed them.

'I don't know, Harry.' I was a bit down. I felt I should be doing something, instead of sitting at home waiting for my wayward man. If I'd any self-respect, I should probably kick him out.

But I didn't want to. I just wanted him back.

'Look,' Harry said, 'would it help if I tried to patch things up with Muriel?'

I was deeply touched. 'You'd do that for me?'

'Yes,' Harry said, swallowing hard and looking none too enthusiastic. I was having more than a sneaking suspicion that he liked his new life better than his old one. 'That's if she'd take me back. And with all the things that she's saying about me . . .'

'Let's keep that one on the back burner for the moment,' I said, letting him off the hook.

I got used to being woken in the middle of the night by Ollie, usually because the stupid eejit had lost his keys. It was a wonder that we hadn't been burgled several times, as there must have been sets of house keys down the backs of seats in half the pubs and nightclubs of Dublin by that stage. Or – and I confess I did wonder – in some other woman's house. But honestly, what woman in her right mind would take on someone like him?

I always went down and let him in. He'd stumble after me into the bedroom apologetically and strip off whatever youthful clothing he was wearing, and get into bed carefully beside me, knowing that if he so much as laid a finger on me, I'd lamp him.

'I love you,' he nearly always said, sounding guilty and confused.

'I know you do, you thick.'

'I know my behaviour is disgustful.' More confusion. 'Disgraceing.' Finally, 'Awful.'

I always hoped he'd fall asleep before he started the drunken it's-not-you-it's-me stuff, like I hadn't copped that already. That was one of the reasons I let him in — otherwise he'd start up in the middle of the street, letting everybody know our problems.

He never got to sleep for long. Muriel would be on the phone early in the mornings, when her boiler went bust, or the car gave trouble; all the little jobs that Harry used to look after, but she could hardly ask him now, could she, after giving out about him to the whole place because he hadn't even offered to take her to her hospital appointment for her bad hip. Hadn't even phoned to ask how she got on.

'I know it's over between us, but I had no idea what a cold man your father really was, Oliver. If it was him going to hospital, I'd have phoned. You know I would have.'

'I know, Mum.' Ollie, weary, hungover again.

Then Harry would be waiting back home, wanting to drink beers and watch the television with Ollie, being all buddy with him and pointing out women on the screen to him with a, 'Whoaar! She's all right!', in a way that was just plain *wrong*.

'Stop it, Dad.'

'Sorry.'

'And you have a dental check-up tomorrow, OK?'

'Do I?'

'Yes. I told you, I made the appointment for you last week, when you forgot.'

And then Maeve and Orla on the phone, giving him more grief. 'Can you not get them into counselling or something, Ollie? Honestly, they can't go on like this. It's crazy.'

'I know—'

'Mum's talking about getting a formal separation. At their age. You're going to have to do something to stop it.'

'I know—'

'And if you don't get Dad to move out soon, you'll be stuck with him for the rest of your life.'

'I *know*.'

No wonder Ollie went a bit loopy. No wonder he went around looking like everything he had known and trusted had just split down the middle.

By then it wasn't a question of whether we would break up, but when.

Chapter Twenty-three

I felt a little warm body wriggle into the bed beside me. Then the singing began in my ear.

'*Happy birthday to you, happy birthday to you*—'

'Cleo.' I reached for her.

'I haven't finished yet. *Happy birthday, dear Mummy*—'

'Give us a kiss.'

'No. Not yet. Get off. Let me finish. *Happy birthday to you.*'

Then I was pushed back on to the pillows and Cleo delivered thirty-eight precise little kisses to my cheek, counting as she went along. 'This is taking a long time,' she broke off once to say, and we both collapsed in giggles. But she made it through to the end, and then fell back into the pillow beside me.

'When you're fifty, I'll be here all day kissing you,' she told me.

When I was fifty, she probably wouldn't be living with me. She'd have moved out to shack up with her boyfriend, and I'd wake up on my blinking own and stumble from the bed to watch Sky News, where the presenters would be the only people I would see all day, and then I might make it to the kitchen, weight permitting, as there was a good chance that depression would have turned me into a twenty-three-stone blimp and, oh God, there was Harry emerging from the living room, the remote control in his hand—

Stop it, I told myself. It was my birthday. I should be having nice thoughts, not bringing myself down with black visions of what my future might hold. Anyway, who said it was all going to be gloomy? I might take over the travel company I worked for and become a (slim) international fecking businesswoman.

Yeah!

'I made this for you last night.' Cleo presented me with a little package and waited impatiently while I tore off the tissue paper.

'Oh, Cleo.' It was a bead bracelet, all different colours, made from a set I'd seen in Sophie's room. Every fourth bead was a pink heart.

She was watching me carefully. 'Do you like it?'

'It's beautiful.'

'One of the hearts is from Dad. I told him on the phone what I was making, and I asked him if he wanted me to put a heart on it from him, and he said yes.'

No problem to Cleo to back him into a corner. She'd be much better with men than I ever was.

'Thank you, pet. Now it's my turn to give you a kiss.'

She gamely submitted to a flurry of kisses and tickles, probably because it was my birthday. She was so lovely and warm and pure that I couldn't resist blowing on her tummy and now she *did* laugh.

Then she was wriggling out from under me. She said, 'Sophie says I have no dad. She's horrible, isn't she?'

'Cleo!'

'Sorry, Mum.'

'No, it's not *you* . . .'

Suddenly Cleo was spouting tears. 'She said she heard Auntie Ellen and Auntie Barbara talking, and that he's not coming back from mad Granny Muriel's. Auntie Ellen called him a bad name too, but I don't think I should repeat that.'

'Best not to,' I told her hastily.

We lay there looking at the ceiling for a while, while I tried to think of the best, most sensitive and child-appropriate way to explain what was happening.

Thankfully, it came to me.

'Do you remember Ron and Amy on *Home and Away*?'

'They weren't on *Home and Away*. Are you thinking of Martha and Jack?' Cleo asked expertly.

'No, no . . .' Maybe it had been Tom and Annie . . . oh, I couldn't remember. 'It was one of those couples anyway. They had two kids, remember? One had glasses and was getting bullied at school and the other one . . .'

'Had she braces?' Cleo probed.

'Yes!'

Neither of us could remember what soap it was, or if indeed it was a soap at all. 'I think it might be *CSI: Miami*,' Cleo eventually said, although I was very doubtful. I distinctly remembered lots of sun and happy people, and nobody got wasted down a dark alley.

'Anyway, do you remember Ron decided that he . . . well, he didn't want to be married any more?' If I'd remembered correctly, he was humping the nanny, but hopefully that bit went over Cleo's head.

Cleo chewed her lip for a bit. 'There was a terrible custody battle over the children.'

'Was there?' Damn. I'd gone and picked the wrong couple. 'The thing is, whoever got the kids in the end—'

'He did. He had really good lawyers who made her out to be a drunk.'

This was going from bad to worse. Now I had inadvertently introduced the idea that Cleo might end up separated from me. And that I was a drunk.

Cleo went on, 'And then she started stealing stuff because she was so depressed over losing her kids and she ended up in prison—'

'OK!' Time to park the soap-talk. I got up on one elbow and looked her straight in the eye. 'There's a strong possibility that Ollie isn't going to be living with us any more, Cleo.'

She lay there, very still, waiting.

'I wish it wasn't going to be like that, but if that's what he wants, then I can't stop him.'

'No,' Cleo agreed sadly.

'But it doesn't change anything between you and me, or you and him. That goes on just like before.'

'Oh, I know,' said Cleo. 'Just like for Pippa and Tom.'

'Who are Pippa and Tom?'

Cleo flounced out of bed. 'God, Mum, am I the only one watching these soaps?'

Barbara had bought me a voucher for a romantic weekend away for two. 'I bought it before you and Ollie broke up,' she said miserably. 'I was going to mind Cleo while you were gone.'

A flash of relief on Cleo's face at the reprieve.

'I wasn't going to give it to you, but I didn't have anything else and I thought it was better than nothing.'

Ellen clapped admiringly. 'Well done, Barbara. Nobody puts their foot in it quite like you.'

I put the voucher in my bag. 'Thanks, Barbara. Who knows, I might. go on my own.' I decided I was going to start saying these kinds of things; some day I might actually believe them.

'Mine next,' Ellen told me, grinning all over her face.

I'd avoided her like the plague for days now. Guilt, of course. Every time I came within a ten-metre radius of her my thigh began to throb.

But nothing had happened. Nothing. Right?

'Wait here,' she told me, hugging herself with excitement, as she went out into the hall and came back with a large box, gift-wrapped. At one point it dipped alarmingly in her hands and a funny noise came from it. 'This is from me and Mark. Well, actually it was Mark's idea. Mark? Come in!'

And now there was Mark too, coming in from the yard to stand in the doorway and watch as I tore the paper off. I didn't look at him. But my face flamed and I was all thumbs, and in the end Cleo had to help me.

I was about to open the cardboard box when a little pink snout poked out through the flaps to meet me.

I got such a fright I nearly dropped the box.

Everybody laughed.

'It's Clyde. One of the piglets,' Sophie helpfully explained. 'But you can't take him home or anything. They won't let you through the airport with him.'

Ellen rolled her eyes. 'What Sophie *means* is that we'll keep him for you. Feed him and look after him and all the rest, but he'll be yours and you'll see him whenever you come over. When he's bigger you can decide what you want to do with him – keep him here on the farm as a pet or maybe sell him for some cash and buy a handbag out of him.'

The children looked appalled.

'Or else we could—'

'Stop!' I knew what she was going to say. *Eat him.* And the day was too nice to have all the children crying.

I cuddled him to my chest protectively. 'I love him,' I said, surprised at how emotional I felt towards a pig. I even preferred him to a new handbag.

Ellen was delighted at my reaction. 'It was Mark's idea.' She turned to give him a smile, the first one I'd seen her give him since we'd arrived. 'He's been watching you down at the sty every day. He says you have a real way with them.'

133

My heart thudded unpleasantly. I just couldn't relax around him any more. No matter how much I explained away the other night, I was uneasy, uncomfortable. I didn't want him watching me at the pigsty. I didn't want him giving me piglets for my birthday.

My eyes locked with his, wary. But he just gave a relaxed grin back, and said, 'Will I make you up a bottle for him? He's due a feed about now.'

'Oh, er, thanks.'

'I'll teach you how to hold the bottle. And how to bed him down. The kids can help too.'

He went to get the bottle and I was disarmed again. Every time I had dark thoughts about him and his motives, he went and did something very sweet and innocent, like teach me how to look after my little piglet – with the kids in tow. Hardly a man with twisted carnal desires, right?

A shadow passed by the window then.

Nick. Old misery guts.

'The poor man,' Ellen told us with a sigh. 'Did you know he was engaged?'

Engaged! This was truly tragic.

'Been together years, just like you and Ollie, Hannah. I think she might have been in insurance too, I'm not sure.'

'Yes, yes,' said Barbara. 'Cut to the chase.'

'Anyway, she was sent to the States for a month as part of an exchange with the parent company. And get this: she got involved in some kind of religious sect.'

'No!' That kind of thing only happened in books.

'A really weird one, too, run by a beardy old man, and where you have to give them three quarters of your wages. But in exchange you get to marry more than once, preferably to your first cousins, and nobody uses contraception, and every Saturday they gather on street corners with placards about how God is only going to save three per cent of the people from a devastating death, and then they have a big picnic.'

We thought about this. 'It doesn't sound too bad,' commented Barbara.

'Not as bad as Catholicism,' Mark agreed. I hadn't realised he'd come back in. 'We only get to marry once.'

He grinned at Ellen. Her smile back was a little tight, I thought. But that was probably my guilt.

Clyde wriggled in my arms.

'Thank you,' I told Ellen fervently. More guilt. 'It's the best present I ever got.'

She looked at me. 'Steady on, Hannah. It's just a pig.'

That night Ellen and I discussed plastic surgery over a glass of wine. We did this every birthday, but now there was added urgency.

'We have to get it done this year,' she insisted.

'Why?'

'I read it somewhere. It's better to pull up your socks when they're just starting to slip down rather than having to hoick them up from around your ankles later on.'

'Jesus.' I was already a bit queasy and we hadn't even got to the medical bits yet.

'They get it in done in America as soon as they turn sixteen. Boobs, nose, chin, forehead. It's no big deal.'

I couldn't imagine myself waving to Cleo in eight years' time as she was wheeled off into surgery: ''Bye, honey! It'll be a whole new you when you get back!'

'I wouldn't be getting all that done myself,' I said, distinctly nauseous now.

'God, no,' Ellen scoffed. 'We said we'd choose one procedure each and we'd go off for a week and get it done together, remember?'

Well, yes, but I thought the conversation had meant nothing, the way we often talked of escaping to a spa resort without the children, or setting up an incredibly successful on-line fashion house. It never came to anything.

I threw down the first challenge. 'What procedure would you choose, then?'

She sighed. 'Well, that's the bloody thing, isn't it? When I was thirty-five, I only needed my eyes done – see these little bags here? – but now *everything* needs to be done.'

'No, it doesn't. And your eyes are perfect.' It was expected that you would heavily contradict the other person at every turn. It was only polite. '*I'm* the one with bags.'

'Not at all! I love your eyes, I wouldn't touch them!' Niceties over with, she admitted, 'We could probably both do with a little jug lift, though. You know, after all that breastfeeding.'

'Oh, I know.' We always blamed breastfeeding for the state of our boobs, and also the fat around our middles (not that Ellen had any) and the cellulite on our thighs, even though there was no clinical link, I believe, between any of them.

'And strictly between you and me? I'd like to do something with my bottom,' Ellen admitted. Before I could protest this time, she confessed, 'It's not the size of it. It's more the way each cheek has kind of divided into its own little bottom. There's a top bit and then a crease, and another bit under that. It's like I have four cheeks.' She saw my face and clamped her hands in horror over her eyes. 'It's only me. I knew it. Oh Jesus. I'm a freak.'

'No, no, calm down. Is it like a hot cross bun?'

'Yes! Only not as symmetrical.'

'I have that too.'

'Really?' She was giddy with relief.

'It's OK, I just buy bigger knickers. Tight ones, to hold it all in.'

I could see that Ellen was finding the bigger, tighter knickers solution unappetising. (Had a sudden, unwanted vision of Mark taking her big knickers off with his teeth. Failing. Trying again. A loose tooth now. 'Hannah told you to get these?' The vision of Mark in the nip was not as enjoyable as usual. Tinged with guilt. Tinged with wrongness now. Badly wished I could switch off my intuition, as that was the only thing getting in the way of my explaining away the hand on my thigh business. Entirely innocent, of course. But my gut instinct was not agreeing.)

'I think it's a toss up between my bottom and my eyes,' Ellen declared.

'Maybe we could get a discount for multiple procedures.' I caught myself on. 'What am I saying? Naomi Wolf would kill us.'

'Ah, feck Naomi Wolf. Feck feminism.'

'But we were feminists once.'

'Were we?'

'Yes. We said we'd never get anything done to ourselves, that we would embrace ageing and all the lines and wrinkles that came with it. Because it means we've lived. If we get plastic surgery, we're propping up the idea that it's not acceptable for women to grow older.'

'I know all that,' Ellen sighed in exasperation, 'but that was back when we were young. It's easy to say you're never going to have plastic surgery when everything is nice and pert and sticky-uppy. But now that I'm thirty-eight, I don't want to look like I've lived. I want to look like I'm twenty-eight again.'

'You can be twenty-eight in your head.'

But Ellen just kept on looking very gloomy and fed up. 'People can't see inside my head, though, can they? All they can see are the old, saggy, outside bits.'

What was with all the misery? Had that Nick chap been in and sucked all the light and happiness out of the house?

'Ellen,' I said sternly, 'you don't even *need* plastic surgery. I could certainly do with some – no, no, don't protest, we both know it's true. But you? You're as slim and trim as you always were. A few lines, maybe, but they're lovely on you. They suit you.'

She was looking a bit better now, so I pressed on, 'And imagine if it went wrong? And you ended up with *six* bottom cheeks instead of four? Or they do your eyes too tight, and you'd end up not able to close them? I read about a woman who that happened to. She said it was hell.'

'Well, she must have picked some eejit out of the telephone directory then,' Ellen said derisorily, but she was back in good humour again. 'I'd only go to the best.'

'And how would you pay for it, anyway? In eggs?'

'Good point.' She was frowning. (I had to resist the urge to tell her to stop.) 'I'd scrape the money together somehow.'

I knew that look on her face. It was a scary look. When she was like that, nothing could stop her.

'You're really serious about this, aren't you?'

She came over all prickly. 'And you're not? Even though—' She stopped herself.

'Even though I'm back on the market again?'

'Sorry.'

'It's OK.' I sighed. The idea of pushing myself back out into society again, to try to meet men, completely depressed me. I didn't care if my bum was surgically lifted to the middle of my back, and looked like Jennifer Lopez's. 'I don't know if I'll bother with another relationship, to be honest.' I meant it too. I was halfway through my life, maybe a lot more if I didn't start doing some regular exercise and cutting out the takeaways on a Saturday night. I wasn't sure if I wanted to go through this whole business again. Not the horrible panic of trying to meet someone before the menopause and get hitched and pregnant, anyway. I really couldn't bear that. But I wouldn't rule out maybe hooking up with some kindly, cultured man when I was in my twilight years, a man who was satisfyingly wrinkly and bald and interesting, and who wouldn't care whether I'd ever had plastic surgery or not.

'Bloody men,' Ellen burst out suddenly and viciously. She saw my startled look, and retreated fast. 'Well, they're who we get this crazy stuff done for, isn't it? And don't give me all that, "Oh, it's for my sense of self; I'd never get myself cut open and stitched up just to please a *man*."'

I wasn't giving her anything. I'd been *against* it, if she could only remember.

I didn't want to go there. Didn't want to mention his name. But Ellen was my friend and something was clearly bothering her. 'Mark's not . . . putting pressure on you or anything, is he?'

She said nothing for a minute, then burst out laughing. '*Mark*, and plastic surgery?'

It sounded convincing, to my ears at least. Only very strange men, usually in Channel 4 documentaries, began getting heavily involved in moulding their wives' bodies to fit their own fantasies.

Usually women did that all by themselves, for a variety of reasons, including fear of losing those men.

'He'd go mad if I went and spent money on my eyes,' Ellen said, 'when we could have bought a muck spreader instead.'

She wasn't telling me the truth about Mark. I knew her by now.

I wasn't telling her the truth about Mark either.

But the pair of us laughed like drains anyway.

Chapter Twenty-four

Nick, a.k.a. old misery guts, wiped the smile off my face by mid-morning.

In normal circumstances he would take the smile off anybody's face, with all that brooding and sulking, and clenching and unclenching of the muscles in his jaw. Jeez! It was like he was trying to choke down a fur ball.

At the same time, I felt I should cut him some slack now that I knew about his fiancée doing the dirty on him, and with a religious cult, too. You couldn't make it up.

He was with Damien. I heard them in the yard before I saw them. 'I'm only thirty-two,' Damien was saying viciously. 'I should be having fucking fun somewhere. Getting laid. Instead I'm dragged to this piss-hole—' He spotted me, on my way to the pigsty with a bottle to feed Clyde, and his face fell. 'Oh,' he said. 'It's you.'

'Having fun?' I said cheerily. I had no idea what the pair of them saw in each other. They spent little time together. Damien passed his days texting all his insurance friends back home, and your man, well, he was always staring off into the middle distance, his hands jammed into his pockets. They were the worst friends I'd ever seen.

Beep beep.

That was Ellen in the Range Rover. I could see Femmie and Denis in the back seat, grimly strapped in and clutching their cameras. Another outing was clearly on the cards.

'I'll take the front seat,' Damien said, brightening up, and trotting off towards the car.

Which left old misery guts with me.

He stood there, dark and intense, and glowering at me from beneath two bushy eyebrows.

Any sympathy I felt for him was waning fast. We were all hurting here, but did it give us the right to go around making everybody else miserable too?

'Can I help you?' I said. I did a bit of chomping of the muscles in my jaw as well, just to show him I could.

He cleared his throat. 'Would you like to come to the planetarium?' His voice was surprisingly nice; rich and warm, and completely at odds with his narky face. Then, a shot of sarcasm. 'It's not a date or anything. We're all going. Ellen sent me to ask.'

Ellen waved at me from the Range Rover and pulled a face. I knew her game. She was on duty with the tourists and hoped to drag me along for the craic.

I couldn't. Even though it was my birthday. I just couldn't hang around laughing with her all day like nothing had happened the other night.

'No,' I told Nick. 'I have to feed my pig.'

One of his eyebrows jumped up sceptically. And I just knew that he saw Clyde for what he was: a big fat excuse.

'If I don't feed him, he'll keel over and die,' I said defensively.

Another long, unfriendly stare.

Feck that. Determined to break the ice, I said, 'Look, I know what happened.'

'I beg your pardon?'

'I've just broken up with someone too. It sucks, doesn't it?'

But my attempt at friendliness was met with silence.

'And if you ever want to . . . you know, talk . . .' I was stuttering a bit now, and sorry I'd ever started it.

'With you? About my relationship?' he asked incredulously.

Put like that, it did sound a bit presumptuous. But I'd only been trying to reach out to a fellow human being with a broken heart.

Bloody miserable git. 'Forget it,' I snapped, my face flooding with colour.

I turned my back on him and walked off.

'There's no sex,' I said suddenly to Barbara that afternoon.

I didn't mean me. Obviously *I* wasn't having any sex. The last time Ollie had touched me, and I'm open to correction on this, was when he had cooked me an enormous chilli to say sorry for a particularly shabby bout of drunken, pretending–to–be–single behaviour, and we'd had awkward, distant relations afterwards because we both felt obliged. Me, because nobody else cooked spicy food as good as he did, plus there was some left over for the following night, and him, because, well, he was behaving like a prat and we all knew it.

'Ellen and Mark.' I turned to Barbara, my cheeks glowing in an unseemly way. 'They're not having sex.'

Barbara checked that Mark was still over in the field, and Ellen still at the planetarium. 'Not at this moment, no.'

'At night, Barbara. Not since we arrived. The headboard hasn't been banging against the wall, and that picture of the Virgin Mary over your bed hasn't fallen down on you even once.'

Barbara looked at me kindly. 'It doesn't always have to be the missionary position, Hannah. There are other ways, you know?'

The cheek of her, trying to make me out to be a sexual hick. But there was no time for that now. 'Unless they're swinging from the light-shade, then they're not having it, Barbara.'

It was clear that Barbara didn't want to enter into speculation about Ellen and Mark's sex life. 'So what? She's tired, she said it herself. They're trying to run a farm as well as look after all those bloody tourists. Plus, they've been together years at this stage. It's natural to slow down.'

'Yes, but to grind to a complete halt?'

Barbara had on her stern face now. 'Hannah, I know both of us have enjoyed certain . . . fantasies about Mark but I think that maybe you're taking it a bit too far now.'

It was on the tip of my tongue to tell. I even opened my mouth and got out, 'Barbara . . .'

'Yes?'

I closed my mouth again.

What could I say? That Mark wasn't having sex with Ellen because he fancied the pants off me, and that him and Ellen were having marital problems that she wasn't telling us about?

Barbara would do what any sensible person would: she'd promptly start rooting through her bag for the portable thermometer she liked to carry around for when people unexpectedly lapsed into high fevers. She would declare me clinically sick, and prone to unintelligible ravings, and send me to bed with two painkillers, also from her bag. 'I won't tell Ellen or Mark about any of this,' she would reassure me, because Barbara was a kind and wise person.

And so I said to Barbara, truthfully, 'I'm just a bit concerned about Ellen, that's all. Do you not think that she hasn't been herself since we arrived?'

'In what way?'

'She wants to get her eyes done.'

'She's been wanting to get her eyes done for years. Both of you have.' Barbara was scathing in her disapproval of any kind of tinkering with what nature had given us. Grudgingly, in my case.

'Yes, but now she *really* wants to get them done. Plus she's gone very thin. You said it yourself.'

'Her mother died. She's taking a long time to get over it.' She had an answer for everything today.

'And now no sex?'

'Can we stop going on about sex?' Barbara implored. 'Because I'm going to start wanting some, and you know I can't while I'm trying to adopt.'

'Did they tell you that?' It wouldn't have surprised me in the slightest.

'Of course not. But if I did, I'd be bound to get caught, and photos of it would go on my file. I'd probably get denied on the grounds of promiscuity.'

She sighed and dragged her hand-knitted, shapeless cardigan around her to further ward off the chill. 'Look, what's all this Mark and Ellen stuff about, Hannah?'

I looked away in case she pulled that trick of hers of seeing exactly what was going on in my head. 'I just think there's something wrong, that's all.'

Scratch that. I *knew* there was something wrong.

Chapter Twenty-five

I got nothing for my birthday from Ollie. Not even a lousy card. Muriel sent one, though, which arrived a day late, and which said, 'Happy birthday, Hannah! Hope you have a great day!' Then, as if realising how inappropriate this might sound, given that she was the one who'd provided my partner with the excuse to ditch me to go back and live with her, she wrote at the bottom, in tiny spidery handwriting, 'I hope you're feeling better,' like I'd merely had a bout of the flu. Then, in even smaller writing, 'If it's any consolation, Oliver is very upset too. He won't admit it, of course, but a mother knows these things.'

Ah, yes, Muriel, the standard bearer for mothers everywhere. The woman who'd put up with a desperate lout – to hear her tell it, anyway – for forty-odd years for the sake of the kids. And wasn't shy about letting everybody know about it, either.

But Muriel wasn't bad. Not *bad* bad, even though I know I've given out about her a lot. In fact I was even starting to feel the tiniest smidgeon of pity for her. She'd been sold a pup, plain and simple. And by whom? I blamed the glossy magazines that she flicked through at the dentist, with their surfacey girl-power articles on having it all. And those frothy, pseudo-feminist afternoon programmes on the telly where women were routinely told that nobody was responsible for their own happiness except themselves (and to hell with everybody else). Mostly, though, I thought Muriel had been completely swindled by Ireland's boom times, where everybody had a new everything – patio, car, holiday home, romance – and if you were standing still, then you were nobody.

Like a crowd of greasy insurance salesman (Damien), they'd all conspired to make Muriel discontented with her lot in life. That's not to say for one minute that Harry was a dreamboat who should be held on to at all costs. Muriel was right: he *didn't* change his clothes. He *did* watch too much TV. But should he have been thrown out onto the street because Muriel imagined there was something better out there – without any proof, mind – just waiting for her?

And now look at poor Muriel! Desperate, really. While Harry was pushing the boat out with his sudden interest in cooking, what was Muriel doing?

'That bloody boiler. Bust again! What am I supposed to do now?'

I could understand her rage. Instead of making a set of new, exciting friends, and joining zany clubs for the over sixties, 'and never having a *minute* to myself, darling,' she was faced with leaking taps and nearby car alarms that went 'woo woo woo woo PISSING WOO' in the middle of the night (she'd been very tired when she'd been telling us this). Normally Harry would have been prodded out of the bed to sort the problem out, but now she had to lie there with earplugs in and a pillow wrapped around her head, and she could *still* hear that blasted alarm.

And then there were people's reactions. *Most* unexpected. She thought she'd be the envy of her friends, who all gave out about their awful husbands too.

'I swear to God, if he asks me one more time to turn the radio up . . . all he has to do is put in his bloody hearing aid . . .'

Everybody had a dastardly story to tell, but nobody had the confidence to actually up and leave the old goats except Thoroughly Modern Muriel.

But instead of people telling her how great and brave she was to have relaunched her life at seventy, she was met with startled looks and concerned enquiries, not about her, but about Harry.

'Where's he living now? With his *son*? Oh dear. And is he all right? What about his calcium supplements, does he remember to take them? Oh, I know he's hopeless, but so long as he can fend for himself . . .' Lots of doubtful, blameful trailing off.

It was maddening. Even when she explained to them about *CSI: Miami*, or the way he never flushed the toilet after himself, even after a number two, they still acted like she'd turned her back on a poor cripple. So she'd had to up the ante, and reveal even more disturbing things about him, such as how he'd once written a letter to Margaret Thatcher back in the 1980s, congratulating her on the way she'd handled those bloody unions.

She got trapped into a terrible pattern of defensiveness. The minute anybody even mentioned Harry, she'd find herself blurting out a stream of his atrocities. 'Bad breath. Awful. Like a dog's. Never brushes, of course. Twice a week, maybe.'

She felt terrible about it herself. 'I don't enjoy saying the things I say. But it's like I can't stop myself. How come *he* gets all the sympathy?'

Some of her tales found their way back to Harry. How could they not have, when they still had the same circle of friends and acquaintances, still did their banking at the same branch? The whole place knew of Harry's infractions. More than they wanted to know. Every time they met him in the queue for the pension at the post office, they didn't know where to look. And certainly not at his feet, because they knew from Muriel that he rarely, if ever, clipped his toenails, and when he did the clippings went straight onto the carpet.

'Hello, Harry!' they would say over-effusively. 'Lovely, um, day.'

Harry wasn't a fool. But he never said anything bad about Muriel, and God knows he'd had provocation enough.

This had Muriel in a bit of a state. '*Why?* Why isn't he trying to get back at me?'

'Because he's mature and kind, and would never say anything to hurt you,' I told her coldly. Time for her to face up to her own reprehensible actions.

But of course I was wrong. Harry wasn't fine with it at all. He wasn't mature and kind. He was letting it all build up quietly inside him and then he would retaliate in a way that left us all stunned.

Chapter Twenty-six

Looking back, the fact that I said nothing about Mark putting his hand on my thigh had been a terrible mistake.

He thought I was up for it.

He chose Ellen's birthday to make his move, as I was to find out.

'Happy birthday to you, happy birthday to YOU . . . !'

We all gave her hand-woven, farmer-ish things, in neutral colours – authentic Irish country scarves and such like, certainly nothing as crass as a gift voucher for the make-up counter in Brown Thomas – and she oohed and aahed over them all and gathered us to her bony chest one by one.

'I could count all her ribs,' Barbara told me, brow furrowed in concern. 'What's worse, I think she's missing one.'

My chat about the no-sex thing must have sunk in.

'This is the best birthday ever,' Ellen declared at least five times, making me wonder whether she was protesting a little too much. Three days ago she'd wanted to be taken apart and completely restitched. 'My two best friends here, my lovely kids – oh, give me a kiss just this one time, Sam; it won't kill you – and, of course, my gorgeous hubby.'

She lifted her cheek and allowed him to kiss her. No jumping up on him and tongues everywhere like they used to do in the early days.

He was all scrubbed and shiny today, and standing behind her possessively. Paying her lots of attention. I'd heard him bring up a cup of tea to her in bed early that morning, when I'd been lying awake listening to Barbara on the flat of her back in the other bed snoring for Ireland.

I found myself being watchful and wary of him. When he was in the house I knew exactly where he was at all times. On the farm, I sensed

146

what shed he was in and gave it a wide berth. Oh, we were fine with each other when it was unavoidable, all chatty and buddy-buddy, but there was something there all right. A knowledge. A discomfort – or, at least, I thought there was. He'd clearly thought it all part of the foreplay.

The kids, all whispery and secretive, fell in from the hall now, the three of them trying to grab hold of one present between them.

'*I'm* giving it to her.'

'No, *I'm* giving to her.'

Ellen whipped it from them before they dropped it on the ground. It was a terracotta plant pot that they'd painted themselves – under Barbara's supervision – half of it covered in lovely pink flowers and hearts, and the other half in black squiggly worms and what was a passable imitation of an AK-47.

'We thought you could grow an acorn tree in it,' Cleo said to her shyly. 'But we lost the acorn.'

'*I* didn't lose the acorn,' Sophie pointed out.

Sam stamped his foot. 'It wasn't my fault!'

'It's OK, it's OK.' Ellen examined the terracotta pot all over and burst into tears. 'It's so beautiful,' she blubbered.

Even the kids exchanged looks at that; like most children, they were used to being told that everything they'd ever produced, even into nappies, was stunningly beautiful, but come on, that *pot*?

Sophie made a screwy motion by the side of her head and Sam broke into loud sniggers. Mark gave him a clip across the back of the head and that took care of that.

Ellen was still crying, even though she was not a cry-ey person. 'It's because I'm so happy,' she kept insisting loudly.

Another birthday, another party.

'Yadda, yadda,' said Barbara wearily. 'No offence, but all this slow cooking is ruining my hair.' The steam from all the pots simmering and boiling since dawn had turned her head into a Brillo pad.

And Ellen wasn't even helping. OK, so it *was* her birthday, but the minute breakfast was over, she'd taken to the couch with a pot of tea and hadn't stirred since. She wasn't even doing anything exciting, like reading the brand-new book on jam-making that Denis and Femmie had presented her with. She was just lying there, pale and wan, and contemplating the ceiling. Periodically, to stave off curiosity, she would call out to the kitchen cheerily, that she was 'having a great time' and 'just chewing the fat'.

'What fecking fat?' Barbara growled. 'That girl hasn't eaten since we've arrived.'

Barbara was worried now. I could see that and it made me feel better. When Barbara was fully engaged, you never felt that anything truly bad would ever happen. She simply wouldn't allow it. Whatever was up with Ellen – and I hoped to Christ it wasn't me – then Barbara would get to the root of it.

All morning we slow-cooked, we baked, we grilled, we marinated, we flash-fried in direct contravention of slow-food principles, and in the end Barbara flung her hands into the air and said, 'Fuck this, I'm calling a caterer.'

'Barbara!' The whole farm seemed to fall silent in shock.

Even the kids out in the yard grew still in their play and tilted their little faces upwards, as if sensing something dark and unnatural in the air.

But Barbara was already on her phone. The second of her three phones, that is, the one she kept for personal use. 'Rosalie? Barbara here. Yes, *bien, bien*. Listen, I've no time for further pleasantries in broken French, because I need food, and fast. I have lots of hard cash to pay. And this is the most important thing: do not tell Ellen.'

We were delighted afterwards. Four of Rosalie's friends were at that moment racing around strangling chickens and lambs and stuffing them into pots to be simmered for eight straight hours, leaving us to the altogether less stressful business of choosing the wine.

This, to Barbara, meant splitting it into red and white. No further differentiation need take place. The white went into the fridge, and the red we lined up beside a row of polished glasses. Done. After looking at the bottles in silence for a moment, drumming our fingers in an hmm-what-do-we-do-now kind of way, we decided it might be best to open one 'just to be sure it wasn't corked'.

'Ellen?' Barbara called. 'How about a little toast to your birthday?'

This was code that it was time to kick-start a day of rampant celebration. We did it every year. Ellen usually led the charge.

But today she just called back, 'I think I'll stick to tea, thanks. Otherwise I'll be on my ear.'

Barbara and I looked at each other. Ellen, saying no to drink?

Definitely something was wrong.

We all got dressed up for the big night. It was expected. This was the annual joint birthday party, and no half-measures would be tolerated. The party wasn't in the kitchen either, like the last shindig. Rosalie's husband,

Marcel, had come over and set up trestle tables in the courtyard, under strings of fairy lights, and we were to dine outside as the weather was so unusually clement.

'It's not normal,' Barbara kept saying, looking to the skies worriedly. 'Usually it's freezing for the whole two weeks that we're over.' She rubbed her hands together in a wizened way. 'There's something brewing, I can tell.'

Yes, and it turned out to be a hideous yellow sundress that she'd packed in her suitcase in the extremely unlikely event that the weather would be good enough to wear it. She emerged from the bedroom looking like an enormous lemon, and could have been squeezed had she not been wearing a pair of runners on her feet. 'Didn't bring any sandals,' she said with a shrug. 'Didn't think I'd need them.'

I wore a new 'normal' dress, as Cleo kept calling it; as in, there were no slogans across the front, no bits artistically 'stressed', and I was free of swinging jewellery, bracelets and bangles. I wore nothing but a simple azure pendant that Ollie had bought me in Spain once, and that remained my favourite piece of jewellery, even if the giver had proven to be a bit of a disappointment.

But, hey – no Ollie thoughts tonight. It was my official birthday party, my first in a very long time as a single woman, and I was determined that I would have a good time.

I wouldn't even let Mark spoil it. I had successfully eluded him all day because the very sight of him at this point was enough to bring on a black mood.

'Wow. *Girls.* The food.' Ellen came into the kitchen now, reincarnated from the wretched, introverted creature who'd lain on the couch earlier. She was glowing – no, *glittering* – in a fabulous off-the-shoulder dress, the kind only she could carry off, due to having boobs that were pointy and pebble-like still, and capable of holding the thing up. Her red curls were pinned tantalisingly on the top of her head, ready to explode at some dramatic moment later on in the night. And as for needing plastic surgery! Oh, she made me sick. The lightest touch of bronzer and lipgloss was all she needed to look absolutely stunning.

'No problem for you to outshine me on my joint birthday party night,' I threw at her. 'Bitch.'

Ellen flung her arms around me, laughing. 'You look nice too.'

'Not as nice as you.'

She took my face in her hands, like she was going to give me an

149

almighty snog, and she said, all weird and intense again, 'I'm so glad you're here.'

Then she let me go, thank God (maybe she'd had a sneaky few in her bedroom while getting ready) and she flung an arm around the kitchen. 'Seriously. The *food.*' It was laid out mouth wateringly on platters, ready to be ferried to the trestle tables.

'Yes, well, we did our best,' Barbara said modestly. 'It's been a long day.'

'You got Rosalie's friends to cook it, didn't you?'

'Yes.'

'I'd recognise that quiche anywhere. It turns up at every blooming country fair for miles around.'

We could see Nick and Damien going to their quarters across the yard. They seemed to be bickering and throwing looks of dislike at each other.

'That poor man' Ellen said with a sigh.

We shook our heads and tutted. Privately, I thought Nick was a hopeless case. Damien, too.

Mark appeared and grinned round at us all. His stripy shirt was new and plastered to him, and he was wearing enough musky aftershave to transfix a herd of cows. I hoped to Christ it wasn't me he'd made the effort for.

When his eyes flickered over me, I looked pointedly away.

'You look gorgeous,' he told Ellen sincerely.

But she just turned and thrust a tray of glasses into his hand. 'Take those out, will you?'

Marcel had organised three of his fellow cheesemakers to provide the music for the night. We were all looking forward to some gentle, indigenous folk songs, played on accordions and the like, and Denis and Femmie had got out the video recorder especially for the occasion.

'They will wet themselves at home,' they told us excitedly. 'One of our neighbours went to India last year and came back with some amazing footage – we had to sit through nineteen bloody hours of it – but this is even better.'

But the three lads pitched up with electric guitars and amps, and began running hundreds of leads from power points in the milking parlour.

'They're a band,' Marcel informed us, in case we hadn't worked it out. 'They're called Stinky Men. Partly because they're cheesemakers, and partly in acknowledgement of the great French punk rock band of the seventies, Stinky Toys. You will have heard of them.'

This was a statement. Like, 'Our food is better than yours and our way of life far superior,' which he'd made earlier, and which we'd all accepted without question. 'I was only winding you up,' he'd said, beaming.

But Stinky Toys? Looks were exchanged. 'Nope, can't say I have . . . anybody else?' No takers.

Marcel was delighted. It probably proved we had no culture. 'You will like them.'

The three Stinky Men got up on the back of a trailer with their instruments, like they were the biggest rock band in the world. 'Good evening, Irish people,' the lead Stinky Man said politely. 'We love you.'

Without further ado, they let rip into 'Stairway to Heaven', knees buckling dramatically and contorted faces turned towards the moon. 'In a TREE by a BROOK, there's a song bird who SEEENGS . . .'

The kids loved it, though, and got candles and went to stand in front of the trailer, waving them over their heads. This got the Stinky Men going even more, and they swiftly launched into 'Highway to Hell'. One of them whipped his T-shirt off.

'My God,' said Barbara, jolted by the unpleasantness.

Damien, who was all got up like a dog's dinner in a shirt and tie, no doubt to impress Ellen, looked a bit shell-shocked. He stood as far away from the trailer as he could, his hands clamped over his ears in a frightened fashion. This kind of thing would clearly never happen in Portugal.

As for Nick, he was watching the Stinky Men with some interest, if not exactly enjoyment, and one of his knees was working the beat.

He caught me looking at him – how come every time I looked at him, he caught me? – and shouted (everybody had to shout to be heard), 'At least it beats talking.'

It took me a minute to realise that he'd massively insulted me.

I shouldn't have risen to the bait, I really shouldn't, but I went over until I was next to him and shouted, 'You're a right little ray of sunshine, aren't you?'

I thought he was going to go mental. His jaw was working overtime on the clenching front, and I was worried it was going to go into spasm.

Then he chuckled. *Chuckled*. 'Yeah. Sorry.'

I was so surprised that I smiled back.

'And sorry about the other day. You know, throwing your offer to talk back in your face.' He raked a hand through his hair. He had nice hair.

'I'm not really into all that talking business. I mean, talking is fine. Just not too much of it.'

'So you're the strong, silent type?' I couldn't believe I was slagging him.

Now he laughed. Janey Mack! It must be all the beer or something.

'So you were dumped too,' he stated.

'Yes.'

Another silence. Emboldened by this new spirit of glasnost, I ventured so far as to say, 'You were engaged? She worked in insurance? Trip to the States? Weird religious sect? Beardy man and multiple marriages? Doomsday scenario where only three per cent of the population is going to be saved?'

I said it kindly. However embarrassing my break-up was, it must be totally mortifying being uncharismatic enough that your other half took up with some fundamentalist loony cult.

He took it on the chin. 'Four per cent, actually. I think she really believes she's going to be one of them, even though I told her the odds weren't in her favour.' A sideways look at me now, and then it was my turn. 'Ollie was his name, right? Drifter? Both of you, that is? Ten years together, but my laddo wouldn't commit? Mad parents who split up, one of whom did something unacceptable on the other, involving a family pet?'

It was damning. There was no doubt about it. 'Who told you?' I said stiffly.

'Barbara.' He looked over at her in her yellow dress, dancing energetic- ally to 'Summer of '69'. Rosalie was pointing and laughing. 'She was on her third glass of wine.'

The treachery.

'So we're both losers,' I stated defensively.

'I'm not a loser.' He was quite definite about this. 'I own my house, I have a good job assessing insurance claims.' He thought for a moment. 'It's a job.'

His eyes were hazel more than brown, I noticed. And he wasn't that short. He was a good four inches taller than me.

'Look,' he said, 'I reckon it's going to take six months.'

'What is?'

'To get over the shock of being dumped. At our age, anyway. Probably less if we were younger.'

For some reason I didn't fly into a panic at my age; I found his matter- of-factness strangely comforting.

'Six months,' he repeated. 'To grieve and all that stuff. Then we'll be ready to move on.'

It was the first time in all of this that I actually felt I had a future. That I would be capable of a life without Ollie.

'Thank you,' I gushed.

But he was prickly again, suspicious that I was making fun of him. 'That's just my opinion.'

We all had a great night. A loud night. We danced and drank and sang our way through 'Born to Run', 'We Are the Champions', and 'My Generation'. Femmie overdid it on the white wine and got sick to the strains of 'Smells Like Teen Spirit'. Damien finally stomped off during 'Juke Box Hero', vowing not to come back until the Stinky Men had gone home.

It was Rosalie who eventually called a halt to the madness.

'Turn that bloody racket down,' she shouted from an upstairs window, having taken the kids up and put them to bed.

The Stinky Men packed up obediently, and unplugged their guitars. One of them got out a mouth organ and began wheezing away on it in a melancholic fashion, and the evening became less LA and more rural France.

'See? It's not so bad, is it?' I teased Ellen. 'Being thirty-eight.'

She was looking more relaxed than she had all day. 'Don't be silly, it's shite,' she said cheerily. 'But at least we're alive, eh?'

I'd baked a birthday cake for both of us. So I hadn't been entirely idle for the day. Now that the food was gone, and darkness had fallen, I retrieved it from Ellen's walk-in larder – she was the only person I knew with a larder, possibly the only person to have one since the 1950s – and contemplated sticking seventy-six candles on it, which was our combined age, but settled for two, slim, elegant ones instead. Yes, Ellen would approve.

'Need a hand?' Suddenly Mark was behind me.

Every cell in my body went on red alert. I knew he hadn't come to help me. He'd watched me come in here and had followed me, and now he was closing the door behind us. Suddenly the larder was warm and stifling and very small.

And he was very big.

'Mark!' My voice came out all high and jolly. 'Actually, yes, you can. This cake is really quite heavy. So if you could just grab it, thanks, lovely.'

He took the cake off me and put it back on the shelf.

What the . . . ?

Now there was nothing at all separating us except the thin material of his shirt, which was hugging his nipples. Which were HUGE. Dear God, they were bigger than mine.

Get me out, get me out.

How could I ever have found him attractive? He was too big, too hairy, too *everything*. Even his nose was enormous.

'Mark,' I began. My tongue was flattened to the roof of my mouth with nerves. 'We should really go back out.'

'In a minute.' His look was hot, heavy. Lusty. Like he'd been waiting for this for days. 'You know we need to talk.'

'Talk!' I forced a laugh, 'About what?'

A disappointed look now. 'Hannah. Please. Don't mess me around.'

'I am not messing you around!' Outraged now.

But clearly he thought I was on some major game-playing binge because he said, 'I know you feel it too. I've seen the way you look at me.'

Oh my God. I felt weak. Well, yes, of course I had *looked* at him, but no more than other women. No more than Barbara. And only in a detached, appreciative way. The way you'd look at Brad Pitt on the telly, for instance – with lots of 'mnon mnons' under your breath but there wasn't the remotest possibility you were going to get up on him and buck his brains out.

'I think I'm falling for you, Hannah.'

I hadn't heard anybody say that to me in ten years. In fact, I don't think I'd ever heard it. Ollie wasn't a great one for the romantic pronouncements. Our 'going steady' conversation was about as passionate as it had ever got, along with the bouts of cooking on a Friday night. Which was a form of love, I suppose.

But Mark falling for me? My best friend's husband? Hearing it from him was perverse, wrong, sick. I wanted him to stop talking, now.

'Mark,' I said, 'listen to me.' It was very important to be clear on this. 'I think there may be some slight confusion here.' I don't know why I was trying to downplay it. Thinking I could salvage the situation, I suppose, even at this late stage.

'Not on my part.' More intensity. More nipples in my face.

I made my voice louder, harder. 'Let's not even go here, OK? Because it's wrong. On *so* many fronts.'

My words got through. He stopped thrusting his chest in my face and deflated a bit. 'I know, OK? But I can't help how I feel. I'm sick of walking around pretending it's not happening.'

'Well, try. Pretend harder. Because it's *not* happening.'

He rubbed his eyes. 'I'm sorry, OK? I'm sorry. But you know how things are with Ellen.'

A crawly sweat broke out down my back. I didn't want to talk about his problems with Ellen.

He saw my reluctance and honed in for the kill. 'Don't say you haven't noticed. You, of all people, know when something isn't right.'

That was low. If true.

'I'm not getting into this, Mark—'

'She's not herself. Not since we moved here. Now it's all stress and aggravation and everything is my fault.'

'So go and talk to her about it. Don't talk to me.'

He was pleading now. 'I just don't know what to do.'

'So you thought you'd hit on me?'

'That was a mistake. I'm sorry. Honestly, Hannah.'

'And so you should be.'

He was confused. His marriage was obviously in trouble. Some insanity had overtaken him and led him down this path of supreme foolishness. But, thank Christ, reason had prevailed finally. He would go away and reflect on this, and the shame of it would make him want to DIE. I felt sorry for him, really.

Then he said, 'But maybe we could have some fun.'

Fun? If we were in a cartoon my eyes would have popped out on little springs with a *boing-boing* noise.

I laughed. I think it was in disbelief. Or nerves, or something.

He gave me a very charming smile. Some women would probably find it irresistible. 'You're having a hard time.' Eyes, dancing into mine. 'I'm having a hard time. No reason why we shouldn't help each other through it.'

The man was unbelievable.

'Mark, I'm going to bring the cake out now,' I said in a voice that would have frozen the heart in any sensible man.

But Mark was too confident in his attractiveness to read the normal signals. He grinned, like I was playing some kind of game, and said, 'Come on, Hannah. You were always up for a bit of a laugh. You know you want to.'

And then he put his hand on my waist. All I saw were lips coming towards me, fast.

I did the only thing that I could. I lifted the two, long, sharp birthday candles and jabbed him roundly in the side of the head with them. One of them broke off.

'Jesus Christ.' He was shocked. Pulling bits of candle from his ear. 'That fucking hurt.'

I was worried for a minute that I'd really done him some damage. Could you get scarred from wax? He was shaking his ear now, like he'd just come out of water, and complaining, 'I can't hear.' Maybe I'd permanently deafened him.

But now was not the time for pity. He didn't deserve it. 'Let this be the end of it,' I told him in a shivery, terrible voice, like they use in *Harry Potter*. 'Now go out to your wife.'

He gave me a look filled with dislike. Clearly he wouldn't be hitting on me again (I seemed to have become catnip for every man within a ten-mile radius of me recently).

Then he went out, rubbing the side of his head, and slammed the door in my face.

Chapter Twenty-seven

'Ellen, I need to talk to you.'

It was 7 a.m. and she was already up, no sign that she'd been partying half the night. It was her turn to milk the cows. They had only five of them. Ellen had explained to Barbara that they didn't keep cows any more for their milk; these five were 'show cows', as in, there to make the place look authentic for the paying guests, and the lambs and the pigs drank the milk.

They were, it had to be said, extremely good-looking cows, like cows from an ad. They had lots of curls at the front of their heads, lovely, shiny coats of brown and fawn, and very sparkly eyes, which looked like they were no strangers to an eye drop or two. Ellen strenuously denied this, although Barbara had caught her taking a brush to their tails in the milking parlour, followed by a pair of curling tongs.

'Although my view wasn't great,' Barbara conceded.

I was forced to trot after Ellen to the milking parlour. My stomach was curdling and my palms slick with sweat. *Don't do it, don't do it, turn back now!* was shouting in my head. But she'd been my best friend for twenty years. How could I not?

She put down her bucket of warm, soapy water, slung on a huge plastic milking apron and tut-tutted at my face. 'You look wrecked,' she said. She, on the other hand, looked all fresh and windswept. And, dare I say it, loved. I wondered if Mark had given her the lash last night. Out of spite.

The thought of him gave me a sour taste in the back of my throat. 'Should he not be doing the milking, and letting you have a lie-in?'

'He's gone to a ploughing championship. Left half an hour ago.'

157

I had a vision of a rat scurrying for its hole.

'He wasn't that keen on going, but it's been booked and paid for for months now. He'll be back in a couple of days. So,' she said. 'What's so important that you had to get out of bed to tell me?'

'Oh! Ah! You see . . .' And my tongue froze. Just like that. Wouldn't budge a millimetre. This had been happening to me all night. I hadn't actually been to bed. I'd changed into jeans and Barbara's super-hairy jumper – for self-flagellation purposes – and had sat on my bed beside Barbara with a little reading light and *Teach Yourself Russian*. More self-flagellation. I was a *cyka* of the worst sort. Bitch, that was. Well, I was more of a bad friend than a bitch, but it was trickier translating two words instead of one so I was grimly happy with the *cyka* label.

'Look,' I managed eventually, 'can we sit down for a minute?'

I didn't think I could tell this one standing up.

But here came the blasted cows now. They were nearly as tame as the dogs, and the minute they saw us coming into the little milking parlour, they got off their beautiful behinds in the paddock next door, so to speak, and began to file into the milking parlour without anyone having set the dogs on them or shouted, 'Get up there, you lazy hoors, before I take a stick to you,' like they do on Irish farms.

Now Ellen was talking to them as she opened the gate for them. 'Morning, Veronica!' For a minute I expected Veronica to say, 'Morning!' back. The rest of them filed past me – more posh-sounding names like Jessica and Ruth – and then Ellen was slapping a big wet cloth from her soapy bucket on their udders, drying them off, then fixing a milking contraption onto their teats, all the time murmuring to them in a strange, farmer-type language: 'You're-all-right-there-now-easy-ara-Veronica!-stop-that-g'wan-you-good-thing.' Eventually each cow had a whole load of pipes swinging out of them and I could see little lines of milk splattering down into a big glass jar. And I have to say, up to that point, I'd never understood how they got the milk out of cows. I resolved to tell Barbara, as she hadn't a clue either.

'Nobody said this was going to be easy,' Ellen announced.

That could apply to many, many things. I just waited.

'Ollie,' she clarified sympathetically. 'It's written all over your face.'

'Oh. Yes. Well, of course I'm still very upset about him.' Was I? I did a quick mental check. Yes, I was. Devastated. This was the kind of tricky situation in which Ollie would have excelled. 'Shop him,' he'd have declared. 'Shop the fucker or I'll do it myself.' He'd never have gone and beat Mark up or anything. Totally not his style. Mark would have flattened him anyway.

I desperately wished Ollie was there. Everything would be so much better if I wasn't on my own.

'But this isn't about Ollie,' I said.

'Oh?' Ellen turned away to do a quick check of all the tubulous things. Everything seemed satisfactory.

A strange notion filtted across my confused headspace: was she engaged in a little time-wasting?

'I was talking to Mark last night.' Best to just blurt it out.

Ellen's face changed. Grew wary. 'Oh?'

I didn't like how this was going from the off. It was all a bit strange.

'So, what did he say, then?' Now Ellen was calm. Almost smiling. Or was it a sneer? 'Bet he couldn't wait to spill his guts. I told him, you know. I told him to say nothing, but you know Mark. Never happy unless everybody's looking at him and telling him how fucking great he is.'

I was taken aback by her bitterness. Also, I hadn't a clue what she was talking about.

'He didn't say . . . anything.' That seemed like the best option. 'Except that maybe things are difficult between you at the moment.' I didn't know how I was going to get back to the bit about him trying to ride me. Right now it seemed best to go with the flow.

Ellen gave an enormous snort at that, so much so that Veronica gave a nervous jump. Ellen absent-mindedly patted her rump. 'Whist-there-now-ochon-tiocfaidh-ár-lá.' Or something like that.

'Difficult,' she repeated, mulling the word over. 'I'd say they are, yes. I presume he means I'm creating the difficulty. Mark, as you may have noticed, doesn't really do difficult. He's more a man for the big idea, or the new trailer that we can't afford, but when it comes down to running a loss-making venture in the middle of the countryside with a pile of kids in tow, well, he leaves that to me.'

I felt very sorry for her. She'd dropped heavy hints this holiday that the gloss may have gone off the venture somewhat, but this defeated air, this bitterness, that wasn't her at all.

But I knew what she said was true. Mark liked to play the part, all right. A man who chose his jeans that carefully surely set a lot of stock on appearances. I hadn't realised, though, just how much he was letting Ellen carry the can.

'Oh, look, I'm sorry,' she said. 'I know you've enough on your mind without all this.'

She didn't know the half.

'I just wish you'd told me before,' I said.

She looked like she was going to protest, but then she just shrugged. 'Yes, well.'

I felt the distance between us then; the miles and the years. All this was going on for her over here, and my slow relationship break-up with Ollie over there, and neither of us able to confide in the other.

'Anyway,' she said, 'what's there to tell? So I've got a husband who can't multitask, leaves a lot of the dogsbody work to me, thinks the kids are my sole responsibility and flirts with the guests. Shock! Horror! We could be talking about half the marriages in the country.' She gave a cackle of laughter, and then turned around to whip Veronica's milking apparatus off. It looked like it hurt. 'I guess we just have to get on with it. No point moaning. But, hey, thanks for listening to him last night.' This was said with a large dollop of irony. 'I'm sure he felt a lot better after getting all that off his chest.'

I stood there, my tongue frozen again. Now I was going to shatter whatever illusions she had left about her marriage, and they seemed to be precious few.

Don't do it! The shriek started up in my head again. *Go home to Ireland and say nothing about it. What she doesn't know won't hurt her.*

Except . . . except . . . oh, there were all kinds of excepts. I'd been through every one of them around 5 a.m. There was no justification for telling someone this kind of news except that it would be criminal not to.

'Ellen,' I said.

But Ellen was doing something strange. Leaning over and gagging or something. I wondered whether Veronica had given her a swift kick when I wasn't looking.

'Ellen? Are you all right?'

She straightened then. Her face was grey. 'Fine.' She looked at me. 'He really didn't tell you?'

'Tell me what?'

There was no joy on her face, no excitement. Just weariness. 'I'm pregnant again.'

Chapter Twenty-eight

'Oh boy. Oh boy, oh boy, oh boy.' Barbara was walking around with her hands buried in her hair. 'You've really done it this time.'

'I've done nothing.' I was filled with panic and fear.

Barbara stopped her pacing. 'How pregnant is she?'

'Three months. She's puking every day and she can't sleep. She thought she was done with kids – they can't afford another one – and now she doesn't know how they're going to cope with a new baby and the farm and the tourists—'

'Yes, yes.' Barbara clearly only wanted broad strokes. 'And a wanker for a husband,' she added in a detached aside.

Barbara hadn't seemed all that surprised at Mark's behaviour. Not satisfyingly, anyway. I'd been looking to let off steam big time, and would have appreciated a little incredulity and genuine horror at the whole thing. But Barbara had listened with a very straight face to it all before announcing, as though she had long and bitter experience of it herself, 'That's men for you.'

'I think I left a mark on his head,' I'd finished up. 'Maybe I've branded him.'

That would be good. Other women then could be alerted.

But Barbara just shook her head impatiently. 'I'd have noticed before the end of the party. He was grand.'

Now she was walking around like Poirot. 'We need to figure out what to do.'

'There's only one thing we *can* do,' I told her. In a way, it was my information, it had happened to me. The decision, I felt, was mine at the end of the day. 'Tell her.'

'Why?'

'Why? Because she deserves to know what she's married to!'

'Why?' Barbara said again.

'So that she can do something about it. For God's sake, Barbara. She's our friend. We can't *not* tell her.'

'We certainly can. If to tell her was to do more harm than good.'

'You'd seriously go home without letting her know that her husband was coming on to her friends?'

'You. Not me.' Barbara was quick to clarify that. She looked relieved. 'And, if you don't mind me saying so, the circumstances are open to question.'

'Barbara, can you stop talking like you're a policeman—' Then it hit me. 'What do you mean, open to question?'

'Don't go ballistic—'

'I can't believe you just fucking said that!'

Barbara wasn't frightened by my unbridled hostility. 'You've just broken up with Ollie after ten years. You admitted yourself that you two were having cosy chats. No, let me finish! He sticks his hand on your thigh and you say nothing about it—'

'Because I didn't want to hurt anybody.'

'Because you weren't sure.' Barbara's face was like a High Court judge's now. 'And now this dalliance in the larder.'

'He tried to kiss me. I told him no. I left him in no doubt whatsoever that I didn't want his advances.' My voice was cold.

Barbara gave up her judge stuff. 'Ah, look, I know. But do you not see how it can all be twisted around? And now there she is, up the spout again. Tired and emotional. And we're going to dump this on her?'

'She has a right to know.'

'It's a tricky business, deciding somebody else's rights. Especially when no good can come out of it.'

'There might.'

'How?'

'They might . . . talk.'

'About what a shit he is?' Barbara scoffed. 'And he'll promise he won't do it again and that'll be the end of that?'

We both knew that was never going to happen. If he'd taken a brief, ill-advised fancy to one of the tourists they hosted, it might be different. That might be forgivable. Explicable.

But to hit on one of Ellen's oldest friends? It was a betrayal too far. The worst kind. There would be no getting over that.

And Barbara and I knew it.

'She'd have to kick him out, wouldn't she?'

'Yes,' Barbara concurred. 'And then she'd be all alone and pregnant, with a farm to run.' She thought of something even more disagreeable. 'And I'd have to fly over and back all the time to give her emotional and practical support.'

'I'd fly over too.' I was stung.

Barbara fixed me with her Poirot eye. 'Do you think she'd want you to?'

God, but Barbara was wise. Wrong, in my opinion, but wise none the less, and more detached from the whole thing than I was. If she said no, then I would go with that.

Also, I was relieved. Well, who wouldn't be? I didn't have to be responsible for Ellen's marriage breakdown. There would be no nasty stuff, no shouting, no crying. We would carry on as normal for a few more days and then we'd all fly home and nobody would ever mention it again.

'Ever,' Barbara repeated, after we'd formulated our plan, rumbling deep in her throat like a Rottweiler. 'We take this to our graves, do you understand?'

'Yes, yes.'

'No getting drunk five years from now, and saying, "Listen, there's something I meant to tell you."'

'I understand, Barbara.'

'You can't even tell Ollie.'

She knew me so well. I really wanted to. Desperately. Even though Ollie and I had broken up and fallen out, etc. Ollie would hoover up this kind of news. 'I always knew there was something about him,' he'd say in triumph, and we'd be off. We could get two weeks at least off the back of something like this.

But I knew where my loyalties lay. 'Not even Ollie,' I promised Barbara.

Chapter Twenty-nine

As if the holiday had been poisoned, things started to go wrong. Femmie came down with a stomach bug that afternoon. All we heard for hours was, 'Eeeuyuucckk.' She blamed Rosalie's friends' food, which was a big mistake.

'Food poisoning?' Rosalie snorted contemptuously. 'How about the four bottles of wine she poured down her throat?'

She rolled up her sleeves and we were all worried that she was going to throttle Femmie. But in fact she had come over to clean, something we'd never seen her do before.

'Are you feeling OK, Rosalie?' Barbara hazarded to ask.

Rosalie fixed her with her glass eye. She didn't actually have a glass eye, it just looked like she did. 'I have no choice. She can't clean, can she –' another contemptuous look, this time in Ellen's direction. She was on fire today – 'since she bought cheap condoms that burst.'

Her displeasure at Ellen's pregnancy was plain. Now that we all knew about it, Rosalie was able to give full vent to her annoyance, shaking her head continually, and tutting under her breath.

'I'm very sorry, Rosalie,' Ellen kept apologising profusely. 'It won't happen again. I'm going to get my tubes tied after this. And I swear I won't ask you to look after the new baby.'

Denis took the heat off Ellen by falling out of a tree while taking video footage of something, nobody was sure what, but ended up having to be taken to the local hospital for an X-ray.

It was just a mild sprain, but he made great drama out of it, and recorded the entire incident for his viewing pleasure, and that of his neighbours, back home.

Sophie made Cleo dress up in her ballet outfit and, when one of the seams split under the pressure, suggested that Cleo went on a low–carb diet.

'No bread, no pasta, no sweets, no biscuits, but you still get to eat meat,' she explained helpfully.

'I don't think anybody needs to go on a diet here,' I managed to intervene in a children's presenter voice, when really I wanted to throttle her.

Sophie threw a cool eye over me, then Cleo. She didn't need to say anything else.

'I want to go home,' Cleo begged me when we were alone. 'Please, can we just go home?'

'Oh, honey . . .' I wanted to go too. But we were there for another five days yet.

'I miss Dad. And Harry. I miss my room. I hate Sophie's room. She says I snore and I *don't*.' There were tears welling up now. I knew that, while some of it was to do with that bloody Sophie, things at home were unsettling her too and she wanted to get back.

'Five more days,' I promised her. 'Then we go home.'

Sam got an ear infection from where the girls had tried to pierce them with a fork. Both his ears swelled up and went red and he looked like a rugby player.

Ellen grew tired and grouchy and sick again, and took to the couch.

Barbara got a phone call on the Dimitri phone and nearly passed out. But it was just Dimitri's assistant wanting to let her know that one of her documents was out of date.

'Not AGAIN, Barbara had screeched (once off the phone, naturally). Otherwise there was no news from Russia. Not a dickybird. 'Are you sure?' Barbara had kept repeating to the assistant. 'Are you *completely* sure?'

Damien discovered a round lesion on his back that totally freaked him out.

'What is it? What is it?' he asked, sitting on a stool in the kitchen and holding up Ellen's make–up mirror to get a better look. Even though he was very good-looking on top, his back was white and spotty and extremely off-putting, Barbara and I both agreed.

'After seeing that, I wouldn't ride him if I was desperate,' Barbara later remarked.

'It's itchy too,' Damien said, panicked.

'This would never have happened if you were in Portugal,' Nick remarked sagely.

Damien gave him a nasty look. The friendship was getting more strained. I noticed now that they didn't even bother keeping up the pretence of speaking. The minute they came out of their converted barn, they went their separate ways.

Barbara, wearing a pair of rubber gloves in case it was contagious, examined his back. He'd wanted Ellen, but she was too nauseous and so he got Nurse Barbara instead.

'I think it's ringworm,' she declared. Being an expert.

'What? What?' He was gone pale now. 'I've got fucking worms?'

'This would never have happened if you were in Portugal,' Nick intoned again.

'Piss off, you.' Damien turned on him viciously. 'I wish I *was* in Portugal, and hadn't drawn the short straw in work and ended up on a saddo holiday with you.'

'I wish you hadn't either,' Nick returned evenly. 'I'd much have preferred Paul, or Anto or PJ. At least they wouldn't whinge all the time.'

'Give them a week looking at your miserable face and they'd top themselves,' Damien spat. He looked at his back again in the compact mirror. '*Worms.*'

'The good news,' said Barbara brightly, 'is that ringworm isn't actually a worm. It's a fungal infection.'

Damien grew more hysterical. 'Fungus? What the hell is that?' More scrabbling at his back in an attempt to see. 'Is it fatal?'

'Not usually. But you'd need to get some cream in the pharmacy.'

Damien flung on his shirt, and optimistically grabbed his phrasebook. 'I'll get the cream, all right. And I'm going to stay in a nice hotel tonight, and then I'm getting the hell out of here, and home,' he snarled.

He was a man of his word. He packed his bags and left without a backwards glance.

'You're a real charmer, aren't you?' I said to Nick.

We were at the pigsty. I was feeding Clyde. Nick was watching. Nobody had invited him.

'Takes one to know one,' he said.

We were good at insulting each other. Actually, I think we both quite enjoyed it.

'So they had a competition in work, did they?' I said, just to rile him.

'To see what poor unfortunate would end up holding your hand on holiday?'

'That's pretty much it. Elaine — the ex — and me, we'd already booked the holiday and paid for it. They all agreed they couldn't let me go on my own, and so they drew lots.'

'You're not exactly close, are you?'

'He's a dickhead.' He sounded quite definite about this.

Clyde was ravenous. He was sucking on the teat like he was mad for it. It was quite uncomfortable to watch, actually.

'Maybe you should go home, too,' I suggested to Nick.

His brown eyes were on me. 'Why? I like it here. The animals are pleasant. The food is good. The company . . . well.' His face said that it could be a lot better.

Oh, just let him feck off then. I was happy to feed Clyde on my own.

I refused to say anything else to Nick as Clyde finished up. I wiped his mouth, burped him — I wasn't sure I was to do this, but it seemed safest — and then cleaned up some of his poop before shaking out some fresh straw for him.

'Now. There, little laddeen.' I felt a bit silly saying that, but I was sure I would get better at farmer talk as I went along.

I saw Nick rock with silent laughter.

'Is there anything else I can help you with?' I asked him coldly.

'No, no, just wish I had a camera, that's all.'

I was fed up of him now, and his sarcasm, and his superiority. I picked up my baby's bottle, said to Clyde, 'Sleep tight now, begorrah,' and swept up the yard.

I was tired. I was wrecked. My heart was sick with guilt and worry, and my lovely Ollie didn't want to be a little family with me and Cleo any more. I could feel tears sting my eyes as I made for the back door fast.

A hand on my arm then. Turning me round.

'Wait. I'm sorry.' It was Nick, his eyes creased in alarm. 'I didn't mean to upset you.'

'Well, you did. You seem to enjoy doing that.'

He looked startled. 'I thought we were using defensive strategies. You know, to cope with our broken hearts.'

'"Defensive strategies?" Is that what you call it? I thought you were just being a prat.'

He raked his hair back. 'God, I'm sorry, Hannah—'

I took it out on him. Everything. I admit it. But at the time I couldn't stop myself. 'It's all right for you. Elaine might be away with the fairies in LA—'

'Minnesota.'

'But at least it's a clean break. You don't have any kids together. You don't have to go home and work out how you're going to deal with each other for the rest of your lives, because that's what I have to do. So quit going around like you have it worse than any other person in the world, OK? Because you don't.'

That took the smile off his face.

Not that he *had* been smiling.

He looked a bit naked or something. All that sarkiness gone. 'What's wrong, Hannah?'

Ah, Janey, was he thick? He knew what was wrong. I'd just told him. 'You look like you haven't slept.'

He'd noticed. Suddenly my eyes were stinging again. Concern wasn't something I was used to. Not lately, anyway.

But this was Nasty Nick and I blinked fast and drew myself up tall. Which was only five foot four, but he was only about five foot eight. 'I'm fine.' I felt obliged to add, 'Thank you for asking.'

I wanted to go now, but he didn't seem in any hurry. 'It'll pass you, you know. All this stuff.' He thought it was only Ollie. 'I know it doesn't seem like it now, but take my word for it. Six months.'

Six months seemed like a lifetime away. I didn't know how I was going to get through the next four days before I could leave this place behind.

But I managed a smile and said, 'Six months.'

Chapter Thirty

❦

'Get it all up. That's the girl.'

Ellen was strewn out on the couch again in her shit-green dress, which pretty much matched the colour of her face. Barbara was solicitously holding a basin aloft, the better for Ellen to puke into.

'Any more, do you think?' she asked politely.

Ellen flopped onto her back again. 'I'm done for now.'

While Barbara fussed around like a midwife – I really think she missed her calling in the medical profession – I found it hard to meet Ellen's eyes.

I know I'd agreed to say nothing to her.

I know the reasons were good and practical and necessary.

But it felt so, so wrong.

'Come here,' she said to me, once it appeared that her sickness had settled. 'Do you think it's a boy or a girl?'

She hoisted up her frock to reveal a washboard stomach. What the hell was I supposed to tell by looking at that? Except that she could do with a good meal or two?

But there was Barbara beside me, arms folded across her chest and giving me the evil eye: *Play along. What she doesn't know won't hurt her. Сделаем это сейчас!*

I was afraid of Barbara and so I gamely said, 'Which would you like it to be?'

'A girl, I think. They're easier.'

I thought of Sophie and wondered what planet Ellen was on.

'But knowing Mark,' she went on, 'he'd prefer a boy.'

I swallowed violently at his name. With some satisfaction, I noted that Barbara did too.

'Well, that's men for you,' Barbara said very heartily. 'An heir and a spare, ha ha.' Her fake laugh came to an abrupt halt, and she refused to meet my eye.

'You're going to have to start looking after yourself better,' I told Ellen. I was worried about her. She was such a scrawny little thing, not enough meat on her to keep herself alive. And now she had to grow eight pounds worth of baby, whilst still keeping the entire show on the road in France.

But Ellen waved me away. 'I'm fine. Very healthy, really, if I could stop the puking. It's more the shock of it than anything.'

We murmured lots of, 'Yes, of course,' and, 'I'm sure,' under our breaths. We sounded very convincing.

'I tried to get Mark to have the snip,' she confided, 'but *men*.'

Barbara started gulping air. So did I.

'Will I make tea?' Barbara interjected suddenly. Anything to get off the subject of Mark's tackle.

Ellen looked at Barbara's stressed face, reached over and patted her hand very kindly. 'I know you're worried about those documents being out of date. But try to relax. You'll get it sorted.'

Barbara nodded tightly. I could see a thin sheen of sweat break out on her upper lip. She wasn't able for this kind of thing at all. She couldn't even eat a bread roll whilst wandering around the supermarket without 'fessing up the second she got to the cash register. Keeping a lid on Mark's infidelity was a challenge too far.

'Have you told the kids yet?' I asked Ellen, to take the heat off her.

'God, no. Sophie would have it named, and a cot put up in her bedroom and everything. And Sam, well, he's still my baby. Let him enjoy it while he can.'

We could see the kids out in the yard. Instead of playing happily, though, all three of them were engaged in their own thing. Sophie was riding violently around on her new bike, shouting, '*Allez, allez!*' to nobody in particular. Cleo had a book which she was trying to read in peace. Sam was beating something with a stick.

All was not well there, either.

'Anyway,' said Ellen, 'there's no sense in everybody getting excited this early on. There'll be so much to do before the baby comes. We haven't even got a proper heating system upstairs yet.'

I could see the discontent setting in again. Her lips grew thin and her eyebrows came together in a frazzled kind of way.

'I don't think I could bear to come home from hospital with yet another baby to a cold house.'

Barbara, shooting a cautionary look at me – what did she think I was going to do, join in with a bitching session? – moved swiftly to put a positive spin on things. 'Mark will fix it up.'

'Oh, right. Mark, who's swanning around at a ploughing championship right now, staying in a hotel we can't afford and hanging out in the bar with other, real farmers, talking the talk?' Ellen gave a short laugh.

'So make a list,' Barbara went on doggedly. 'Give it to him. You're pregnant, Ellen – he's going to have to pull up his socks.'

Ellen digested this. Her eyes flickered to me. 'You're not saying much.'

Treacherous heat worked its way up my face. 'Barbara's right,' I stuttered. 'Maybe he just needs to be told what to do. He wouldn't be the first.'

'We'll come over for the birth,' Barbara announced suddenly.

I looked at her askance. What new foolishness was this? I'd planned to extricate myself somewhat from their lives, not become more embroiled in things.

But Ellen was looking at us, face wreathed in hope. 'Would you? Oh, that would be so brilliant. Even just to mind the kids for a day or two while I'm in. I'm sure Mark could cope, but just in case.'

Barbara had done it now. 'No problem,' she said gamely. Madly avoiding my eye.

I could see Ellen turning to me again. I had to smile and nod. 'Just say the word.'

'And you're going to have to cut down on the tourists,' Barbara ordered. She was always most comfortable when she had a plan. 'You can't be cooking fry-ups when you're on the verge of puking all the time. And no more milking.'

Ellen was delighted. 'It's lovely to be bossed around.'

'Let Mark do everything,' Barbara thundered.

Lazy, randy fecker, we were all thinking. Well, not the randy bit, in Ellen's case.

Ellen sighed. Her hand drifted down to her flat belly. She started to stroke it unconsciously. 'And to think that I was dreading you two coming over this time.'

'Thanks a bunch.' It was out before I could help myself.

'It wasn't you, it was me,' Ellen clarified quickly. 'Feeling I had to put on a front the whole time. Lying about how great things are. And then to go and do something completely stupid like get *pregnant*. Completely unplanned. That's the kind of thing . . .' She trailed off.

'That I would do?' I supplied.

Ellen looked at me. 'Yes.'

We all laughed. There was so much buried tension in the air that it was a great release and we rolled around, even though it wasn't that funny.

'I love laughing at someone else's expense,' Barbara said, wiping her eyes.

'It's great, isn't it?' Ellen agreed.

'Well, I'm delighted for you both,' I said.

We continued to grin at one another, just like old times. Ellen put one hand on Barbara and another on me, and went a bit doe-eyed.

'Don't get all icky on us now,' Barbara warned.

'I'm not. I just wanted to say thanks. For being there for me.'

'What did I just say?' said Barbara crossly, trying to shake her off.

But Ellen wouldn't be stopped. It must be all the pregnancy hormones or something. 'For the first time I'm actually starting to get excited about this baby now.'

She looked so hopeful that all I could do was squeeze her hand back, even though I had an uneasy premonition. 'That's great, Ellen. It's really great.'

Chapter Thirty-one

Mark came home the following afternoon. I knew the minute he stepped into the kitchen behind me because my stomach rose.

Then it was a flurry of activity. 'I'm home!'

The kids came running in. He picked up Sam and swung him round in the air, Mr Happy Family Man, to hoots and cries of, 'Put me down!'

'He'll be sick,' Ellen warned tolerantly. She'd just finished puking half an hour previously, and had showered and changed, and looked very beautiful and frail in a fresh billowing dress. She was rewarded with a peck on the cheek and a box of handmade chocolates that he'd picked up at the championships.

Fucking phoney.

For a second I was petrified I'd spoken aloud. But, no, my lips were jammed tight over my teeth. Barbara had instructed me to do that. She was worried I was a loose cannon. 'You're being swayed by all this baby stuff. I can see it in your eyes. "Oh, we'd better tell her before she gets in any deeper." Well, it's too late for that. So I'm warning you now, unless you want to cause a miscarriage, shut your mouth and don't say a word to him. Not even hello.'

I felt his eyes on my back now. I knew I had to turn around. It would be odd otherwise.

'Hi, Hannah,' he said. Bland and smooth. No hint that he was worried at all that I might have spilled my guts while he was away.

I didn't say anything. I just lifted my chin and offered him a twisted, closed-mouthed smile, and a stiff nod.

It seemed to do the trick. His eyes slid away from me — no threat there, I knew he was thinking.

And somehow that was worse. He had known I wouldn't turn him in; had counted on my years of friendship with Ellen saving him. He dismissed me like I didn't matter.

I felt spineless. Weak. And so angry that I had a hard knot under my breastbone.

Now he was bending to Cleo. Taking something out of his bag.

'I got you a book. I know how much you like reading. It's *Babar the Elephant*, a famous French story.' He handed it over with a grin. 'Don't look so worried. It's in English.'

She was delighted with it. Thrilled. 'Thank you,' she said, her face pink with pleasure.

I stood there, wanting to rip it from her hands and throw it back in his face.

But he smiled over at me as though to say, 'See? All friends here. No need for any nastiness.'

'What about me?' Sam demanded, furious.

'I've got you and Sophie a book too.'

'A *book*.' He was even more furious.

'Sam. Pick that up *now*.'

'Thank you, Papa,' Sophie chimed in demurely, always one to know when to pick her battles. And a poxy book wasn't one of them.

Barbara arrived in from the yard then, and I knew she found it hard to look at Mark too.

But she gave him a brusque nod, which wouldn't be out of character for her, and said, gruffly, 'I see you're home.'

'Barbara,' Mark said, with an easy smile. He seemed to have plenty of them today.

Barbara's eyes bounced off me flintily, keeping me in my place.

Then Ellen put her hands on her hips and announced to Mark, 'The girls know.'

I enjoyed his face. The split second of uncertainty, the 'what the fuck is she talking about?' You could almost see the sweat burst from his pores in little, frightened spurts. Or maybe that was just my wishful thinking.

'Know what?'

Ellen flicked a glance at the kids. Sam was thumbing the pages of his book furiously. 'I *hate* reading.'

'Go get ice pops for yourself and the girls from the freezer while I talk to Dad,' she told him placatingly.

When they were gone, Ellen said, 'About the baby. I told them.'

Mark's expression didn't change. He was smooth. Only I noticed the way his eyes climbed down a gear. 'Oh. Great.'

Now we had to launch into the expected congratulations. Barbara was first off the starting blocks, moving forward to give him a perfunctory peck on the cheek. It looked like it hurt. 'Delighted for you, great news, et cetera, et cetera,' she told him.

He laughed, thinking she was just being Barbara. If he looked into her eyes for any length of time at all, he would see quite a different story.

Now it was my turn. I forced myself forward, watched by a benign Ellen. 'Congratulations, Mark.'

His lips were cool and dry on my cheek. I managed not to kiss him at all, pecking instead a pouch of air near his ear.

'Thanks,' he said, as neutral as me.

We all got back to our own corners of the room fairly pronto. Did Ellen notice the peculiar atmosphere? Barbara's scarcely hidden glower in Mark's direction? My inability to maintain eye-contact with anybody for more than two seconds?

'So,' said Barbara. Her eyes came to rest on Mark. 'We were just saying that Ellen is going to have to take it a bit easier.'

Fair play to her. She even managed to sound polite.

'Absolutely,' said Mark, putting a protective hand on Ellen's back. She, in a great humour after our chat earlier, let him.

'Really easy, Mark,' I added.

Mark's head went up now. His eyes tennis-balled from me to Barbara. Instantly, he knew that Barbara knew, and that we were ganging up on him.

Ellen, though, wasn't one to stand by while somebody else fought her battles. 'Don't worry,' she said, mock threateningly. 'I'll make sure Mark knows that.'

'Good,' I said, keeping it all nice and light. 'Plenty of rest. No heavy lifting. A few lie-ins in the morning. I'm sure you can manage that, can't you, Mark?' I softened this with a jokey smile.

His own smile didn't reach his eyes. 'You don't need to worry about Ellen. I can look after her.'

Ellen gave me and Barbara a back-off look. I was unapologetic. After all her whinging – deserved whinging, it had to be said – had she really expected us to say nothing?

'Anyway,' said Mark at last. His hand was still on Ellen's back. 'If it's OK with you two, I'm going to make Ellen a cup of tea.'

Get lost, in other words. He'd had enough of the pair of us looking on like two she-devils with a bad case of wind.

'Great,' said Ellen. 'Start as you mean to go on.'

Mark turned the full force of his charm on her. 'The girls are right,' he said. 'You do need to take it easy. And that means listening to me when I tell you to sit down, OK?'

She fell for it. Or made herself, anyway. She smiled up at him. Mark, as though throwing two fingers up at me and Barbara, turned his back on us and nuzzled her hair like he used to do in the old days, making gooey noises and looking like he was about to suck her face off at any moment.

'Mark,' said Ellen, embarrassed, but she didn't slap his face either.

I wondered when Ellen had become so easy to fool.

We left, and they didn't even notice.

Chapter Thirty-two

'Hannah! Wait up.'

It was Mark, hurrying after me down the farmyard.

I turned round to him, my arms across my chest, my face flat and cold. His own wasn't much warmer. 'What the fuck was that all about?'

'I beg your pardon?'

'That stuff in the kitchen. Were you *threatening* me?'

He didn't like it. He didn't like it at all.

I looked as innocent as I could. 'If you're asking whether I've told Ellen, obviously I haven't.'

That set him back a bit. Better mind his p's and q's, he was thinking. Keep her onside. 'Obviously, I'm glad we can put the other night behind us.'

'I'm sure you are.' I couldn't hide my disgust.

He had on a mature face now, as though he was dealing with a spiteful teen. 'I knew you'd do the right thing.'

'As opposed to you.'

'Let's get one thing straight here. There were two of us in it.'

'*There were not.*' I said it so loudly that the dogs looked over.

If the kitchen window had been open, Ellen would have been looking to see what was going on.

But Mark just smiled. 'Come on, Hannah. You were gagging for it. If it wasn't for Ellen, you'd have been in there like a shot.'

My face burst into colour. He saw.

'Maybe you were wondering what a real man was like, after ten years of Ollie.'

'Shut up,' I said. I knew I was letting myself down but I couldn't help it.

177

'Well, you needn't worry, Hannah. It won't happen again. You can be sure of that.'

I realised I was being dumped, a bare three days after an attempt had been made to pick me up.

Good thing my ego was already in tatters. I could sink no lower, I told myself.

Driving the hurt home, Mark went on, 'Maybe I was just curious too. To see what it would be like to have a roll with a bohemian chick like yourself.' He made the bohemian bit sound derogative and sleazy. 'I figured you'd put it about in your time. At it like rabbits in those resorts, aren't you, all you lot? Maybe I thought you might have a few tricks up your sleeve once I got you in the sack.'

I was so shocked at his venom that I couldn't think of a thing to say. Just stood there, mouth agape, taking his insults.

Eventually I managed, 'You're sick, do you know that?'

He threw back his head and laughed like I'd said something funny. For the first time, I noticed his teeth, all pointy and sharp, and huddled together at the front. He was repellent; his size, his thick neck, his chin, which was also pointy and sharp and lent him a wolfish look. No, not wolfish; fox-like. Sly and opportunistic. He was *horrible*.

'Still, better luck next time,' he said in commiseration.

Then he turned away. I was dismissed once again.

'Mark. Wait.'

He turned. 'And, oh,' he said, 'don't ever lecture me in my own kitchen again, OK? And you can tell Barbara that too.'

'She knows. I told her.' It came out pathetic and puny.

'Yes, I bet you couldn't wait. Well, I hope the pair of you enjoy your moral high ground.'

I wasn't going to let him walk away on that note. I couldn't. 'I want to know how you could do something like that to Ellen.' My voice was shaking slightly. 'Especially when you knew she was pregnant. It's disgusting.'

But if I'd been hoping to prick his conscience with mentions of his wife, I was in for a disappointment.

'My marriage is none of your business.'

'Ellen's my friend.'

'Ellen has lots of friends. What makes you so special? She didn't even tell you about the pregnancy.'

That hurt. He saw.

'She didn't tell anyone.' My voice shook slightly. 'She's cut off over here, she's working too hard, and all because of your stupid pipe dream to run a farm which you're not even capable of doing.'

I had wanted to cut him to the quick. But he didn't seem to care that I knew that his farming skills left a lot to be desired. That he was better at schmoozing the tourists than getting his hands dirty.

He just smiled. 'I bet it killed you not to tell her.' His lip was lifted slightly at the corner. 'You'd have loved it if she was in the same boat as you. A relationship fuck-up. That way you'd have company in the kitchen for your tea drinking and your whining about the pathetic men you landed.'

I didn't say anything. I couldn't.

'Well, I'm sorry to disappoint you, but Ellen is in a totally different league from you. I think you're just jealous that you chose a deadbeat with an allergy to marriage, whereas she got all this.'

He flung out a hand, laying out the beautiful green farm, the peaceful animals, the lovely children over near the tree house sucking ice lollies. He was clearly also including himself in this; a prize.

'It sucks, doesn't it, Hannah?'

I knew what he was trying to do. If he humiliated me enough, and put it all down to jealousy, then maybe I would slink off back to Ireland and spend my time obsessing about what a pig's dinner I'd made of my own life, and I wouldn't have any time left for poor Ellen's.

Well, as far as I was concerned, Mark had been accommodated enough in this whole thing.

For my own sake as much as Ellen's, I told him, voice steady but venomous, 'I'm going to be watching you. I didn't say anything to Ellen because she's pregnant. But I'm coming back in three months' time. And then for the birth of the baby.'

I hadn't planned anything of the sort. But I knew that I would. The look on his face was satisfying. He didn't want me anywhere near the place.

'Barbara's coming too.'

'Yeah, right,' he said. Dismissing it as bravado.

'We've decided that, as Ellen isn't that well with this pregnancy, and is clearly over-worked, we're going to come over to help as much as we can. In fact, we're going to be here so often that you'd better convert another barn for us.'

He wasn't keen on that. I could see his hands balling into fists of frustration. Now he'd have two of Ellen's eejity friends following him around the farm, giving him the evil eye, making snide cracks about men who couldn't keep it in their pants. I wouldn't fancy it much myself.

'And after the baby is born, next year we'll come over for the whole summer,' I lied. Well, we might come over for a week. 'So if you think you're getting away with this just because we care too much for Ellen to hurt her, then you're mistaken. And the next time you put a foot wrong, I'll go straight to her. I swear.'

'I warned you not to threaten me,' he said.

I made my last stand. 'You haven't got away with this, Mark. I'm not going anywhere and I'll only keep my mouth shut for so long.'

A funny thing happened then. Instead of tossing his head like a cornered schoolboy, he gave me a small, queer smile.

'Fine. If that's the way you want to play it.'

He turned and made for the farmhouse.

Chapter Thirty-three

The night that Ollie left me, I had actually thought he was going to propose.

That sounded so stupid now. Mortifying. How could I possibly have dreamt that, when everything between us was going so badly?

Maybe I was just desperate. I was fed up of the drinking and the tight trousers and the distance between us.

Plus, I knew that he still loved me. It was himself he couldn't stand. And possibly his parents. Which was OK, because I couldn't stand them either.

What got my hopes up was Harry's extraordinary announcement that he was going over for a peace dinner with Muriel.

'You what?' said Ollie.

Harry had been prowling around the previous night for hours, crossing between the telly and the kitchen. I'd heard him, and now I wondered if lack of shut-eye had disturbed his brain waves.

But no. 'I'm going to cook her a special meal to show her how much I've changed,' he announced steadily. 'I'm not the slob she threw out all those weeks ago.'

'Steady on, Dad. Anyway, you pretty much are. You've just learned to cook, that's all. You still leave your underpants on the bathroom floor.'

'Give a man a break. One step at a time. Anyway, she's more likely to be impressed with a beautiful meal.'

We were, understandably, flabbergasted. There had been few indications of a thaw between them. If anything, Muriel had been more energetic than usual in her denigration of Harry. Only that week she'd gone public about his penchant for systematically clearing out hotel rooms of all their

181

sachets of tea, coffee and sugar. He even took the little containers of long-life milk, 'even though we never use them! They go in the bin!' Similarly, he failed to utilise the disposable shower caps or the little bottles of moisturising body lotion.

'I wouldn't mind, only he could have done with some of that,' Muriel had said, amid much flinging of eyes to heaven. 'I've been hoovering up his dry skin for years.'

'We paid for it,' was his dogged argument (according to her).

All this had been brought on by Muriel's discovery of one hundred and thirty-nine sachets of out-of-date ketchup that she'd discovered at the back of the cupboard that Harry had apparently been robbing and stashing from McDonald's restaurants over the course of years.

'We paid for it,' Harry merely repeated when she rang up to complain.

We believed he'd thought no more about it. For months now he'd absorbed all her indiscretions and veiled insults that another, less detached person, would have found hard to swallow. At least, he gave no indication that the condiments insult was the one that would push him over the edge. All was calm on the surface.

Besides, other matters overtook the week. Susie went out for her morning wees and didn't come back, even though she'd seen Muriel opening a tin of lamb and beef in gravy for breakfast (Susie could read, apparently). Muriel called her for hours, then walked around the entire neighbourhood but there was no sign.

Nobody was unduly alarmed, least of all Harry and Ollie. 'That damn dog,' Harry swore energetically. 'Do you know how many times she's gone missing over the years? And it's always to do with some pumped-up Alsatian. Muriel thinks she's off sniffing daisies, but I know she's sniffing something else. Disappears off for a whole day sometimes, then comes back like butter wouldn't melt, and Muriel goes rushing off to buy her tins of steak and Bonio chew-chews, the stupid woman.'

But Susie didn't come back that day. Muriel rang up at eleven o'clock that night, inconsolable.

'Fourteen years, I've had that dog. Fourteen. I won't be able to sleep a wink without her. Not here all on my own.'

That was Ollie's cue to go over for the night, to fend off any marauding gangs of intruders that Susie would normally have taken care of with her annoying little high-pitched yap.

But he was tired and cranky, and I suspect the hectic socialising was taking it out of him. As was sharing a house with a wayward father, a resentful partner (I did resentful very well) and a child who was wondering why Daddy always had to go over to Granny Muriel's house instead of making curries and watching telly like he used to.

'Go and find that fecking dog,' he ordered Harry tersely. His eyes were bloodshot.

'I don't know where she is.'

'So *look* for her. She has to be somewhere.'

'Is he going to look for her?' Muriel rang up again to ask plaintively. 'He always goes to look for her when she goes missing.'

Harry got on the phone. 'You can't have it both ways,' he informed her. 'You can't feck me out and then ring me up the minute that long streak of misery goes missing for ten minutes.'

But he went. He put on his coat and boots the following morning and spent a couple of hours looking in the streets around Muriel's house. Well, what else was he supposed to do, comb Dublin inch by inch?

'You didn't even search the park,' Muriel said.

'I did.'

'Knowing you, you probably went for a coffee and didn't look at all.'

'I looked. The dog's gone.'

Muriel's loss, I have no doubt, was what made her speak so harshly. Well, there had to be some excuse. 'You're a selfish, miserable man, Harry O'Mahony, and it was the best thing I ever did in my life, getting rid of you. I'm sorry I ever married you in the first place!'

So no, there had been no hints that either was seeking an improvement in relations. Muriel didn't ring again. Harry retreated into himself again, spending lots of time with his growing collection of cookbooks. I was pleased, thinking that a little time in the kitchen would take his mind off things.

'I don't think a dinner for Mum is a very good idea at the moment,' Ollie declared of Harry's completely unexpected plan to descend on her for a social night. 'She's still very upset about Susie not coming back.'

Susie had never been gone this long before. It wasn't looking good. Muriel wasn't sleeping well and Ollie was running out of excuses not to go over.

But Harry just said, 'She'll need something to take her mind off things.'

He must have seen our naked fear that someone might end up dead because he sighed. 'Look, I know there's been a lot of water under the bridge between Muriel and me. I know it's been difficult on everybody. But there's no sense in carrying on like this. Right now Muriel needs someone and I should be the person to go over there.' He looked at Ollie. 'Not you.'

Sense, at last! One of Ollie's parents was finally beginning to act like one.

Now, if only Ollie could start to act like a man instead of a teenager then we'd be all sorted.

I turned to look at him, willing him to see reason too. If Harry, who'd been insulted, denigrated, fecked out and humiliated by his wife, could find it in himself to reach out to her in her hour of need, then why couldn't we, too? Couldn't we put all this stuff behind us, and move on?

Ollie flicked a glance at me – it was hard to know what he was thinking, but at least he didn't seem hostile – before telling Harry, 'Go on, so. But don't expect too much, OK? Just cook her dinner and leave.'

'That's exactly what I intend to do,' Harry assured him.

The air in the house lightened. I felt like we had reached some kind of turning point, all of us. Harry was willing to swallow his pride for Muriel. And maybe, just maybe, Ollie might see that there was hope after all if people were just prepared to face up to things.

Right?

First we had to get around Muriel. Not an easy task. 'I don't want him over here,' she said on speakerphone. 'I'm going out to look for Susie again.'

Ollie must have felt the same desperation as me to get rid of Harry for the evening because he told Muriel, quite forcefully, 'If Susie's going to come back, she'll do it on her own. It's more important that you stay and thrash things out with Dad.'

'But I don't want to thrash anything out.'

Just do it, you contrary old cow, I wanted to bellow. I felt like I was grasping at my own relationship with sticky fingers; if she didn't let Harry go over and cook for her, then I knew that Ollie would retreat on me again and my chance would be gone.

Ollie must have known this too, somewhere in his pickled brain, because he was very persuasive on the phone, as only he could be. 'Come on, Mum. Just talk. Please. And you won't believe how good he's got in the kitchen.' He shot a sly, playful look at me, just like he used to do before. 'He might even be better than you.'

Well, Muriel wasn't having that. 'I doubt that very much. I suppose he *could* come over. But only because I'm hungry. I haven't eaten a thing all week, what with poor little Susie missing. Oh, do you think she's all right out there? I keep having this feeling that something terrible has happened to her.'

Neither Ollie nor I gave a shite about the dog at that point. We were giddy just at the thought of getting the television to ourselves for the night.

'Go, go, before she changes her mind, you silly old fool,' Ollie hissed at Harry as he faffed about in the kitchen. 'What are you bringing all that stuff for?'

Harry was flushed and strangely excited as he packed up the car with his wok, his spices, his herbs, his tortillas, and a covered tray of what he called 'special ingredients' that he'd got for Muriel. He knew exactly the kind of thing that she liked. Then he set off in a cloud of dust.

Ollie and I were finally alone.

'So,' he said.

I just looked at him. It wasn't up to me to do the talking. I'd done nothing wrong, after all, except stand by while he fell apart.

Cleo was in the living room, with the couch all to herself minus Granddad. She had a big bowl of popcorn in her lap, the remote control in her hand, and we could hear her programme choice floating out:

'Jeer Rachel indid it with Jack?'

'Y'kiddin. We oughter go over.'

I pulled the door quietly closed and left her in Aussie heaven.

'Would you like me to cook you something spicy?' Ollie eventually offered.

No plans to go out tonight then. No drinking, no stumbling home full of shame and beer.

My heart rose. 'How spicy?'

'Very spicy. I was planning to use two whole chillies.'

Two. I was tempted. Since he'd been gone, dinner had been pasta and potatoes and shepherd's pie – awful boring stuff, with not a hint of heat.

'Go on, then.'

I watched as he went to the fridge and began to take out wilting courgettes and past-it peppers, a testament to how long it had been since he'd last cooked for me.

We ignored the incriminating vegetables. I sat up on a stool at the kitchen island and he handed me a beer, like he would on a normal Friday night. That was usually my cue to launch into a complicated and no-details-spared account of my week, and whatever the latest disaster was that had fallen into my lap from Holiday Rep Land. I had a good one that week too: a rep who'd allegedly fallen in love with one of her married, middle-aged tourists and had absconded in a boat to Crete with him. A very, very rare occurrence, I must add, and no reflection on the conduct of holiday reps in general, who were usually too busy to have anything other than rushed sex with tourists.

In turn, Ollie would tell me about his latest bookings and what level he'd reached on World of Warcraft, if it was the slow season.

But tonight we were too far from normality to do the usual news swap. And, with Harry there for the past few months, too out of practice. So we sipped our beers, he chopped, and it was like we were on an awkward date.

'I wonder how they're getting on,' he eventually said.

Indeed. Maybe Muriel was watching Harry doing his chopping thing too, amazed at how much he'd come on. 'Why, Harry! I had no idea,' she might say, the scales falling from her eyes as she fell in love with him all over again.

Or maybe not. Small steps.

'I don't know,' I told Ollie. 'But I suppose we can't let our lives revolve around what Muriel and Harry decide to do.'

That brought me a look. I didn't care. All this had gone on long enough.

'They're my parents. It's kind of hard to stay out of it.'

'Yes, and they're doing their level best to make sure we get dragged in as much as possible.' I stopped. I hadn't got into the blame game so far and I knew it was unwise to go there now.

Ollie retreated too. 'You never know. They might get back together.' He said this like it was the solution to all our problems. 'Dad will move home, and everything gets back to normal.'

Did he honestly believe that? 'Maybe they will.' I indulged him. 'And maybe they'll break up again in six months' time. Do we have to go through all this again?'

He knew what I meant: not Harry on our couch, or our kitchen trashed, but him. Ollie.

He stopped chopping. Took a breath. Looked me in the eye for what seemed like the first time in months. 'I'm sorry, Hannah. For . . . you know. I don't know what's been going on.' He shook his head a little, as though he was coming round from an anaesthetic. 'I know I'm forty. I know I'm supposed to be taking this on the chin. But I always thought they were the most perfect couple in the world, how crazy is that?' He gave a sudden smile.

I had to smile too. Harry and Muriel? They'd never be winning any prizes.

'Looking back now, of course, they've been bitching at each other all their lives. But I never really saw it. I just thought it was their little way, and they were grand, and they'd be together until one of them kicked the bucket.' He looked a bit embarrassed at his idealism. 'Now it feels like my family has fallen apart.'

'We haven't. Cleo and I, we're still here.' We just hung around like gobdaws in the background while he had his crisis of confidence. Again, I felt it would be unhelpful to say this.

He said something then that made me want to cry. 'I don't know who I can trust any more.'

'You're saying you don't trust me?'

'I do, I just . . .' He suddenly looked embarrassed. 'Christ, I'm sorry about the leather trousers.'

'So you should be. If Cleo was much older, she wouldn't have been able to go to school and face people.'

'And the drinking. I'm sorry about that too.'

'All right. Absolved. Your liver needs a break anyway.'

I could feel myself holding my breath. It was like Ollie was coming back to me, slowly; he'd been lost for months, but was now back on the same planet as me, talking sense.

'I need to tell them to shag off,' he declared suddenly.

Yes! I wanted to punch the air but contented myself with a casual swig from my beer. 'Well, I don't know if I'd tell Muriel—'

'She's behaved very badly,' he stated seriously, as though nobody else had realised this and he was regretfully informing us of a dreadful truth. 'And my father. He'll have to move out.'

Oh, Cleo, I thought, our world will soon be put to rights.

'I suppose we could help him look for a flat or something eventually,' I said, very maturely. Somebody had to temper this conversation or, the way Ollie was going, Harry might find his bags packed on the pavement when he got home tonight.

Ollie was in full self-revelatory mode, though. (I was a bit worried it was the beer. He'd drunk it very fast.)

'And as for you and me and Cleo, we need to get back to being a proper family again.'

187

I found myself holding my breath. Things had reached a delicate stage. 'It'd be nice to have some normality again,' I hedged.

Now he looking at me with a fervency that I hadn't seen before, except maybe back in our pot-smoking days. 'I can't believe you've put up with me.'

'Why wouldn't I? I love you.' It was the simple truth.

And that's when I felt the strange electricity in the air; the sense that he was going to make something happen between us, push us on from our decade of living together and pottering along.

I knew that Ollie felt it too. It was now or never for us. Did we commit to a permanent future together tonight?

'Hannah.' The way he said it made my heart stop.

The shagging phone rang.

We should never have answered it. Why, oh why, did we answer it?

It was Muriel. Her voice burst out of the receiver, high and hysterical and hoarse. 'I've eaten Susie. Harry has cooked the dog.'

Chapter Thirty-four

Nick had seen the fight between me and Mark in the yard.
'What are you talking about?' I barked at him. Best defence is offence.

'I wasn't spying—'

'So how did you see it, then?'

'I was cleaning the windows in my converted barn and I happened to look out—'

'Cleaning the *windows*?' I'd never heard such codswallop in my life.

'To be honest, the windows were manky. They've been bugging me since I arrived. But rather than ask Ellen to clean them, what with her being pregnant—'

'Yes, yes, yes. Good deed done for the day. And by the way, we weren't having a row.' I was smarting. Caught mid-brawl.

'It's none of my business—'

'Damn right it's not.'

'Is there any chance at all that you'd let me finish a sentence?' He looked exasperated.

'Finish then. Go on.'

'I was *going* to say, that while it's none of my business, I just came out because you seemed a bit upset.'

Oh. Talk about taking the wind from someone's sails. Mind you, he didn't look that concerned. He looked like his usual cranky-arse self.

'Thank you for asking,' I told him, as nicely as I could, 'but I often look upset when I'm not.'

I was hardly going to fill him in on the Mark/me scenario.

His eyebrows did that thing where they nearly disappeared into his hairline again. He had very flexible eyebrows. 'Really?'

'Yes. And often when I look happy, I'm actually totally miserable.'

He took a moment to digest this. 'You're an incredibly complex woman, Hannah. I don't think I've met the like of you before.'

'You're taking the piss out of me.'

'Yes.'

'You know, I'm not surprised Elaine left you for some weird cult,' I threw at him.

It had no effect. 'The only surprise, really, is that she didn't leave me sooner,' he agreed sagely.

'You're a very dour man, very sarcastic, and you're not even tall.'

'No. But I'm taller than you. You're a bit of a shortie yourself.'

This was true. There was no sense denying it. 'OK, yes.'

We both felt better after the insults – letting off steam, if you like – and things calmed down a bit.

'Look,' he said. 'I just came out to say that I'm making a fresh pot of coffee in my converted barn – why do we all keep calling it a converted barn? It's a bit of a mouthful – and if you fancy a cup then, well, come on in. We don't have to talk or anything,' he reassured me. 'In fact, it would probably be better if we didn't. I have several grisly murder books that you might like to leaf through.'

He didn't look like a man who enjoyed murder books.

He saw my doubt.

'I'm full of surprises,' he assured me, with a sudden grin.

I remained suspicious. 'Why are you being nice to me?'

A sigh now. 'Why would I *not* be nice to you?'

It seemed perfectly reasonable. Or, at least, I couldn't find fault with it.

'So, just you and me in your converted barn?'

'Yes,' he said. He waggled a finger at me. 'So don't go getting any ideas, OK? Feet to be kept on the floor at all times. I'm just over a relationship, you know.'

My face burst into colour. As if! With him! So why was I blushing then?

'Um, OK, thanks. Coffee would be nice.'

His eyes rested briefly on my face. 'Great. See you in a few minutes.'

Off he went, just avoiding Barbara, who'd also observed the confrontation with Mark from her bedroom window. Had everybody seen it, including Ellen?

'No,' Barbara assured me. 'She's too busy puking again.'

I filled her in on the row. She was unimpressed with Mark's head-throwing and veiled threats to back off. 'What's he going to do, tell her himself? She'd throw him out on his ear. No, don't mind him. Full of hot air. Like a big fart.' She sighed, and blessed herself like some old crone from a cottage in the west of Ireland, then mumbled hoarsely, 'Dear God. What have we done, keeping it from her?'

'The only thing we could do,' I snapped. The last thing I needed was Barbara having doubts too.

But I was still sick inside. I didn't like confrontation. I also wasn't that keen on having to act like some demented Victorian aunt every time I came over to France, watching Mark's back all the time and giving him withering looks.

'I just want to go home,' I told her plaintively.

'Me too,' said Barbara with a sigh. 'This is the crappiest holiday ever.'

We heard a scream then.

It came from the tree house. After they'd finished their lollies, the kids had gone up there with several of Sophie's baby dolls under their arms, and swaddling clothes. Sophie had had a nurse's uniform on and a plastic stethoscope around her neck. 'Hurry up,' she'd ordered Sam, as he'd struggled again to get his foot on the lower, broken rung (Mark's shoddy workmanship). 'It's nearly time for your epidural.'

Here came Sam now, back down the steps as fast as his short little legs would carry him. His progress was slowed by the fact that he had twin babies tied to his back in a pink blanket, like an African lady. 'Sorry,' he panted to the babies as he dropped from the last rung and fell back violently upon them.

Then he was running over to us, round cheeks bursting with terrible news.

'She bit her! She bit her!'

Bit her? As in . . . ?

'She wouldn't push the baby out like she was supposed to. There are teeth marks and everything!' He thought for a bit. 'Five of them.'

I swung to Barbara, shocked. This was a new low. Poor Cleo! How dare Sophie? You'd expect it from a two-year-old, but *this*.

'Keep your cool,' Barbara advised. Already an expert, and she hadn't even got her baby yet. Wait till somebody thumped junior in playschool and *then* she'd see. 'We don't know what happened yet.'

No, but from the tensions between the two girls recently, I could have a good guess.

The girls were coming down the ladder as we steamed over, Cleo first. She was calm, if pale, and the heartbroken sobs we could hear weren't hers; Sophie, of course, laying it on thick for the benefit of the adults.

I ignored her and threw my arms around Cleo. 'Are you all right? Show me. What *happened*?'

Cleo just stood rigidly in my arms. 'I didn't want to have a baby. I've had seventeen babies since we came here, and I didn't want to have any more.'

'Well, of course you didn't!' My heart rose. 'Seventeen is enough for anybody to cope with.'

'But she kept saying that it was her house and that I was only a guest and that I'd have to do what she said or she'd make us leave.'

All the time I was trying to find the bite mark. Thank God it wasn't on her face. A quick inspection of her hands and arms showed nothing either. Had that devious little witch gone and bitten her somewhere in the hope that nobody would see?

'Show me where it hurts,' I instructed Cleo.

Sophie was now hobbling down the tree house ladder, howling fit to beat the band. Barbara hurried over to minister to her, wisely sensing that it wouldn't help matters if she left it to me.

'Nowhere,' said Cleo.

'Cleo, stop it now. I need to see the bite so just show me, please.'

Sophie, meanwhile, was clutching her backside and screaming, '*Maman! Papa!*'

Cleo turned and gave her a look. 'I didn't mean to. I was just so angry.'

That's when the penny dropped.

'Cleo. You . . . didn't?'

Sophie turned to look at Cleo, and stretched out a finger in accusation. 'She bit my bottom!'

Now Ellen was coming from the house, striding towards us. Mark was behind her.

From the look on her face, and his, I knew that I was sunk.

Sophie's bottom had five angry teeth marks in it.

Ellen, her face like stone, said, 'Barbara, would you mind taking Sophie in and putting some cream on it? And maybe some TV for Cleo and Sam. Thank you.'

Barbara didn't want to go. She knew something stank, and she didn't want to leave me to face the music on my own.

'Go on, Barbara,' I said. It was best the kids weren't around for any fallout.

'I'll be back in five minutes,' Barbara warned us all. 'Three, even.'

Off she went, dragging the three kids behind her, Cleo shame-faced and Sophie still howling like the sky had fallen in.

'Go on, pet,' Ellen told Sophie encouragingly.

Then she turned to look at me. The look on her face was so odd, so wrong, that I felt the blood go cold in my veins.

Mark, meanwhile, had peeled away to stand behind her like he was on guard or something. Against who? Me?

'I'm sorry about the bite,' I began. Maybe I was reading too much into things. Maybe that's all that was upsetting her. 'I have no idea what got into Cleo. She's never done anything like that before. I'm going to *kill* her—'

'How could you?' Her voice lashed across me.

I looked behind her to Mark.

I knew she knew.

'Ellen—'

'You come here to my house, to my home, and you make a play for my husband?'

I don't know which was bigger: the shock of his lies, or the shock that she automatically believed him. Twenty years we had known each other and in an instant it counted for nothing.

'I didn't.' I said it loud, strong. 'He made a pass at me.'

She threw her head back, fiercely defensive. 'Oh, please. Don't start that. He told me what happened and I believe him, OK?'

I felt like I was drowning. And all the time he was standing there, a malevolent, controlling presence. If it was just me and her, then maybe we might have had a chance.

All I could do was repeat the truth, steady and calm and hope that she came to her senses. 'He made a pass at me, Ellen. Twice. I couldn't tell you because you're pregnant.'

'Don't.' She put her hands to her ears. I could see the incredible strain she was under. Her husband telling her one thing and her best friend another. 'Just don't, OK?'

'Ellen, I know this is hard for you. I know this is the last thing you want to hear. But I'm telling you the truth and you've got to believe me. Mark told me that you were having trouble and he tried to get me to have an affair with him.'

She wasn't listening. She'd taken her hands from her ears all right, but I knew by her face that she wasn't hearing a word I was saying. She wasn't going to let herself. Nothing I could say to her was going to count.

'I would never, ever do anything to hurt you.' It was all I could say; the only way I knew to get through to her. 'I would never try to sleep with him. What do you take me for?'

I thought I saw a flicker of reason in her eyes. I was Hannah, for God's sake, her mate. I would never even let her leave a pub on her own, never mind steal her husband behind her back.

But Mark shifted in the background. Sensing this, she cast a small look over her shoulder. He gave her an 'I'm right behind you, honey, if you need me' look, and I had never hated him more.

He looked back at me now, cool and steady. His marriage saved, and it didn't matter at what expense.

'I want you to leave,' Ellen said rapidly, breathing hard. Her hand was on her belly protectively. 'Now, please.'

'Ellen—'

'Just go, Hannah. Don't come back.'

I just stood there, staring at her so hard that eventually she was forced to meet my eyes.

'You know I'm telling the truth.'

Suddenly she got ferociously angry. 'I know what you did, OK? You want me to go into the detail? I took you in when Ollie threw you over. Now get out of my life. I never want to see you again. Do you understand?'

I did. Utterly.

Into the silence Barbara came barrelling out of the house. Tears were pouring down her cheeks. I wondered for a shocking minute whether Cleo had turned on her too, and chomped her on the arse.

She waved a phone above her head, like it was on fire. The Dimitri phone. 'I just got the call,' she croaked queerly. 'I have a baby.'

Chapter Thirty-five

Nick was marvellous.

'Everybody strapped in?' he asked. We were in the Range Rover, our hastily packed luggage piled into the smelly boot. He'd asked Ellen if he could borrow the car to drive us to the airport from where we would be hastily expelled back to our country of origin in disgrace. Otherwise we'd have had to walk, or rent a hot-air balloon or something.

Nobody bothered answering him.

Barbara was crying silently in the back, clutching the Dimitri phone to her chest and stroking it in a disturbing fashion. I was still in shock. Cleo was trying to get the taste of Sophie's bottom out of her mouth.

'Right-e-o,' said Nick, unfazed at our general rudeness. He started the engine. 'Let's hope I'm insured to drive this thing, eh?'

He gave a little laugh. Nobody joined in. He stopped laughing and tried to turn it into a cough instead.

I looked back at the farmhouse. Ellen and Mark and the kids were inside. All the doors and windows were shut, and the blinds pulled down. It was like the whole house had thrown two fingers up at us. At me.

'I'm going to drive off now,' Nick informed me, as though giving me one last chance to gallop to the house and beg for admittance and understanding.

'Go,' I managed. There would be no point.

Amid much clashing of gears and exclamations of 'Damn', Nick managed to get the car into first, and off we set across the yard.

'Wait! Wait!'

'Brace yourself,' said Nick.

It was Femmie and Denis, hurrying out of the back door from the kitchen. Great. Just what I needed. An audience to witness my shame.

Nick had to stop, or else mow them down. And I have to say he looked tempted.

'What's going on?' Denis demanded upon reaching the driver's window. His glasses were all fogged up with the excitement. 'Ellen said you were leaving.'

'Yes,' said Femmie. 'What was the big bust-up about? We heard there was a cat fight in the yard between you and Ellen.'

I could feel Nick looking at me. He must think I was a desperate thug, starting fights with everybody in public. As with the row with Mark, he'd missed the row with Ellen too, because he'd been busy making me a delicious pot of fresh coffee. It was brewed just in time for him to step out of his farmhouse and hear Ellen throw me off the property.

Nice.

I didn't know what he was thinking now. Maybe that I had tried to filch the family silver. Which was preferable to him thinking I'd tried to filch someone else's husband.

He surprised me by telling Femmie and Denis, 'We have to go. It's an emergency.'

He revved the engine. He wasn't used to the accelerator and the car reared forward alarmingly.

Denis and Femmie jumped back. 'What, is someone sick?'

All three of us, by the looks of us; could they not tell?

'Yes, it's terrible,' Nick said.

Barbara surfaced at this point, from whatever planet she'd been on. 'Goodbye, Femmie. Goodbye, Denis. I hope I'll never see you again, but enjoy the rest of your holiday,' she said through a spectacularly blocked nose. She'd had a very hard hour. One minute she was trying to contain her elation over Dimitri – 'Oh my God, oh my God, I have a referral, I have a REFERRAL!' – the next she was wading in to try to sort out things between Ellen and me – 'Can we just sit down, please? Can we just talk this through like mature adults?'

Meanwhile the kids were all crying in separate rooms. Sophie's bottom had been washed and covered in ointment, and once the redness had died down there was really only one small tooth mark on it, not the savaging that we'd all been expecting. Cleo was bawling in mortification and shame. Sam was crying because he didn't want to be left out.

But Ellen wouldn't even engage with Barbara. She'd flung around accusations about Barbara 'sitting on the fence'. Then Mark had stepped in, all manly and protective, putting an arm around Ellen's sobbing shoulders and telling Barbara and me sternly that he wasn't having any more of this, that we were upsetting Ellen — we! — and that he was taking her off for a rest.

He led her into the house, shut the door and that was the last we saw of them.

Eventually Barbara said to me, 'Look, I think it's best if we *do* go. We can try and sort this out at home once everybody's calmed down.'

I let her pack for all of us while I sat with Cleo on the bench outside, two lepers.

'I'm sorry about biting Sophie.' Cleo was crying too. 'And now I've gone and upset Auntie Ellen and she's thrown us out.'

'What? No . . . No! We're not being thrown out because you bit Sophie.' But what else could I say? 'It's just . . . it's best that we leave.'

And we were trying to, if we could just shake off Denis and Femmie.

'Give us your address,' Denis told Barbara.

'No,' she said.

'We might be in Ireland next year and we could visit you.'

'No!'

Nick did a magnificent thing then. He put his foot on the accelerator, hard, and the Range Rover jumped forward like it had just received an electric shock. We shot through the gates at the bottom of the yard like a bat out of hell, leaving Denis and Femmie engulfed in diesel fumes.

'Wait!' Cleo sprung forward from the back urgently. 'Clyde!'

My piglet. Little fat Clyde. I hadn't said goodbye. They might even eat him very soon out of some sort of sick revenge on me. The memory of what Harry had done to Susie sprang afresh to the front of my mind. 'Ha, ha, let's eat her pig, that'll teach her. And we'll send her a photograph of it, too.'

'I'll look after Clyde,' Nick promised Cleo.

Cleo sighed. It was better than nothing. 'OK.'

I gave Nick a grateful look. I wondered would he be as accommodating when he eventually found out that we'd been ostracised because of my voracious sexual appetite for other women's men.

We drove back the way we'd come, down flat country roads towards the motorway, passing by fields upon fields of sweetcorn and artichokes. There was a deafening silence. I would have to make the effort. All this was my fault, after all. Or so it felt like.

'Barbara,' I said. 'I'm sorry, but I didn't even ask. What did you get matched with?'

She met my eyes over the car seat. 'A baby,' she said in wonder.

'Well, yes, we know that. A boy or a girl?'

'Oh.' A narky look now. She was coming back to normal. 'A boy. I already told you but you clearly weren't listening.'

'What's his name then?' Cleo enquired, in a challenge. That Dimitri fellow continued to be highly unreliable, in her book, and she obviously wouldn't be surprised if the whole thing was a stitch-up.

'Sergei.'

'Age?' Cleo fired off.

'I don't know. I didn't think to ask anything at all, what with all the drama going on in the background. They're going to fax me the paperwork and it'll be waiting for me when I get home. And photos and everything.'

Paperwork. Photos. This thing really was happening at last.

'When will you get him?' Cleo wanted to know.

'It'll be months yet.'

'Months!' Here we went again.

Barbara sighed. This was the problem when you dealt with amateurs. 'I can't just fly over there tomorrow and pop him in a car seat and make off with him. There are legalities, court appearances, I have to have a medical.'

'Another one!' She always seemed to be at the doctor's, ruling out horrible diseases.

Barbara ignored this. 'And I have to make two trips over.'

That was enough for Cleo. She flopped back into her seat with a look at me that said, 'See? She's *never* going to get this baby.'

It was up to me to say, 'I'm delighted for you, Barbara. You deserve it, after all this time.'

'Thanks.' Barbara looked a little emotional. 'I still can't believe it. I'm going to be a mum.' She turned to look out the window a tad nervously. 'I just hope I don't muck it up.'

'Right, well, erm, have a good flight.'

Nick had set us down in an area that was strictly no set-down. I could already see several uniformed officials in the distance growing highly agitated, and getting onto their walkie-talkies, probably to summon the airport police.

'Thank you.'

Cleo and Barbara were hauling luggage from the boot, bickering over who took possession of the wheelie suitcase.

'Can I get you anything for the flight?' Nick shifted awkwardly. 'Water? A sandwich? Bottle of vodka?'

I managed a small smile. He was being very nice again, which was most unusual for him.

But there was nothing he could do to help. I was still in semi-shock at Ellen's rejection. It had given me a jolt that was in some ways more upsetting than Ollie walking away.

With men, boyfriends, you somehow expect that awful things will happen. Passion does that, right? Makes people behave very badly. Any magazine in any dental practice in the country will tell you that lovely fathers-of-three routinely stun their wives by absconding with their secretaries, or having love-children with their sisters-in-law. We all knew people – sensible women and men – who'd fallen out spectacularly with the loves of their lives, and ended up setting fire to their cars. Were we surprised? No. Because we all knew from bitter experience that people once in love often treat each other spectacularly badly afterwards.

But *friendship*. That's supposed to be different. Enduring. Loyal. Thick and thin, and all that. We'd seen each other at our absolute worst and best, and still we phoned each other up twice a week and said, 'Fancy a coffee and a chat?' The whole world might fall apart, you might lose your job and your hair, your bank might threaten foreclosure, your jeans mightn't zip up, your children might despise you, but your friends were always there.

That was the rule.

And now it was shattered. Ellen had turned on me. Because she believed I had turned on her.

Over a man.

The natural order of things had been overturned, and I didn't know if they could ever be fixed again.

Barbara had won the tussle with the suitcase, and she trundled forward with it now, and squeezed my shoulder in solidarity. One friend left. I knew I should be glad.

'Will we go?' she said.

'Yes.'

Part Two

Chapter One

There was something burning in the kitchen.

'Relax,' Harry called cheerfully. 'I've taken the batteries out of the smoke alarm.'

'Harry,' I said to him, 'shouldn't you be packing?'

'Plenty of time for that. Here, try one of these. They're lovely. Made with cream, from that nice Nigella Lawson's recipe.'

Harry loved Nigella Lawson. He had all her cookbooks. Sometimes I found him slumbering on the couch with one of them open across his crotch, his fingers splayed playfully on Nigella's picture on the front.

I'd put on half a stone in the four months since we'd come back from France. And it was all down to Harry's cooking. The good news was that he didn't burn things so much any more, except when he got distracted by the TV and forgot to put the timer on. The bad news was that he'd discovered Nigella Lawson, and cream.

'It's amazing,' he would tell me feverishly. 'It can make anything taste better. Even porridge.'

He was currently in the grip of its intensity. You couldn't even eat a slice of his homemade brown bread without discovering afterwards that he'd snuck in half a pint of double cream before lashing it in the oven.

Now he was trying to foist meringues on me. 'They're for dessert, Harry. We haven't even had dinner yet, you silly old goat.'

I scolded him often and vigorously. He enjoyed it, I enjoyed it, it let off a little steam. The alternative was taking a frying pan to the back of his head some day and burying him under the patio.

But it was all coming to an end today, our little arrangement. I didn't know how I felt about it. In one way I was dying to get my house back to myself. No more hairs in the bath; a couch, without his backside on it; a full night's sleep without being startled awake at 4 a.m. by the sound of him tripping over the rug on his nocturnal ramblings. Bliss.

But of course I would miss him terribly. For all his faults, he'd been the one constant in my life since Ollie and I had broken up: a small, brown, furry presence in a house that was otherwise stunningly empty except for Cleo and me.

'What time did you tell Ollie?' he asked officiously now.

'Seven. Is that OK?'

'Perfect.' He lifted the lid on a pot with a bit of a swagger. 'The boeuf bourguignon should be ready just about then.' He even tried a French accent, showing off – 'buff' bourguignon.

Ollie was coming over for the farewell dinner. He came over for dinner quite a lot. Shortly after I came back from France, we sat down and agreed that it would be good for Cleo if we continued to do certain things together.

'We don't want her thinking that just because we've split up, we can't sit down at a table together and have a meal as a *family.*'

'God, no. After all, we're both still her parents—'

'Totally, and, as such, tied to each other for the rest of our lives—'

'Well, more intertwined. "Tied" sounds a bit harsh—'

'Oh, look just come over for a bowl of pasta on Friday night, will you?'

'Sure. I'll bring the wine.'

It had been a little awkward at first, with a lot of, 'Um, where will I sit?' from Ollie, even though nobody had actually taken his chair, but he obviously felt it would be inappropriate to just slap his arse down into it like he'd never left. He also made some stilted offers to do the washing-up afterwards, which I took him up on, and he made sure he left fairly promptly after dessert just so everybody knew where they stood.

All this lasted about two weeks. Then he just began to roll up on Fridays, he stopped offering to wash up, I stopped making him, and he hung around chatting until we ourselves were ready to go to bed.

Dangerous.

Occasionally he invited us over to his. As in, Muriel's. Yes, he was still there. No big move out into a lacquered black bachelor apartment with leopard-print bed-throws and a huge wardrobe for his crotch-hugging jeans. I think he might have attempted it once, as in, he'd arranged a viewing of some place, but Muriel had gone along with him and trailed around after him, intoning witlessly, 'Did you know that ground-floor flats are forty-five times more likely than anywhere else to get burgled?' and, 'Someone got stabbed up the road from here last month.'

Then, following one of these viewings, she'd experienced a 'high-blood pressure incident' at home and maintained that she might have died only that Ollie was there.

'It was indigestion,' Ollie told me tersely. 'I made her cajun meat pie for tea. The doctor gave her some Rennies and told her to calm down.'

I could feel his growing frustration. Served him right, of course. When he'd moved in with Muriel, he'd had no idea that she'd never let him move out again.

But things were tetchy between them. Very tetchy. When we were over for dinner in her sparse, tiled kitchen, with all the ceramic ducks on the wall suspended in startled mid-flight, he'd be positively short with her.

'Let's push the boat out and stick on the heating for our guests, will we, Mum?' he'd say sarcastically. Muriel, like a lot of older people, was extremely cagey with her oil tank. She only put it on for special occasions, and Cleo and I didn't rank. We got the heating that night, though.

Then there was the shrine to Susie, which drove Ollie mad. Susie's little basket was still in the corner of the kitchen, 'untouched since the day she left,' Muriel always said sadly. There was a half-chewed Bonio in the corner of the basket, and even a tiny poop that had clearly taken Susie by surprise on the morning of her disappearance, and which any other sane person would have flushed down the toilet, but which Muriel went over to gaze at reverently several times a day.

'For God's sake, Mum. Not while we're eating.'

His tone made Muriel blink rapidly several times. 'I still miss her, you know. I can't help it.'

'Yes, we know. Maybe we can find you some pet bereavement classes or something.'

Oooh. Even Cleo looked up at that: *mean.*

I felt a bit sorry for Muriel as she bowed her head and took her place at the dining table. I could see her face fall as Ollie dished up; something spicy, again. Her windpipe was shot to hell by his vindaloos and jalapeno soups and fecking salsa chicken. But she said nothing, just began to pick out bits of vegetable and scrape the sauce off it in a dignified fashion with her knife.

She cornered me in the kitchen afterwards, her eyes a bit watery. I didn't know whether it was from the food or not.

'I know what you're all thinking. That it's not right for a forty-year-old man to be back living with his mother.'

'It's sick, actually, if you want to know.'

I said it half in jest, but she seemed very taken aback. Fragile, almost. 'What's wrong, Muriel?'

'I don't know . . . I suppose I just didn't think it would be like this.' I thought she was going to bang on again about missed spa weekends and exciting new hobbies that she'd never taken up. But she said, 'Me, I mean. When I threw Harry out, I was so sure of what I was going to do. How I would change. I never for a moment thought I'd be afraid to sleep on my own in the house at night, or that I would miss Susie so much.' She looked upset. 'I feel like I've let myself down.'

'Oh, Muriel.' Half of me wanted to shake her, the other half to make her a cup of tea. 'Look, it's done now and I suppose you're just going to have to make the best of it.'

'I don't know how. It's like I'm stuck.'

'Why don't you try making plans? Be more proactive, like Harry.'

It probably wasn't a great idea to have held up Harry as a shining example. But he was the big surprise in all this. Who would have thought that he'd discover a passion for cooking, and was now moving, of his own volition, into a flash apartment?

Well, it wasn't that flash. But it was an actual apartment, in an apartment block in a gated community for retirees.

No wonder Muriel was somewhat subdued. She was the one who'd wanted to transform her life, yet she got stuck in the family semi with its overgrown garden and sharing the bathroom with one of the kids again.

But of course Harry had gone over to the dark side. Muriel had researched this thoroughly on the Internet. Clearly he was dabbling in some very strange and subversive practices if he was capturing and killing innocent animals, and serving them up for dinner.

'Oh, for the love of God,' Harry would howl when he heard this. 'It was a JOKE. I didn't cook the bloody dog. The dog ran off. I was mad at you because you were saying all those things behind my back and so I pretended to feed you the dog. It was only rump steak from the butchers.'

'It was not. It was all stringy and tough.'

'It was cheap rump steak.'

'I can't talk about it any more, or I'm going to be sick.' Muriel would start fanning herself furiously at that point, and looking quite green. 'Married to a monster all these years and I never knew.'

The news of Harry the dog killer had spread through the community like wildfire. People couldn't believe it at first but, as they said to each other after mature reflection, where was the darn dog? Gone! Never been missing for more than a few days before. And Harry had always hated that dog . . . Plus, who could blame him, after all? Many a man might have killed and cooked Muriel herself after half the things she'd said.

'It's always the quiet ones,' they would whisper as Harry would pass by them in the supermarket, in his shiny trousers and V-neck jumpers, and a pound of unsalted butter under his arm. 'Oh, hello there, Harry! Lovely day!' Always best to keep on the right side of these nutters, or they might pay you a visit too.

Harry took no notice of his new notoriety. He was more upset that people didn't get his sense of humour. Orla and Maeve were still cold-shouldering him from Canada and Australia. When they'd been over at the end of the summer to visit, they'd stayed with Muriel. Anytime that Harry dropped by to say hello, they kept their kids very close to them at all times, for fear that they might end up in a frying pan.

'It's OK,' he assured them. 'I have a strict policy of using local produce only.'

'Dad!' Appalled looks and much Muriel-type fanning of faces. 'That's not even *funny*.'

'Oh, lighten up. What is it with the women in this family? No bloody sense of humour.'

They would look at him like he'd mutated from some doddery old fool into Jack Nicholson.

'They were always mammy's girls anyway,' he'd whispered to me, not put out in the slightest. 'They'll come round.' A little pause. His forehead puckered. 'It's you and Ollie who are killing me.'

He never normally broached the subject of me and Ollie. Anything to do with emotions generally had him scurrying for the safety of the TV. He hadn't even been able to discuss what had happened with Ellen, even though I'd landed in on him from the airport several days early, distraught, and caused his cheese soufflé to droop horribly in the middle.

'A bad business,' he'd blustered when I'd told him what had happened. Mark he roundly dubbed a 'bozo'. Ellen was 'confused'. I, on the other hand, was 'a decent girl'.

I enjoyed the simplistic labels. It was like we were all cartoon characters in a book, or something.

And it helped to make it hurt less that I had been cut off so comprehensively by Ellen that I might as well be dead.

But now he appeared intent on discussing his son and me, even though his eyes were racing around all over the place in a clear bid to avoid eye contact.

'I was just wondering,' he began. He faltered. Then kick-started himself again. Eyes going mad now, almost in circles. I was getting dizzy looking at him. 'Whether you two should give things another go. You know, now that I'm moving out. It can't be easy when you have no privacy.'

Well, he'd fairly put the kibosh on our sex life, that was for sure. But it scarcely followed that we'd kiss and make up the second he was gone.

'I appreciate the thought, Harry, but—'

'Butt out?'

'Yes.'

'I suppose I'm the last person who should be giving anybody advice,' he sighed. His fingers unconsciously fell to his copy of *Nigella Bites* where they began to stroke her long, dark hair. She seemed to have a soothing effect on him because his eyes quit their crazy avoidance tactics and met mine squarely. 'The last thing I'll say is that I know he's behaved like a total fool –' he saw no irony in calling anybody else a total fool – 'but anyone can see you're made for each other.'

'Harry.'

The doorbell rang. Through the frosted glass I could see Ollie – tall, probably scrubbed, undoubtedly smelling of something nice.

Very dangerous indeed.

Chapter Two

'One folding laundry basket. Sixty-five centimetres by forty-five by forty-two. A house-warming gift.' Ollie put the laundry basket down ceremoniously in front of Harry. 'Perfect for used underpants.'

Harry cackled appreciatively, and gave the laundry basket a prod with his toe to see how sturdy it was, the same way that men walk around each other's new cars giving the tyres vicious kicks in the hopes that one of them might fall off, or deflate or something. 'Thanks, son.'

'And this is from Mum.'

We all waited to see what pointed present Muriel might have sent over for Harry. Deodorant, perhaps, or a receptacle for toenail clippings. But it was a rather sedate DVD holder, for his considerable collection of back episodes of crime series.

'Lovely,' said Harry, genuinely pleased, giving it a few prods too, which, thankfully, it withstood.

Ollie had brought me a bottle of my favourite white wine, and a chocolate rabbit for Cleo. 'Not before dinner,' he cautioned.

'Why do people keep telling me things I *know*,' Cleo exploded unexpectedly before slamming her way out the door and up to her room.

Ollie looked at me, alarmed. 'She's not pre-pubescent already, is she?'

'She's just a bit out of sorts because Harry is leaving, that's all. It'll be a big change for her.'

Harry puffed up a bit. Missed already, and he hadn't even gone yet. 'The beef's got ten minutes yet,' he decided after some careful totting up on his fingers. 'I'll go up to her. I meant to tell her that there's a playground in the park next to the old folks' flats for when she comes to visit.'

He jokily referred to his new abode as, variously, 'the check-out hotel' or the 'end-of-life facility', which always made Muriel draw in her breath disapprovingly, even though anyone would think she'd be delighted to see him pop his clogs, after everything.

Off he went to make Cleo feel better, his little beaver head bent over industriously.

'You'd never think he was the kind to make fajitas out of people's pets,' Ollie remarked.

'If you want to know the truth, I think Cleo's mad at us. Well, you,' I told Ollie bluntly.

'Oh?'

'In school today they had to make a family tree.'

'Oh.' Already his face was falling.

'Yes. And because she's so honest, she separated the photos of you and me in case anyone thought we were still a couple, only then she realised she'd have to separate Granny and Granddad as well.'

'So it looked like carnage?' He winced.

'We look fickle, to say the least.'

The worst bit was that she hadn't told any of her classmates about me and Ollie, even though we'd obviously been in to see the teacher. With the family tree, she unwittingly unleashed a storm of curiosity in the other, mostly soap-watching, children.

'Did he have an affair? Your dad?' Much shaking of eight-year-old heads.

'Mid-life crisis, was it?'

'Let's hope it doesn't go to a custody battle.'

Then someone piped up, 'It's nearly always the dad, isn't it?'

Ollie was looking very pained as I recounted this to him. 'Maybe I should go up to her myself.'

'No, don't. Maybe talk to her on Sunday.'

Ollie always took her on Sundays. He'd be able to explain himself then. I wished I was a fly on the wall.

'I'm sorry,' he said, in such a way that I knew he was talking about more than the damage to Cleo.

'Beer?' I said. I didn't want to go there. I wasn't ready.

He took the hint, accepted a beer and threw himself down at the kitchen table, long legs stretched out in a pair of old jeans.

I gave them a pointed look. 'Not going out tonight, then?'

'A jibe,' he said in admiration. 'I don't go out every Friday night, you know. Not any more.'

'That's because you've run out of places to go.'

He was enjoying this, a little back-and-forth. 'There's a new place in town just opened up that I might try out.'

'Knock yourself out. I hope you get lucky.'

'Who said I was looking to get lucky?'

Our eyes met over the beer bottles. I moved on quickly with – and I don't know what possessed me, I really don't – 'Maybe next Friday night you can take Cleo, and *I'll* go out on the town.'

'You?' His eyebrows jumped up. They weren't as flexible as Nick's.

Now, where had that thought come from? I hadn't seen Nick in four months. Not a phone call, nothing.

He still came into my mind at odd moments, though. Like now.

'Ahem?' said Ollie. He knew my mind had drifted.

'Barbara and I would go,' I informed him airily. I had no idea why I was pursuing this fantasy. The very idea of tarting up and heading into some dark pub in town in the hope that somebody would take pity on me horrified me. But I wanted him to know that I was game; that I had some kind of notions for myself, instead of just entertaining him and Harry at dinner every Friday.

I wanted him to know that I was over him.

'*Barbara?*' Ollie threw back his head and had a good old laugh for himself. 'Good luck, stuffing her into a frock and a handbag and getting her into town.'

He was right. She'd have a cow. Anyway, she would be in Russia, which was a bit of a logistical problem.

'Tell you what, I'll come with you,' Ollie offered generously. 'Show you the ropes. Things have changed a lot since our day. Like, there are no slow sets any more – I know, I know, it's incredible – and when someone says you're fit, it has nothing to do with actual stamina. But don't worry. You'll soon get the hang of it.'

'You're hillarious.'

'We might even find you a bottle of Ritz.'

More hilarity on his part. I found myself reluctantly smiling along with him. I'd laughed plenty at his tight trousers – 'Look at that teeny, weeny bulge! So *sweet!*' – but only when he was stocious drunk and wouldn't remember anything I'd said the following morning.

'Shouldn't we be fighting?' I said suddenly. It troubled me, usually about 4 a.m. when I would wake up with a chill, knowing something was wrong. A burglar in the house? No. Forgot to pay the credit card bill? No.

Then: Ollie had been over and we'd had a great old time.

'Fighting?' Ollie was genuinely puzzled.

'Most people who break up fight. Why don't we?'

He shrugged. 'Because we're friends.' An uneasy little pause now. 'Aren't we?'

'Well, yes.'

Relief now. 'God, I'd hate to fight all the time. Like Christine and Tommy.'

'Jesus, yeah.' They were awful. They'd broken up three years ago, a couple of kids between them, and they were still pretending they'd never received the other's twenty-seven texts about little Andy's football match on Saturday morning, or having drunken brawls at family reunions. *Awful.*

'Or Mum and Dad.' He was serious now. 'Although they've calmed down.'

'I suppose.'

Why was I so upset that things had worked out so well? What had I wanted? The break-up from hell? Would I have felt better if, upon my return from France, things had got all bitter and nasty, and we'd found we couldn't stand the sight of each other?

Instead ours had been the break-up of dreams, if that wasn't a contradiction in terms. No sudden, sharp shock, but rather a slow dying, where everybody had plenty of time to get acclimatised before the final, quiet, demise.

The way back up hadn't been that far at all. And now here we were, in my kitchen, Ollie's third time in my house that week, now that I thought about it, and we were getting on almost as well as we ever had.

We just weren't sleeping together any more.

I let that sink in for a bit. Everything was the same as always, except for the exchange of bodily fluids.

And unless somebody did something, I knew with a sudden sharp shock that it wouldn't be long before we were back doing that, too.

Chapter Three

The part of Russia where the orphanage was located was eight hundred miles beyond Moscow, and so cold that Brittany would seem like Las Vegas in July.

'Not that I'm complaining. I'm just stating a fact.' Barbara was always at pains to sound positive; she knew how lucky she was, compared to the people who were still at home, waiting, waiting for the phone call that never came. 'And you wouldn't believe how beautiful it is. Very wild and unspoilt. See?' She held up a series of photographs in front of me like flash cards, and I felt under pressure to memorise them. No doubt she already had. 'No, the main thing now is just to source some decent thermal underwear. And ski boots. Apparently they do great ones in those discount supermarkets, I'll have to get up there early tomorrow because the flight's on Thursday morning and I can't believe I'm so behind on the packing—'

'Breathe, Barbara.'

'I am breathing.'

'I meant more slowly. You're starting to hyperventilate again.'

'Am I? Yes, I am. Shit. Now I *can't* breathe.'

'I'd slap you only I know you'd enjoy it.'

Barbara put down the photographs and took a few wild snorts, her nostrils flaring. 'Christ on a bike,' she said. 'I don't know if I can do this. Can I do this? Yes, of course I can. Sorry. I'm being silly again.'

Her knuckles were white. And to think that we'd believed that once the referral came in, it would be nothing but unadulterated joy and excitement; all the stresses and strains and unknowns of the last five long years miraculously swept away as Barbara set out on a new phase in her life, she and her little Russian baby. And it *was* joyous. It just hadn't quite turned out the way any of us had expected, that was all.

'You should have let me go along with you,' I told her.

'You have Cleo.'

'Ollie would have minded her.'

'And there's your job,' Barbara said doggedly. 'You can't just up and leave all those holiday reps for ten days to go to court in Russia with me. Look at the grief I've got.'

Barbara's chauvinistic boss had nearly had a canary when he discovered that his star employee was about to become a mum, and it wasn't even a conventional route. Barbara had nearly had to lay out employer legislation on his desk before he'd agree to her taking a week off to fly out.

'Plus there's all the schlepping around with the translators, and the meetings with Dimitri and the agency, and then the judge. It'd be no fun at all,' Barbara went on.

'And the orphanage visit,' I reminded her. The most important thing.

'Yes, of course. Of *course*, the orphanage.' A pause. I thought I saw pinpricks of sweat break out on her upper lip like little bullets. 'Maybe I could have done with you there for that.'

'Did you send the care package finally?'

She'd had one ready for the past year; all her little hairy hand-knitted cardigans, some cuddly toys, teething rings, that kind of thing. In general colours, because she didn't know whether she'd be getting a boy or a girl, obviously, and in a variety of small sizes. Once she got her referral, she'd planned to send off the package to the orphanage to give to the baby before she flew out. I wasn't sure of the psychology behind it, but it was a bonding thing anyway.

Of course, once she got the referral everything in the care package turned out to be obsolete, but I'd made her go out and buy new things. It was important to carry on preparations just as before; the parameters had simply changed, that was all. Expanded, so to speak.

'Yes,' Barbara confirmed, 'although I don't really know if Sergei will like any of it.'

'He will! He'll be delighted.'

'And I sent him a photograph of me too. God only knows what he'll make of me.' She sounded gloomy. 'He might want to run a mile, and who can blame him?'

We all knew what a surprise photographs could be.

'I hope you were smiling in it,' I warned her.

'Yes. I got Jane at work to take it. You know, with me in my white coat holding test tubes and things. I thought he might like that. Boys do, don't they?' She thought about this. 'Or he might think I look a bit unbalanced. He might think, feck this, I'm not going to Ireland to live with *that* one.'

'Or he might think, she's very interesting, I wouldn't mind having her for a mum.'

'He hasn't got any choice now, has he? Anyway, the test tubes will be something to talk about.' She thought about this, and amended it to, 'Or to draw pictures of, or something.'

There was a slight problem in that Sergei didn't speak any English. Barbara's Russian was still slow in coming on, even though since the referral she'd hurriedly embarked upon an intensive audio course and went around with earphones jammed on all the time, muttering feverishly under her breath.

'Give him six months home and you'll be chatting away to each other nineteen to the dozen,' I assured her.

'Whatever that means,' Barbara said. God, she was a right bag of misery today. I watched as her hand went absently to her purse. She'd developed the same fascination with it as she used to have with her phone. She stroked the purse, then withdrew her hand uncertainly, but within five seconds she'd be back pawing it again. And it was a big plastic orange yoke too, not a thing you'd want to touch of your own volition.

'Let me see him again,' I encouraged her.

'Are you sure?'

'Of course I'm sure. He's going to be your son.'

'I know, but I don't want to bore people. You know those mothers who stick photos of their kids in your face without you even asking to see them? The ones you end up next to at a dinner party? Kill me if I ever turn into one of them. I mean it.'

She opened the hideous orange purse and carefully extracted a photo. She had two photographs of Sergei. One she kept at home in a blue frame on the kitchen table so that she could see him at all times. At night she brought the frame upstairs and put it on her nightstand, and sometimes she took him on a visit in to the bathroom if she was doing a particularly onerous job like peeling the corn on her right foot, 'just for the company, like'. Then she'd look worried. 'Don't ever tell him I do that.'

'I can't decide what colour his eyes are,' she said now. 'Sometimes I think they're brown, but then other times I think they might actually be green.'

She propped the photo up against the sugar bowl on the table. Sergei looked back at us out of his brown/green eyes. To me, it wasn't the colour that always struck me. It was the seriousness of them, like he'd momentarily forgotten how to smile.

'He's very cute,' I said.

'Yes.'

'And his hair is nearly the same as yours.'

'Do you think so?' Barbara's hand went to her mop of hair.

'Just the colour,' I assured her. 'Not the texture.'

We stared at him again intently. Back in Russia, he must have had a crawly feeling around the back of his neck, or maybe a strange, unsettling chill around his calves (he was wearing shorts in the photo), what with these two maddish Irish women gawking at him in a kitchen in the Dublin suburbs, scrutinising his freckles — he had a smattering over a handsome, straight nose — and studying his lips and wondering where he got that tiny little scar just over his right eyebrow, and whether it might have been from chickenpox.

'I can't bear it,' Barbara burst out. 'I can't bear that he might have needed calamine lotion and they didn't have any, and there's me with rakes of the bloody stuff in work. Gallons of it.' We'd discussed the chickenpox thing before and it had clearly got in on her.

Then she took a breath, fanned her face, and said, 'There, I'm grand again now.' She looked at Sergei again. Stayed looking. 'You know,' she said quietly, 'I think I'm getting used to him.'

She looked at me and I thought, wow. She'd come a long way.

You see, Sergei had been a mistake. A mix-up, rather. Well, he must have been, because Barbara had requested a baby. A toddler at a stretch. 'Up to thirty-six months,' her application had clearly specified. Hence all the mad knitting of miniature hairy cardigans for the poor little devil. But Dimitri, he of the no phone calls or contact, had clearly been very busy behind the scenes after all, mostly confusing people's files, because instead of referring her a baby, he'd matched up Barbara with Sergei.

Sergei wasn't a baby. He wasn't even a toddler. Nor could he be described a tyke, a chisler or little 'un.

Sergei was five years old, and very tall for his age, and in the first photo Dimitri sent on, Sergei was in a school uniform with a severe tie and a severer haircut, all of which had the unfortunate effect of making him look like he was a smallish man off to work for the day.

'Oh my God,' Barbara had cried. She'd immediately thought Dimitri was double-jobbing. 'Is he running some kind of mail-order groom thing on the side? I don't want a husband, I want a baby.'

But there was no mistake. Sergei was matched with Barbara. She'd had no idea he wasn't a baby until we got home from France.

Naturally, she got on the blower straight away, me at her elbow. 'Give it to him straight now, Barbara. Tell him you're going to turn the referral down. And you won't be using his services again, either.'

'*Out*, Hannah. Now. Oh, hello, Dimitri?'

There followed a half-hour conversation with Dimitri. When Barbara came off the phone I expected her to tell me that she had a new referral, for a lovely, chubby six-month-old with curls. But she didn't. Dimitri said that he'd matched her with Sergei for several reasons: referrals, already slow, were nearly grinding to a halt and the wait for a baby would be much longer. She could wait if she wanted, but it would be a while yet. Then there was her single status. He felt she would do better with an older child. He finished off by saying that there were many, many older children waiting for a family, because almost everybody wanted babies, and nobody came to Dimitri looking for tall, gawky boys of five, with crew-cut hair and eyes that had forgotten how to laugh.

'Don't listen to him. That's just emotional blackmail. He's laying it on thick. Here, give me that phone. I'll ring him.'

Five years of waiting and toil, and now this?

But Barbara was looking very thoughtful and far away, and I had a bad feeling.

'How can I say no?' she agonised. 'How can I turn Sergei down?'

'But you can, Barbara. I don't mean to sound cold, but how can you take on a child so much older than what you were expecting? He'll have spent years more in an institution – how is that going to have affected him? You can't take him on just because you feel bad. What if it turns out that you can't cope? He'll be the one who'll suffer at the end of the day. You're not a do-gooder.'

'But I am! That's exactly what I am. A bloody do-gooder. Oh, I wish I'd never started this in the first place.'

'You don't have to go through with it. You can turn the referral down. Dimitri said so. You'll get a baby if you wait just a little bit longer.'

Barbara was shaking her head like a dog who'd just come out of a bath and was wet and confused. 'I don't know. I don't know. Just stop talking to me, please. No offence. But I can't bear it.'

Of course everybody else chipped in too as the news spread – 'Barbara, you'd be *mad*' and, 'That Dimitri! I knew it' and, 'I'd hold out, Barbara. You wouldn't know what you'd be getting into.'

In the end Barbara packed up her tent and disappeared for a weekend. Told nobody. Just found a music festival somewhere and set herself up on the fringes of all the youthful drinkers. She took Sergei's file with her, and slept on the hard ground for the weekend, ate over-priced, cold burgers and somehow came to a decision.

'I'm going to accept the referral,' she told us all when she arrived back, eerily calm-faced and very smelly. 'So from now on, I don't want to hear any more bitching about Dimitri, or remarks about Sergei's age. He's going to be my son. We both need love and support, people, OK?'

But first her social worker had to be consulted. She'd been assessed to adopt a baby, not a five-year-old child. There was some back and forth for a while but this time things went speedily, and she rang one evening and said, 'It's going ahead.'

On the surface Barbara was great. She wrote to the orphanage and got all the final paperwork in order. She organised her flights for the first of her two visits out – and she got on with the momentous preparations for having a new person in her home and her life.

Scratch the surface, though, and I could see all her insecurities and fears, and I was glad in a way. She wasn't going into this totally blind.

'You're the only one who knows I'm having mini-wobblers,' she said now, as we continued to stare at Sergei's photo.

'I know. Which gives me the right to say that it's not too late to change your mind.'

'It is. He knows I'm coming. I won't let him down.'

We absorbed this.

'It's going to be OK, you know.' I strove for reassurance.

'I know. I mean, it's not like I haven't got experience of older kids. There's Cleo, Sophie.'

I felt a small pang at the mention of Sophie. I hoped her bottom had recovered.

But mostly, of course, I thought of Ellen. It had been four months now since I'd last spoken to her and I missed her every day.

Chapter Four

Barbara had remained in contact with Ellen.

'I'm too old to take sides. You're my friends, and I love you both – eek, did I just say that? – and so I'm going to stay friends with the two of you. But – and I mean this, so please don't ask, because it may cause offence, just like when you ask for credit in those little shops – do not keep pumping me to find out if she said anything about you. We are not twelve. If you want to know what she thinks, you'll have to ring her up yourself. I can't say fairer than that.'

Barbara had maintained a steady string of phone calls and text messages to France, even before she'd left the country. At the airport I could hear her in the loo next to mine, whispering away. '. . . Of course not . . . Mark wouldn't . . . you have to mind yourself . . . Hannah may have picked it up wrong . . . that business with Ollie . . .'

I confronted her by the hand basins afterwards. 'I bloody did not pick it up wrong.'

Much rolling of eyes. 'I know you didn't, OK?'

'So why are you giving her all that rubbish about poor, deluded, jealous, sex-starved Hannah, imagining that every man in the world must fancy her because she's suddenly single?'

Several other women looked over with interest, whilst pretending to wash their hands. For once I had a racier life than anybody else.

'You're white-washing things,' I insisted to Barbara.

'What else can I say? She's chosen to stick by the creep and I have to support her in that.'

'You could tell her the truth. There's a novel idea.' I was very hurt. Barbara could have put an end to this whole thing back at the farmhouse.

219

If she'd told Ellen, 'Well, actually, I believe Hannah. Your husband is a bona fide slimeball who hit on her while you were pregnant,' then none of this would be happening.

But she hadn't said a word! OK, so she'd got her referral in the middle of it all and it had semi-scrambled her brain, but she could have clarified the situation at the first available opportunity afterwards, couldn't she?

It might be easy to dismiss me as a jealous, bitter friend – well, actually, not so easy, but Ellen had done it anyway – but it would be a lot harder to dismiss Barbara too.

'She doesn't want the truth, Hannah,' Barbara told me emphatically. 'She's pregnant, she's desperately trying to keep her family together. I can't ruin that for her.'

'So instead you're going to make me out to be some kind of pathetic liar?'

'Oh, Hannah. You know I believe you. But it's the best way. It's the *only* way.'

For Ellen, maybe. She got to live in her bubble, and keep her husband, and have Barbara as a loyal friend.

Me? I got banished back to Ireland, tarred with the terrible brush of having tried to steal my best friend's husband, while she was up the duff, just to add another new and low twist.

Jesus, even *I* hated myself, and I hadn't done anything wrong.

I thought maybe she would soften with the passage of time.

But nothing.

'Please tell me what's wrong,' Ollie said one evening after our Friday dinner. Harry had gone to his new apartment the week before, Cleo was in bed, and we were alone.

I froze.

'You've been home four months. You and Barbara are always whispering in the kitchen together. Nobody's talking about Ellen, and I know from Cleo that something happened in France. You came home days early, for God's sake.'

Yes, but I'd made up some excuse about accommodation and tourists and over-booking. I thought he'd bought it, especially as we hadn't seen him till the following Saturday anyway, as planned, and I'd sworn Harry to secrecy.

'Look, I know I've no right to pry into your life any more, Hannah, after . . . well, after what I've done. But maybe I can help.'

Why hadn't I told him? Mostly because on one level I found the whole episode demeaning and shameful, and something that just didn't happen to women like me. It happened to – and I was aware I was probably being snobbish here – floozies who drank too much and whose bra straps always showed, and who would make at least one appearance on an afternoon confessional show under the title, *Girlfrien', Watch Out 'Cos I Stole Your Man.*

So I'd been going to keep the whole sordid business to myself. But now Ollie was there, offering me sympathy and a shoulder to cry on, and he had such nice, broad shoulders. Before I knew it – two bloody glasses of wine – I was letting the whole saga tumble out.

'Jesus.' Even he was shocked, and Ollie was pretty unshockable. '*Mark?* Dirty fucker. Dirty, rotten fucker.'

I lapped it up. 'Say it again.'

'I can't believe he did that.' Much shaking of his head and dark looks and testosteroney snorts. It was gratifying. 'God, poor you, Hannah.'

I began to feel better and better.

Then he said, 'But, you know, it figures.' He saw my supremely defensive look because he added quickly, 'Knowing him, I mean. Look at the kind of guy he is: intense, obsessive, extremely low boredom threshold. Always chasing something new. Or someone.'

I blushed. I didn't know why. I wasn't used to being the kind of woman that men chased. I thought those days were behind me.

But now it struck me. I'd been pursued by someone, even if it was by yucky Mark. Was I still slightly dangerous, slightly mysterious, at the grand old age of thirty-eight?

I snuck a glance at Ollie to see if he was thinking, Christ, what did I throw away here? But he was too busy staring off into the middle distance and waxing lyrical about Mark.

'Plus, he's far too fond of himself. Name one other guy that we know who does fifty press-ups every morning before breakfast.'

'Well . . .'

'And his hair. Jesus Christ! He must keep the hair product people in business.' He looked particularly animated at this. 'And have you ever noticed the way he keeps giving people his profile?'

'What?'

'Like this.' Ollie lifted his chin in a poncy kind of way and turned his head to the side, so that I could see the line of his nose. 'I swear, that guy has worked out his best side. You could be in the middle of a conversation with him, and he'll turn his head just so you can admire his fucking nose.'

'It's a nice nose.' I was annoyed now. What was he saying – that only weird, hair-obsessed narcissists fancied me?

'It's a *nose*. I'm telling you, that guy is so far up his own arse, I'm surprised he can find his way out in the mornings.'

'You sound like you're jealous.'

'Jealous? Of Mark?' He laughed loudly, slapping his thigh for good measure. 'Yeah, sure. I was really jealous that week I spent in France fixing his roof while that fucker surfed the Internet downstairs.'

'Ollie!' But I was all ears. 'He was *surfing*?'

'I didn't want to bad-mouth him, but . . .' He pulled in his chair eagerly. 'There I was, dragged over like the poor relation to make that kip habitable before Ellen got out of hospital. Oh, man. Mark was supposed to know what he was doing, but I've seen five-year-olds with a better grasp of engineering. He was useless, Hannah. Fucking useless. Couldn't tell one end of a nail from the other. Every time he got up that ladder . . . do you know how many times he nearly had a fatal fall? In the end we banned him, me and that Marcel bloke, but he still had to be the big man, standing at the bottom shouting up these useless instructions. We tried to get him to do practical stuff, like clear out the kitchen, but no. He went on the Internet, looking up shit like how to turn tractor tyres into attractive raised beds.'

I couldn't help it: I laughed.

So did Ollie.

We laughed and laughed, and Mark became more ordinary – stupid, even – and the nasty words he'd dished out to me suddenly had less bite.

He was a bit of a plonker, I was beginning to realise.

'We felt so sorry for Ellen, me and Marcel,' Ollie confided. 'Moving to France with that idiot. I think that's when Marcel decided that he and Rosalie would have to take them under their wing.'

This character assassination was so deliciously devastating that I almost wanted to hug Ollie.

Thankfully, I managed to refrain from complicating matters further.

'You should have said something. You shouldn't have let me think you came home early because . . .'

'I wasn't up to the job?' He saw my face. 'You actually thought that!'

'Well . . .' I was mortified.

'Such a low opinion of me.' He enjoyed my face for another long minute before saying, 'I left when it became apparent that if I stayed much longer, yours and Ellen's friendship would have been severely strained. Anyway, I didn't want to ruin it for Ellen. They'd only just arrived.'

Ellen, being protected again. Why did everybody persist in thinking that she couldn't handle any kind of truth? She was the last person on this earth who needed to be mollycoddled.

I noted that I was going a little short on the mollycoddling front too. While this bitch-fest about Mark was highly satisfying, Ollie didn't seem too put out that someone had tried to have their way with me. In fact, he didn't seem put out at all.

'So he's finally shown his true colours,' he was saying. He was just one step short of rubbing his hands together in glee. 'I could have predicted this, you know.'

'If you could have predicted it, then why didn't you say something before they got married?'

'Ah, Hannah—'

'No, seriously. If you knew Mark better than any of us, why didn't you spare me and Ellen all this grief by putting your hand up in the beginning and saying, 'You know something? This guy's a fuckhead. Run a mile.'

He was looking at me, taken aback. And things had been so friendly up to now, too.

Intimate, even.

'But you didn't, did you? No, you took him out drinking in that chalet, and you got him to do that stupid quiz and then you told Ellen that he was a great guy.'

I knew I was being unreasonable. I knew by his face he was wondering why I was getting so excited over Mark.

I wasn't. I was wondering about Ollie, and where his passion was. What was between us any more? Was there any emotion that might suggest a spark? I wasn't looking for him to jump up in a fit of jealous rage and make a voodoo doll of Mark, but it would have been nice.

It would have meant that we were more than just friends with benefits. People who gravitated towards each other because it was our comfort zone, and who were in danger of drifting right back there again because it was too scary to do anything else.

'I had no idea then how he was going to turn out, Hannah.' He knew we'd gone beyond Mark; he just wasn't sure where.

'No? Actually I'm starting to think now that if we look hard enough, we get a pretty good idea of how people are going to turn out. And maybe we could all spare ourselves a lot of grief by not getting together in the first place.'

His face was tight and closed now. He stood. 'You can stop right there, Hannah. Because I can hear you loud and clear.'

Chapter Five

Cleo's birthday was 5 October. A padded envelope arrived in the post for her with a French stamp on it.

'It's Sophie's handwriting on the front,' Cleo informed me. 'She still puts her Es around the wrong way. Only don't say that to her because she gets mad as hell.'

I stared at the envelope. Cleo did too. The day she'd sunk her teeth into Sophie's backside was still fresh in her mind. Once or twice she'd come into my room in the middle of the night and whispered urgently, 'I had that dream again. Where I ate Sophie.'

'Oh, honey.'

'Only this time I had a bite out of Sam too, and the new baby.' She looked stricken. 'They tasted like marshmallows.'

'The pink or the white kind?'

She looked at me reproachfully; when would I learn that she had no sense of humour?

'Anyway, there's no need to explain to me that it's only a dream. I know that because Auntie Ellen—' She pulled herself up short. 'Is it still OK to call her that?'

'Of course it is. Of *course* it is.'

'She hasn't had the baby yet.'

'No.'

'When is she having it?'

'In two months' time. She's seven months pregnant now.'

I had her estimated due date up on my calendar. I have no idea why. It wasn't like I was going to be asked to be the birth partner or anything. Barbara had already been asked to do that, as Mark apparently wasn't great in these situations (quite good at getting women in the family way, though) and anyway, he would be needed to mind Sophie and Sam, as Rosalie didn't look after people's children while their parents gave birth. Something to do with a labour – not Ellen's, but some previous employer's – that had gone on for ninety-six hours.

'Why the blazes did she ask me?' Barbara had fretted. 'I *hate* all that stuff. And I'm not looking down at her fiddly bits to find out how much her cervix is dilated. I don't care how much she begs me.'

I'd have loved it. All the drama, the hospital smells, the panting. Being able to shout, 'Nurse! We need an epidural in here, pronto!' Maybe even taking a little dip in the birthing pool, although I suspect that might be for the pregnant partner only.

And then being there, actually present, when a whole new person was pushed into this world, all sticky and wriggly and tiny, and Ellen and me looking at each other, and going, 'Oh my God, oh my *God*,' and knowing this was the most special moment we'd ever shared.

Let's face it, it would be completely wasted on Barbara. 'I'm going to the crisps dispenser,' she would probably say, the minute it was all over.

'Sophie wants a girl,' Cleo advised me now. 'She wants to dress it up and stuff, and put it into her doll's pram and take it for walks.' She thought about this. 'She's going to be really raging if Auntie Ellen has another boy.'

'I don't suppose there's much she can do about it.'

Cleo looked at me quickly, then away. 'We're not going to see it, are we? The new baby.'

I had a cold feeling in my stomach. 'I don't know. Maybe not right away.'

'We won't see it because Auntie Ellen is cross with you, and I probably won't see Sophie or Sam again either, until they're grown-ups and then I won't recognise them anyway.'

My heart broke for her. And for me. 'Do you miss Sophie?'

Her reply was swift. 'Actually, no. She was very bossy. I was quite glad to get away in the end. I might like to see her again sometime in the future, though, when she's calmed down a bit.'

I had a feeling that Sophie would never calm down; she would undoubtedly end up as the CEO of some international company where she would rampage through people's lives, ordering them about and earning herself some colourful nicknames behind her back.

We looked at the envelope again. 'Aren't you going to open it?'

Cleo picked it up and felt it. Gave it a shake. 'I hope it's not a jumper,' she said worriedly.

She'd already got one of those that morning, from Barbara. Barbara had flown out to Russia on Thursday as scheduled, but had maniacally knitted through the day and night before her flight out in order to finish Cleo's present. 'It takes my mind off things.' She may well have been too distracted, though, because the jumper was a bit strange in the end. Technically it was a hoodie – 'I don't want her to be embarrassed in something mohair' – but the actual hoodie bit was smaller than the rest of the jumper, and when Cleo had pulled it up over her head it had fit so snugly that she looked a bit like a tadpole.

'I think I'll leave the hood down,' she decided in the end. 'Don't tell Auntie Barbara.'

I imagined that Cleo's birthday was the furthest thing from Barbara's mind at that moment. Actually, I wasn't sure what was on Barbara's mind. Communications weren't great from her part of Russia, and I'd got several terse texts saying things like, 'Landed. Bloody freezing,' and, disconcertingly, 'Dimitri a dote. Meeting his mother this afternoon.'

There had been no texts about Sergei or the orphanage or meeting him for the first time, but I was assuming that she simply hadn't got there yet.

Or else she had, of course, and it was all going terribly wrong. But no, I wasn't going to allow myself to go down that road. Barbara had been prepared for every eventuality, including Sergei running from the room screaming upon the sight of her, to *her* running screaming from the room, to them both deciding that, while it was a nice idea on paper, in reality it was never going to work out.

I would hear from her soon, I was sure of it.

'Open it,' I urged Cleo.

She took a deep breath. 'OK.'

If I'm being honest, I was slightly worried about the contents. Ellen must have organised it. And she was furious with me. Would Clyde's ear pop out? One of his trotters? Or a court summons for Cleo's arrest for oral assault of Sophie?

I knew I was being stupid. But Ellen and I had never fallen out before and I just didn't know what to expect.

In the end the contents of the envelope were harmless. Sophie and Sam had made cards, and coloured them in in crayon, and they were very pretty even though Sophie's card was quite violently red and the pig (Clyde, I presume) she'd drawn on the cover seemed to have abnormally long teeth. They were practically fangs.

But Cleo didn't notice and she put her cards up on the mantelpiece, delighted.

'Oh, look, Cleo.'

Ellen had put in a beautiful embroidered top for her. Very rustic, obviously, and no doubt every fibre in it was natural and hand woven, but the colours were pink and purple and girlish, and Cleo exclaimed, 'I want to put it on straight away!'

Thank you, Ellen. I couldn't say it out loud to her, but I said it in my head.

Somehow, the present seemed very hopeful, or something. She hadn't cut us completely off. Or Cleo anyway.

When Cleo had run upstairs to put the top on, I tipped the envelope up, wondering if there was anything else in there. A note for me, maybe.

But there wasn't.

Chapter Six

Ollie, Muriel, Harry and I took Cleo to the circus for her birthday. 'It's years since I've been to the circus,' said Muriel happily, not looking at all out of place in her purple eye shadow, skinny jeans (what the hell?) and knee-high boots. There was something so wrong about it all that it was almost right. 'Oh, come on, let's sit near the front,' she said skittishly.

I was suspicious at the effort she was making. It was just the circus. Could it be the first part of an offensive to win Harry back?

'No idea,' Ollie said tersely when I put this to him.

Here came Harry now, in his usual non-circus clothes of V-necked jumper and well-worn pants, plodding through the crowds – 'Excuse me, excuse me, oops, sorry' – before joining us on our bench. 'Home-made peanut brittle!' he announced, and doled out little brown paper bags.

We all peered in cautiously. Hard, orange nuggets nestled within, sporting vicious protrusions that would take the mouth off you, and with the peculiar sheen of nuclear waste.

'Mind your dentures,' he called to Muriel cheerily.

She went brick red and bristled. 'Thank you, Harry.'

He never learnt. He also didn't seem to notice Muriel's glamorous new look; he just squashed in beside her, creasing her skinny jeans and stamping on her new high-heeled boots. She extracted her foot painfully and rearranged her hair, which she'd clearly had done professionally, possibly with an instruction to the stylist to, 'Gimme a Farrah.'

'How's your new apartment?' she cordially asked him. 'Working out well for you, I hope?'

I leant in closer. I didn't want to miss this.

Harry gave the question his usual due consideration. 'I think so, yes,' he

229

replied after an age. 'I have nice neighbours. Lots of single people like myself.'

Muriel tutted sympathetically. 'It must be hard, moving into a community like that, from such a settled area. And all those old people.' You'd think she was thirty-five herself. 'Well, whenever you get lonely, you must pop by some evening and I'll make you your tea.'

Tea! I thought cooking, and food, was completely off limits after he'd sautéed Susie.

Harry's brow puckered. 'I don't think I have any evenings free,' he said.

Muriel chuckled. 'Don't be silly, Harry.'

'Well, I do cookery classes three nights a week. Then there's dinner at Hannah's on Friday nights. Saturday is poker.'

'You play poker?' She couldn't hide her surprise.

'And on Thursday I see my chiropodist. I used to have Sunday nights free, but Pete — he's in 4C — he started up a pub crawl. We go to a different pub every week, and we have half a pint of Guinness with blackcurrant, and then we rate the pub on these little cards that he's drawn up. You know, cleanliness, service, friendliness, value for money.' Harry's cheeks were rosy now. 'I bring the pencils because somebody always forgets—'

'Oh, just stop it, Harry.' Muriel's nicey-nice attitude had frosted over. 'You're just trying to puff yourself up, making out that you're so exciting and . . . and *happening*.'

'Well, I'm sorry. I didn't mean to,' said Harry, confused.

'I was only asking you over because I felt sorry for you. It's not like I'm sitting around twiddling my thumbs myself.'

I shot a look at Ollie; I thought that's exactly what she was doing.

'I never said you were—' Harry began.

'You're not the only one with a busy social schedule, you know!' she finished rather triumphantly, giving her big hair a savage adjustment.

But she refused to say any more. Just angled her skinny-jeans-covered knees towards the ring and gave a secret smile.

'What's she talking about?' I whispered to Ollie. I suspected she was involved in some heavy game-playing to pique Harry's interest.

But he was already poking about in his paper bag, extracting peanut brittle. 'I don't know,' he said.

'But you live with her.'

'Doesn't mean she tells me everything.'

Of course, he was still mad at me since our row. Relations had cooled dramatically. He hadn't even come over for dinner on Friday, citing a work do. Which was a bit rich, given that he was the only employee in his company – what had he done, gone out on the piss with himself?

He was clearly unhappy now at having to sit next to me on the bench, but Cleo had decided upon the seating arrangements. He sat there like a school mistress beside me, his thighs clenched in tight like I had some communicable disease.

I suppose in a way I couldn't blame him. I'd more or less told him that us getting together ten years ago had been a nasty mistake. Naturally he was hurt. But I was hurt too. *He'd* hurt me, good and proper. And now things were all horrible and stiff between us again, and maybe I should have shut my trap and said nothing.

But at the same time it had stopped the slow drift. Wasn't that what I'd been afraid of? Of the two of us gravitating back together like a pair of old, turned-up shoes under the bed because, until proven otherwise, we were more friends than anything else?

I snuck a glance at him.

He didn't look too friendly now. He was aloof and distant, and not at all like his usual easy-going, beer-swilling, spicy-food-making self.

'Oh, look,' I said to him, 'how long are you going to keep this up?'

Haughty eyes transferred to mine. 'I beg your pardon?'

'This sulking.'

Temperature dropping to freezing now. 'I'm not sulking.'

'Well, whatever you're doing. Please. Can we just get back to normal?'

He shook his head slowly, as though marvelling at the sheer neck of me. 'What, just because it suits you? You can't have it every which way, Hannah.'

Cleo leant over. Her little cheek was bulging under the strain of the peanut brittle. 'When's it going to start?' She was missing a bunch of soaps for this and was naturally anxious.

'Any second now.'

She nodded to me and warned Ollie, 'You'll have to hold her hand when the tigers come out.'

'Don't worry,' Ollie assured her, 'I'm on the case.'

When the lights came down Ollie moved away another inch and crossed his arms tightly over his chest and kept them there.

I told myself I was glad, even though I *was* afraid of tigers.

★

We stumbled out into the darkness two and a half hours later, on a sugar high, semi-deafened, and with our hands sore from clapping. The ring-master had been very insistent that we give every single act 'a big hand, now, folks! A bigger hand! I can't HEAR you!'

'How about we go see the animals being fed round the back?' said Ollie, enthusiastically.

'Sounds great!' I said.

'OK!' he said. 'Let's go!'

We were being Completely Normal. For Cleo's sake, of course. If we sounded jolly enough, I'd discovered, then we didn't have to make too much eye contact, which was a relief all round.

'Come on then, Dad!' boomed Ollie. 'And Mum!'

Muriel was scrabbling about, trying to inspect the back of her jeans. Some little fecker in the row behind her had put down a half-eaten toffee on her seat when she wasn't looking, and she was concerned that it had attached itself to her buttock.

'Not me,' she said. Ah! The offending toffee. It was discovered, unpeeled, and hurled to the ground. 'I have a date.'

We all ground to a halt.

Eyes swivelled from person to person, startled.

A date? Muriel?

'What was that, Mum?' Ollie said. He rummaged about in his right ear with a finger, as though suspecting some kind of blockage.

Muriel gave another tremendous flick of her hair, almost injuring a man behind her, and announced, 'I'm going for a drink.' A pause. A look at Harry. 'With Anthony.'

Anthony. More swivelling eyes, even though the chap was bound to have a name.

So Muriel hadn't dressed up for Harry at all. Her excitement was nothing to do with him.

'Well,' said Ollie at last. 'Well, well.'

Harry said nothing at all. Maybe he was terribly upset. Whatever about separating, the idea of either of them dating someone else, well, that was a whole new development.

For us all. There was no chance of reconciliation at all now. Or little, anyhow. If Muriel was casting her eye about elsewhere, then what hope did Harry have?

He looked up suddenly. 'Anthony? Anthony Jackson? Who reads our gas meter?'

'I knew it!' Muriel exploded. 'I knew you'd try and make fun of him!'

'I wasn't—'

'What's wrong with someone who reads gas meters? Someone has to do it, don't they? Otherwise none of us would get bills. Anthony is a lovely, lovely man who helped me with my boiler last week, when the men in my own family wouldn't lift a finger!'

A look between Ollie and Harry: oops.

'Why *shouldn't* I go on a date with him?'

'No reason—'

But she cut Harry off again. 'Why shouldn't I have some company in my life, now that my Susie is gone?'

Not Susie again. Please.

'So he's picking me up outside in his van and we're going for a drink in the hotel.'

She looked around at us all, defying us to take the gloss off it.

'I hope you enjoy yourself,' said Ollie at last.

'Absolutely,' I weighed in. 'You and Anthony.'

'Go, Gran,' Cleo announced.

Muriel gave a final adjustment to her hair, and hitched her handbag further up on her shoulder. Her parting words were for Harry. 'You're not the only one who's moving on, you know.'

She turned and threaded her way through the crowds, heading towards a white van in the distance that had a power company logo emblazoned across the side. Then we lost sight of her.

'So,' said Ollie, flatly. His mother embarking upon a new romance seemed to have knocked him back a bit.

Or maybe it was the realisation that everybody else seemed to be moving on except him.

And me . . .

We were all relieved when my phone began shrieking in my pocket. It was Barbara. From Russia.

'Barbara! I thought you were never going to get in contact!' I took advantage of the fuzz on the line to get in a quick, 'Tell me absolutely everything about Sergei before I burst.'

But the line was terrible and Barbara's voice just came out of the phone in disjointed bubbles. '. . . Can't talk . . . at the airport now . . . flight just been called . . .'

'But, Barbara, you're not due home for two more days.'

I was worried now. Something had gone wrong. Dimitri, maybe. The courts had found a problem – sometimes they did. Her file had a piece of paper out of date, and they had told her to get the next flight home and sort it out.

Or . . .

She had gone to the orphanage to meet Sergei and somehow it hadn't worked out.

'Barbara, are you OK? Barbara, what's happening?'

Her voice suddenly burst into my ear, as clear as a bell. 'I'm absolutely fine. It's Ellen. The baby's coming early. I'm flying to France now.'

Chapter Seven

It was interview day. I only did three days of interviews in Dublin for holiday rep staff during the entire year, and the very next day was one of them.

My timing, as usual, sucked.

Right now there were two hundred and eighty-nine young hopefuls sitting in a conference room in a hotel near the airport rehearsing in their heads how fabulous/hard-working/willing to work for shite money they were. Some of them were wearing 'fun' clothing, like clown's shoes, obviously in the hopes of imparting just how much craic they were. Others had guitars, and probably woeful renditions of Oasis songs, ready to pull out at the drop of a hat.

As for me, I was next door in another conference room, with two bottles of sparkling mineral water and a man called Duncan.

He was from the English arm of the travel company, based in Telford. They always sent him over for the interviews on the very real chance that I might hire a load of alcoholic Irish idiots.

'They do not,' he'd said, scandalised, when I said this to him. 'We need an interview panel. We can't have a panel with only one person on it.'

He made it sound like that would be totally illegal.

'It's OK, Duncan, I was only joking.'

I'd met Duncan three times a year every year for the past five years. We hadn't really got beyond the pleasantries, no matter how hard I tried. For a good while I had persisted with the jokey thing, like, 'Hey, Dunc! Another roomful of wasters out there for us to weed our way through!' but this only seemed to upset him and so I stopped.

He shuffled his papers now. He always had the same list of questions that he asked applicants, such as, 'Where do you see yourself in five years' time?'

This, to an eighteen-year-old potential holiday rep. In a pub, probably, and some of them were naive enough to say it.

But Duncan routinely came armed like he was recruiting for NASA, and put a great deal of stock by appearances. He didn't like nose rings, or odd-coloured hair, and he got very unnerved at the sight of a tattoo.

'Shall we get started?' he said. He checked his watch. His flight back tonight was at precisely eighteen twenty, as he had reminded me four times already.

The problem was, my head wasn't there today. It was in France, and a hospital somewhere, and poor Ellen spread-eagled on a table and covered in a thick layer of sweat. Or maybe even being cut open inch by inch. I'd never seen a Caesarean section, but I could imagine what it would be like.

'Fizzy water?' Duncan offered a little worriedly.

'Yes. Please.'

I'd had a feeling of dread in my stomach since Barbara's call yesterday evening. No further information had ensued, even though I had continued to shout into the phone, 'But she's only seven and a half months gone!' and, 'What did she say on the phone? Did she give a reason?' Eventually, when I could hear nothing from Barbara's end, except fuzz, I was forced to hang up and take to chewing my fingernails instead.

Something must have gone wrong. She wasn't due for weeks yet. What had happened that she was having the baby now?

Too damn thin, that was the problem. Or too low in iron, or something. Or maybe she'd got pre-eclampsia, and had swelled up like a puffer fish.

Or maybe the problem was the baby. Maybe there was something wrong with it. I hoped to God not, but these things happened.

I tried to reassure myself with the knowledge that she was in the best place. As in, a hospital. Barbara might even be there now, and everything would be OK.

Deep down, I couldn't shake the feeling that it was somehow to do with me. That all that business with Mark had shaken her so much that her already rocky pregnancy had taken a nose dive, and that her ending up in hospital was entirely my fault. I may well be listed as a cause on her medical notes. *Reason for premature labour: her horrible friend Hannah, who accused her husband of dropping the hand. Accused denies all charges.*

Ring, Barbara, ring.

But she didn't, of course. I'd checked my phone every five minutes last night, and then slept with it under my pillow all night long. I was sure I'd get a call. If it was an emergency, then she'd probably have the baby during the night – they usually arrived around 4 a.m., didn't they? – and I'd get a phone call before dawn broke.

At eight I gave up and rang Barbara. She didn't pick up. Then I rang Rosalie. I had her number for emergencies. She didn't pick up either.

Then – and this is how desperate I was – I rang Mark. His number was still on my phone. I probably should have deleted it. It's not like I ever used it much, as Ellen was always the first port of call. But it was there as back-up, the way I had the numbers of most of my friends' husbands and other halves.

I let it ring once and then I hung up.

He probably wouldn't have answered it anyway. Not to me, the she-devil. Plus, he could well be up to his oxters in a delivery suite and be quite unavailable to take my calls.

But just in case Barbara had texted in the meantime, I ducked beneath the table under the pretext of getting something from my handbag, and sneakily checked my phone.

Nothing.

What was going on in France?

'Hannah?' It was Duncan, stooping down beside me.

I came up so fast that I bumped my head on the table.

'I really think we should get started,' he said.

'Yes, yes, Duncan, let's get started.'

And so in they trooped, one hopeful after another, clutching sweaty CVs and bottles of water and references from other jobs, often not good ones.

'Hello there!' I began cheerfully every time, fair play to me, even though in my head I was breathing in and out like I was in labour myself. 'Tell us a bit about yourself.'

It always stumped them. For some reason they never expected it. They thought you'd make them stand there while you went through their CV and asked forensic questions like, 'So tell us now, Geraldine, tut tut, how come you only got a D minus in your Irish exam in the Leaving Cert?'

But ask them to talk a little about themselves . . . They would look at you like it was a trick question, and often I would have to help them along by pressing, 'Well, why are you here today after a rep job?'

Their faces would clear happily. 'Oh, the rep job! I *really* want this job, I can't tell you how much, I'm a real people person, you can probably tell that, and I *love* children, and everybody says I have this massive sense of humour, will I tell you a joke? No, no, I have a really good one, it won't take a minute. Three men walk into a bar, right? . . .'

I made notes, pages and pages of scrawled words on CVs and photos, such as, 'Total pain in arse' and, 'Would have to order outsize uniform at great cost to company'. Or sometimes just, 'No, no, NO.' Hopefully the freedom of information act would never come to bear on my scribblings.

On one of the CVs I'd written, 'Ellen is in labour fourteen hours and thirty-two minutes now.'

And no phone call from Barbara.

'Will we press on?' said Duncan, my light ray of sunshine.

'Yes, Duncan.' I tried to swallow my worry. 'Let's press on.'

'Hannah? It's me.'

'BARBARA! Oh, thank Christ. Where are you?'

'I'm standing outside the—' Her voice was drowned out by the wail of an ambulance. I gathered the missing word was 'hospital'.

'What's happening? Just tell me, please.' Suddenly I felt frantic. I had a feeling of foreboding, like Barbara was going to say something shocking, and that I would never get the chance to make things right with Ellen again. For no reason at all I pictured Barbara wearing a blood-spattered green apron, and panting hard.

'It's a girl!' Barbara announced. 'Don't ask me what weight – I'm crap on all that – but she's a bit midgety, comparatively speaking, what with being early, so she's in an incubator in the special unit and they'll keep her there for a while until she fattens up a bit.'

A baby. A *live* baby. A girl.

I felt wobbly with relief.

Sophie would be delighted.

'Oh, and she's yellow. Jaundice, or something. They said it'll wear off in a couple of days, but right now she looks like she's been hitting the Jack Daniel's hard.'

'Yes, yes.' I confess I had lost interest in the baby. Well, not so much lost interest, but why wasn't Barbara saying anything about Ellen?

'She's going to be called either Amelia or Tania.' The sneer in Barbara's voice let me know exactly what she thought of those. 'Ah, well. Each to their own.'

'*Ellen*, Barbara,' I butted in. I couldn't help myself any longer. 'How is Ellen?'

'Great,' said Barbara, sounding surprised. 'Well, obviously she's a bit knackered after forcing out a five-pound baby – oh, so I *do* know the weight – but when I left her ten minutes ago she was sitting up eating toast.'

Eating *toast*? What about all the drama? After getting everybody so excited, wouldn't you at least think she'd be in an incubator too? Or after losing a satisfying amount of blood? Not that I wished it on her or anything, but after twenty-four hours of being in the horrors with worry, I expected something a little less pedestrian than some toast-eating tale.

But then Barbara said, 'Well, she needs to build her strength up, after going into labour so suddenly like that. They don't really know what happened. She was at home, she said, not doing anything special, just swilling out the pig shed—'

'Swilling out the pig shed? At seven and a half months pregnant?'

'Oh, I know, the doctors took the head off her too, but she maintained it was a gentle swill; that she found it therapeutic. Anyway, there she was, swilling away, when her waters broke all over the place. Apparently there were gallons of the stuff. Anyway, she wasn't alarmed. Why, I don't know. If it was me I'd have been calling in the SWAT team to get to hospital. But she mopped it all up, cool as a breeze, apologised to the pigs, and was thinking about phoning the doctor for a bit of advice when the first contraction came. She said it was like being hit on the back of the knees by a sledgehammer. When they found her, she was face down in the pig trough, eight centimetres dilated.'

How they knew this was anybody's guess. Possibly she had measured it herself. I wouldn't put it past her.

'Anyway, by the time they got her to the hospital her blood pressure was all over the place and they were threatening a C-section. She wouldn't, though; kept insisting that she'd have a natural birth. In the end they let her get on with it herself because they were worried about the baby's lungs, what with them not being mature enough at only thirty-whatever weeks, so they stuck a needle into her and pumped her full of steroids – not for her, for the baby – and she was able to hang on for another twelve hours and that's when I got there.'

'So you were there for the actual birth?' I was pierced with envy.

'Yes,' said Barbara in disgust. 'I thought I'd have missed it. And I was jet-lagged to hell, so I wasn't much in the mood for all that hand-holding stuff, as you can imagine.'

Yes. I could just picture Barbara telling Ellen, 'Oh, just *push*, for heaven's sake.'

'Will you tell her I said congratulations?' I said.

'Hannah . . .'

'Fine. Don't, then.' I felt a bit teary. Could a simple message of goodwill not be passed on for fear that it might be misconstrued as something else?

Barbara said gently, 'Look, she's very tired, and she's had an awful fright, and she's on her own in there. I'll tell her in a few days, OK? When she gets home.'

'All right.' Then, 'Why is she on her own?'

'Mark's minding the kids. He'll be in later.'

'He wasn't there for the birth?'

I knew Barbara was the assigned birth partner and all that – something that was now striking me as odd.

'He was there at the beginning,' Barbara said, 'and then he turned up afterwards, but no, not for the actual event itself.'

Definitely very odd, even if he wasn't very good in hospital situations, or whatever that claptrap was that Ellen had fed us.

'What man isn't there for the birth of his own child?' I questioned Barbara.

But Barbara, as usual, wasn't going to get involved in anything remotely resembling gossip. 'I don't know, Hannah. Obviously it's something they'd already decided.'

Yes, some weird, sick arrangement. But who was I to comment?

Barbara was once again on hand to pour big buckets of cold water on my conjecture. 'Anyway, I saw him earlier and he's absolutely delighted about the baby. Brought Ellen in this massive bunch of flowers and chocolates and everything.'

I let it go, even though I thought the whole thing was strange: Ellen going into premature labour, and asking Barbara to be the birth partner. That *anybody* would choose Barbara to be a birth partner was in itself very odd.

'Barbara? Barbara, are you still there?' In all the drama, I'd nearly forgotten to ask. 'What about Russia? And Sergei?'

Another ambulance squealed by in the background. 'I'll be home tomorrow,' she shouted over it. 'I'll tell you everything then.'

Chapter Eight

I came home from work three hours later to find a strange man on my doorstep. Given that I had just loaded Duncan onto a plane, his complaints still ringing loudly in my ears, my mood wasn't the best.

'Be off with you,' I said haughtily, as I got out of my car. 'I have no intention of changing my electricity, telephone or satellite television provider so go harass somebody else.'

This usually worked. I felt no qualms about my rudeness. How would these people like it if I turned up on *their* doorsteps at dinner time and tried to flog them a holiday rep job in Greece? Not blooming much, I'd bet.

I was about to announce that I had a large Rottweiler out the back, straining at a leash, when the man turned. I noted he was missing the usual greasy sheen of the door-to-door salesman, and the well-palmed clipboard. But the biggest giveaway was his eyebrows, which were dark, incredibly supple and already inching up his forehead.

'*Nick?*'

'Hey.' His smile was like the sun coming out from behind the clouds. I don't think I'd ever seen him smile before.

And then I realised it was for me.

'I was in the area,' he said. 'I thought I'd drop by.'

My mind was scuttling about all over the place. We'd exchanged numbers and addresses at the airport that day, along with vague post-holiday promises to 'meet up sometime'. But had either of us really meant it?

He saw my face. His own fell. 'You didn't really mean it, did you? About meeting up?'

'Yes! Of course I did! Christ, yes!' I was overcompensating now. 'Great to see you!'

I stumbled forward to give him a kiss on the cheek. Somehow, in my haste, I missed and got him on the nose.

He got me on the chin.

'Sorry—'

'No, I'm sorry—'

We took a moment to disentangle ourselves, and to wipe the saliva from our faces.

He looked me up and down. 'I hardly recognise you with your clothes on,' he said at last. 'Your work clothes, I mean.'

I was all got up in high heels and a trouser suit. The interviewees expected it, even though they turned up in frightful stuff themselves.

'I could say the same for you.'

He was in a jacket and what could only be described as a pair of slacks. He looked down at himself with a sigh. 'I know. I've been out assessing claims. Calling people blatant liars, that kind of thing. Generally I only get away with it when I'm in a shirt and tie.'

'I can imagine,' I commiserated.

Apart from the awful clothes, he looked . . . good. Not half as miserable as he used to be, anyway. Also, he wasn't as short as I'd remembered, and I was wearing heels. I snuck a quick look at the heels of his shoes, but thank God there was no evidence that they were built up in any way.

'Well!' I said. It was a little awkward now. 'What brings you to the area, then, claims?'

'No,' he said.

For a second I thought he was going to say that it was me. That he'd been thinking of me compulsively and had jumped into the car before he knew what he was doing.

'A stag party,' he said.

I made sure to keep smiling. 'Very good.'

'Someone from work. They're always getting married. I think we're starting off in Temple Bar with the intention of ending up in Bad Bobs at about three o'clock in the morning completely ossified,' he said bravely.

'Good luck with that.'

'Thank you. Even though I know you don't mean it.' He looked down at his shoes – black, plain, insurance-type shoes – and then back at me. 'The thing is, I have a couple of hours to kill first.'

I had two hundred and eighty-nine CVs in my bag to shortlist and then fax through to Duncan by Monday. I also had a hot date with the local Chinese takeaway facility and the TV remote control.

'Would you like to come in?'

My kitchen looked different with Nick in it. Maybe it was because I was so used to Ollie sprawled at the kitchen table, or else cooking and leaving a trail of destruction behind him.

Nick was contained. He sat rather rigidly on the couch as we waited for the takeaway food to arrive (he'd confessed a weak spot for chicken chow mein). The jolly talk about Bad Bobs had died away and he seemed a little uncomfortable now, shifting a bit and crossing and recrossing his legs. I wondered whether he thought he may have made a mistake after all, coming to see me in Dublin, like one of the those holiday romances that you follow up back home, only to realise that the tanned, witty, gorgeous creature you shagged in Torremolinos was really a fat, plain, uninteresting girl with a skin problem once you got her back in Crumlin. Not that I'd been tanned, witty or gorgeous to begin with.

Best to tackle it head on. We were both adults here, after all. 'Listen,' I said, 'if you want to go . . .'

Now he was wriggling about on the couch like he had worms. Dear God. And sort of *scratching* at himself. With one final violent twitch, he reached under himself and extracted a Barbie doll from beneath the sofa cushion. She had only one arm, but the one that she had was fixed rigidly over her head in a salute, which might indeed have caused him some discomfort.

'Your daughter's,' he stated.

Well, it wasn't mine. I could see him look around now, wondering where she was.

'She's with her dad tonight,' I told him. 'She won't be back till the morning.'

I had just meant it as information. Honestly. But somehow it immediately took on a different connotation in the confines of the living room. I might as well have hissed sleazily, 'We're all alone, get your kit off, I can go three times, how about you?' What kind of a brazen hussy must he think I was, that I was laying out my stall before the food had even arrived?

But it turned out that this was all in my head because he said casually, 'Ollie, right?'

There was no hint of recrimination in his voice. No underlying snide tone that said, 'Oh, yeah, that laid-back bastard who left you because his mammy kicked his daddy out and he was terribly confused.'

'Yes.'

He took another slug of beer and watched me. 'How's that working out?'

'OK, I suppose. Civil enough. Well, it has to be really, for Cleo's sake. And how about you and . . . um . . .' Fuck. I'd forgotten her name. And there he was, so interested in me, and I couldn't even remember who he was heartbroken over.

'Elaine.'

'Elaine. Of course.'

He gave a laugh. 'We're not civil. Can't stand the sight of each other. Thankfully, we don't run into each other often, but she was home recently for a funeral and I saw her in the car park and I told her what a creep she was.'

I was mildly shocked. 'You didn't, did you? Can you even call a woman a creep?'

'I don't see why not.' He sounded entirely reasonable.

Which was why it was a little disconcerting to discover that he'd let rip in a church car park after a funeral.

'I can't tell you how much better it made me feel.' And he grinned proudly like a five-year-old who had upended the sandbox just for the hell of it.

I found myself laughing. 'You're full of surprises, aren't you?'

'Try me,' he said.

It came out as a challenge. The air was suddenly thick again, only this time he had made it happen. We watched each other across the living room, the atmosphere all crackly and weird and kind of sexy, and I don't know whether I was relieved or disappointed when the doorbell rang and Andy, from the local takeaway, who could find his way to my house blindfolded and in the dark, roared through the letterbox, 'Open up, Hannah. It's half cold already.'

We ate at the kitchen table, me wishing I hadn't ordered barbequed ribs, as they were a bitch to eat whilst trying to remain remotely attractive-looking.

I nearly choked altogether when Nick commented casually, 'Lovely baby they had, wasn't it? Tania.' My eyes must have been like saucers because he faltered a bit. 'You *did* know?'

'Yes, of course I did, God, yes. Barbara rang me immediately,' I bragged.

'The spit of Ellen,' Nick commented comfortably. He must have a sister or two, because, unlike most men, he was clearly well versed in all the right things to say in these situations. In a minute he would comment on the birth weight.

Another rush of jealousy my end. 'You've seen her?'

How could that be? The child had only been born that day, so unless Nick was a dab hand at the old transubstantiation . . .

'Here.' He was taking out his phone, and finding something on it, and passing it across to me. 'Mark sent it on to me earlier.'

Mark. The name sent a cold stab of dislike into my stomach.

Nick put his phone into my hands. It was warm from his body. I found myself looking straight into Ellen's tired, but slightly crazy eyes. I recognised that post-birth look, having had it myself – when you were knackered, high on drugs, flattened by pain, and with a birth canal so stretched that it would give the Suez one a run for its money. But, overriding all these emotions was the sheer YES factor of having produced the wondrous creature that now lay in your arms, and that's exactly how Ellen looked as she beamed/grimaced into the camera.

The baby was beautiful. She looked like a little old man, of course, all scrunched up and shrunken in a pale blue blanket but I could see wisps of auburn hair poking out, and her mouth was definitely Ellen's.

I had no idea I was crying until Nick said, in alarm, 'Hey!' and then I found a man's handkerchief pressed into my hand and he was patting my back awkwardly like I was having an asthmatic episode. 'Are you OK?'

I buried my face in his handkerchief to give us both time to recover. 'I just haven't spoken to her since . . . you know, since we left France.'

I handed his phone back to him, and the picture of smiling Ellen, feeling more bereft than ever.

Nick was silent. He must be putting things together in his mind: my fight with Mark, my second fight with Ellen, the order to leave the farm, and now the discovery that I hadn't been in touch with her since.

'I didn't make a pass at him,' I blurted.

He said nothing.

'I know that's what you're probably thinking.'

'Actually, it never occurred to me—'

'Or maybe Mark said something to you, I don't care. Because you might as well know. He tried it on, I turned him down, and then he turned the whole thing around on me to save his marriage.' I lifted my chin. 'So there you have it.'

245

Well, that pretty much killed everything stone dead. All the little hints of flirtation, the warm looks, the shared companionship over the barbequed ribs – I'd forced him to accept one – it all fizzled out like a bottle of flat champagne. Nick was looking around, probably for the door. He'd been invited in for a nice chicken chow mein and a beer, and now this.

Well done, Hannah, I congratulated myself. Well shagging done. For the first time in ten years, I had an eligible, attractive man in my house, both of us single – *single* – and probably gasping for sex if we would only acknowledge it, and I had gone and blown it all by bleating on about my embarrassing ejection from France.

'Anyway,' I said, trying to take back something that couldn't be taken back, 'water under the bridge.'

A lot of men would be delighted to leave it at that. It got them off the hook.

But Nick scarcely flinched. 'It's not, though. You're clearly upset over it. You and Ellen have been friends for a long time.'

'Two decades,' I said, and I was off again, crying my eyes out. 'I miss her so much. I mean, Barbara's great, but she won't go to chick flicks with me, and she hates shopping, and she won't talk to me at all after I've had three glasses of wine because she says nothing I say is fit for human consumption.'

'She's a hard woman, all right,' Nick agreed. I realised that his hand was still on my back. It was very nice.

'I feel like someone has died or something, which is ridiculous, because neither of us has. And you know something? I'm raging, too, because it's so unfair. I did nothing wrong, but she wouldn't listen to me. Wouldn't do me the courtesy of hearing me out, after twenty years of friendship. She went and believed him when anybody with half a brain can tell that he's a slithery, selfish bollocks.'

Nick's hand stilled a little – he clearly wasn't expecting such fruity language – but after a moment it resumed its cathartic patting.

'I don't blame you. For being angry.'

'Thank you!' And, actually, I was surprised by my anger. It wasn't something I'd given any space to so far. Maybe I'd felt I had no right to be angry. But right now I was blindingly, furiously angry with Ellen, and the way she'd turned her back on me.

I did a bit more crying, Nick did more patting, and at some point the congealing takeaway food was removed and replaced by a nice cup of tea.

'Are you feeling better now?' he murmured.

God, he should be bottled and sold.

'Yes. Sorry. You probably want to go now.'

'Not at all.'

'You don't have to be polite.'

'I'm rarely polite,' he assured me. 'I'd just rather hang around here than go to that stag party.' Then he looked anxious. 'That was a joke, by the way. Please don't start crying again. I mean, do if you want, obviously. I just don't want to be the cause of it.'

'I think I'm OK for the moment,' I told him. 'Anyway, I need to give my nose a chance to go down. I can't breathe.'

'Probably best. It's always handy, to be able to breathe. Couldn't do without it myself.'

I squinted up at him through my puffiness. 'I'm still trying to decide if you're just a smartarse, or whether underneath it all lurks a heart of gold.'

Our eyes were locked together now.

'My mother says I'm lovely.'

'She's probably biased.'

'Your mother would think I'm lovely too. Mothers tend to.'

'Is that really a recommendation?'

Our faces were very close. Inches apart. And his hand was still on my back, pressing me to him.

Then I realised. We were going to *kiss*.

I thought he would be a good, if restrained, kisser. Clearly he had a few notches under his belt. But he was also wearing a shirt and tie, and worked in insurance. The omens weren't great.

But I was wrong. When our lips came together, it was with a tremendous smack. We were kissing like our lives depended on it. Not politely either, but wet, slobbery, needy snogs, his hands on either side of my face, and mine clamped on his midriff like I was kneading dough.

'Nick.' At one point I had to come up for air, due to my nose being so blocked, but it was only for a split second before we got dug in again. *Wow.*

I had no idea what we were doing: probably some mad rebound stuff, that we would regret as soon as one of us came to our senses. All I knew at that moment was that it felt great, and I wanted it to go on for ever. Actually, no, I didn't, I wanted to go to the bedroom and whip off all my clothes, and his, and bounce up and down on him until my thighs gave out.

247

Neither of us heard the front door open and close. Ollie still had his own key, as he came and went with Cleo so much.

The next time I came up to gulp air, like a seal with a sinus problem, it was to find Cleo looking at me in shocked disapproval. '*Mum.*'

Ollie stood behind her.

He didn't need to say anything at all.

Chapter Nine

There was an appalling moment where everyone waited while Nick and I disentangled ourselves. I removed my hip from his groin, while he took a step away and lowered his hands to conceal what can only be described as a very impressive erection.

'Hello, there!' he said to Ollie.

Ollie just stared. He looked a bit stunned or something. His eyes went from Nick to me, dark, accusing, hurt.

I felt terrible. Which was ridiculous. I was simply entertaining in my own home. It was nobody's fault that my daughter and ex had walked in on me engaged in enthusiastic relations with a man wearing slacks.

But Ollie's face . . .

I could feel Nick's eyes on me; he was waiting to be introduced. We were two consenting adults, right? It was over between me and Ollie, right? So why was I behaving like a child who'd been caught with her hand in the cookie jar?

The silence stretched.

In the end Cleo did the honours. 'You're Nick, right?' she said. 'From France?'

I could see Ollie's eyebrows snapping together. Who was this Nick from France? And how come nobody had mentioned him before?

'Yes,' Nick said cautiously.

They studied each other for a minute,

'It's OK,' said Cleo. 'I'm not going to bite you.'

'Phew,' he said. 'That's a relief.'

A tiny smile from Cleo.

Finally I found my voice. 'What's happened? What are you doing home?'

I tried not to sound as guilty as hell.

Cleo gave a deep, middle-aged sigh and announced, 'I have a sick stomach. Haven't I, Dad? I chucked up after having my dinner. It was awful.'

She did look kind of grey.

'She hasn't been feeling well since I picked her up from school,' Ollie said tersely. 'She wanted to come home so here we are.'

And we didn't expect to find you about to mount your new boyfriend on the kitchen table, his eyes said reproachfully.

Nick was stirring restlessly beside me. He was in danger of being forgotten.

'Ollie,' I said, having put it off for long enough, 'this is Nick. Nick, this is Ollie. Cleo's dad.'

There was a tiny moment of male shape-throwing by the pair of them – chins jutting out an inch, hips thrusting forward a tad, a little under-arm scratching, that sort of thing. Long, suspicious looks were cast across my living room.

Finally, Nick stuck out his hand and said, 'Pleased to meet you.'

Ollie took his hand and shook it violently. I almost heard the bones in Nick's hand crunch but, to his credit, he hardly grimaced, just set his jaw and squeezed back as hard as he could.

When they let go they were both red-faced and hurting, but *so* not admitting it.

'So,' said Ollie, rocking on the balls of his feet.

'So,' said Nick. Not rocking.

And that was that. Conversation over. Ollie continued to stand at the door like a bad-tempered bouncer at a nightclub, just waiting for the cue from me to grab this Nick fellow in his fucking *slacks* and hurl him out on his ear, imposter that he was.

Nick, on the other hand, was standing possessively over his mug of tea, waiting for the cue from me that this little interruption was over and we could continue drinking, and, when his hand recovered, making out on the table.

Me? I stood there, paralysed. I hadn't planned any of this, clearly, and now that I was in the middle of it, I hadn't a clue what to do. *Choose?*

Naturally, I bottled it, turning to Cleo instead. 'Cleo, darling. We need to get you to bed.'

Her forehead crinkled. 'Why are you calling me darling? You never call me darling.'

'Oh, just . . . get upstairs.' I'd been trying to impress Nick with my mothering instincts. Thanks, Cleo. 'I'll be up in a minute.'

Off she trudged up the stairs, throwing a, 'Good night, Dad' over her shoulder, and, 'See you, Nick.'

Now it was just me and the two lads. Each of them waiting for their instructions. Who would be sent away with a flea in their ear? The bad, feckless ex, with too much respect for his mammy, but who would always have his feet under the table by virtue of the fact that he was the father of Cleo?

Or Nick, fresh into all this mess, bringing with him the promise of a new start and who was a very, very good kisser? Didn't I deserve a second chance, after everything?

In the end Ollie startled me by saying, 'I'm sorry for interrupting your evening.'

He didn't sound that sorry, but I inclined my head stiffly in acknowledgement.

Then he turned to Nick. 'I realise that you haven't finished your tea –' His eyes flickered, not over the mugs, but over Nick's crotch, which still required camouflage – 'but I have urgent business to discuss with Hannah regarding Cleo, which simply can't wait.'

Clever. Very clever.

I'd always put him down as a nice, easy-going lad, never believing for a second how manipulative and cunning he really was.

'I'm sure we can talk in the morning, Ollie.' I was determined to get back control in my own home.

Nick, of course, had been rendered powerless in the proceedings. As Ollie had intended.

'I'm afraid we can't,' Ollie said pleasantly.

That was me finished, too. If I protested any more, it would look like I was putting carnal desires over the welfare of my own daughter.

The evening fizzled out fairly spectacularly after that. Nick adjusted his slacks, found his car keys and I escorted him to the door.

'Enjoy your stag night,' I said miserably.

He didn't try to make me feel bad. 'Thank you.'

I didn't want to leave it like that. I liked Nick. More than liked him. And nobody had kissed me like that in a long time. Maybe ever. 'Can we meet up again sometime?'

He gave me a small smile. 'Sure. When you get things sorted with Ollie, give me a call, eh?'

'Oh, he won't be here long, half an hour at most,' I assured him.

'I kind of meant when he stops having keys to your house.'

My faced exploded into colour.

'See you, Hannah.'

He touched me lightly on the arm and was gone.

'What's this "urgent talk" we have to have then?' I threw at Ollie. I was raging at him. But mostly at myself. 'You just made it up, didn't you? To get rid of Nick. God, you're pathetic, Ollie. You think I'm somehow not entitled to a private life? That I need your permission before I can start dating again?'

'Hannah—'

'And this thing of swanning into my house without even doing me the courtesy of ringing the doorbell? Key, please. Now.'

I'd expected all kinds of protests, but he just took it out of his pocket and handed it over.

'Thank you. Boundaries are important. Because we're too mixed up with each other, you and me. I know some of that is unavoidable, what with Cleo, but do you not feel that sometimes it's all a little unhealthy?'

'Hannah—'

'Friday nights, for instance. I think we should start by cutting down to every second Friday night. Just so that we get a little breathing space.'

'Hannah.' This time he was insistent, and I stopped.

His face was a bit peculiar, like he had indigestion or something.

'Will you marry me?'

Chapter Ten

'Everything's very *brown*, isn't it?' Barbara whispered to me, scandalised. 'Or grey, or green.'

We were in a large department store, in the boys' section, down in the basement. This was a part of the shop that neither of us had ever strayed into before in our lives, and we were both very uneasy amongst the racks of combat trousers, shirts, underpants and hoodie tops. No sparkly bits anywhere, no bows or ribbons or the odd bit of a flounce. It was like we'd stumbled into some strange, cheerless world, where an apocalypse had already picked off anything pink.

'Do boys not wear any other colours?' Barbara asked.

'Technically I think they're allowed to wear blue as well. Oh, look, there's a blue hoodie over there. He'd like that, wouldn't he?'

We approached the rack of hoodies with extreme caution. They all had aggressive things emblazoned across the front in neon writing, like, 'Born to be BAD' and 'Are You Looking At Me?' accompanied by a picture of a large fist.

'No,' said Barbara, very decisively. 'He definitely wouldn't like those.'

So far, all we'd managed to put into her shopping basket was a six-pack of plain socks and a pair of runners that were Sergei's size, but obviously she wouldn't know whether they fit properly until he tried them on. He had his own clothes, of course, in Russia, but they would be too heavy for the weather here, and also they looked a bit different to what Irish kids were wearing. He would probably feel out of place enough already without pitching up at school in an enormous padded coat that, if you fell over in it, you would beetle about on your back in until someone came and helped you up again.

But given that Barbara had spent the past five years skulking about in the baby section of Mothercare and Mamas & Papas, feverishly pawing tiny babygros and furry hats, she was ill-equipped for the less glamorous world of boys' clothing, and so I had come along for moral support.

'Well, what's his favourite colour?' I asked. That would be a good starting point. So long as it was green, brown, grey or blue.

'Purple,' said Barbara decisively.

'*Purple?*'

'Have you got a problem with that?'

'Absolutely not, no.' So aggressive! Real tiger mum material, and she hadn't even got him home yet.

She was going back in a few weeks to finalise the adoption. She had a calendar up in the kitchen, upon which she religiously crossed off each day with a massive purple marker. When I saw it, it said everything about her and Sergei that I needed to know.

Which was just as well, as she was annoyingly light on detail. She guarded the particulars of the orphanage visit to her chest fiercely, and the hours that she had spent getting to know Sergei. 'Fine,' she would tell people, closed-mouthed. 'It went as well as could be expected in the circumstances.'

She wouldn't even tell me. 'But *why*? I'm not going to tell anybody else.'

Her face grew all red and flustered then, and she said, 'I just can't. It's all too . . . personal. Sorry. We're both just feeling our way. Is that OK?'

Of course it was OK. I'd just never known Barbara to be stuck for words before, that was all.

I got a better idea of her first visit through the photos she brought home. She took hundreds and hundreds, nearly all of them of Sergei, but some of the two of them together, taken by the staff. I remembered one in particular where they were at a kids' table in one of the orphanage's playrooms, Barbara with her knees up around her ears as she gamely squatted on the tiny chair. They were drawing. That was how they communicated, through pencil sketches and dashes of crayon on one of the many pads that she'd brought over with her. In the picture, Barbara had sketched something that Sergei clearly found puzzling. In fairness, she'd never been noted for her drawing talent. He was holding it up to the light like it was the crappiest thing he'd ever seen, while Barbara looked at the camera in a 'Well, at least I gave it a lash' kind of way. So far, so pedestrian; but if you looked under the table their feet were touching. Just ever so slightly, angled in towards each other, Barbara's encased in big brown boots, and Sergei's slim and small in well-worn runners.

He was very good at drawing, Sergei. 'Gifted' was the word Barbara had used, and she wasn't one to throw it about lightly. Of all the things she'd brought over – a blooming suitcase full of stuff – he'd brushed aside the electronic games, the puzzles, the books, to get at the packet of markers she'd got in the pound shop.

She'd brought home a folder full of his drawings. She hadn't shown me many – again, she'd been tetchily secretive about them – but I'd got a glimpse of a drawing he'd done of her. It was gas. It was more a caricature than anything; he'd given her rakes of puffball blond hair, and many more freckles than she actually had. But her eyes were beautiful in it, clear and direct, and they were looking suspiciously out from the picture, and I thought, good man, Sergei, you got her in one.

'Here,' she said rapidly now. 'He'll have those.'

She grabbed a pair of camouflage-patterned combat trousers, bulging with pockets for penknives and gobstoppers and all manner of other boyish things, and thrust them into her basket.

'Are you sure, Barbara?' They didn't look like his kind of thing. They'd swamp him for starters, he was so slender. Maybe he could put his pencils in the pockets. Now she was picking up a T-shirt to go with it, some horror of a thing with some shouty slogan on the front. I couldn't imagine Sergei, so still and self-contained, strutting about in stuff like that.

'He'll have to get used to it,' Barbara said rapidly. 'They'll all be wearing this kind of gear. If he doesn't he'll get picked on.'

She worried incessantly about this. She'd done quite a lot of research on five-year-olds in the past few weeks, mostly by hanging around school-yards at home time and loitering with intent at the shopping centre on Saturday afternoons. She'd reported back tersely, 'some of them are fucking monsters. Chucking chewing gum and pushing each other, and demanding to go to the toy shop.'

Sergei did not chew gum or push people around. The idea of him demanding to go to the toy shop in his combats was so *wrong*.

'No matter what you say, he'll be different.' Barbara was chucking in more unsuitable clothing. 'Not because he'll be adopted, although they might pick on him for that too. But just because of the way he is.'

I knew what she meant. A quiet, gentle, beautiful boy.

'He'll have so much to cope with.' She was getting herself in a right

knot now. 'A new country, a new mother – that'd be me, by the way
– and a new school.' Her face hardened. 'Plus, little shits in shopping
centres.'

'Won't he have you there to beat them to a pulp?'

'Yes.' She breathed a sigh of relief. 'You're right.'

'That was a joke, Barbara. Look, you're going to have to let him get
on with it. He'll find his own way.'

'Will he?'

'You both will.'

Barbara sighed. 'You're right, you're right, I know you're right.' She
took the offending combats and dumped them back on the shelf. 'Nobody
told me it'd be like this. Becoming a parent. I just don't think I can cope
with the worry.'

'Too late now.'

'Cheers.'

'Come on,' I urged her. 'Buy the blooming socks. Although would you
not get him more interesting colours? Look. Here's a pack with a purple
pair in it.'

Barbara swooped on them in delight and we went to pay.

'The bridal section is upstairs,' Barbara commented, when we were done.

'Go away, Barbara.'

'Just if you wanted to have a look. I hear the empire line is all the
rage these days.'

'I'm not getting married.'

'Your mother would be delighted.'

'Stop stirring it. She doesn't even like Ollie.'

'She'd like him a whole lot better if he did the decent thing by you.'

'But that's just it, isn't it? He's doing what's expected of him. He knows
he fucked up and the best way to win me back is to ask me to marry
him.'

'So? What's wrong with that?'

'Because he's not the marrying kind. He wouldn't even have asked if
he hadn't seen me with Nick!'

'Hmm, yes, Nick, yum.' Barbara rolled his name around her tongue
dirtily.

'Stop it.'

'Chicken chow mein, yum, yum.'

'*Barbara.*'

'You know, I don't feel a bit sorry for you. Six months ago, you were comprehensively dumped. Now you've got one man wanting to marry you, and another beating his breast and checking his phone every five minutes in the forlorn hope that you've rung. So boo-hoo, not.'

'He isn't checking his phone,' I returned hotly. But God, wouldn't it be lovely if he was?

'Probably not,' Barbara agreed, knocking that one on the head.

I found I was disappointed, even though I knew instinctively that Nick wasn't the type to make an idiot of himself over a woman. Certainly, he hadn't phoned me. His message had been pretty clear; when I had moved on sufficiently from Ollie to have a new relationship, then we could hook up. Not before. Otherwise we were both wasting our time.

I found I liked him more because of this.

I liked him, full stop. I liked his eyebrows, his smile (but maybe that was because it was so rare), his dryness. I had liked his kisses and the hard feel of his body under my hands. I even liked his slacks.

'Look at you,' Barbara said in disgust. 'All lusty.'

I couldn't deny it.

'If you want him that much, then for God's sake go for it.'

It sounded so easy. There was just one problem: Ollie.

Chapter Eleven

The next time Ollie asked me to marry him was in a branch of McDonald's as I was about to sink my chops into a Big Mac.

'I was hoping you'd forgotten about it,' I told him.

'I'll take that as a no, then,' he said bravely.

Cleo was at a birthday party two tables over. Afterwards, Ollie was taking her for the weekend and we'd met up to exchange bags, teddies, roller blades and at least three dozen other things that were apparently essential between now and Monday.

'Is it because I haven't bought a ring yet?' he asked. 'I was going to, but you always say my taste is awful, and you'd go mad if I came back with something that looked like it came from a vending machine.' He thought about this. 'Although obviously I wouldn't have bought it if it did.'

'It's not about the ring.'

'I know! We could go together and choose it. Plus, it would be very handy to have your finger with us. You know, for the sizing. I know what you take in clothes, but I haven't a clue when it comes to your finger.'

'I don't want to go shopping for a ring, Ollie. Especially as we're not getting married.'

He put down his own Big Mac in let's-thrash-this-out fashion. 'Give me one good reason why.'

'Just one?'

'You seem to enjoy hurting me today,' he said very sadly. 'And what have I done? Nothing, except beg you to spend the rest of your life with me.'

I couldn't help myself. 'As opposed to six months ago, when you couldn't get me out of your life fast enough?'

He met and held my accusatory and vindictive gaze, in fairness to him.

258

'I know,' he said. 'I won't go on again about my confusion and immaturity and fickleness, because we both know it's not pretty.' Now he pushed his fries away too, a measure of his seriousness. He *loved* fries. 'But all that time that I was being stupid, I never stopped loving you, Hannah.'

I knew he meant it, too. That's what was so difficult about all of this.

'And you love me too,' he insisted.

'So modest.'

'You can rudely reject my marriage proposals, you can insult me all you like, but I can see it in your eyes.'

'I admit to a certain fondness. That's all.'

'Look,' he said, 'can we be serious for a minute?'

I didn't want to be. It was much easier to be jokey and laid-back, and put off what I knew I would have to do.

'Is it this Nick fellow?'

He was never just Nick. Always 'your man Nick' and 'that Nick guy' and once, with magnificent put-on memory loss, 'whatever his name is'.

'Ollie—'

'I know, I know, it's none of my business. But at the same time I'd really appreciate it if you were straight with me.'

Fine. If he wanted the truth, then he was going to get it. 'It's not Nick.'

For a moment he looked relieved: if there was no competition, then it was simply a case of grinding me down.

'It's you, Ollie.'

He sat very still. 'That doesn't sound too good.'

'Would it have even entered your head to ask me to marry you if you hadn't walked in on me and Nick kissing that night?'

'You were doing a bit more than kissing.'

'OK, whatever—'

'In fact, his hand was—'

'Ollie.'

'Fine! You've got me!' He threw up his hands very dramatically. 'I admit it. I haven't exactly had a lifelong hankering to get married. I've never felt the need for a ring on my finger to prove my commitment to someone, nor have I ever wanted to fit in with what everybody else is doing.'

No kidding.

'But I know that your mother has bought an outfit and so I think we should get hitched for her sake before it goes out of fashion. That was a joke, by the way. I just felt the need to lighten things for a moment.' He sucked in his breath and gave his head a little shake. 'OK. The thing is,

259

Hannah, I know that you want to get married. No, no, don't protest, I can pick up vibes, I'm not entirely thick. And I know that you've never put any pressure on me – although I suppose your mother has dropped enough hints for both of you – but if we're going to get back together, then I feel that I have to go the extra mile for you, seeing as I was the one in the wrong.'

By now the food was stone cold. Neither of us noticed.

'So you're doing it for me?'

'Well, yes, but I want to get married, too.'

'But you just said you didn't.'

'Hannah—'

'I don't want you asking me just because you're trying to make it up to me, Ollie.'

'I'm not a martyr. I'm not going to drag myself up the aisle against my will. I asked you because I meant it.'

'Because you're afraid I'll go off with Nick.'

'Why are you being so crooked?'

'Answer the question.'

'No. Yes. Yes, all right, I *am* afraid you'll go off with that . . . slacks-wearing person. And he has funny eyebrows, too, I don't know if you've noticed. Come on, Hannah. You don't want to get saddled with a guy who works in insurance. How much fun is that? But you and me, now *we* have fun, and laughs and good times, don't we?' He was very persuasive. He reached out and tickled the underside of my wrist, the way he knew I liked. 'We're good together, Hannah. We have ten years under our belts already, so try and tell me something's not working. We have a great kid, even though she mostly has my genes. And, best of all, I think I would look seriously good in a monkey suit.'

That drew a smile from me. 'You wouldn't wear a monkey suit?'

'You're right. I wouldn't.' Then he caught himself on. 'But I will if you want me to. This wedding, it's yours, baby. If you want to walk up the aisle in a massive meringue and have twenty bridesmaids, then go for it.'

OK, so now I was touched. 'I can have twenty bridesmaids?'

'You can have forty.' A shadow passed over his face. 'You don't want forty, do you?'

'I don't even have forty friends.'

Ellen popped into my head, as she always did when the word 'friend' was mentioned.

I wondered how she was getting on. Her and the baby. More than anything I wanted to pick up the phone to her and tell her that Ollie had proposed, and ask her what the blazes was I to do? She'd have dissected the situation in five minutes flat, and then I wouldn't constantly feel that I was making a big mistake in turning him down.

Ollie saw my indecision. Magnificently, he brushed aside Big Macs, fries and Cokes to take my hands in his. It would have been romantic had it not been a burger joint. 'Marry me. Go on. You know you want to say yes.'

He was right. I did. Marrying Ollie would be the most natural thing in the world.

'Do it,' he coaxed.

It would also be the easiest, a little voice in my head said.

'What's wrong now?' he said, grimacing. Victory had been so close.

'I don't know.' It was true: I didn't. Six months ago I'd have been over the moon at a proposal from Ollie. But six months ago, he would never have dreamt of proposing. He was only doing it now because he figured it was the only way to get me back.

But was that so objectionable? People often didn't realise what they had until they lost it. Could Ollie be blamed for taking ten years to have his epiphany?

It was a bloody long time, ten years.

Then there was Nick.

I barely knew him but already I was afraid that I was falling for him. I wasn't sure I'd ever felt that way about anyone so early on. Not even Ollie.

Ollie seemed to realise that the vultures were circling on his proposal because he said urgently, 'I know I've been a prat. I can't tell you how sorry I am. But please believe me when I say that losing you has been the worst thing that's ever happened to me.'

The intensity was so much that I had to look away.

'Promise me that you won't say no. Promise that you'll at least think about it,' he insisted. 'Please.'

'Yes, OK, Ollie . . . *what* . . . ?'

That's when I saw him.

He was on the street outside the restaurant, striding through the crowds with his unmistakable cocky gait.

'It's Mark!'

'What?'

'Out the window. Look! There.'

'Where?'

I didn't wait. I jumped up and ran out after him.

261

Chapter Twelve

By the time I got out into the street, he was gone. Vamoosed. Skedaddled. Of all the slippery characters . . .

'Excuse me.' I accosted a street entertainer. In other words, a scrawny, unwashed-looking youth murdering 'Wonderwall' on his guitar. About fifty-seven cents, mostly in coppers, was strewn on his guitar case. 'Did you see a man walking by a minute ago?' I realised I would have to give him more than that. 'Very tall, thick neck, far too much hair product? Adulterous? Although you probably can't tell by looking. He would have passed right by you.'

'No. Sorry.'

I threw the poor creature a couple of euro – 'Eat something' – and continued my search.

I walked up and down Grafton Street so many times that the security men on the shop doors began to lift their walkie-talkies upon my approach, no doubt to warn other security men that there was a possible bag snatcher coming their way. I even called, 'Mark!' once or twice in the hope of startling him and he would look around before realising that it was me, and that he'd better fucking run, and fast.

But he was gone.

I even began to wonder whether it was actually him at all. I'd only seen him from the side, in a crowd, through a window. I'd caught one quick glimpse of his arrogant nose and square, bullshitty chin and that was all.

A lot of men had arrogant noses, after all, and bullshitty chins. It mightn't necessarily have been Mark.

And what would he be doing in Dublin anyway, a few weeks after

Ellen had given birth to their premature daughter? I knew they hadn't come back to Ireland yet to show off the bundle of joy. Barbara would have said.

But I knew it had been him. I just knew.

'What did you want him for, anyway?' the guitar guy said. I'd ended up back by his pitch again.

Good question. What *would* I have done? Had a good old shout at him? But I'd already done all that, in France. I could hardly accuse him all over again of being a slime ball, even though he still was; just because he was in Ireland didn't absolve him of that.

I would only look like a nutter, shrieking at someone in the middle of the busiest shopping street in the country. 'God love her,' people would say, and walk around me in a big circle. 'Is he her boyfriend? Oh, no, he's walking away from her, shaking his head sadly. Poor man. Out doing his shopping, only to be attacked by someone with mental health issues. Is that *ketchup* on her chin?'

It wasn't fair, I realised.

He'd got away with it. He could saunter down the Grafton Street in the bold light of day, while me, the wronged party, the one who'd lost a friendship over him, could do nothing about it. Without looking foolish, that was.

The lad on the guitar started up again, this time butchering the Beatles. 'This is for you,' he said.

My two euro had just kicked in. God, he was bad.

I chucked in another euro, just to get him to stop, and made my way back to McDonald's.

Chapter Thirteen

Mark bothered me all week. What was he doing in Ireland? Or had I been seeing things?

'Ring Ellen,' I urged Barbara.

'No,' said Barbara flatly. But she was very tetchy these days. The closer her trip to Russia got, the shorter her temper became. Nerves, of course. But, frankly, we were all a bit sick of her.

'Please, Barbara. Ask her if he's in Ireland.'

'What the hell would he be doing in Ireland? And them with a premature baby at home? And anyway, even if he *was* in Ireland, so what? He's Irish. Maybe he came home for a visit. Have you thought of that? His mother might be having an operation or something.'

'His mother lives in Scotland.'

'His father, then. Whatever. He might be over for a stag night, or for a school reunion. There are millions of reasons why he'd be in Dublin.'

'Not millions, Barbara.'

I could see her getting crosser by the second. 'What's it to you, anyway?'

'Apart from the fact that he made a pass at me and ruined my friendship?'

'Supposing he *is* here? What are you going to do about it?'

'I don't know, do I?' Again, I felt that familiar sense of impotence; the unfairness that he'd got away with it.

'Well then, shut up about it!' This even startled her. 'Listen to me. I'm like a fishwife.'

'You're like two fishwives.'

'Sorry. It's Sergei. Well, it's not Sergei, he's great. It's me. I'm going to be a mum in a matter of weeks and I'm freaking out.'

'You're freaking out? What about poor Sergei?'

She managed only the weakest of smiles. 'Look, can I ask you something?'

Rather regally, I prepared myself: yes, I would *love* to be godmother to Sergei.

'Can I ask Ollie to look after my fish when I'm away in Russia?'

I deflated. 'I thought we agreed boundaries, Barbara?'

'Oh, don't go all coy on me – he's practically family again, isn't he?'

'How many times do I have to tell you? I am not marrying him. I simply promised to think about it.'

'That's as good as.'

'What is wrong with you people? We are not getting married, OK?'

'Hannah?' It was Muriel. She sounded uncharacteristically coy. 'I was wondering. Would it be OK if I brought a guest?'

'To what, Muriel?'

'Oh, I know it's not official yet or anything, but Anthony has to book his holidays with the gas people and, well, I was kind of hoping I might bring him to your wedding.'

Jesus Christ. This was getting totally out of hand.

'What wedding, Muriel?' I made my voice icy cold.

She had the decency to backtrack. 'I know you haven't said yes yet—'

'*Yet?* What, you think I'm holding out?'

'Well, he's asked you twice.'

She made it sound like I was being very unreasonable. And that, the way I was playing it, he might not be inclined to ask me again.

'Muriel. I don't know how I can make this any clearer, but we're not getting married. I simply said—'

'That you'd think about. He's on tenterhooks, you know. I heard him up last night – Anthony and I got in late – and you know what a good sleeper he normally is.'

I knew what she was going to say next: 'And then there's Cleo.'

'And then there's Cleo. You know I've never had a problem with you and Ollie not being married.' Thoroughly Modern Muriel was on the loose again. 'But I think it's hard on Cleo, not having things formalised.'

I really wanted to hang up on her, but I was curious to know what the explosive sounds in the background were. There it went again. *T-chewww.*

'Are you OK, Anthony?' Muriel was all concern. 'Maybe try a drink of water.'

I could hear Anthony now. He sounded very nasal. 'That's for hiccups. Not sneezes.'

Ah. So that's what the noise was.

I'd never met Anthony. Hardly anybody had. He seemed to work very odd hours, reading meters. 'Most people are out during the day, so it's best to catch them in the evenings, or else very early in the morning,' he'd explained to us. Well, via Muriel. We'd have accused her of making him up except that Ollie had met him – only once, though, at about 2 a.m., when he'd run into him outside the bathroom, fresh from reading meters. It was dark, and he didn't get a good look at him, plus Anthony was wearing a peaked gas company cap. Then Ollie had to avert his eyes sharply when Muriel had thrown open her bedroom door, wearing some kind of skimpy nightie, and had spirited the cap-wearing Anthony inside.

She was mad about him, by all accounts. She loved his unpredictable comings and goings – so different from Harry – and his handiness with cars and troublesome boilers. Most of all, though, she loved his descriptions of people's side passages and back gardens. He had unfettered access, you see, what with his meter reading. And the *dirt* of some people, he said to Muriel. It would shock you. Overflowing bins; millions of empty wine bottles; broken yard brushes scattered about just waiting to trip him up and land him in hospital with a broken leg. Another time he'd come across a woman sunbathing nude. No shame at all! Didn't bat an eyelid when Anthony had to step over her to get at the meter.

No, there was very little Anthony hadn't seen in the course of his work, and he had a very eager audience in Muriel. They'd open a bottle of wine and he'd regale her with what went on in suburban back gardens. Then, all fired up, they went to bed, judging by the big bags under Ollie's eyes, whose room was next to theirs.

I heard another violent sneeze in the background now. 'Damn!'

'I don't know what's wrong with him today,' Muriel told me worriedly. 'He's been at it since he got up.'

'Maybe you need to hoover more,' I said, tongue-in-cheek.

She ignored that. 'Anyway, listen, will you think about the guest thing. If you're getting married,' she added hurriedly. 'Look, it's not really about Anthony's holidays, although they *do* like them to book early. It's more Harry, really. I wanted to prepare him.'

'For what? He's fine about Anthony.'

'He's not really.'

'Muriel, he is. He said he's a very nice chap.'

'You see?' Muriel cried. 'How patronising is that! If Anthony was a doctor – oh, get a tissue, Anthony, don't be sneezing all over the furniture – then he wouldn't be "a nice chap", would he?'

'He might well be.'

'No, that's just Harry looking down on him. Anthony has noticed it himself.'

They'd run into each other the previous week, in the supermarket. Even though Anthony had been reading Harry and Muriel's gas meter for twenty years, it was the first time Anthony had met him as Muriel's 'toyboy' – Harry called him that because he was eleven years younger than Muriel. Anyway, it had all gone swimmingly until Harry had clapped Anthony on the back. All kinds of things had been read into it. Ollie thought it was in commiseration at being landed with Muriel. Muriel was insistent that it was as condescending as giving Anthony a tin of USA biscuits at Christmas. Which she used to do when he'd read their meter, Ollie pointed out, to her mortification.

'In fact, Harry is quite fond of Anthony,' I impressed upon Muriel now.

'I can read the signs,' she said curtly.

She was just cheesed off that she'd got a new man and wanted to rub Harry's nose in it, but Harry didn't give a damn. He was too busy. He was beginning to miss Friday night dinners at mine because he had previous engagements.

Anthony was sneezing so hard now that he seemed to be in some distress. 'Something's setting me off,' he was gasping to Muriel. 'Have you cats?'

'Hold on, Hannah.' Then, to Anthony, 'Cats? No. Why, are you allergic?'

'Yes,' Anthony wheezed. 'Cats, parrots, horses, squirrels. Rabbits, they kill me altogether. But it's mostly cats that set me off. Oh, and dogs.'

'Well, we don't have any of those here,' Muriel said sadly.

She'd even thrown out Susie's basket and the fossilised poo. There wasn't a trace of the critter left in the house (God rest her soul).

'Are you sure you have no dogs?' Anthony sounded very poorly indeed.

'No, Anthony.' She was very snippy now. 'And, frankly, I think your enquiry's in very poor taste, given the circumstances.' Anthony had been informed within five minutes of meeting Muriel's about Harry's murderous deed.

267

She gave him no further hop. Back she got on the phone to me, ignoring him entirely. 'You never told me Ellen and those had moved back to Ireland,' she said chattily.

I was shocked at the casual dropping of Ellen's name into the conversation. 'I didn't, because they haven't.'

'Well, I saw that husband of hers jogging when I was out in the car the other day. What's his name again? Michael?'

'Mark.' I said the name dully, even thought my heart was thumping hard.

Jogging. In Dublin. Two weeks after I'd first seen him.

'Are you sure it was him?'

Maybe Muriel was delusional too. And she didn't know Mark that well. She might have made a mistake.

'Oh, yes, I'd know him anywhere. Wears a lot of stuff in his hair . . .' She was gone again. 'Anthony . . . are you OK?' Then she was back. 'Hannah, I'm going to have to call you later. Anthony's gone a bit blue.'

'Do you want me to ring an ambulance?' I was getting a bit concerned too. It'd be just Muriel's luck to land herself a new man, only for him to expire on her living-room floor.

'I don't know . . . Sit up, Anthony.' I could hear several thumps now, and deduced that she was slapping him on the back. Then, nothing.

'Hannah?' After an age, she got back on the phone. 'No, I think he's OK, I've sent him outside for some fresh air and it seems to have done the trick.' She trailed off. 'Oh my God. Oh my *God*.'

'What's happening? Muriel?' Had he got belly-up on the lawn?

But Muriel's voice burst out of the phone, suffused with joy. 'It's Susie! She's back! She's just walked in the door! Oh, my baby!'

Now that Anthony was OK, I could go. I didn't really care about Susie. 'That's great, Muriel. I have a plane to catch.'

'But . . . where are you going?'

'France.'

Chapter Fourteen

It was a great idea until I was on the plane. As we began our descent
– well, the pilot did, I just sat there with my tray up and my seat in
an upright position – my gullet began to tighten unpleasantly. Barbara's
words came back to haunt me, as they so frequently did:

'At least let me warn her.'

'No. That'll just give her time to set the dogs on me. Best if it's a
surprise.'

'I don't even know why you're going.'

'Because he's jogging around Dublin, seemingly having abandoned her,
and I want to make sure that she's all right.'

Ollie was minding Cleo. He, at least, had been more understanding.
'Do what you have to do.'

I knew from his face that he was desperate for some indication about
the marriage thing. But, to his credit, he didn't press the issue. Just leaned
in and gave me a kiss on the forehead that managed to be both tender
and rather erotic at the same time – no mean feat. I was, I admit, impressed.

'See you when you get back,' he said. Again, that questioning look:
hopefully all the organic food and bracing air would sort me out and I'd
come home with an answer for him.

Cleo presented me with 'Bead Extravaganza' – her newest and best set
of beads, no fewer than four thousand of them, in a range of magnificent
colours, some of them so sparkly they'd nearly take your eye out. She
loved those beads, so much so that she'd only made one bracelet out of
them so far, eking them out.

'For Sophie,' she said gravely. 'To make up for her bottom.'

'Are you sure?' I was also a little worried that the box might burst loose in the luggage compartment; I would be a long time picking up four thousand beads.

'Yes.' Then, as if I were heading off on a very dangerous mission, which I could well be, she told me, 'Come back safely.'

So there I was, in France, with a bead-making set, a tiny outfit for a new baby, and a sat nav that spoke only in French. Oh, and a hire car with all the controls, including the steering wheel, on the wrong side.

The foolishness of my plan was only now coming home to roost. If I ever managed to reach Ellen's house – and it was looking dodgy – who was to say she was even there? And what was to stop her closing the door in my face? Mark might be there too, fresh from his jog in Ireland, and he might shout, 'She's come to make another pass at me! Dear God, when will it *end*,' and that would really put the kibosh on any emotional reunion we might have.

I'd better get realistic; stop hoping for some kissy-kissy make-up like in the movies. Ellen and I had parted on very bad terms. It would take a lot more than a box of chocolates from the duty free (Butler's, in fairness) to make things right again.

I set off.

The countryside looked different in November. Not that I could see much of it, in the dark and the rain. Everything looked a bit squat and threatening. I drove on, feeling more and more apprehensive as I got nearer the farm. I could have picked a better time to land in on them than a cold, wet evening just as they were probably about to sit down to dinner.

The village!

This time I was right. The sat nav lady was quite insistent, in any case. I drove through it and out the other side and then past Rosalie and Marcel's house. I slowed down, harbouring some wild notion that Marcel would be out tending his goats, but of course the man was sensibly inside with his blinds drawn.

And now there was the farm. The lights were on in the house; someone, at least, was home. The yard lights were on too; loads of them. Driving in there would be like arriving on a runway. The whole place would be alerted.

In the end I chickened out and parked outside on the road. I decided not to take my bag out of the car. I might be leaving in a hurry.

The converted barns were in darkness when I walked into the yard; no guests staying, then.

My eyes were drawn to the one that Nick had stayed in. I wondered how he was. If he spared me a thought at all. At this stage, he must be giving up hope.

Sorry, Nick, I told the converted barn. Still faffing around. But hang in there, if you can.

The door to one of the sheds was open. A squealing noise came out. The pigs!

I hurried across the wet yard and in, before I'd even thought of the possibility that someone might be in there. But it was just the pigs, penned in and squealing like billyo when they saw me.

I'd expected them to be babies still, cuddly and cute. But I was very disappointed to find that months of chowing down on nuts and milk and whatever else they scoffed had turned them into burly, broad-backed porkers, with big meaty heads and chubby bellies.

'Girls, seriously, you're going to have to watch that,' I told them, shocked. 'And boys,' I added, not wanting to be sexist.

Then one broke away and came trundling over, snout raised to sniff me. Clyde!

'Hey, boy! You remembered me!' I was surprised at my emotion.

I was tickling his ears when another one came up, and also started sniffing me affectionately. This one looked very like Clyde too.

'Clyde?' I said to him, but got no reaction.

Now a *third* pig, the spit of Clyde, trundled up. Feck it, I was hopelessly confused.

'See you later, lads,' I said, in defeat, and stepped back outside.

I could put it off no longer. Also, it was getting quite late to find a hotel, if I needed one. I didn't much fancy the idea of sleeping in the hire car, with only the sat nav lady for company, although she did sound quite friendly.

I turned off the light on the pigs and shut the shed door against the elements. Back across the wet yard I ran. It was raining hard now, and my hair was plastered to my face as I stepped up to the door. At this rate she mightn't even recognise me.

I rang the bell, badly wanting to gag.

The sound of the bell triggered movement inside, and dark mutterings: who could be calling at the farm on a foul, wet November night, only thieves and blackguards?

I braced myself to be confronted with a baseball bat. Through the rain-spattered glass I could see a figure coming towards the door. It was too dark to see who it was. Next thing the porch light snapped on, blinding me, and the door was flung open.

I had to blink several times before my vision was sufficiently restored to recognise the door-opener.

Ellen.

We stared at each other for what seemed like half an hour.

She didn't slam the door in my face. She didn't even scowl at me. Mind you, neither did she look ecstatically happy. Mostly she looked tired.

First things first. Even before we greeted each other I had to ask, 'Where's Mark?'

I was still worried he was going to spring out from behind her and shout something about bunny-boilers.

Her face shut down. She gave a long sigh that sounded very final. 'Gone.'

Chapter Fifteen

'Auntie Hannah! Auntie Hannah! Hurrah!'
Sophie and Sam bounced up and down on Sophie's bed, despite my efforts to quieten them.

'Sssh. You'll wake the baby.' I'd crept up to see her but had been ambushed on the way.

'Pah,' said Sam. 'Nothing wakes her. I dropped a plate by her head yesterday and she didn't wake,' he said in disgust.

'She's very small,' Sophie advised me, as though this explained everything.

I was warmed by their welcome. Clearly they held no grudges, at least not against me.

Testing the water, I produced the bead set from my handbag. 'This is from Cleo.' I handed it over. 'To say sorry.'

Sophie grabbed the bead set. With a dismissive flick of her hand, she said, 'Tell her my butt is fine.'

'I'm going to tell Mum you said butt,' cried Sam.

I could see he was waiting expectantly for his present. Shite. How could I have forgotten to bring him something?

I was forced to palm him off with the box of chocolates I'd got for Ellen. 'I didn't have much time at the airport,' I began apologetically.

He turned the box over in his chubby little hands. 'This is for me?'

'Yes, I'm sorry, I'll bring something better the next—'

'All of them?' He clasped the box fiercely to his chest now. I saw a little pool of drool gather at the corner of his mouth.

'All of them.'

'Thank you, Auntie Hannah, thank you, thank you,' he said fervently, and he went scurrying off to his own room, and slammed the door shut.

The baby was in Ellen and Mark's room, in a crib at the bottom of the bed. I tried not to look around avidly as I went in. But I couldn't help myself, of course. The bed was an unmade mess but the rest of the room looked sparse and, well . . . *uneven*. Ellen's things were strewn across the dressing table, but only over half of it. Little rings were visible in the dust on the other half, where somebody had recently lifted bottles and canisters off it: Mark, unless a third person shared their bedroom.

He'd taken everything of his from the dressing table. I could see none of his shoes; no clothes, either. Everything was gone.

The baby stirred. I looked in cautiously. She was so tiny that I was afraid my very breath would disturb her. Ellen had her all swaddled up in a blanket, so that only a patch of downy, auburn hair was visible, and a tiny, doll-like face. She made a sucking motion and then lapsed back into sleep.

She may well grow up to be very tall, with a thick neck and an unhealthy fixation with hair gel, but right now she was beautiful.

Ellen had opened a bottle of wine and put out some bread and cheese and olives.

'Sit down,' she said at last.

So far we'd said very little. Nothing, really. If I'd been expecting a rush of emotion along the lines of, 'Hannah, I'm so fucking *sorry*,' then I'd be a little disappointed.

But at least there was drink. As in alcohol, not just endless pots of strong tea. I grabbed the glass and knocked back half of it before my backside had even hit the kitchen chair.

Ellen sat too. She looked wrecked. Really wrecked. And skinny as ever under her sickly green frock, even though I was delighted to note that she had a little paunch left over from the baby. Knowing her, though, it'd be gone in two weeks' time without her having to do a single sit-up or be forced into the purchase of a pair of control pants.

We eyed each other over the vast kitchen table.

'I was going to ring you,' she said at last. 'Only there never seems to be time. The baby, she has to be fed every two hours, on account of being premature, and then winded and changed, and I've hardly finished before it's time to start all over again. And Sam just started school, and he hates it, and I have to prise his fingers off my leg every morning one by one. He's figured out that if he says he's sick, they'll ring me to come and get him. So he pulled a sickie every day for two weeks before someone copped on and stopped ringing me. And Sophie has just started intensive ballet classes twenty-five miles away, and I have to drive there three times a week with the little witch. And then there're the dogs and the cows and the sheep . . .' She trailed off. 'You know something? I'm actually too tired to go on.'

I hated to break the news to her. 'You left a light on in the pig shed. But I turned it off and closed the outside door.'

'Thank you.' She was pathetically grateful. Christ, she really *was* wrecked. She took a big glug of wine. Good to see that her swallowing reflexes were still lively enough. 'So that's why I haven't phoned you. And also,' she said, her eyes skirting mine, 'because I figured you must hate me.'

'If I hated you I wouldn't be here.'

That seemed to loosen something in her and she looked a little less like she was being lined up for a stoning.

'So tell me. How are you?' she asked cautiously. 'Barbara rings, of course, but you know her.'

Yes: completely useless at passing on any kind of decent tittle-tattle.

I intended to waffle on about my job a bit, and Cleo, of course. Ice-breakers, if you will.

Instead I blurted out, 'Ollie asked me to marry him.'

Christ, where had that come from? What was wrong with me? Why couldn't I play it cool, like normal people, instead of spilling my guts at the first opportunity?

Ellen didn't go 'Great!' like everybody else. She just gave a little nod, as though she wasn't surprised at all, and said, 'You obviously haven't said yes, or else you'd be telling me you were getting married.'

Suddenly we were back in groove, talking about men, like we hadn't had an almighty bust-up at all.

'I've promised him I'd think about it,' I confessed.

'So you haven't said no either.'

'Well, I did the first time. He asked me again. Oh, I know it makes me sound flaky and indecisive, all the worst things about myself that I vowed I was going to change, and yet here I am, doing it again.'

'You're not. You're just trying to decide what's best for you, and that sounds very sensible to me.'

'Thank you!' I said, delighted at this analysis. It made me sound so much better.

Then I think we were both a bit embarrassed at the chumminess, in the circumstances, and we took refuge in our wine glasses again.

Ellen put her glass down with a clunk and said in a rush: 'When I said I didn't believe you that day, I was lying.'

I was completely shocked. She'd been so outraged. So righteous as she'd turfed me off the farm and out of her life.

She looked very upset. 'I knew you were telling the truth, Hannah. I just didn't want to face it.'

'But . . . how did you . . . ?'

'Because he'd done it before.'

Chapter Sixteen

It was just a feeling. Women's intuition, maybe – that old chestnut. Or maybe it was the way he smiled too readily and too long at some of the holiday guests who came to stay. The female ones, that was, and generally only those below a certain age. He probably gave them a good old grope, too, and stuck his tongue down the throats of more than one, but Ellen had never seen that.

No, all she could pinpoint was a sense of unease about Mark that developed over the course of a couple of years – right around the time it became clear that they could sow all the organic carrots they liked, but the farm would never make them a decent living.

'He just lost interest. And it was his idea in the first place. I sat him down and went through ideas to bail us out – the farm tours, taking tourists in, all that malarkey – but do you know what he said? "Let's just go home." Let's just go *home*? After everything we'd given up, after all the work we'd put in, he'd have been happy to just throw in the towel and feck off home, no harm done?'

We'd drunk one bottle of wine. We were onto the second. We sat at the table like two female warlords, battle-scarred and weary. And tipsy too.

'Do you know what his problem was?'

'Tell me,' I said eagerly.

I knew it was probably the wine, but it was so good to talk to her. So good to have her back. Some part of me was still fuming, of course, but I would deal with that later. Probably after the third bottle of wine, but I made a mental note that it wasn't to get nasty.

'In his head, he was going to be some kind of gentleman farmer, selling his produce at fairs, that kind of shit, and making wine at home in his spare time that he could open to impress friends when they came over: "*Gorgeous*, isn't it? Made with grapes that we ship up from Bordeaux. Ellen juices them with her bare feet.''"

We had a bit of a snicker: she was very good at taking off his Southside Dublin accent.

Now she got vicious again. 'The problem is, there *is* no spare time. He hadn't reckoned on that, had he? And when I told him we'd have to work even harder, what with the tours and all that, and that there was no more money for his fancy equipment, well, I think that frightened the life out of him altogether. The dream of life in France was officially dead.'

She put her glass down hard on the table. I worried for it.

'The farm wasn't the only thing he lost interest in.' She eyed me. 'He didn't want me any more either.'

'That is not true, Ellen.' I wasn't just saying that. I really meant it. They were always having sex – Barbara would have agreed.

Ellen held up her hand like a policemen to stop my protests. 'I was going on thirty-eight, Hannah. Lately I was too tired for sex any more. I was getting wrinkles around my eyes and my hair was growing grey. That kind of thing doesn't suit Mark at all. The only thing going for me was that my arse didn't look like the back of a bus.'

That's when it struck me. 'The plastic surgery . . . ?'

Ellen squirmed. 'I know. Stupid. But I felt so unattractive, so rejected. Imagine thinking that if I dragged up my forehead two inches that he'd stop looking at other women.'

She looked so sad that I was furious at what he'd done to her. 'Oh, Ellen. Apart from anything else, you'd probably look really weird if you dragged your forehead up two inches.'

She thought about. 'Christ, yeah.'

She started to laugh. She laughed and laughed and then it segued seamlessly into big, noisy sobs that racked her. 'It's pathetic, isn't it? Even though I knew he was probably making a play for other women behind my back, I still tried to hold on to him. I didn't even *like* him any more. But there were the kids to think about, and we were all the way over here in France, no family or friends, nobody to rely on except each other, and I should have confronted him but I never did. I just kept my head down, and pretending that if I didn't notice it, then it wasn't happening. And even when I walked in one day on him and this Spanish tourist, I can't even remember her name, and I just knew I'd interrupted something, I still said nothing. What does that make me?'

She sobbed like her heart was breaking.

'You were just trying to do the best you could.'

She shook her head hard. 'I used to look down on women like me, do you know that? I used to think, why has she so little self-respect? Why is she putting up with that idiot, when everybody can see he's making a fool of her? Does she not have any friends who would tell her the truth?'. She gave me a bleak smile and looked around for a tissue. There weren't any, so she grabbed a tea towel and roughly wiped her face with that instead.

Calmer now, she went on, 'But then, the thing with you . . . Oh Christ, I couldn't believe it. Didn't want to believe it. I thought, surely he couldn't sink that low. To hit on my best friend? That's when I should have thrown him out. I should have packed his bags and shown him the door. But he was clever. He got in before you. And was so convincing, Hannah. So hurt on my behalf. He even tried to defend you, saying you were confused after the break-up with Ollie, and that I shouldn't be too hard on you. When I think of it now . . .'

Another swipe at her face with the tea towel. I sat there, frozen, sick as I heard the details of what he'd said behind my back.

'There I was, pregnant again, sick as a dog, and so bloody tired. And he was promising to look after me, to take over on the farm, that everything would be fine if we could just get rid of one problem. You. *He* was the problem, only I refused to see it.' Her eyes met mine square on. 'I'm so sorry, Hannah. For ruining everything.'

I knew what she meant: twenty years of friendship, of trust built up, of loyalty and closeness.

I had my own transgression to confess to, too. 'I should have told you the first time it happened. When he put his hand on my thigh.'

Surprise flared in her eyes; he'd conveniently omitted to tell her that. 'But I chickened out.' I took a big breath now: here came the bad bit. 'He was being so nice, you see. I kind of enjoyed it.' Now, the *really* shitty bit. 'I think I might have led him on.'

It was like something my mother would have said. I felt like I was 'that kind of girl'.

But Ellen just flicked a hand. 'I don't blame you. That's Mark. Always flirting. He can't help himself. He even flirts with Rosalie, even though it's water off a duck's back with her. Being nice to women is Mark's default setting. I'm not surprised he was being extra nice to you. It's called softening you up.' She gave a sigh and shook her head. 'And you fell for it, you eejit.'

Oh! She was being so *decent*. Well, it wasn't that decent, calling someone an eejit. But still. I was really glad she hadn't broken a chair over my head.

'I used to think he was handsome,' I gushed, high on all this confessional stuff. I'd probably end up telling her about that time I shoplifted a Curly Wurly when I was ten.

'Most women do,' she advised.

'But when you look at him, his neck is actually obscenely thick, and his chin is horrible and his *hair* . . .' I ground to a swift halt. Ellen had married him, after all, so at some point she must have thought he was gorgeous, and I didn't want to go calling her a blind fool.

And now for the big question. 'I know he's in Dublin. What happened?'

Ellen picked up the second bottle of wine, as though trying to figure out if there was enough left to finish out the sorry saga. She sloshed more of it into our glasses in an ominous kind of way, and I had horrible visions of him being caught straddling a nubile young woman from a coach party, which had happened to stop by the farm. I wouldn't be surprised if he'd been caught with a sheep, that's how low my opinion was of him.

'Nothing much,' Ellen said, exploding my little theories. I found myself deflating just a little. I wanted the ending to have a little more oomph. Baddies were never dispatched with a 'nothing'. They were always blown up.

I realised then how badly I wanted Mark blown up. He deserved *something* nasty to happen to him. Instead he was jogging around Dublin, being admired out of car windows by elderly ladies like Muriel.

'It was mostly you,' Ellen said.

'Me?' I stuttered. Hang on a second. I'd been in Ireland for the past however many months, trying to sort out my own catastrophic love life. I'd hardly been in a position to cause any more damage.

'I could dismiss all the others. That Spanish girl, the Scandinavian, the Italian.'

Christ. He'd worked his way halfway around Europe.

'It was easy to pretend everything was fine because they were strangers, here for a week and then gone and we never saw them again. They didn't affect me; does that make sense?'

It did. For Mark too: a holiday romance, short and sweet, what people don't know won't hurt them, right? That's the proposal he'd made to me, anyway.

'But he crossed a line with you. He didn't care any more. Not about your feelings and definitely not about mine. How could he have known you wouldn't tell? In fact, the chances were you would. He risked everything: our family, me, my friendship with you. In fact, I think maybe he wanted to get caught. He mightn't have known it at the time, but he did. He was fed up of France, sick of me, and he wanted to go home.' She pushed away her wine now. 'And I wanted him gone.'

I don't know how long we'd been sitting there. But I knew it was very late. My bum was numb but I was riveted to the chair.

'I was so angry, Hannah, that I couldn't even hide it any more. The week after you went home, I kicked him out into the spare room. Then I put my head down, and got through the pregnancy as best I could. I still needed him because someone had to run the farm and look after the kids.'

'That sounds awful, Ellen.'

'It was. But I figured I had six months to get things sorted before the baby came and then I'd have options.'

'And then the baby came early.'

'Yes. It was no surprise, really. Poor little thing, I was so stressed and furious and tired that it was amazing she survived at all. Anyway, Barbara came and said useless things like, "Will I ask them for a couple of paracetamol?" and everything was OK.' She took a shaky breath. 'A week after I got home from the hospital I kicked the fucker out for good.'

That demanded something. An acknowledgement. It was, I decided, almost a religious moment. So I opened my mouth and shouted, 'Halleluiah! Praise the Lord!'

Ellen looked to the ceiling, 'For feck's sake, Hannah, you'll wake the baby.'

'Oh. Sorry.'

But she was smiling now. 'I threw all his clothes into the cow dung at the bottom of the yard. You should have seen him prancing around trying to rescue his Gucci jeans from a pile of poo.'

We had a cackle at that. I told her about mine and Muriel's sighting of him in Dublin.

'He's back working in his old job,' Ellen confirmed. 'Took him back with open arms, apparently,' she commented wryly.

'And what about the kids . . . ?'

'Oh, he'll see them, all right. I'm not going to interfere with that. We haven't worked anything out properly yet, but for the moment he'll fly over some weekends.'

She leant back in her chair, spent now.

'So he's gone. And I've been trying to work up the nerve to ring you ever since.'

Chapter Seventeen

Susie trotted back into Muriel's life with no indication at all of where she'd been the entire time she'd been missing. According to Muriel, she was still wearing her collar, but was bedraggled and dirty, and stank to high heaven. She was immediately popped into the bath, a tin of the finest dog food was opened, and Muriel wrapped her in a soft towel and cuddled her to her chest for the rest of the evening.

'You naughty, naughty, lovely, lovely girl! Where have you been all this time? Tell Mummy. Did someone kidnap you? I bet that's what happened. Someone saw you and thought, look at that beautiful little dog! I must have her for myself!'

Nobody knows what exactly Susie responded with, but possibly something along the lines of, 'Yip! Yip! Yip!'

A new basket was hastily purchased, and a new blanket, and Susie was installed in the corner of the kitchen like a queen, just like she'd never left.

'I can't believe it,' Muriel rang me up in France to tell me, ecstatic. 'I prayed every night, you know, long after people told me to give up. I knew she was out there somewhere, and it was just a matter of time before she showed up.'

'But weren't you sure you'd eaten her?' I felt I had to point out.

As always, the memory of those fajitas elicited a gagging noise from Muriel. 'There's no need to bring that up,' she said frostily.

'I'm just saying—'

'That was just Harry's stupid sense of humour. I never really believed it. As if he would cook a *dog*. Honestly, Hannah. And I really wish you'd stop going on about it all the time.'

I bet she did. Wait till word of this got out amongst all of her and Harry's old cronies. Talk about mortification. They'd be saying that Harry had been right all along; silly little Susie had most likely run off with some bowser, or several of them, and never been near a frying pan at all. That daft old Muriel, falling for a joke like that, and having panic attacks and being put on Valium for her nerves. Still, there was no doubt that it wasn't entirely undeserved, after all the things she said about Harry. Disgraceful. Although imagine being taken to Sellafield for your wedding anniversary . . .

'See? I told you! I knew that little bitch would come back.' Harry also rang me up to gloat. 'Worse luck.'

He went over to see her with his own eyes. Even gave her a poke with his foot to make sure she was real.

She retaliated by biting him roundly upon the calf.

'OK,' Harry growled at her. 'Now we're quits.'

So elated was he at this blot, this stain, being wiped from his character that he rang everybody up to tell them the news, including Orla and Maeve in Australia and Canada.

'She's alive,' he burst out breathlessly down the phone.

They got a terrible fright, of course, thinking that Muriel had almost croaked it.

'The dog. Susie. She came home,' Harry clarified.

'That's great, Dad.' Maeve, very frosty. 'But it's three o'clock in the morning here.'

'Is it? Sorry. I didn't check the time difference.'

He celebrated Susie's return by cooking dinner for all his buddies in his apartment block, which went on until four in the morning. Muriel wasn't invited.

'I got a letter from the management company complaining about the noise,' he told me, delighted.

So everybody was happy – Muriel, Harry, Susie. In fact, the only fly in the ointment was Anthony.

Anthony had nothing against Susie, although a lesser man might object to his new girlfriend's insistence on plonking the canine between them on the sofa as they watched *Coronation Street*. Susie often snuck into Muriel's bedroom too, apparently, and would watch Anthony with jealous, beady eyes, which quite put him off his stride. Luckily Harry had warned him about the pooping in the shoe business – they got on very well, those two – and he put his slip-ons in the wardrobe now, so she hadn't caught him out on that front yet.

All in all he could have lived with Susie if it wasn't for the sneezing.

How Anthony sneezed. Two hundred and thirty-seven times in one single afternoon. His head hurt from the sneezing, his nose was raw, his eyes were permanently bloodshot.

'It's his heart, though, that we're most worried about.' Muriel said, in another of her phone calls. 'Did you know that when you sneeze, your heart stops for a millisecond?'

'I don't know if that's actually true.'

'It is,' she insisted. 'The same way that it's impossible to keep your eyes open when you sneeze, or else they'll pop out. He's tried doing that, keeping his eyes open, and he can't.' She recounted this as through laying out medical proof. 'Anyway, we've worked out that, what with all the sneezing, his heart must be stopping for *minutes*.'

'Yes, but not all at once. That's even if it's true that your heart stops when you sneeze.'

'He's taking a huge risk even coming round here,' she insisted.

'Look, never mind about his blooming heart. If he's that allergic to Susie, he must be miserable.'

'Well, yes, of course he is. There isn't a moment's peace, for either of us. The minute he pulls into the drive he starts up, the poor man. And he's not a quiet sneezer, Hannah, not like Harry. It's like an explosion. If you didn't know he was in the room with you, you'd get a terrible fright. I just don't know what we're going to do, except get the doctor to ratchet up his antihistamine medication.'

Only once she'd finished talking about herself was she able to move on to other people. 'How's Ellen? She must be feeling better by now, is she?'

'She's still very upset.'

'I know, it's terrible how it all ended with Mark, but she must realise that you can't stay for ever. Obviously, it's very kind of you to give her moral support, and help out with the new baby and all that, but you've been gone two weeks. You have to think about Cleo.'

'Cleo is fine. I speak to her twice a day. She knows I'm coming home soon.' I tried to keep the defensiveness out of my voice. 'Anyway, she's having a great time with Ollie. They went on a ten-mile trek earlier.'

I could just imagine the scene in the hallway at home: dirty wellies, wet raincoats, rucksacks, all strewn on the ground. Ollie would probably be making hot chocolate with marshmallows in the kitchen, oblivious to the necessity of hanging things up to dry. But they'd be having a great old time.

He'd moved back in – temporarily, I hasten to add – to look after Cleo while I was in France. Cleo didn't want to stay at Muriel's, what with the ceramic ducks, Susie, a sneezing Anthony, and a freezing cold house. It'd be less disruptive for her if she was in her own bed at home, with her things around her, especially if I was going to be gone for a little while, and so I'd asked Ollie to come and look after her. He was pathetically grateful, as there was no peace to be had at Muriel's, and he'd been round in fifteen minutes, his things hastily thrown in a bag.

The slippery, slippery slope.

'How long more will you be gone, do you think?' Ollie probed on the phone. Ultra-casually, of course. Everything was softly-softly, don't push, and whatever else you do, don't bring up the blooming marriage thing again.

He didn't.

And I certainly didn't.

'I'm not sure. Ellen's still very upset.' But I'd been saying that for days now and felt I needed to up the ante. 'Crying and carrying on, that kind of thing. Won't get out of bed.'

'She won't get out of *bed*? Even with a new baby?'

What had I started? But I'd no option except to plough on. 'I bring her in the baby to be fed. Then, if she stops crying long enough I, um, make her breakfast and give her a sponge bath.'

A shocked silence on the other end of the phone. 'God, Hannah, it sounds like you have your hands full.'

'So you see why I have to stay on.'

'Well, yeah, you couldn't leave her in that state. And I don't want to interfere or anything, but maybe she needs to see a doctor? Or a counsellor or something?'

At that moment Ellen turned towards the open kitchen window and bellowed heartily, 'Come on, Hannah! We're playing Frisbee!'

I left a small moment for us all to digest that. 'Weirdly, though,' I told Ollie, 'she often has half an hour where she feels marvellous, and wants to do all kind of crazy things. It never lasts, though,' I finished sadly.

A stern silence now. Then: 'Hannah, what's going on?'

'Nothing. Look, she's not that bad—'

'Obviously.'

'But she's still having a tough time, Ollie. And she's got a new baby to take care of, and the farm and everything. She needs the company.'

All of which was true. New babies were a lot of work; I'd forgotten that they never slept the same time as anybody else. Ellen was up with her most of the night – she'd been renamed Jill, after a false start with 'Tania'; Mark's idea, I learnt – then I took over during the day to let Ellen sleep. Marcel was in charge of the farm for the moment, which was brilliant, and Rosalie came and banged pots and pans around in the kitchen every morning, and told me I was holding the baby wrong. I always conceded on the matter to keep the peace. In return, she changed Jill's number twos.

At least Sophie and Sam were on their best behaviour. They'd deduced that the baby was a direct threat against their positions, and that they'd better launch a charm offensive in the hope of hanging on to their mother's affections. And I have to say that so far it was working.

'I just hope she's grateful,' Ollie said gruffly. Ellen didn't really deserve so much of my time and energy, he meant, after the way she'd expelled me from the farm as a floozie and a liar (although I didn't mind the floozie bit so much).

'She is,' I said firmly. I wasn't going to go there. As far as I was concerned, that was between me and Ellen, and nobody else. 'Look, give me another few days, OK? Just until I'm sure she's back on her feet.'

I wonder did he suspect the truth: that I was hiding out? That I didn't want to go home, because going home meant giving him an answer?

And I wasn't ready yet.

Chapter Eighteen

Ellen was recovering a little more every day. I made lots of hearty soups, until she begged me to stop. Most of the time it seemed like she only nibbled on things, but maybe she was having secret midnight feasts, because her body seemed less swamped by her lady-farmer dresses. Barbara phoned most nights with advice to eat things like chips, because generally nothing was so bad that you couldn't eat a lovely bag of vinegary chips. Once again, she was right. We began to eat plenty of *frites* (my French was coming on), and Ellen's face filled out just a little, and she readily partook of our 'evening constitutional': i.e. a bottle of red.

We talked about everything: premature babies; the shockingly low price of milk; the children and how they would cope with the separation – I had plenty of advice to offer there. We spoke about Mark (we were still in the early, name-calling phase: shit, cad, creep, how-could-he, that kind of thing), Clyde (whichever one he was; Ellen didn't know either), her episiotomy, Marcel (a dote), Rosalie (not a dote, but completely indispensible), and how Ellen was going to face the future as a single mum. At that point, we usually broke into song, nearly always 'One Day at a Time'. Sweet Jesus.

During these chats, Ellen would regularly trail off in the middle of a sentence, clasp her hand to her forehead and blurt, 'Christ, I'm so sorry.'

'Ellen—'

'No, let me say it.'

'But you've already said it. Dozens of time.'

'I need to say it again. I'm so, so sorry for not believing you, Hannah. For taking the word of a *man* –' at that point we'd both spit

288

contemptuously on the floor – 'over that of my best friend of twenty years. Can you ever forgive me?'

'Yes, ten Hail Marys and a couple of Our Fathers, my child. And he wasn't just "a man" in fairness. He was your husband.'

This was dismissed with a violent flick of her hand. 'I lost my way for a while, Hannah. Turned against my friends, turned against *myself*, and all for what?'

'You had extenuating circumstances.'

She sighed. 'You're very kind, to try to make me feel better.'

'It's true.'

'You've been a great friend to me, and I've been a terrible one to you,' she said sadly.

'Is this going to get mushy?' I asked in alarm.

'No. Just one more mushy thing, though. I'm going to make it up to you. I promise.'

'OK. I'll have a Stella McCartney handbag so.'

I suppose I was keeping it jokey because I didn't want to admit to the extent of my hurt over what she'd done. There was enough hurt going around already. And even though we talked for hours, there was an underlying awkwardness that would take more than an apology to put right.

For the moment, though, our friendship had been salvaged, even if it carried a health warning. Without getting too mushy about it, it was enough for now.

'Right, what do you want to talk about tonight?' I asked her. I'd just opened the bottle of red wine and we'd settled ourselves at the Table of Moans. 'Mark? What's the best way to treat bovine mastitis? Whether you're going to get Jill christened or not?'

'I couldn't bear it,' she confessed. 'Why don't we talk about you instead?'

'Me? God, no. I'm really not that interesting.'

'Oh? With one man wanting to marry you, and another one getting frisky over a Chinese?'

'That Barbara,' I said viciously.

So much for her lofty, 'Oh, I don't talk about either of you to the other person.' And there she was, squealing about my intimate business with Nick the minute my back was turned.

'I made her,' Ellen confessed. 'I was desperate for news of how you were getting on.' Admiringly, she said, 'And you've been quite busy, haven't you?'

I gave a modest shrug: what can you do?

'I thought Nick had a bit of an eye for you, all right.'

'He's nice,' I said cagily.

'Just nice?'

'Well, more than nice. Interesting, I suppose. I'd like to find out more.'

Ellen was frowning. 'That's hardly a ringing endorsement.'

'What else can I say?' I felt like I was letting Nick down horribly behind his back by condemning him with descriptions of 'niceness'. Particularly as he was a moody fecker. 'We've had one sort-of date, and I haven't been in touch with him since.'

'Think harder,' Ellen ordered. She was moving into control-and-command mode. This was the kind of thing she excelled at: dissecting emotions, unearthing motives, turning the screws on you until you had no place left to hide. 'What is it about him that turns you on?'

I tried, I really did. Was it his eyebrows? His sarcasm? His moodiness? His mega-watt smile, whenever he grudgingly managed one?

'God, Hannah, if you can't think of a single thing . . .'

'I can! I'm just trying to decide which one!'

'So he's an all-rounder? That's good.'

'Yes, but it's not *that*.'

'What, then?' I could tell she was getting pissed off that I wasn't coming out with nice clean statements like, 'He's confident, compassionate and mature in the areas that matter' or, 'He has a stonking great willy.' *That* we could discuss, and it would get us through until the second glass of wine.

But the problem was that I hadn't been around him long enough to make statements like that.

Then it hit me.

'I like the things I don't know about him more than the things I do.'

Ellen gave me a suspicious look. 'What the feck is that supposed to mean?'

'You know when you meet someone new? And it's about the possibilities? The excitement? The future?'

'I'm trying to cast my mind back,' said Ellen with a sigh, 'but it was all so long ago . . .'

'You've only just met him but immediately you know that you want to find out more?'

'Yes, yes,' said Ellen excitedly, some of it coming back to her. 'And it's all about the good bits, and none of the bad bits, because you don't know yet that they're pretentious gits with the attention span of goldfishes and who think fidelity is a suggestion, not a requirement. Sorry,' she finished up very apologetically. 'I really didn't mean to bring up Mark again.'

We both turned and spat on the floor. If Rosalie knew she would kill us.

'Let us continue,' Ellen said. 'That's if you want my humble opinion.'

'I do, I do,' I said eagerly. I was desperate for someone to make sense of it all for me, preferably before they clubbed together back home to send in a search-and-rescue team, due to my continued non-appearance.

Ellen brought her chin to rest on the tips of her finger. She loved this bit, when she made her pronouncements, a bit like Judge Judy, whom we all greatly admired, both for her certainty that she was right, and her acid tongue.

'I think,' she said, slowly for effect, 'that you like Nick.'

I looked at her gravely. 'You're a genius. I don't care what anybody else says.'

'I haven't finished yet. I think that you like him, and indeed from what I've seen of him, he seems like a very nice man. *I haven't finished yet.* You sound like you'd really like to get to know him better—'

'Would you like to tell me something I *don't* know at this point?'

'BUT – Christ, it's difficult to talk to you, do you know that? So impatient – *but* I think you like him mainly because he's not Ollie.'

I digested that for a minute. 'That's a load of rubbish.'

'I'm not saying you'd choose just anybody—'

'Well, clearly my standards are very low.'

'He's a very fanciable man. Good luck to you if you do end up with him. But I think we can deduce from your own words that the thing you find most attractive about him is that he's offering a fresh start.'

'Go on, O wise one.'

Ellen fixed me with her best, don't-fuck-with-me Judge Judy stare. 'In my opinion, this thing isn't about Nick at all. It's about Ollie.'

And she sat back, delighted with herself, sure that she had got to the nub of the issue.

'Well, maybe I don't want it to be about Ollie,' I burst out viciously. 'Why *should* it be about him? He was the one who went and spoilt everything.'

'So he had a bit of a wobbler, Hannah. Happens to a lot of people. The important thing is that the whole experience has made him realise what's really important to him, which is you. He's matured. Grown up. And now he's trying to make it up to you in the best way he knows how, which is to ask you to marry him.'

I couldn't believe she was being his cheerleader. And after her own husband turned out to be a right creep. Wouldn't you think she'd have been on the side of Nick, and all the possibilities that came with him, the excitement, the fresh start?

'He doesn't really want to, though. Get married. He's only doing it to make me happy.'

That still rankled.

But if Ellen's eyes got any bigger she would have to rethink that plastic surgery. 'He wants to make you happy.' She spelt it out slowly. 'Isn't that great? Isn't that *fantastic*? If I met a guy who wanted nothing more than to make me happy, I'd grab him with both hands.'

'You're just saying that because Mark turned out to be a shit.'

Another quick hawk and a spit on the floor.

'I'm not, Hannah.'

'Next thing you're going to tell me how lucky I am.'

'Why, because Ollie's the kind of man who believes that when people love each other, they stay together for life? So much so, that when that belief was blown to smithereens by his own parents, he goes a bit loopers? You're not just lucky, girlfriend.' She did that whole wagging her index finger from side to side sternly, like they do on confessional TV shows, while her head wagged in the opposite direction. 'You're *blessed*.'

'And the leather pants?' I challenged her hotly, because someone had to put a stop to the canonisation of Ollie.

'Well, they were a mistake,' she admitted. 'But do you not see, Hannah? His parents aren't reconciling. There's no happy ending for them. Yet he's still prepared to overcome his natural fears, and ask you to marry him. If that isn't love, I don't know what is, sister!' More wagging of fingers and general triumphalism.

'Pack it in now, Ellen.'

We quietened down, refilled our glasses, had a good sigh, and sat back.

'So, basically, you think I should marry him,' I concluded.

And it was hard to contradict her. I had a prickly feeling on the back of my neck.

'Look, I don't know, Hannah. It's just that you seem to have an awfully hard time putting him behind you.'

It was true. I did.

Chapter Nineteen

Sophie and Sam wanted to come to the airport too, but they had school, even though it was useless and stupid, and anyway, Jill didn't have to go, did she?

'That's because she's a baby,' Ellen patiently explained to Sam.

Sophie went happily enough, because she'd made herself an enormous necklace and matching bracelet out of Cleo's bead set, and was quite confident that she looked stunning and that the other girls would be 'jealous as hell'.

They submitted to my kisses and promises that we would all see each other soon.

'Not next weekend, though,' Sam clarified. 'Daddy's coming to visit. He's going to sleep in the converted barn and come up to the house for his dinner.'

This was all said with great practicality. He was taking the news very well, apparently. So well that Ellen was worried that he'd have a meltdown in six months' time and have to go into therapy until he was twenty-seven.

Sophie, meanwhile, had gone to school and announced to the class that, very sadly, her father had died over the weekend. Naturally, everybody had been horrified, and she'd been taken to the secretary's office, and someone made her hot chocolate, while the teachers wondered in the staff room whether he'd met some grisly end in a slurry pit, or under the wheels of that dodgy tractor he'd bought, because, let's face it, the man was a liability on a farm.

The principal herself had driven Sophie home, and had commiserated tearfully with a confused Ellen on the terrible loss of a fine man. Sophie, in the meantime, had slunk off to her bedroom rather rapidly. The principal, once she got over her disappointment that Mark was alive (it was a quiet school, not much excitement), assured Ellen that Sophie's fibs weren't an uncommon reaction to parents divorcing or separating, and that Ellen might want to handle the situation delicately.

'It's because I heard you saying to him that he was dead to you,' Sophie explained afterwards, and began to cry her eyes out.

The poor child! Ellen, guilt-ridden, had been extra nice to Sophie for days — treats, hugs, lots of mum/daughter time. She'd even got Mark on the phone to prove that he wasn't dead. Obviously Sophie was taking this far harder than anybody had thought.

Then Ellen heard that Sophie, in town shopping with Rosalie, had been overheard wrangling free sweets from one of the shop owners 'because my poor father has died'.

The kids waved me, Ellen and Jill off early that morning, while Rosalie stood in the doorway, her arms folded implacably across her bosom.

'See you, Rosalie!' Ellen waved ingratiatingly at her from the Range Rover. 'I won't be late back, I promise! Thanks!'

We drove off quickly before she could change her mind and go home. It had happened before, apparently.

'I suppose you won't miss her too much,' I commented.

'Rosalie?' Ellen looked panicked. 'Why, is she going somewhere? Has she got a new job?'

I smiled. 'I meant when you move back home.'

Ellen continued to look mildly confused.

'Obviously not now. Not straight away. I suppose you'll have to sort things out here first. But listen, don't worry — Barbara and me will come over to help with the transition.'

I had pleasant visions of the two of us sorting through stuff, and putting it into piles to be recycled, thrown out or packed for home.

'Out!' we would decree, holding up Ellen's shit-coloured dresses. I was really looking forward to doing that, actually.

'I'm not moving back to Ireland,' Ellen announced.

I indulged her for a minute. She wasn't thinking straight, not after all that Mark stuff. And she was still hormonal after the birth.

'I can understand you wanting to be as far away from him as possible, but—'

'It's nothing to do with Mark.'

I saw now that her jaw was set. She was really serious.

'I love France,' she said. 'I love my farm. And yes, it's hard work, and the house still isn't finished, and we're completely broke, but that will change. I've put so much work into this, Hannah. I can't walk away now.'

Someone had to talk sense into her. 'Yes, you can. It's called being reasonable. Look, you've tried your best. There's no shame in admitting failure.'

'This is my *home*. Just because Mark has left doesn't mean I have to too.'

'It wasn't even your idea! It was his.'

'I know that.'

'And it's always raining.'

'It is not. You and Barbara just manage to come at the wrong time.'

'Ellen, you're crazy.'

'So what?'

I made a last-ditch attempt, jerking a thumb at the sleeping baby in the back. 'Look at her! An innocent child.'

'I know,' said Ellen fondly. 'I think she looks like a farmer, don't you?'

Chapter Twenty

'Maybe she can hawk her skinny body on the village square to bring in a few quid,' Barbara said, practical as ever. 'I'd say she knows a trick or two.'

She'd picked me up from the airport. Cleo and Ollie had wanted to come, but she'd beaten them back. 'I need a dry run,' she insisted. 'I'll be flying to Russia again in a few week's time and it's best to be as familiar as possible with the airport because I'll be so nervous on the day I might end up getting on a flight to Singapore.'

Totally weird. But that was Barbara for you. So she'd come two hours early, even bringing an empty suitcase, and had staked-out the airport, doing a mock check-in, and security run, even buying those rip-off plastic bags. When the whole thing went off without a hitch, she rewarded herself with a massive McDonald's and a giant-sized Mars bar.

'I think I'm ready,' she'd told me nervously. 'Well, as ready as I'll ever be.'

She'd booked the full whack of her adoptive leave off work, and would be going back next year part-time, once Sergei was settled in. Her boss still hadn't got over his consternation, so much so that he'd actually tried to talk her out of the whole thing. He'd cornered her in the staff kitchen one day and gone on about how awful his own children were, how demanding and selfish and smelly, and was Barbara really sure about what she was letting herself in for? Then he'd hinted, extremely vaguely of course, because the firm had very good solicitors, that any future promotions might be compromised.

'And the really weird thing was, I didn't give a shite,' Barbara had told me, almost laughing. A year ago she'd have dragged him by the unmentionables into an employment court.

We were heading down the M50 now, Barbara pressed up against the steering wheel like a very elderly person and rarely straying above fifty kilometres an hour. The way she drove, it'd be nearly dinnertime by the time we got home. I'd be lying if I didn't say I was hoping that Ollie had planned something hot and spicy, and had a cold beer in the fridge.

'We're going to have to talk some sense into her,' I told Barbara. 'She can't stay there on her own with three small kids.'

'Why not?' said Barbara.

'I *hate* it when you start this devil's advocate stuff.'

'It's her life.'

'Yes, and we're her friends, Barbara, and it's our duty to stop her descending into madness and destitution.'

Barbara shrugged. The car nearly went off the road. 'If anybody can make a go of that place, it's her.'

'Do you not think that it's some kind of demented response to what Mark did? Some misguided "I will survive" rubbish? And that really, she should come home to Dublin, put back on her skinny jeans and Ugg boots, and take up a nice job as a producer again?'

'Not if she doesn't want to,' said Barbara, infuriatingly. Honestly, that girl would disagree with anything.

'And what happens when the baby gets sick, or the one of the cows breaks into the paddock next door?' Not that I could ever imagine that happening; they were such well-behaved cows. 'There could be any number of emergencies, and she's there on her own, in the arse end of nowhere?'

'Doesn't she have Rosalie and Marcel three fields over? Doesn't she have a car, and a phone, and a reasonably practical brain?' In contrast to mine, her look said. 'She's an intelligent, capable, hard-working business-woman. Just because she kicked Mark out doesn't change that.'

'I wish I was as wise as you, Barbara.'

'I bet you do,' she said modestly. 'Oh, fuck. Look at that! We just missed your exit.'

Now she was all in a lather. Barbara didn't really do roads, or directions, or any of that stuff.

'Go on to the next one. We'll just turn back.'

Barbara grimly drove on, her nose nearly pressed to the windscreen now. 'Anyway, we can't do anything about it, except visit more often. I'll go over with Sergei, and you'll go over with Cleo. And maybe Ollie?' She gave me a wink. Again, the car took a sudden swerve.

'Ollie and I are none of your business,' I told her haughtily.

'The poor lad,' said Barbara, clucking. 'Doesn't know whether he's coming or going. I was over during the week – he cooked me lovely spicy kebabs – and he was very down in the mouth.'

'Stop trying to stir it, Barbara,' I snapped. 'Why does everybody want me to get back with Ollie? I know it'd be the handiest thing for everybody – including you. No, no, don't deny it, I know he still fixes your car for you. But nobody seems to care that while Ollie was off doing his naval-gazing, I might have been doing some of my own!'

'And what did you find?' Barbara enquired kindly.

'Well, that . . . that I'm not just going to *settle* for something just because it's nice and easy.'

Barbara's eyebrows shot up. 'Easy? I've never seen two people make getting back together more complicated. In fact, if you want my opinion—'

'Oh, why not? Everybody else has had a go.'

'If you don't want to marry him, fine. I don't care one way or the other. But for God's sake, just tell him no. Put us all out of our misery.'

I was raging.

Mostly because she was right.

Barbara was peering at a road sign ahead like she was extremely short-sighted. I'd been so engrossed in our conversation that I hadn't noticed that, at some point, Barbara had made a daring dash, or crawl, off the M50.

'Fuck,' she exclaimed, predictably. 'I don't know where the hell we are.'

The sign ahead directed us either towards town, or back to the M50.

'Back, I guess,' said Barbara, gloomily.

I suddenly recognised the area. An unseemly impulse overtook me. I was powerless to resist it. 'No, Barbara,' I urged her. 'Keep going straight on.'

When Barbara finally pulled up outside a swish, personality-free building, she was fit to be tied, what with the rush-hour traffic, and my dodgy directions.

'I'm sorry, Barbara, I knew the office was around here somewhere, I just got a bit confused as to exactly where.'

I'd only been here a couple of times before, usually on the way to the pub on a Friday night. I'd never been invited inside. Probably because I'd usually be wearing jeans and something sloganed on top. Ollie wouldn't be much better.

'This is a very, very bad idea,' Barbara said sourly.

'Just two minutes, Barbara, OK?'

'I'm not even parked legally!'

We were on double yellows, near to the automatic glass doors of the building. Barbara was nearly having conniptions. I, on the other hand, was watching keenly as the glass doors slid open, disgorging smartly dressed, cool-looking people, into the start of their weekend. I scanned each face. Nope, not him.

'Anyway, we might be too late. He might have already gone.'

'And he might not. Let's just wait and see, will we?'

'What are you going to do, anyway?'

This time I had a plan. I wouldn't stand there powerless and impotent, that was for sure.

Barbara began to look worried. 'You're not going to break the law or anything? Because if you do, I'll get implicated too, and it'll go on my file, and it's not too late for them to pull the plug on me, you know—'

'Relax, OK? It won't have any repercussions for you.'

More people spilt out into the Friday evening busyness. I began to deflate. We were probably too late: it was ten past six.

Maybe it was for the best. Ellen would go mental once she found out. And what would it achieve at the end of the day? Nothing, except to make me feel better, in a childish sort of way.

There he was! Just coming out of the glass doors now.

Mark.

He was in his city slicker IT garb: striped shirt, no tie, cool jeans, loafer-type shoes, man bag. He was chatting to three or four other city slickers. I could hear the self-satisfied laughter from here.

I felt a roar in my ears.

'For God's sake, don't do anything stupid.' Barbara was scrunched down behind the steering wheel, like something from a cop movie.

'Keep the engine running,' I told her dramatically, and before I could think any more about it, I threw open the passenger door, and strode towards him.

His back was to me so he didn't see me coming. He was having a great joke with his friends.

'Mark,' I said, very calmly, as I stopped behind him.

He turned. His face froze for a split second, and then, almost immediately, I saw a kind of amused insolence. 'Well, if it isn't Hannah.'

His friends were turning now to have a look. And people were watching idly from their grid-locked cars on the road beside us.

I didn't speak to him. I had nothing to say. Instead I lifted my hand and slapped him hard across the face.

'That's from Ellen.'

His friends sucked in their breath hard. I saw the shock on his face; the pain. The public humiliation.

I was about to turn away, then I thought, feck that. And so I slapped him again, this time on the other cheek, harder. The cracking sound filled the air.

His friends made a collective 'Ooooh,' sound.

'And that one was from me.'

The feeling was wonderful. I left him there, clutching his red cheeks, in full view of Dublin 4.

I raced back to the car, jumped in and, like something from *Thelma & Louise*, shouted at Barbara, 'Let's go!'

Chapter Twenty-one

Someone had mown my front lawn. The lawn hardly ever got mowed (which was why there was so much moss, according to Harry. Not that he'd been any great shakes at mowing it either, while he'd lived here).

Ollie opened the door. The first thing I noticed about him was that his stubble was gone. He'd had that stubble for years. It was cool and sexy and, just, *him*. I wondered whether he'd had a run-in with a rusty razor or something equally nasty. But it seemed rude to ask.

'Hi,' he said.

'Hi yourself.'

Then there was a squeal of 'Mum!' and Cleo was barrelling past and throwing her arms around my middle and squeezing me like she was never going to let go.

'What did you bring me back?' she asked breathlessly.

Ollie rolled his eyes. 'Cleo.'

But I was ready for it – I figured three weeks of being absent deserved some kind of compensation – and I handed over sweets, a pair of fancy flip-flops and some over-priced toy I'd bought in the airport.

'And Sophie sent you this.'

It was a necklace, made out of the beads Cleo had given her. There had been letters in the bead set too, because she'd spelt out, on the necklace, 'BEST FRIENDS FOREVER'.

Cleo looked at it for a moment, uncertainly. 'Is that, like, an order?'

I met Ollie's eyes and we both smiled.

'I didn't bring you anything back.' I'd meant it as a joke, but it came out a little bitter and twisted.

'That's OK,' he replied bravely, and I knew that some small part of him had hoped that I'd arrive on the doorstep with the best present of all: a big fat, 'YES! I'll marry you!'

The awkwardness grew.

And I noticed now that he was wearing . . . dear God, *slacks*-type trousers. What was going on? Where were his faded jeans?

He caught me looking intently at his nether regions and looked down too, to check that his flies weren't open.

Breaking up all the awkwardness was a familiar, annoying yip.

I looked at Ollie. *Susie?*

'Yes,' he confirmed with a sigh. 'We've shut her in the utility room. The noise of the blender drives her mental, you see. Every time it goes on she tries to jump up and attack it.'

More furious yipping.

Then, a roar: 'Shut up, you daft dog, or I'll go in there and tan your lazy backside for you, do you hear me?'

Harry.

The yipping stopped. Now he was coming from the kitchen wearing one of my aprons and smelling of thyme. 'Hannah! You're home.'

'Harry.' I was enveloped in a hug. 'What's Susie doing here?'

Then I knew: Muriel must have called over too, for the great homecoming.

Harry saw me craning my neck. 'Oh, Muriel's in Miami with Anthony,' he said comfortably. 'A ten-day cruise. Having a whale of a time, aren't they, Ollie?'

Ollie was wearing shoes, I noticed. Proper black leather things, with laces. Holy cow. What was going on?

'Yes,' he confirmed politely, as we walked into the kitchen. He was acting like a host, or something else a bit stiff and strange. 'Is the lamb nearly ready, Dad?'

I had a little moment of disappointment. It was a Friday night, after all. But Ollie wasn't cooking tonight, and it was lamb, which I'd always found a little greasy.

'Ten minutes,' said Harry. Everything always seemed to take ten minutes with him, I'd noticed. I think he only said it to look cook-ish and brilliant. 'It's got a herb crust,' he told me in a very Nigella Lawson way. 'You must be starving after the journey.'

I was actually hungry after belting Mark in his ugly mug, but Barbara and I had decided that it was best to keep the incident strictly to ourselves.

It reflected no credit on me, she said stemly, and he would be well within his rights to press charges.

'But I bet the bollocks won't,' she finished up with great satisfaction.

'How's Ellen?' Ollie asked. He was opening the fridge now; getting me a lovely cold beer. But no. Instead he poured me a glass of crisp – and expensive – white wine.

'Good,' I said. 'Well, not *good*, obviously, but OK. I said I'd ring later on just to check in.'

The table was set – crikey, usually it was a fork and piece a kitchen roll – and there were some flowers from the garden in a mug and it all was so mature and grown-up that I almost felt out of place in my own kitchen.

Yip, yip, yip. Susie again, from the utility room.

'You're very good to look after her for Muriel, Harry.' I was almost glad for something to talk about. Because Ollie didn't seem himself at all – and certainly not in that stripy shirt. He looked like it hurt him around the neck.

'Oh, I'm not looking after her.' Another stern roar towards the utility room: 'Keep that up and there won't be any Doggie Yum Yums later on! Do you hear me?'

He nodded in satisfaction when she fell silent.

'She's living with me now,' he finished up sunnily.

I think my jaw literally dropped.

'It was poor Anthony, you see. He couldn't control his allergy. They tried everything. Bathing her, putting one of those jacket things on her, putting her out in the garden. But nothing worked. He was in a terrible state towards the end, his nose shot to bits; he couldn't even go to work. Muriel knew she'd have to choose between them, so she did the sensible thing and threw him out.'

Ollie chuckled. Then, as if he'd farted, he pulled back on his mature, grown-up face quickly.

Harry took a peek in at the lamb. 'Ooh, lovely! Anyway, I felt I couldn't stand idly by and watch her squander her chance at happiness—'

This time Ollie couldn't contain himself. 'Rubbish. What he really means is that he didn't want her bothering him about boilers and alarms and stuff—'

'That is not true—'

'Especially if Anthony was there to do it. Very handy for you, wasn't it, Dad?'

'I offered to take Susie out of the goodness of my heart,' Harry declared, but with a twinkle in his eye.

'But you hate her.' It was Cleo who pointed out the obvious.

'Hate is a very strong word,' Harry counselled. 'I simply refuse to put up with her nonsense. There's no special treatment, no baskets in the kitchen or gourmet dog food or any of that rubbish that Muriel was so fond of. But I take her for walks twice a day, and I throw a ball for her, and she gets all the scraps from the kitchen.' He said this as though we were all supposed to be very impressed, what with him being a master chef now.

'Muriel can still come to see her whenever she likes. 'Plus,' he reluctantly conceded, 'I do have the very odd night at home, and I quite like the company.'

Which made me wonder whether he'd been stitching Muriel up when he maintained he didn't have a single night free.

But if so he wasn't letting on. 'So really, it's all worked out very well.'

And, strangely, it had – for Muriel and Harry, anyway. Muriel had finally discovered the adventure and passion she'd craved with the gas man, while Harry, former couch potato and all-round non-achiever, had spectacularly reinvented himself, and acquired a dog into the bargain.

So that just left Ollie and me, really.

But then again, we were always the last to get our acts together. Why change the habit of a lifetime now?

I felt him looking at me now, intently. But when I turned to him, he was all politeness and distance again, and pulling out a chair for me.

He'd never pulled out a chair for me in my life. For a couple of years after we'd bought the house, we hadn't even *had* any chairs, making do with cushions on the floor.

He gave me a mature smile. 'Will we eat?'

Chapter Twenty-two

Harry finally bumbled off into the night with Susie yipping around his heels and almost tripping him up – deliberately, Ollie said. It seemed that Harry, also deliberately, gave her a poke in the behind as he loaded her into the boot of the car. On reflection, they were very suited, that pair.

Cleo, yawing, condescended to being put to bed by me.

'Don't go away again, Mum.'

'I won't.'

She was asleep before I'd even left the room.

I went back downstairs to the kitchen, where Ollie was holding up the expensive bottle of wine.

'Another glass?' he enquired solicitously.

'No, I'd better not.' I didn't want to be squiffy. Not tonight.

He deflated a bit. 'I'll just get my stuff then.'

I didn't know what he was talking about for a minute.

'To go back to Mum's,' he clarified.

Of course. His time in my house was officially over. Plus, I could tell he was dying to get out of his 'good clothes'.

'Ollie, wait. Can we . . . talk?'

Barbara was right: it was time to sort this thing out once and for all.

Ollie's shoulders crept up around his ears, and his face tightened with tension. 'I guess.'

First things first. 'What happened to your beardy bits?'

'I shaved them off.'

'I can see that.'

'Do you not like my new look?'

305

I wanted to tell him I hated it, that I liked his beardy bits, but he looked a bit anxious and so I said, 'Well, it's different.' My eyes flickered downwards. 'And the trousers, and the shoes.'

Ollie looked down too. 'Just fancied a bit of a change,' he said nonchalantly.

'I see.'

'Oh, and I mowed the lawn, like I should have done regularly all these years, but could never be arsed to. So I went out with the lawnmower this afternoon, like a regular guy, and I mowed it. I got some funny looks from the neighbours, what with it being November, but I think it looks good.'

'Yes, it does, it looks great . . .'

'You don't like it,' he stated. He was trying to hide his disappointment. 'Or the lamb or the table arrangements or anything. I thought, well, after being away for three weeks you deserved something special, instead of my usual old stuff, thrown together, and so I asked Dad if he'd come over and do his magic.'

'And it was lovely—'

'Oh, come on. You can't fool me, Hannah.'

He gave a big sigh. His new shoes creaked. We both looked down at them.

'They look like they hurt.'

'They hurt like fuck.'

He kicked them off. He was wearing a pair of tartan socks underneath. And for the first time since I'd arrived home I felt that he was the old Ollie again.

'What's going on?' I asked softly.

Losing the shoes seemed to have a cathartic effect on him too. 'Look, I know you don't want to marry me – no, it's OK, I don't blame you. I'm obviously not the kind of guy you're looking for any more, what with the shorts and the sandals and all that shit, and never making a commitment to anything. Just drifting along like there's no tomorrow.'

I didn't know what to say. I felt stricken that he believed I rejected everything he stood for, everything he was.

'But I'm going to change. Dress properly. Behave like someone who's efficient and practical and knows what time the 39A is due at.'

He perpetually missed it.

'I might even give up the website business and get a proper job.'

'Don't,' I blurted.

He looked taken aback.

'You love that website. Don't.' I back-pedalled slightly. 'Anyway, there aren't any jobs out there any more, so you're better off sticking to it.'

'True,' he said. 'And I'm not sure how long the slacks will last, to be honest, but I'll give them my best shot.'

'Why slacks?' I asked, trying not to smile. 'Why not, say, corduroys? They'd have looked equally awful on you, but they're a whole lot more comfortable.'

He looked embarrassed. It quickly turned to defiance. 'You liked them on that Nick person.'

Part of me wanted to laugh. Another part of me was in a crazy flux. He was doing all this for me? He'd asked me to marry him, even though it went against the grain, and now he was trying to transform himself − pretty unsuccessfully, it had to be said − into the kind of person he thought I wanted.

Maybe I'd thought I'd wanted it too.

Seeing him now, all trussed up and behaving like a more strait-laced, diligent version of himself, made me appreciate even more how much I loved the old one.

But I'd always loved Ollie. I'd never made any bones about that. And he loved me. Throughout this entire mess, that was the one constant. We'd just let everybody else's stuff get in the way.

'Oh, Ollie. For God's sake, take off the trousers. And that shirt too. It looks like it's choking you.'

He looked at me. He knew there was something different in the air: all that promise and excitement that I was so hot on. 'Is this some cheap trick to get me into bed?' he asked at last.

'Don't push it.'

He didn't actually strip off in front of me. He ran upstairs and was back in less than two minutes, in his faded jeans and his T-shirt, and with bare feet. He couldn't do much about the stubble, but that would grow back.

He stopped just inside the living-room door, as if he wasn't sure whether he was staying or going.

'Listen,' he said, 'are you really sure you don't want a regular guy? I can't promise anything, but I'll do my best. I mean it.'

He looked kind of weary, and I felt like my heart would burst. He'd put me through the wringer, there was no doubt about that, but he'd turned himself inside out trying to make it up to me, and it must seem to him that nothing was working.

307

'No. I don't want a regular guy.'

Nick floated there between us, still full of possibilities and intrigue, and then he gently floated away. He was lovely, but I had everything I needed right here.

Ollie was still watching me warily. 'Does that mean . . . you might want to give things another go? Us?'

I thought of what 'we' were: people who'd gelled from the moment we'd met, ten years ago. We were people who'd never had a row, a *serious* row. We were people who laughed, quite a lot, actually, and larked about and generally had a good time. We were friends, lovers maybe twice a month – must do something about that, a nurse's outfit, maybe – parents, companions and hopeless gardeners. We were people who would do anything for each other, including stick by while one had a serious crisis of confidence when their parents split up, and who would propose to the other as a measure of our commitment, even though we weren't at all pushed ourselves.

We were people who were great together. And maybe the reason it felt so easy to get back together – the easiness I'd be terrified about – was because it was so right.

'Yes,' I said.

Ollie looked a bit dumbstruck: surely he had to do more?

'I *would* like to give things another go. Preferably as soon as possible.'

'Um, gosh, OK,' Ollie said. Then he scratched his head. 'Did I just say "gosh"?'

'You're emotional,' I assured him.

He took a cautious step into the room, as if he still expected me to say the whole thing was just a joke. 'I'm so sorry, Hannah. About everything.'

'I know.'

'I know you know, but I need you realise just how sorry I am—'

'So you went off the rails a bit. You didn't kill someone.'

'No, I didn't,' he confirmed.

'You didn't lie to me, or sleep with someone behind my back.' A pause. 'Did you?'

'Who'd look at me in those awful leather trousers?' he complained.

'Well, we *did* try to tell you.'

'I'm getting a bit of a reputation for awful trousers.'

He took another step into the room now, just a small one. 'If you agree to take me back, I'll never, ever do anything like that again. I swear.'

'And I'll never make you feel like you have to change for me again. Because you're perfect the way you are.'

He looked taken aback and very touched at that.

Then he conceded, 'Well, no, I'm not.'

'Actually, you're right, you're not.'

'But I'm close.'

'You're very close.'

Now *he* was very close. So close that I could see his poor, raw-looking pores, having been run ragged by a razor, and I wanted to stroke them.

He said, 'Can I mention the marriage thing?'

'And things were going so well.'

'You don't want to get married?'

'I'm not against the idea.'

'Neither am I,' he said. 'And your mother does have that outfit.'

'To hell with my mother. And *definitely* to hell with yours.'

'I wouldn't spit on her,' he declared. 'Obviously.'

Wedding ring or not, I was certain now that we were built to last. And if we *did* get married, it'd probably be in some dosshouse in Tenerife owned by one of his mates, who also happened to be a justice of the peace. No doubt we would party for three days and it would be tremendous fun.

'I've missed you,' Ollie said, his voice all husky and thick.

I put my arms around him, his body as familiar to me as my own, and it felt like coming home.

'Not half as much as I've missed you. And I think that's enough talking for now.'

'Definitely.'

Chapter Twenty-three

The airport was jam-packed with people coming home for Christmas. 'I can't see a thing,' Cleo complained.

'Will I lift you onto my shoulders?' Ollie offered.

'Dad,' Cleo said sternly. 'I'm *nine*.'

In the end we managed to bully our way to the front of the barriers. People were streaming out of the glass doors of Arrivals, pulling suitcases and small children behind, to be greeted with shouts of, 'Kate! Over here! and, 'Brian! You langer!'

'I hope they're not delayed,' Cleo said. She had a banner, handmade, all ready to wave in the air the minute we saw them. I had a bouquet of flowers. Ollie kept trying to take them from me, saying they were too heavy — heavy! — but I hung grimly on.

'Do you want to go and sit down?' he asked. Again.

'No, Ollie. I'm perfectly fine.'

Cleo looked up, alert. 'Why do you keep asking her if she wants to sit down?'

'I don't.'

'You do. Like, in the supermarket yesterday. You don't *sit down* in the supermarket.'

I rolled my eyes behind her back: well done, Ollie.

We were spared by a commotion behind us, followed by some annoyed voices: 'Take it easy', and 'Stop pushing!'

'Oh, chill out.' It was Ellen, followed by Sophie and Sam. She efficiently elbowed her way through the crowd towards us. 'Keep going, kids. There's Auntie Hannah.'

She carried a bunch of helium balloons. They all said, 'Happy Birthday!' on them.

'They were the only ones they had,' she explained breathlessly to me.

'It's the thought that counts,' I assured her. Besides, she'd organised the really important stuff: the video camera, which was on full battery (she'd checked five times), and two separate cameras: one digital, also on full battery, and one of the ancient ones with real film in it, 'just in case'. Not a moment of this could be missed.

'I can't believe it's finally happening,' she said.

'I know. After all this time.'

A fresh burst of people emerged from the glass doors: another flight. But not the one we wanted. We all sank back down from tippy-toe again.

'Move over,' Sophie told Sam.

'I can't! I'm squashed!'

Then a peculiar thing happened. Cleo looked at Sophie and smiled. A wide smile, almost like she was . . . dear God, was she *baring* her *teeth*?

Sophie looked quickly away from Cleo. 'Oh, just leave it then,' she muttered to Sam, backing down.

I looked at Ollie, horrified. He just grinned.

Luckily, Cleo and Sophie wouldn't see much of each other over the Christmas period. Mark was taking Sophie and Sam for almost the whole two weeks, and was at his father's house with Jill right now. Sophie and Sam had insisted on coming to the airport with Ellen, to get a good look at this boy who was coming home.

Ellen was staying with us for a week, in the spare room. It had twin beds, and after the first night, I abandoned Ollie and moved in with her. It seemed like the right thing to do, as she was on her own, her kids away with Mark, and it was a tough time for her. Within five minutes we were giggling, and preparing a raid on the fridge, and it was like we were back in Mrs Dullard's tasselled house again.

She was the first to cotton on, of course, when she'd brought up two glasses of wine for us, and I'd professed myself too tired to drink mine.

'You're pregnant, aren't you?' she said instantly.

'You're not supposed to guess!'

'Oh my God! That's fantastic, Hannah.'

'I'm only six weeks, that's barely pregnant, anything could happen. Please don't say anything,' I begged. 'We're not telling Cleo yet.'

'Of course I won't.' A stern look now. 'But I hope Ollie's looking after you.'

Ollie was doing more than that; he was practically suffocating me. If he asked me one more time if I wanted to blooming sit down . . .

But he was thrilled. We both were. It was a little secret we were hugging to ourselves for the moment. And there had been no further mention of the marriage thing, upon my insistence. It was all I could do to keep my breakfast down, never mind party for three days. But at some point, in the future . . .

The glass doors opened again. We all drew in our breaths. Was it . . . ? No. Everyone exhaled again. For feck's sake. What was keeping them?

'Do you think they got held up at immigration, what with Sergei having a Russian passport and everything?' Ellen wondered.

We looked at each other, hoping there wouldn't be a problem. There had been no problems so far. Everything had gone smoothly; so smoothly that Barbara kept expecting something terrible to happen, probably involving paperwork, and would send regular gloomy texts, such as, 'Am anticipating problems at Moscow Airport.' But there weren't any.

'It's a shame you can't stay longer than a week,' I told Ellen impulsively. 'You know, seeing as she'll just be home with Sergei.'

'I know. But I don't want to ask Marcel to look after the place for any longer. And anyway, I'll get loads done while the kids are away.' She'd have Jill with her, but Mark wouldn't be flying out until after Christmas to bring Sophie and Sam home.

'We could kidnap you,' I said lightly.

She squeezed my hand tightly. 'It's all right over there, you know. It's a bit lonely sometimes, but it's all right. So you needn't worry about me.'

'But I do.'

'Well, I suppose that's nice to know.'

Ollie leant in. 'Ladies, if you keep nattering away like that, you're going to miss the big event.' I could feel his hand on my back, warm and steady. 'By my reckoning, they're due any minute now.'

'It's Auntie Barbara! Look!' Cleo squealed. Her eyes grew round with wonder. 'And Sergei.'

And we all turned to the glass doors to welcome them home.